Finley's Tale – Bo

C000076100

The Bond of Love

Church Mouse
Musings at
Historic St. Peter's

Sandra Voelker

THE BOND OF LOVE
FINLEY'S TALE - BOOK III

This is a work of fiction. Names, characters, places and incidents either are the product of the author's imagination or are used fictitiously, and any resemblance to actual persons, living or dead, businesses, companies, events, or locales is entirely coincidental.

Print ISBN: 978-1-4866-1668-8
eBook ISBN: 978-1-4866-1669-5

Word Alive Press
119 De Baets Street, Winnipeg, MB R2J 3R9
www.wordalivepress.ca

Cataloguing in Publication may be obtained through Library and Archives Canada

This book is dedicated to my Robert, my husband, my love. I treasure the way you are, especially that you give and receive God's grace, through Christ our Lord, cheerfully, thankfully, and persistently. You give me strength to do the same.

"I would be happy just to hold the hands I love."

—Gordon Lightfoot

Greetings!

Imagine, at this moment, you are standing on the front steps of a highly regarded historic church. Beneath your sturdy snow boots, shiny black wingtips, plastic flip flops, soft deerskin moccasins, waterproof rain boots, brown penny loafers, trusty sneakers, soft ballet flats, or whichever type of sensible or fashionable footwear you are currently wearing, is a cheery welcome mat. Please take a moment to wipe the dust off of the soles of your shoes, but more importantly, clear away any troubling thoughts that cause you to become emotionally flustered or anxious. I give you this advice because my mouse sense tells me that having an untroubled frame of mind will highly intensify your delight in reading *The Bond of Love*. Very quickly you will ascertain that the people and mice that belong to Historic St. Peter's are far from being bystanders, spectators, or sofa spuds. It is a pleasure to broadcast that they are full of zeal, zip, zest, and zing!

Now that you are standing at the threshold of the arched wooden church door that was constructed ages ago of mighty oak, you will notice an eye-catching, but time-worn, golden crucifix doorknocker. A bronze plaque inscribed with the words "Historic St. Peter's Lutheran Church, Erected 1842" is prominently placed underneath the stout doorknocker. Go ahead, reach out, and give it a rap. Immediately the door will open to welcome you inside. Very similar to the image I just conveyed to you, I invite you to step into my tale, an absorbing world that can be called "church life." Please make yourself at home by plunking down in your favourite chair to take the load off of your feet. As you begin reading my tale, shortly you will be in the thick of things. You will not walk away achieving a major or minor in the subject of church life, but you will come across a treasure trove of grace. By the way, grace seems to be a very significant word at St. Peter's because we have heard Ephesians 2:8a spoken many times. It goes like this: "For it is by grace you have been saved, through faith."

Some of you have steadily followed my first two recordings, *In the Beginning* and *Heaven on Earth*. While reading my final journal, please keep in mind that you will be covered with honest-to-goodness *Gemütlichkeit,* a German-language word that encircles all sorts of good cheer and light-heartedness, where there is an abundance of love and acceptance.

Let me take a microsecond to introduce myself to the newcomers unfamiliar with my tale. Finley Newcastle is my name. I am a church mouse living and working at Historic St. Peter's. During the unfolding liturgical church year I have been steadily recording a journal. This compilation unintentionally became three separate journals due to the vast supply of information. From reading entries in my journal, you will instantly become acquainted with Historic St. Peter's delightful clergy family, the thought-provoking parishioners, and the many mighty mice that reside at Historic St. Peter's, which commonly is shortened to St. Pete's or HSP. Residing at Historic St. Peter's, along with my gem of a wife, Ruby, we have found that it is a perfect place to live. The church environment fosters a flourishing and intriguing way of life. Ruby and I are members of a thriving mouse village that appreciates dwelling in God's house, too. The village has concluded that human beings are highly intelligent, perceptive, and extra good-looking. In the back of my journal I am keeping a list of the many mice and people at St. Peter's in an appendix. This should ward off any slight confusion as to who exactly is who!

Being wholeheartedly thrilled, let me say a word of thanks for spending your free time with me as minutes and hours are precious, something not to be treated carelessly. There happens to be twenty-four hours in each day but what we choose to do with those hours, minutes, and seconds is up to us! Since it is wise not to waste time, let's constructively plow forward by using some of the 86,400 seconds that are in each day to explore what's found in *Finley's Tale - Book III: The Bond of Love*. Keep in mind that while you are learning about the primary news and events at Historic St. Peter's we are united in fellowship with one another. Our hearts will be linked with endearment and fondness, just like the verse about love found in Colossians 3:14 where it says, "And over all these virtues put on love, which binds them all together in perfect unity."

It is a full time job to observe Pastor Clement Osterhagen, his lovely and practical wife, Aia (pronounced I-ya), and their three children, Gretchen, Marc, and Luc. The children are adored by their parents, parishioners, and the entire mice village. The Osterhagens reside in the parsonage that is connected to the church proper by a long-windowed breezeway surrounding a well-landscaped courtyard. My wife Ruby and I have a small dwelling right next door to the parsonage in an old storage room. Fortunately, there is a small crack in the parsonage dining room wall directly behind their wooden hutch. It is there we are able to peek into the parsonage to see and hear what is happening in their home. Trust me, you will not read very far into my journal before you develop a fondness for this clergy family.

It was on Monday, September 21, the Feast of St. Matthew, Apostle, Evangelist, that the last recording was made in *Finley's Tale – Book II: Heaven on Earth*. Entries into my journal once again came to a halt because every single sheet in my notebook was overflowing with handwriting. Thankfully I enlisted help from the mice village and within a short amount of time two brothers, Wayne and Calhoun, stumbled upon a new journal in the church library that had a yin and yang drawing on the cover. We are aware that a yin and yang symbol is not exactly churchy, but it was an emergency, the only notebook that they could find. Remember that the depiction on the cover of the journal is of no mind, the interior paper is the vitally important component to continue my writing.

As I've said before, I have a tale to tell and you may follow my tale. Oodles and oodles more will be presented. My writing is not scholarly, intellectual, or perfect in punctuation like most great writers of the world that include Leo Tolstoy and Laura Ingalls Wilder. Please take into consideration that I am a mouse and English is not my first language, my native tongue is Mouse. I admit that I do not possess a university degree in writing so my sentences will not be written like an academic. Every so often my tale gets messy and complicated, overwhelmed with details, but it will be told in a straightforward manner involving no fish tales that always taste far better with a dollop of cocktail or tartar sauce.

In the evenings when Pastor Osterhagen and his family are asleep, my wife Ruby and I usually travel to the parsonage kitchen to see if we can find a late night snack. We are curious to know what the other rooms in the parsonage look like, but we do not satisfy that hankering. We only venture into the dining room and kitchen. Owing to the fact that Aia is such an excellent cook, almost daily we happen upon itty-bitty nutritiously yummy morsels that have accidently dropped on either the dining room floor or kitchen floor from one of their three daily meals. Rarely do we venture over to the church through the breezeway to look for morsels dropped in the kitchen or youth room.

I encourage you to stay with *The Bond of Love* to see how the remainder of the liturgical church year unfolds. God bless you!

Your old friend or your brand new friend,
Finley Newcastle
(F.N. for short)

P.S. Earlier on when I encouraged you to rap on Historic St. Peter's golden crucifix doorknocker, one portion of a Bible verse dawned on me from Matthew 7:8. It reads like this,". . . and to the one who knocks, the door will be opened." I have a sneaking suspicion that two of the words contained in that particular Bible verse could be expressed in another way. Perhaps the word "knocks" really means to pray, while the word "opened" might actually mean to be given an answer. Bear with me as I loosely insert these two substitution words: And to the one who prays, answers will be given.

Friday, September 25

It was last January when Humbly, a timid and easily frightened mouse in our village, overheard Priscilla Larkin inquire about the various colours of St. Peter's embroidered liturgical cloth hangings that dress the altar, pulpit, and lectern. He remembered that it appeared critical that she find out the exact colour and shade that would be used on Saturday, September 26, the date of her daughter's upcoming wedding. Pastor Osterhagen revealed to her that it will be the season of Pentecost so the green altar cloths, commonly called paraments, will be in use at that time symbolizing renewal and promises of a new life in Christ our Saviour.

Crestfallen to hear about the vivid shamrock green liturgical paraments, Priscilla (Cilla for short) inquired if a softer, more gentle peaches-and-cream type of colour could be substituted for Penelope's wedding so that the colour of the paraments will not jarringly clash with the dewy bridal colours that Poppy (for short) has meticulously chosen. Revealing to Pastor that the bridesmaid's gowns are a delicate cameo blush-pink, Cilla appeared even more uneasy. She also added that the bridal bouquet will consist of white roses, pink calla lilies, and silver drop eucalyptus. Over and above all she is unquestionably certain that the professional photographer will frown upon using the sanctuary as a photography venue because of the glaring mismatch between the soft-hued wedding colours and the dill pickle green chancel linens. She anticipates that he will recommend that the wedding photos instead be taken at Emsworth's Manor House Grand Banquet Hall and also in their passionately manicured garden area, weather permitting, of course.

Humbly noticed that Pastor perceived Cilla is vigilantly overseeing her daughter's wedding by even seeking to customize the colour of the chancel paraments to better compliment the delicate hues of the wedding attire. Humbly later told Ruby and myself that he was proud of Pastor when he kindly told Cilla that the paraments are not changed for weddings held at Historic St. Peter's, but are only changed as the liturgical church year progresses. Cilla's face looked terribly disappointed when she heard that news, but she quickly offered a generous suggestion. She began speaking about Rita Hines, a local woman known for her sewing handiwork skills who has been commissioned by the current Governor's wife, Mrs. Margo Silbertson, to sew the chic and sophisticated clothing that she wears to a wide variety of state functions. Cilla offered to commission Rita to sew a new set of paraments in a high quality blush-pink fabric. At that point, Humbly noticed that Pastor did not know what to say. He guessed that Pastor might have assumed that far less skill is needed to sew straight seamed lines on altar cloths than sewing fancy dresses, fitted skirts, and blazers. It must be tricky to sew the occasional evening gown worn by Mrs. Silbertson when she attends formal dinners where Caesar salad, pan-seared filet mignon slathered with peppercorn sauce, and green beans with almonds are likely served. Humbly told Ruby and myself that sewing that type of clothing with an abundance of detailed fancywork would definitely require persistent patience combined with a plenitude of expertise. Thinking of a compromise, Pastor asked Cilla to come to his office and take a look at a church supply catalogue where various paraments are shown. Without delay, Cilla claimed that the ones featured in the catalogue were constructed of top quality fabrics, tastefully adorned with colourful appliqués, and stitched with artistic Swiss-style embroidery. Cilla thanked him for pointing out these pre-made parament sets, asking to borrow the catalogue so that she can show them to her husband. Telling Pastor that she had some thinking to do, she assured him that she would speak to him later about what she now has dubbed the "parament predicament."

Two weeks later, Cilla and Pastor had a conversation overheard by Hawthorne, a mouse as robust and healthy as a hearty geranium. Cilla revealed to Pastor that when she telephoned the church supply company headquartered in Allentown, Pennsylvania, she found them to be exceptionally helpful. They recommended that their pastel rose-coloured brocade paraments embellished with golden embroidery would be the perfect choice. Assuring Pastor that she and her husband Raymond plan on purchasing the set along with a matching clergy stole for him, all she needed was his approval so she could proceed. Hawthorne told me that Pastor had a bittersweet expression on his face while he noticed Cilla trying so hard to achieve the perfect aesthetic ambiance at St. Peter's for Poppy's upcoming wedding. Since this gift would be a glorious addition to St. Peter's, Pastor encouraged her to go ahead and place the order. He told her that just this once he would make an exception and take down the green paraments and replace them with the new set for the wedding. He also was glad to point out that the new paraments would be used on Rose Sunday, as Historic St. Peter's does not have special paraments for the Third Sunday in Advent. After hearing that, Cilla was so overjoyed that she hugged Pastor and thanked him numerous times for helping her solve the "parament predicament."

After that discussion, Cilla asked permission to use the church's long-windowed breezeway to host a short champagne gathering immediately following the ceremony, just prior to the guests heading out to Emsworth's Manor House for the wedding dinner. She added that sweet-rosé champagne will be served alongside nut cups containing a medley of pink Jordan almonds, jumbo cashews, and macadamia nuts. After hearing the description of the champagne and nut event, Humbly jumped to the conclusion that Pastor might be a nutso not to let them use St. Peter's breezeway for a short reception.

Pastor has kept an eye out for the new paraments to arrive at St. Peter's. He was concerned about them, so a few days ago he telephoned the supplier in Allentown, Pennsylvania. They assured him that the paraments were on their way and will arrive shortly. Pastor was so at ease when they finally arrived. After opening up the box, he became horror-struck when he saw that the paraments were altogether the wrong colour. They were supposed to be a gentle pink, but they were strikingly blood red with an abundance of golden embroidery depicting the burning fire of the Holy Spirit. With lightning speed Pastor searched for the church supply catalogue to find their telephone number. While on the phone with the customer service clerk, she looked up Historic St. Peter's order form. Clement later told Aia that the clerk actually gasped when she realized that a mix up had occurred in the company's mailroom, admitting that the rose-coloured paraments intended for Historic St. Peter's were accidently sent to the wrong church and St. Peter's got that church's order. Being that the wedding is tomorrow, Pastor needed to quickly come up with a solution. Realizing that Sunday is St. Michael's and All Angels (Observed) he knew that the white paraments would be used. So, he changed all of the liturgical cloths, knowing that the only tricky thing yet to do would be to call Cilla and explain what had happened.

Ruby and I heard Clement telephone Cilla after he returned to the parsonage. We thought he might be as nervous as a student facing a physics test who pauses to pray before the exam. But, he remained calm while explaining to her exactly what had transpired. After he hung up, he told Aia that Cilla told him that he was a hero, a real giant who solved another "parament predicament." Adding that she is feeling anything but calm and relaxed, she wondered if Pastor would pray for her because her mother-in-law, Harriet, arrived a week early and has been getting under her skin. She revealed to Pastor that on their wedding day thirty-one years ago, Raymond's mother told him to "not marry that woman." Before they hung up, Cilla said that she hopes to enjoy Poppy's wedding, so one good thing is that she put her mother-in-law's place card right next to Denver Wickstrom's. If Denver cannot sweeten her up, then no one can.

At 10:30 p.m. Ruby and I travelled to the parsonage finding only a sweet gherkin under the dining room table. Ruby especially enjoyed it because it was deliciously sugary. We will have trouble sleeping tonight because we are so looking forward to coming across snippets of the various nuts on the breezeway's floor following tomorrow's champagne wedding reception. We have not tasted any of these nut flavours before, having been only familiar with the simple peanut. It's just too bad that they are not serving cheese and crackers instead of nut cups. Our village ranks cheese with a perfect five-star rating in comparison to the humble peanut that lands only a one-and-one-half star rating.

– F.N.

Saturday, September 26

Ever since Marc and Luc were born, five-year old Gretchen tries very hard to be a good sister by helping care for her twin brothers. Her assistance is even there when it is time for diaper changes. If their diapers are simply wet, she throws the disposable diapers away and fetches two fresh ones for her brother's tiny bums. When the diapers are soiled, she stands by Aia's side, pinches her nose, and frantically fans the air with a Spanish folding fan that she keeps handy at the changing table. Over and over again she theatrically exclaims "PU" in a long drawn out way by voicing "Peeeee-yoooooou."

Gretchen recently began kindergarten. Her favourite part of school is learning all twenty-six letters of the alphabet, which she often sings to her brothers. Gretchen asked her mother a couple of days ago if they could go shopping at Bill's Dollar Bill to purchase a sparkly notebook along with a matching pencil bag and pencils. She intends to put them in her church activity bag that she carries to worship every Sunday morning. Recently discovering that the expression "PU" is actually two letters of the alphabet, Gretchen has taught herself how to print these two letters.

This afternoon when Aia was in the washroom, Gretchen slid a little slip of paper underneath the door with a handwritten "PU" on it. After Aia opened the door, Gretchen doubled up with laughter, asking her mama if she liked her "PU" note. It was last May when Aia's cousin, Shane Borg, stopped to see them after finishing his sophomore year at "P.U." (a.k.a. Purdue University.) Shane apologized for accidently tooting, blaming it on the cafeteria food as well as the anxiety of his finals. When Gretchen heard Shane use that expression she thought it was fun to say, so she added it to her vocabulary. She evidently thinks it is more fun to say toot than to say beeped your horn or passed gas. Clement and Aia smile when she uses that phraseology. Now that Gretchen knows how to spell "PU," she runs to get her notepad and writes a "PU" note to slip under the door every time the washroom is occupied. Gretchen's purpose in shopping at Bill's Dollar Bill is because she is running low on supplies due to heavy duty usage.

Yesterday the school children participated in a field trip to a nearby dairy farm to learn about dairy production. When Clement and Aia asked Gretchen to tell them about the outing, her main comment was that she saw lots of smelly cow plops and had to say "PU" many, many times. She also mentioned that one of her friends called them cow pies and the other friend called them meadow muffins. Her favourite part of the field trip was when the farm couple served vanilla ice cream cones to all of the children at the end of the tour.

Because Clement is now making supper every Monday he's gotten interested in the art of cooking and is expanding his cooking repertoire. Checking out library cookbooks is part of his expansion of knowledge. Lately he has been cooking outdoors so he doesn't dirty-up, greasy-up, stinky-up, messy-up, or sticky-up the oven, stove, or the kitchen counters.

Having purchased three large heads of cabbage, Clement is experimenting at fermenting shredded cabbage, an attempt to make homemade sauerkraut just like his grandmother Martha Kuehnert prepared when he was a boy. The cabbage is busy fermenting all right, but during that process the parsonage garage doesn't smell very pleasant due to the strong vapours. We suspect that the unpleasant pungency might shortly creep into the parsonage and the breezeway, prior to wafting towards the sanctuary. Clement said that he hopes the smell doesn't reach the sanctuary interior before he can pack the sauerkraut into sterilized glass jars. Gretchen persistently says PU every single time she enters the garage.

United in Holy Marriage this afternoon was Penelope (Poppy) Larkin and Anders (Andy) Rasmussen. The most talked about part of the ceremony in our village was when Pastor gave his wedding sermon. Pretty close to that was when Nita Janssen sang the Irish wedding song, "May God Bless this Couple" using her colourful soprano voice. Because Pastor delivered such an excellent sermon, I decided to include part of it in my journal. It went like this:

> "God's Word is joining you together today. You have been a couple for a long time, engaged quite a while, but now you are joined, one flesh, one new family, one new home. And since you believe in our Lord Jesus, sent as our Saviour from our sins, you are not just two becoming one together, but are as Ecclesiastes 4:12 reads, 'a cord of three strands that is not quickly broken.' The law affirms it, your vows proclaim it, and the Church confirms it here that you are one as long as you both shall live."

Following the ceremony Pastor attended the breezeway champagne reception before travelling to Emsworth's Manor House for the wedding dinner. It was easier for Aia to stay home with Gretchen, Marc, and Luc than to hire a babysitter. Plus, they seem to need their mama every single minute.

At 6:30 p.m. Ruby and I travelled to the breezeway where we came upon a few dropped nuts. We selected the cashew as our favourite nut. Lately, we have been avoiding the parsonage due to the fermenting sauerkraut with its strong foul air. Ruby and I fear that we might lose consciousness by breathing in the potent fumes, so until further notice we look elsewhere throughout the church building to find our treats. Rarely do we come up empty.

– F.N.

The Eighteenth Sunday after Pentecost (St. Michael & All Angels, Observed) ~ September 27

AIA AND THE CHILDREN SETTLED INTO ONE OF THE REAR PEWS DURING WORSHIP THIS morning. Near the back pew was Maverick, a refreshingly free-spirited member of our village. After the church service Maverick came to our dwelling and told us about the free-flowing banter between Mr. Ambrose Beckman and Gretchen. It began when Mr. Beckman walked into the sanctuary and sat down in the pew directly in front of the Osterhagens. Aia visited briefly with him while Maverick listened. Maverick heard Mr. Beckman say that he happens to live three and one-half blocks from Historic St. Peter's. When the weather is pleasant with no chance of snow or rain, he rides his twenty-six inch adult tricycle to church. Wheeling it inside the church's entryway, he parks it directly underneath the coat rack. To deter theft, even while at church, he uses a padlock that comes equipped with an adjustable length of about six feet of cable so it can be secured to the heavy duty coat rack. For safety reasons, Ambrose dons a shiny silver helmet that coordinates with both his hair colour and his tricycle. Our village is certain that Mr. Beckman, who we refer to as the Silver Fox, proves to be a safety first gent. Maverick overheard him tell another parishioner that several months ago he completed a community class on bicycle safety. Riding his adult tricycle nearly every day of the week, on Sundays he heads to church. The other six days of the week he takes another route and rides to his favourite pub for a glass of beer at four o'clock. He is such a fixture at the establishment that the employees watch for him to arrive at 4 p.m. If he has not arrived, one of the employees will pick up the telephone and call him to make sure he is all right. Employees have shortened his first name to "Bro" in favour of using his formal name, Ambrose. After Bro enters the pub, he parks his tricycle at the end of the bar and padlocks it to the foot rail. He revealed all of this to Gretchen after the worship service. Maverick noticed that today the two of them became devoted friends. Their solidarity is due to a slight bomb erupting from Mr. Beckman. Gretchen's response to this incident is what resulted in them becoming chums.

During the reading of today's Epistle lesson, Maverick revealed to us that Ambrose accidently broke wind, loud and clear. After that, Gretchen stared at her mother in disbelief with saucer-sized eyes while plugging her nose and wildly fanning the air. Everyone seated in close proximity looked like they were being overtaken by whiffs of the vapour. Because Aia had her hands brimming full holding Marc and Luc, she did not notice that Gretchen was busy with her church activity bag. Standing up on the pew and leaning forward, Gretchen tapped Mr. Beckman on the shoulder, waited a second for him to turn around and then gave him a homemade "PU" note. Aia did not scope out what was happening until Ambrose chuckled while reading Gretchen's message. His laugh was subdued because he was noticeably trying to be well-mannered following this hugely embarrassing moment. Mr. Beckman turned around and thanked Gretchen for the note. Gretchen told him that he could keep it and tape it to his refrigerator. Gretchen spoke softly again to Mr. Beckman and told him that everybody is windy, not just him, and that even snowmen pass gas, but they are snowflakes, which are pretty and don't smell stinky like his does. After hearing this fresh news about snowmen blasting forth gas, Mr. Beckman resumed laughing, but appeared as though he was trying to muzzle it to a muffle.

Returning home after church, Aia and Clement began a head-to-head conversation about Gretchen's perpetual flow of "PU" notes. Aia broke the news to Clement that this behaviour has got to stop. She reminded him that when her cousin Shane visited last May, Gretchen was bewildered as to why he attends a "PU" school in Indiana which she said "must smell stinky." Ruby and I are aware that Aia has her highest regard for her own *alma mater,* Trinity College, but also is a fan of Purdue University since three of her relatives have graduated from that school. Explaining to Gretchen that "P.U." is an illustrious, esteemed, and creditable university (First Note: Aia's Trinitarian lingo) that does not smell unpleasant, she pointed out that the campus air is altogether scented with a totally distinct type of air that is highly academic, educational, and scholastic. (Second Note: Aia's Trinitarian terminology continues.) After Aia's first point, Ruby and I noticed that Gretchen's eyes and mouth opened so widely that we deduced she did not comprehend her mother's clarification about three differing types of campus air quality. Gretchen simply moved forward from Aia's Trinitarian attempt to explain the difference. Instead, she started singing "The Diarrhea Song," having the most fun singing about sliding into first and feeling something burst. Aia also told Clement that it wasn't helpful when her folks visited them when Marc and Luc were born to bring along the book, *The Stink of Love: Pepé Le Pew's Guide to L'Amore,* in addition to a Pepé Le Pew colouring book. Aia said that a far superior book choice would have been a *Madeline* book, noting that it is far more pleasant to hear words about twelve little girls in an old house in Paris than Gretchen concentrating on offensive, strongly unpleasant, and foul-smelling odours. (Third Note: Aia concluded her Trinitarian speech.)

Clement listened to Aia and followed up by interjecting something that she was unaware of, a detail about the expression, PU. Explaining to Aia that PU is a shortened form of the Latin word, *puteo,* he said that it means smelling bad. Clement also pointed out that Gretchen is just being very human, recognizing that some odours are unpleasant, stinky, and putrid. Gretchen's actions of holding her nose, wildly fanning the air, saying PU in a long drawn-out way, along with writing PU notes are just part of a phase that she is going through. Besides, Clement added, it must have been the highlight of Ambrose Beckman's day when he received his very own PU note. He probably hasn't had a child give him a note to tape on his refrigerator door in eons or maybe even ever. We heard Clement mention that a life without a sense of smell, either due to an illness or an accident, would be heart-rending. He spoke also about Job and how he was thankful that as long as he had life within him, the breath of God was in his nostrils. Aia thanked Clement for listening, hugged him, but then hurried off as she needed to get a kettle of eggs on the stove. She watches them carefully since she does not want to overcook them. If she is not attentive to the timing, the eggs will produce a sulfur stench when they are peeled that will stink to high heaven. She does not have the first idea how to neutralize this type of odour except to open all the windows. Ruby concluded that most stinks are better prevented than neutralized.

After supper tonight Clement helped clear off the dining room table. While Clement and Aia were working in the kitchen, Ruby and I heard their conversation centering on the new towels in both the kitchen and washroom. Aia happily explained the reason why there are decorated Christmas towels now hanging in both rooms even though it is not currently the Christmas season. A few days ago she and Gretchen shopped at the discount store in nearby Beeker County. The two of them came across a wide variety of Christmas towels that were on a seventy-percent off sale. Since their towels are so run-down, washed-out, and thread-bare, Aia and Gretchen decided to stock up on this bargain, reminding each other that their abundant supply of drab beige and white striped towels will be a useful addition to the rag bin. The old washroom hand and bath towels have been replaced by festively-decorated Christmas towels embroidered with snowmen, reindeer, Christmas trees, the word "*Noël*," and the expression, "Baby, it's cold outside!" We noticed that Clement appeared very positive after hearing Aia's explanation, plus he mentioned that it will now resemble Christmas every day of the year at the parsonage. After that remark, he washed his hands, ran a Granny

Smith apple under the kitchen faucet, and wiped both his hands and the granny using a one-hundred percent cotton kitchen towel printed with dozens of Christmas candy canes.

At 9:30 p.m. Ruby and I travelled to the Youth Room and snacked on a plethora of popcorn scattered on the floor from the youth group gathering this afternoon. We were careful to shy away from the old maids, the un-popped kernels, or are they called old bachelors? As we munched, we tried to approximate the exact number of calories contained in one kernel of oil-popped popcorn. Ruby guesstimated five calories per kernel, but I thought it more in the ballpark of around two calories. If we have time, tomorrow we will call on Dr. Theodore Simonsen, village head librarian, ask him our "Q" and anticipate that he will come up with an "A."Meanwhile, we are highly suspicious that consuming this treat just might produce a chunky tummy, so we exerted willpower and cut back a bit. We also learned from the empty popcorn bag that this popcorn is distributed by a company in Indiana, the same state where Shane attends P.U. We have no idea where Indiana is but when Shane visited Gretchen and Aia we heard him refer to himself as being a Hoosier. That makes no sense at all to us because we know that Clement and Aia have a free-standing piece of furniture that they refer to a Hoosier in their kitchen that once belonged to Clement's great-grandparents. But, Shane is a living and breathing person, not an antique oak cupboard that has a flour sifter, a beautiful blue and white speckled porcelain workspace, along with plenty of places to store food supplies. An additional "Q" we will ask Dr. Simonsen tomorrow is to explain how and why a person and a piece of furniture can possibly share the Hoosier name. We can hardly wait to hear his "A."

Ruby and I spent a little while pondering just what other types of Christmas kitchen towels will we see when we travel to the parsonage for our late night snacks. Ruby predicted towels with gingerbread men and I reckoned we would see holly and ivy.

– F.N.

Monday, September 28

Bramble is a peculiarly tenacious mouse in our village who keeps current on Lake Harvey's recreational fishing report by seeking out a copy of the "Rod, Line, & Hook" column published every Saturday in the Oswald County Gazette. Spending most of his time in the parsonage garage, he is keen to jump into the recycle bin after Pastor has tossed the Gazette aside. Having found the latest edition, Bramble's curiosity was intrigued when he spotted a fifty-year-old black and white photograph. At our village meeting tonight, Bramble reported that after much concentration he concluded that the photograph of this particular gent, who was delightfully clasping a weighty fish, is definitely a member of St. Peter's. Bramble carefully managed to tear the photograph from the Gazette, and without being spotted, ran like wildfire to our village meeting while clenching the photo in his teeth. All in attendance gathered around the photograph. Immediately a guessing game began to put a name to the familiar face. I thought they were frittering away their time, so I pointed out that it was far more conducive to simply read the caption printed underneath the photograph: "Fifty years ago Sportsman Palmer (Pike) Hallgrimsson landed a 24-pound northern pike on Lake Harvey." Our village is aware that Pike and his easy-on-the-eyes wife, Dorothy, are life-long members of St. Peter's. All were amazed that Pike's appearance is no worse for wear after fifty years. Comments were uttered that Pike still retains the same inviting smile, a steady twinkle in his eyes, but most remarkably, fifty years later his blonde head of hair has not taken on a drab silver shade or even lost a bit of luster.

While on an outing earlier today, Bramble was relaxing underneath the backyard shrubbery at St. Peter's when he overheard a lively conversation between Pike and his fishing buddy, Roland Robinson. While the gents were sitting on an outdoor bench, Bramble heard what seemed to be a continuation of an earlier discussion that was hatched one afternoon while fishing on Lake Harvey. Bramble told us that Roland complimented Pike on the fine article printed in Saturday's Gazette which told about his fishing success fifty years ago. Pike went on to tell Roland more details that were not published in the article. He conveyed that on his confirmation day his parents hosted a celebration dinner that included all of his relatives. After coffee and dessert the relatives headed home, while Pike and his Dad, Hálfdan, eagerly headed out to their favourite fishing spot on Lake

Harvey. Pike went on to say that his Dad grew up in the picturesque little village of Vik, Iceland, adding that his veins must have been permeated with fish blood. To this day, most of the locals are certain that there has never been a fisherman as successful in Oswald County as Hálfdan. That memorable day after Pike reeled in a twenty-four pound northern pike, Hálfdan started up the boat motor pointing it toward Custer's Cove Bait & Ice Cream Shop. After they arrived, his fish was weighed and measured, as well as a photograph taken of Pike holding his prized fish. Back then, when the photo was featured in the Gazette, it was the editor of the paper himself that crowned Pike with a new, catchy name. He has proudly gone by Pike, instead of Palmer, ever since his confirmation day.

Now that Pike is retired, he and Dorothy are presiding over a newly started circle of retirees at St. Peter's. The group's mission is to re-vitalize, re-organize, re-do, re-model, re-vamp, re-generate, re-work, re-vise, re-make, and re-focus Historic St. Peter's. Bramble mentioned that so far the only thing the group has accomplished was to re-ject many name ideas. All re-joiced when they agreed to call themselves The Grace-Filled Re-tirees. They find fun and fulfillment while being together at St. Pete's.

Ready to tackle a fishing endeavour, Pike mentioned to Roland that he planned on proposing an idea during today's Grace-Filled Re-tirees gathering. Bramble listened intently to Pike's words since realizing that mice are thoroughly unfamiliar with the topic of fishing but surely will be eager to learn about it. However, Pike mentioned a specific type of fishing that he referred to as "fishing for men." Pike pointed out that this type of fishing does not need a trip to Lake Harvey or the Sea of Galilee, but is done right here in the local community. He hopes to be a guiding light by helping and encouraging the retirees to become Christ's disciples, right here, right now. This involves putting on the armour of God and picking up the shield of faith. Pike's ultimate goal is to get more people in the pews on Sunday mornings to hear God's Word. Bramble noticed that when Pike said those words, Roland nodded his head up and down in abundant agreement. Pike finished his thoughts by reciting to Roland a memory verse from the King James Version, Mark 1:17, where it reads, "And Jesus said unto them, 'Come ye after me, and I will make you to become fishers of men.'" Being so intrigued after hearing that Bible verse, Bramble decided to attend the Grace-Filled Retirees meeting held this afternoon in Woolcox Hall. Thankfully, he straight away found a hiding place in the far corner of the podium while all of the retirees were going through the potluck line, which Bramble said looked like a mouth-watering spread at a scrumptious buffet. Not long ago, the Grace-Filled Re-tirees funded the purchase of an amplifying microphone for Woolcox Hall so all in attendance will hear what is spoken at an event. The microphone is a true blessing because today's words clearly spoken by Pike enlivened and fired up everyone to get out there and go fishing.

During the group discussion about becoming fishers of men, Bramble noticed that there was an aura of hesitancy, a murmuring, and misgivings about this being a grand plan. It was pointed out by several retirees that they truly have the heart to invite people to attend church but not the skill, adding that when they try to become fishers of men they end up feeling as though they have flopped and have become nothing but a squeezed-out lemon. Also voiced was that it is far easier to encourage complete strangers to attend St. Peter's, but more difficult to urge your relatives or friends to turn up at church. As the meeting neared the end, Bramble told us that the Grace-Filled Re-tirees put the fishers of men project on hold for a year or so. They will instead put their efforts into hosting a November Fish Fry at Jake and Georgia Lambton's year-round cottage on Lake Harvey, who have also generously offered to provide a keg of beer. All hands shot up in agreement for this event. Volunteers to provide coleslaw, buns, potato salad, lemons, dessert, and the like were plentiful.

Shortly before today's meeting was adjourned, Brad Barretto voiced a creative idea that caught everyone's attention. All listened to his proposal where St. Pete's could hold a "First Annual Fishing Contest." He pointed out that there are several parishioners who own fishing boats, extra fishing poles, and life jackets, so those who enter the contest would have no apprehension being part of the event. The only cost to the Grace-Filled Re-tirees would be the purchasing of minnows and worms. Awards could be divided into four distinct categories: First Fish Caught, Largest Fish Caught, Smallest Fish Caught, and the Last Fish Caught. Brad suggested that the contest could be held on a Sunday morning from 10:30 a.m. until noon simply because most parishioners have that time off. The winner in each category would be awarded a gift certificate to the Sweet Dreams Ice Cream Shoppe redeemable for a triple scoop ice cream waffle cone, generously provided by Brad and his wife, Estelle. (After the Barrettos retired, they took up a new occupation by opening up the ice cream parlour.) Brad mentioned that between his four teenage grandchildren and two other trusty employees, he and Estelle rarely need to work at the shop. All of the retirees were enthusiastic about this contest, so it quickly came to a vote and passed unanimously. The only details left were to choose a particular Sunday morning for the event and to post a signup sheet. Bramble said that this turn in direction from being fishers of men, to not only planning a fish fry, but also a fishing contest, seemed to perplex Pike, but it did not seem to annoy or irritate him. Instead, he encouraged the fishermen/fisherwomen in the group to spend time fishing for northern pike or walleye on Lake Harvey, even if it means they will need to occasionally skip church on a Sunday morning in order to come up with enough fish to host the fish fry.

At 11:30 p.m. Ruby and I travelled to the parsonage. We could not find a crumb tonight so we just sat in a corner of the kitchen quietly visiting about how Pike's main goal was to fill the pews but it completely backfired on him. We thought the meeting had a boomerang moment because now less people will attend worship on Sunday mornings, the far opposite of Pike's original goal. Now on several Sunday mornings Lake Harvey's north cove will be full of St. Peter's members resting on boat cushions beside trusty thermos mugs and sacks of muffins bursting with blueberries, instead of sitting in the pew beside friends they have invited to church. What transpired today is so bitterly sad that I can hardly even write about it. Ruby and I are heartsick that the foremost scriptural plan of becoming fishers of men somehow altogether shifted to catching fish that will simply end up sizzling away in a cast iron skillet. I do not want to be a critic, but in analyzing the new fishing plans, I must write that it does not seem very evangelical, devout, or churchy to tempt parishioners to skip worship services by offering them fishing opportunities. Ruby and I wonder if Pastor might put on his clergy robe, hop on one of the fishing boats, and conduct a church service right there on Lake Harvey, similar to what is found in Luke 5:3: "He got into one of the boats, the one belonging to Simon, and asked him to put out a little from shore. Then He sat down and taught the people from the boat." Heavenly days, if it does even come to that point, we will need to send two watchful members of our village to be aboard one of the fishing boats.

– F.N.

St. Michael & All Angels ~ Tuesday, September 29

This morning's conversation among Clement and Aia, witnessed by Ruby, was anything but saintly because it had nothing at all to do with St. Michael or any of the heavenly angels. Sitting at the breakfast table, Clement, once again, inquired as to what specifically Aia would be preparing for tonight's supper. After Aia replied that she planned on serving Philly cheesesteak sandwiches, Clement conveyed his disappointment while requesting that she prepare something else, simply a supper that does not incorporate onions. Aia revealed to him that she already had done much of the prep work by slicing onions and a green pepper, shredding cheese, and thawing out the beef from their deep freezer. This onion topic has been occurring frequently between them ever since Clement told her that he cannot arrive at church meetings sporting strong onion breath. Even if he chews several sticks of cool minty gum at a fast and furious pace before the meeting begins, he is not able to completely refresh his breath. Aia did touch upon the fact that onion breath is far worse than morning breath, adding that she was in full understanding of Clement's anxiety about having halitosis. But, she also took this opportunity to dream out loud about their future days of retirement when she can cook onions any day of the week. Aia went on to mention a long list of meals that will contain the humble onion (which Ruby tried fervently to write down, but could not keep up with Aia's dictation.) Her verbal list included Coney islands, California hamburgers, onion rings, Granny's onion jam, tacos, and her side of the family's favourite onion recipe: French onion soup.

To plan ahead, Aia revealed to Clement how she takes St. Peter's monthly church calendar and uses it as a meal planning tool. On evenings with scheduled meetings she will prepare onion-less foods that are humdrum, while on the other evenings she will arrange suppers that incorporate onions. Clement thanked Aia. Both brightened up when Clement mentioned that after tonight's meeting plans are to open the pre-packaged onion ring snacks that are currently calling out from the depths of the pantry. Clement finished by saying that no arm-twisting is needed to answer that inviting call.

At 11:15 p.m. Ruby and I were under the Osterhagen's dining room table conversing about the importance of September 29 being listed on the church liturgical calendar. Admitting that she did not know much about the day designated to honour St. Michael and All Angels, I told Ruby that I might know just a little bit about it. Mentioning that it might be vaguely tied to the wildflower daisies that grow on Scotland's Isle of Skye, I told her that I have a distinct recollection of my dad, Ellis Newcastle, recalling his memories of sweetly dozing underneath his favourite autumn flower, the purple Michaelmas daisy. Ruby complimented me on my large brain capacity for recalling details. After that, she suggested that we equally divide a single crumb of a cheesesteak sandwich that completely lacked onions. Together we undeniably agreed that onions can be considered optional when it comes to making a pleasant-tasting Philly. After arriving back home we discussed Aia's usage of the word halitosis. We reckon it just might be an elaborate and far more ladylike term to describe bad-smelling breath.

– F.N.

Wednesday, September 30

Last Sunday Sister Bernadette from Holy Angels Catholic Parish attended worship at Historic St. Peter's. She was instantly identified as a nun by her black habit. Hanging around her neck was a sterling silver rosary with colourful acrylic beads. Gumi, one member of our village, overheard Sister Bernadette mention to several St. Peter's members how much she appreciated the mass, especially the solid Gospel-centered sermon, along with the traditional music played on the pipe organ. In an odd sort of way, many parishioners felt honoured by her presence.

When Sister Bernadette shook hands with Pastor Osterhagen after church, she asked him if she could make an appointment to meet with him. Pastor agreed. The appointment was scheduled for 10 a.m. today. Wheel and Barrow were hiding in Pastor's office closet, behind his clergy robes, so they were fully cognizant listening to the doctrinally thought-provoking discussion.

Sister Bernadette began by briefly opening up about her vows to dedicate her life to the Catholic Church. She said it was necessary that she centered her faith in God when she made her choice to become a nun. But convent life is not always strict, prim, and proper, as though the nuns are locked away where there is no laughing or hugging. Neither is it similar to nuns in the movies belting out one melodious song after the next. There is moderation and self-discipline, of course, and her tummy has shrunk. For over four years she has been totally content and comfortable to consume a small apple for lunch each day. In her time spent at the convent, she has eaten close to 1,500 apples. Sister Bernadette also mentioned a seasoned nun, Sister Carmella. This particular nun has lived at the convent for over thirty-three years and has eaten over 12,000 apples. Just for fun, Pastor asked Sister Bernadette if any of the apples consumed by Sister Carmella were caramel apples.

Sister Bernadette smiled but quickly returned to the reason for this appointment. First of all, Sister Bernadette said that the six- minute sermons at Holy Angels are so condensed that they never even get started on proclaiming the Holy Gospel. Secondly, she said that the contemporary Catholic music seems almost hollow, noting that the style and leadership is markedly different since Vatican II. Holy Angels does have a magnificent *Casavant Frères* organ from Saint-Hyacinthe, Quebec, but the instrument is rarely used. The trend has been to avoid the pipe organ, substituting musical leadership with guitars, a keyboard, tambourine, and a drum set.

It was at this point that Sister Bernadette asked Pastor Osterhagen if she could worship at Historic St. Peter's on Sunday mornings. She added that she will attend mass at Holy Angels Monday through Friday, plus twice on Saturday, emphasizing that all week long she will look forward to Sunday mornings at Historic St. Peter's. Pastor told her that she is welcome and did not need any type of permission to attend St. Peter's. Sister Bernadette emphasized that she will not partake of Holy Communion, attend Bible Studies, or any social functions, but that she would appreciate worshipping here where there is solid doctrine and traditional music.

Clement went home for lunch and shared a bit with Aia. She chuckled when she heard about the "Sister."One of St. Pete's homebound members, Gabrielle Charpentier, has trouble remembering Aia's first name, so she just calls her "sister." (Mrs. Charpentier is the lady with a Québec French accent that kisses Pastor's hands each time he comes to bring her Holy Communion.) Aia added that now St. Pete's supposedly has two "sisters," but in the days to come there could possibly be three. She backed this up by pointing out that parishioner Marie Crogan has a lot of natural nun qualities and tendencies. Ruby looked at me and spoke three words, "Trinitarian Aia, again."

At 6:20 p.m. Ruby and I travelled to the church kitchen where we discovered that the recycle bucket had been tipped over. We actually had a feast because the empty cans had not been rinsed. Traces of food were stuck on the sides of the cans, which we were able to get loose. The fruit cocktail can was my favourite while Ruby's was the crushed pineapple. We are guessing that the ladies who play bridge the first Wednesday morning each month whipped up a simple ambrosia salad that contains only five ingredients: mini marshmallows, mandarin oranges, pineapple chunks, coconut, and sour cream. When their competitive game stops at 12 noon, the ladies put the card deck away, retrieve their sandwiches from the refrigerator, and pull out the ambrosia salad. Lunching together, in this manner, has been repeated so many times it is simply second nature.

– F.N.

Thursday, October 1

When Gully, a far from gullible mouse in our village, overheard the side door of St. Peter's being unlocked late this afternoon, he straightaway went out of sight behind the children's book rack in the narthex. Pastor Osterhagen was there at the time, but thankfully was not aware of Gully's presence because he had his back turned when Gully scooted into hiding. Pastor was carefully positioning an old-fashioned portrait in the dead centre of the bulletin board. Gully peeked out to see what was happening and spied the portrait of an unidentified gent holding an unusually large Bible. Gully later told me that the portrait must be of an influential historical figure, someone scholarly, prestigious, dignified, and worthy of great respect. Ruby and I were curious to see this portrait, so before our snack tonight we ventured to the narthex to see it with our own eyes.

Every afternoon Leona Wilkes arrives at St. Peter's and takes a little hike around the building to see if everything is orderly. It is on Fridays that she picks up the upcoming Sunday bulletins, taking them home to fold and stuff with inserts. Most members realize that Leona is the church's self-proclaimed "Bulletin Examiner, Bulletin Folder, and Bulletin Board Overseer." She scours the contents of the bulletin board to remove any obsolete papers, tacks up recent obituaries, and repositions the entire contents to match her preference. It is as if she has invented her own Ten Commandments of the bulletin board. On Fridays, Leona arrives feverish to check over the contents of newly printed weekly bulletin. Before going home she sits down in the Fireside Room, armed with a red pen and her tortoise shell reading spectacles, fully excited to scour the bulletin's contents in hopes of finding any typos. When she finds anything, she promptly knocks on the parsonage door to inform Pastor and Aia of the blooper she has spotted. Before Leona exits the building, she slips a corrective note underneath the secretary's door to notify her of her typing booboos.

Just when Pastor finished tacking the portrait on the bulletin board, Leona was at his side to post a newspaper clipping of Elmer Walsh's obituary. Since Elmer transferred away from St. Peter's many years ago, Pastor told her that he had never met Elmer because it was before his time serving at St. Peter's. Leona revealed that Elmer had once been a faithful member of St. Pete's, but that came to an end due to a falling out with another member, Allyn Clarke. Leona spoke ceaselessly, revealing that the gist of the dispute was over the addition of pew cushions. She continued by saying that Elmer generously had offered to oversee the ordering and purchasing of tailor-made padded pew cushions. At first Elmer was certain that the comfort provided by the pew cushions would be appreciated by all members of St. Peter's. He later wised-up by realizing that he was mistaken, all due to Allyn Clarke's persistent broadcasting that the addition of pew cushions would ravage the aesthetic beauty of Historic St. Peter's. Leona also said that Allyn was determined that St. Peter's should focus on adding kneelers, which definitely did not need padding. He pointed out that when our Lord Jesus Christ was hung on the wood of the cross, which lasted three-full hours, he was not comfy. Allyn suggested that the members of HSP can at least sit on hard wooden pews for one hour a week. Elmer ended up transferring away from St. Peter's, a church he once loved and cherished. Unfortunately, after the verbal explosion between Elmer and Allyn, the improvements of adding pew cushions and/or kneelers came to an end.

After Leona provided these details to Pastor, Gully reported that it was just seconds before a ripsnorter of a conversation transpired between the two of them. Leona took one look at the newly hung portrait and insisted that Pastor take it down. She pointed out that it is not inspiring to look at a person that appears so sad and downtrodden, but that if he wants to display a portrait on the bulletin board, it should be one where the person is radiantly beaming, one that is a true reflection of a satisfied, blissful, and happy life. Pastor attempted to enlighten Leona that this person had anything but an untroubled life, but she was not open to learning anything. At that point, Gully said that Pastor stopped talking and stuck several more thumbtacks on the portrait to secure it even more tightly to the bulletin board.

Gully said that as long as Leona had Pastor's attention she brought up the subject of prayer, the prayer requests that are called in to circle through the church's telephone prayer chain. Leona is on the prayer chain and receives calls to pray, but she told Pastor that she does not receive enough information to pray thoroughly. She told him that he should stop shilly-shallying and dilly-dallying with his words and to just spit out the full information. It is not enough to say that one certain person is in the hospital and needs our prayers, but that he should be more direct concerning their afflictions. Everyone on the prayer chain needs and deserves to know the exact medical condition of the people that they are praying for. Leona said that it is better to spell it out, like so-and-so is having bladder reconstruction, a hemorrhoid-ectomy, or double bunion removal.

Gully told me that Pastor excused himself from Leona by telling her that he had an appointment. Gully followed him down breezeway and watched as Pastor once again breathed heavily, returning home to Aia. Ruby and I heard him tell her that he needed a counselling appointment with her to seek some relief. As they were sitting at the dining room table, Clement explained the annoying and exasperating conversation he just had with Leona. He told Aia that he felt like he was behind a customer service counter being chewed out by an irked customer. When he was finished, Aia gave him some good advice by pointing him to Jesus words. It says in John 12:8, "You will always have the poor among you." Aia added that clergy life will always have critics who find something to question, scrutinize, and judge. She said it is a losing battle, but do not get too worried and end up having a stomach ulcer over it. Aia winked at Clement, told him that she would be honoured to be his personal counsellor. It was at this point that she changed the subject and asked three "why" questions, Trinitarian-style. 1) "Why is it that Leona Wilkes has the title of being St. Peter's Bulletin Examiner, Bulletin Folder, and Bulletin Board Overseer when she does not attend the worship services held on Sunday mornings?" 2) "Why is it that Leona Wilkes can drive to church Monday through Saturday to examine the facility, but does not drive here on Sundays?" 3) "Why is it that Leona Wilkes thinks she is entitled to learn the details of everyone's health problems?" She finished her thoughts by telling Clement that there is a lot of customer service in church work, pointing out that there is a good reason why "customer service" rhymes with "nervous." After that, she told Clement to take off his clerical shirt, put on his old college sweatshirt and tennis shoes, and that all five of them were going for a walk. Aia said that they would walk down to Grocer Dan's to pick up three items: a pound of butter, a can of cream-style corn, and diaper rash ointment. Ruby and I saw the return of Clement's warm and loving smile all because of the love he received from his Aia.

At 10:30 p.m. Ruby and I scooted to the parsonage. Finding only a single shred of cabbage from tonight's coleslaw, we felt blue. Knowing that it is only a pittance of a snack, we deliberately turned away from sniveling. After arriving home we discussed a "Who" question: "Who in the world is this renowned historical figure spotlighted on the narthex bulletin board?" We had a hunch it just might be Saint Peter, Paul, or Valentine, or maybe Gustavus Adolphus, but remain completely stumped, so we instead closed our eyes and sang "Sourwood Mountain." The striking portion of the folk song is not about chickens crowin' or my true love, but is found in the refrain that contains the extra-snappy, fun to sing words, "Hey-ho diddle-um day."

– F.N.

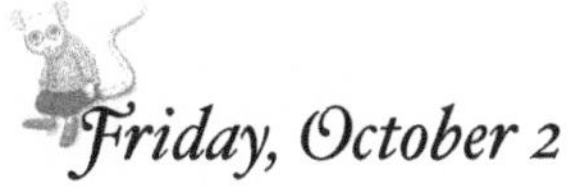

Friday, October 2

IT WILL NOT BE LONG FROM NOW WHEN GRASS MOWING SEASON WILL COME TO A HALT. Four dedicated parishioners from St. Peter's, Gil Green, Reid Miller, Lanny Foster, and Tim Payne have kept the church landscape looking like a golf course. HSP's Treasurer, Simon Thompson, is especially relieved that the volunteers only ask to be reimbursed for the gasoline they have purchased to run the lawn mowers. All four men arrive at church on Fridays so that the grass has a fresh haircut before Sunday rolls around. As been their practice this summer, they have taken turns bringing along a cooler containing ice cold beer. After the mowing is complete, they sit on two benches in the garden area and reward themselves for accomplishing the mowing and trimming. Two mice in our village, Rosetta and Wallaby, have been observing their behaviour week after week. The four men have also done many other helpful outdoor projects like putting up bird houses, planting bushes, and tending a large vegetable garden on the back lot at Historic St. Pete's. From the open back of Lanny's freshly washed brown pickup truck, parishioners have purchased cantaloupe, eggplant, watermelon, onions, honeydew melon, spinach, Swiss chard, kohlrabi, and four colours of peppers following Sunday's worship services this summer. Their gardening efforts produced a whopping success because they have raised over $700. The funds are earmarked to be given to the current District mission project, "Plentiful Harvest," based on Matthew 9:37.

The discussion at our last mouse village meeting centered on the recently drafted no alcohol policy drawn up by the church council. At the heart of our discussion was that these same four men, Gil, Reid, Lanny, and Tim, all hold a position on the church council and helped create this policy. But, they themselves go against it by enjoying a beer while on church property. The "No Alcohol Policy" is so strict that there cannot even be wine at wedding dinners served in Woolcox Hall, which makes no sense to our village. We are fully aware that Jesus himself turned water into wedding wine, which could very well have been Pinot Noir or Sauvignon Blanc.

At 8:30 p.m. Ruby and I travelled to the church kitchen and found a little bit of pastry dough. Today several of the ladies made beef and turkey pies for two families in the church that are struggling to make ends meet. It is a good thing that they were busy crafting pies and did not witness the brief Bavarian *Biergarten* unfolding in the church garden area after the yard work was completed.

– F.N.

Saturday, October 3

The first one of four scheduled Underground Railroad historical tours began today at St. Pete's. Abundant interest has been generated throughout the entire state and beyond because of this historical discovery. According to what we heard Pastor mention this morning, people are anxious to see for themselves the sight. With the good people at HSP working so diligently and faithfully these last weeks in preparation to host these tours, Clement and Aia cannot help but exclaim far and wide how very proud they are of the dear parishioners in their church!

The State has been divided up by Finn Larssen, State Historical Society Representative, into four separate sections. A charter tour bus arrived today from the Northeast section of the state at 10:30 a.m. While many mice from our village were posted on the window ledge in the church basement to see the arriving visitors, we noticed that Finn Larssen was in the lead with excitement written all over his face. He had so much enthusiasm that it rubbed off on the visitors, the parishioners, and the entire mice village! Finn did a marvelous job as tour guide giving those in attendance nothing short of a detailed history of the Underground Railroad, taking his time to explain the vast help given to the escaped slaves by Historic St. Peter's. Following his presentation, Finn asked the group to line up to take turns viewing the actual hiding spot where the escaped slaves once hid. Three people volunteered when he inquired if anyone in attendance would like to experience the hiding place first-hand. Finn asked the volunteers to enter the horizontal hiding spot, advising them to rest quietly on their backs. The movable floor boards were then laid down gently. Those in hiding experienced a snippet of what it was like to be an escaped slave during those life-threatening times. Organist Josie Johnson had been hired to play "Shall We Gather at the River" on the keyboard. After introducing the spiritual, the tourists sang the words that were printed on their song sheets while the pretend escaped slaves rested quietly in the hiding place. After the spiritual ended, Finn lifted up the movable floor boards. Instead of getting out of the hiding spot, the three volunteers stayed flat on their backs and handed Finn their cameras, asking him to take their photograph while they were in the actual hiding spot, a memento of their one-of-a-kind experience.

Josie also played numerous spirituals very quietly, much like a prelude, while the tourists were settling into the pews. Ready to calm down her anxious nerves, she again was in possession of her tea tumbler. Tissues were handy in case she needed to cover her mouth when anyone spoke to her in order to prevent them from getting a whiff of her breath. Pastor Osterhagen had an odd look on his face when he spoke with Josie, evidencing that he just doesn't know what to do about her problem. She never seems to be without her tea tumbler, similar to a baby's security blanket, and her pockets always have a tissue handy in case anyone visits with her. Her tumbler and tissues are starting to look like evidence, something most helpful in forming a conclusion, but Pastor doesn't want anything to do with being a lawyer or a judge. Perhaps Josie's condition as a tipsy organist at Historic St. Peter's is a problem that will be revealed soon enough to everyone. At that point he will not be alone. It might take care of itself and come to a head shortly.

The luncheon, prepared by the Ladies' Guild, was ready at noon in Woolcox Hall when everyone gathered there for lunch. Following that, the tourists were scheduled to return to the tour bus for their trip back home. A few mice heard that the bus driver was going to stop the bus half-way at a casino for two hours to break up the lengthy trip back home.

Today the ladies prepared wild rice soup, chicken salad and egg salad sandwiches, and brownie sundaes. The high cost of ingredients in wild rice soup led to a big ruckus among the ladies a few weeks ago. Some of them argued that wild rice soup is far too fancy and expensive, emphasizing that they should prepare a simple soup, like chicken noodle, which is far more economical. Darla Bungard piped up and told them that this was no time for plain old chicken noodle, the standard soup served to those who are suffering from the common cold or to those who have just recovered from a bout of the flu. Stating that they needed soup that is impressive and extra special, Darla was convinced that only wild rice soup would do, suggesting that they prepare a fresh kettle of it on all four Saturdays. Reminding them of the recognition given to Historic St. Peter's as a landmark church, she emphasized that HSP has been placed on the historical map of the entire United States. Because of that, it would be disgraceful, dishonourable, and shabby to be serving plain old chicken noodle soup. She told the girls to think of this opportunity as four celebration occasions in which they need a fancy soup. As far as the expenses were concerned, Darla volunteered that she would gladly donate enough wild rice for all four Saturdays. Her friend, Trina Davey, who is not a member of St. Pete's, came to her side and volunteered to donate fresh mushrooms for all four Saturdays, as well. Trina pointed out that the addition of mushrooms would enhance the wild rice soup bringing it a notch closer to being a gourmet soup. Because Trina has tight connections with the Ferguson Family Mushroom Farm located just outside Oswald County, she will purchase the best mushrooms available. She explained to the ladies that this mushroom operation transports small truckloads of top quality mushrooms to fancy restaurants up and down the East Coast. There are standing orders for these sought after mushrooms as chefs at posh restaurants rely on their excellence, quality, flavour, and freshness. Trina also put in a plug for the Elkridge Mansion on nearby Lake Harvey by telling everyone that their exceptionally talented chef-in-residence, Chef Axel O'Gara, uses only Ferguson Family Mushrooms in his creations. Because of the great savings on wild rice and the mushrooms, it quickly became settled by the ladies that they had the answer to their soup query, removing all of their doubts about expenses. The ladies commented that although they were not running a restaurant and are simply home cooks, not chefs, these Saturdays at St. Peter's will appear similar to a fancy restaurant that features wild rice soup as their soup du jour.

One of the Ladies' Guild members, Claire Dahl, spotted Finn Larssen when she served him a bowl of wild rice soup. Mandarin, one of the sweetest mice in our village, happened to be hiding behind the old upright piano when she peeked out and saw Claire nonchalantly stare at Finn's left hand, noticing that he was not wearing a wedding ring. Throughout the luncheon Claire's curiosity about Finn Larsson was sparked, so she glanced his way, several times, careful not to make any ado about it, but Mandarin said that she obviously found him to be remarkably attractive. She wasn't the only one in the room that found his looks captivating. Some of the tour bus ladies told him that if he ever tires of working for the State Historical Society he could be a movie star. Claire confided to her dear friend, Janet Woods, that Finn Larssen was blessed with more good looks than any man she had ever seen. His well-groomed six-foot something height, chiseled, but kind facial features, broad shoulders, and his strawberry blond hair made him a masterpiece of a man. But more importantly than his good looks, his personally and demeanour seemed to be topped off with a lighthearted, jolly, and exuberant smile. Claire again mentioned to Janet that Finn was so breathtakingly handsome that she needed to talk about it, so she spilled all of her thoughts to Janet. Claire told Janet that he looked like a Viking except for the brown State Historical Society uniform. Janet admitted that he is amazingly striking as far as good looks are concerned, but added that she much prefers her Ronnie, who looks much more like a teddy bear than a Viking. Janet told Claire that she likes her Ronnie just as he is because he is kind, cozy, and super-cuddly.

At 11:30 p.m. Ruby and I travelled to Woolcox Hall and snacked on an especially tasty morsel of a fancy mushroom. I guess it tasted so divine because it was grown locally. We concluded that everyone should purchase local ingredients to nourish themselves instead of choosing food items that are shipped into the state from some far, far away place like Tibet.

– F.N.

The Nineteenth Sunday after Pentecost ~ October 4

Today at Historic St. Peter's we remembered and honoured St. Francis of Assisi, the patron saint of all animals and lover of all of creation. The Feast of Assisi was technically yesterday, October 3, but, due to the fact that St. Pete's was extra busy with the presence of the State Historical Society, the celebration was moved to today, which many parishioners referred to as "Noah's Ark Sunday." Parishioners arrived this morning with their pets. Dogs, cats, birds, hamsters, a bunny, two hedgehogs, a turtle, and a guinea pig were in attendance to receive a special blessing from Pastor Osterhagen. This year, the mice village was honoured for the very first time. In a white cage, Billy Parker brought forward his two little white mice, Pearly and Alabaster. When Pearly and Alabaster received their special blessing, our mice village was delighted.

For safety reasons, the Feast of Assisi is being held for the first time outdoors because of last year's repulsive experience. It was then that Dallas Whittingham brought his donkey, Don Quixote, to church for a blessing. Much too large a creature to parade down the aisle at St. Pete's, Don Quixote, after having received a blessing, was led back down the aisle by Dallas. Unfortunately Don Quixote, a little stressed by everyone staring at him, did a big stinky splat on the sanctuary carpet. The parishioners gasped and even a year later are still talking about it. The church bully, Herman Jenkins, successfully hurt another person's feelings by standing up and yelling at Chuck Brownton, the custodian, using a sharp and threatening voice. He warned him to get busy, clean it up, and to hurry like H-E-double toothpicks to fix the problem. The tone of Herman's voice scared many of the animals and frightened the parishioners in addition to Chuck.

Chuck Brownton looked terribly downcast after being admonished. But, at the same time, steam was coming out of his ears after he had been yelled at in a very demeaning manner. Later that day, Pastor Osterhagen received an envelope that Chuck had slid under his office door. It contained his church keys along with the expected "I quit and I give up" letter adding that he had enjoyed his work at St. Pete's. He wrote that he always tried to give extra effort to make certain the church was spotless, to keep the quality of his work high, taking pride in his work, never minding to clean up more than what was expected of him. Pastor Osterhagen telephoned Chuck right away after receiving his resignation letter, telling him that he was not expected to clean the carpet. Pastor recognized that it needed a well-qualified carpet cleaning company that uses professional products plus the equipment to clean it up. At the end of their telephone conversation, Chuck rescinded his I-quit-and-I-give-up letter. He was so thankful for Pastor's kind and caring words, but mostly grateful that he did not have to go down to Grocer Dan's to rent a carpet cleaning machine in order to sanitize the carpet. Chuck told Pastor that he just couldn't do that job because he didn't have the stomach for it.

So, after all of the above, it was decided last year by the church council that every time the Feast of St. Francis of Assisi rolls around, the event will be held outdoors, and if it rains, it will be cancelled. Dallas was so embarrassed by Don Quixote's movements last year that it has prevented him from returning to church since that dumpy day because he has felt profoundly humiliated.

After blessing the two hedgehogs this morning, Hedgie and Hedgiette, the two dogs, Nip and Tuck, were ready to receive their blessing but appeared jittery when it was their turn. It was at that point that Nip and Tuck started to go at each other. Pastor tried to pull them apart, but in the process he got nipped. After he got them off each other he saw the bleeding wounds on both of his hands. The village assumed that Pastor probably couldn't wait until church was over so he could go home and try to repair his newest botheration.

Most of the village mice were hidden and tucked so far into the corners of the church today because Nettie LaFontaine brought her cat, Midnight, to church. A small team of mice went briefly to see what was going on, but when Midnight arrived, they headed for the hills.

Near the end of the worship service, Pastor wrapped his clean handkerchief around his wounded bleeding hands and when all had quieted down, he ended today's blessing of the animals with this specially selected Bible verse. "How many are your works, O LORD! In wisdom you made them all; the earth is full of your creatures." – Psalm 104:24

I must bring up that today was also St. Peter's First Annual Fishing Contest held on Lake Harvey. Two weeks ago a signup sheet was posted. Faster than a New York minute it was filled with contestant's names. Turner, the most nimble and fastest runner in our village, heard Pastor speak last Sunday with Brad Barretto, the organizer of the event. Brad agreed with Pastor that it was unfortunate that the event was scheduled during the Sunday morning worship service. Thankfully, instead of being held from 10:30 a.m. to 12 noon, Brad and Pastor changed the timing to 4:30-6 p.m. Turner mentioned to us another benefit of the time change. He said that Brad told Pastor that fish often bite better in the early evening. After all, he admitted that during that time, usually an hour before sunset, he personally has reeled in the most fish. Two mice in our village, Hop and Scotch, were able to hop into Stu Lazzarin's fishing boat while it was parked in the church parking lot. Stu had hitched the boat onto a trailer and was towing it with his truck. He only stopped at church to pick up three parishioners who were going to carpool with him to Lake Harvey.

Today's First Annual Fishing Contest winners were the following:

First Fish Caught by Josh Nowak: 3 lb. 3 oz. Walleye
Largest Fish Caught by Fred Berger: 6 lb. 3 oz. Northern Pike
Smallest Fish Caught by Ava Halvorson: 0.8 lb. Bluegill
Last Fish Caught by Stan Bakken: 2 lb 5 oz. Bullhead

Hop and Scotch reported to us that after the winners received their ice cream gift cards they decided to split and head to the Sweet Dreams Ice Cream Shoppe. Not only did the four winners go after ice cream, but everyone else in attendance at the First Annual Fishing Contest decided to go along, too. Scotch said that there must have been thirty or forty people standing shoulder to shoulder ordering their favourite flavours of ice cream. Ruby and I assume that Brad and Estelle Barretto must have raked in a bunch of dough at their ice cream parlour today.

At 11:30 p.m. Ruby and I travelled to the well-lit church yard and snacked on morsels we have never tasted before. We also sampled generic chicken jerky dog treats and dog biscuits. There were also some carrot tops and an entire iceberg lettuce leaf on the grass. We are very familiar with those two vegetables, as Aia continually uses them in her cooking. Being curious to know exactly what we were eating, we travelled to the church kitchen and peeked in the recycle bucket to learn from the empty containers exactly what unusual treats we had the opportunity to sample.

Ruby and I talked about how we, too, received a blessing at St. Pete's today even though we were hidden in the background. Knowing that some human beings think mice are a nuisance, God must not agree with that. Surely all creatures that God made have His blessing, just like when Pastor mentioned Psalm 104:24. After that, we spent the rest of the day being full of anticipation waiting for Hop and Scotch to arrive at our dwelling to reveal details about today's fishing contest. We were so overjoyed that Gretchen's friend, Ava Halvorson, was awarded a prize for catching the smallest fish. When Ruby heard that news she lunged forward and did a perfect cartwheel. Ava is just five years old and it was the first time she has gone fishing. We did wonder how someone so small could possibly consume three scoops of raspberry ripple ice cream packed in a waffle cone. We dare say she must have buckled down and given it her best shot.

– F.N.

Monday, October 5

Pastor Osterhagen's wounds are not healing. His hands are still oozing and continuing to swell. Running them under water several times yesterday and today, he followed up by applying dabs of antibiotic cream on his wounds, over which he placed several extra large sterile adhesive bandages. Aia has continually worried about his injuries since yesterday because she is certain that Nip and Tuck actually bit Clement, as she sees the bite marks on his hands, which she declares are not just bad scratches. They know that germs are quickly multiplying and both are worried about his safety.

This morning I heard Aia blurt out that she positively shudders when Historic St. Peter's blesses parishioners' pets. Pointing out that it brings out far too much realism, she brought up last year's event when the donkey, Don Quixote, attended St. Pete's. Because of the nitty-gritty consequences of that day, Don Quixote's owner, Dallas Whittingham, has not returned to church. What transpired that day is so vividly memorable it is though it happened just yesterday. It might take years for the blather to cross the great divide. Don Quixote probably could not help it that he deposited something far too earthy and repugnant on the sanctuary carpet. Just then Aia's comments to Clement were interrupted by a telephone call. Petal Duff, the owner of Nip and Tuck, called to advise Pastor that her dogs were exposed to rabies last Friday, two days before the Blessing of the Animals. After Clement hung up the telephone, he told Aia that he is petrified he has rabies. Instead of calling the clinic to make an appointment, Clement rushed down there faster than lightening.

While he was seated in the clinic waiting room, he later told Aia, an almost forgotten childhood memory popped into the forefront of his mind. One particular summer afternoon everyone in his family safely remained inside the house because a rabid skunk was unceasingly turning circles across the street in his friend Brucie's driveway. Clement recalled that his entire family had their noses pressed against the living room window staring at the odd actions of this skunk. He got an even better view after he retrieved his binoculars, a Christmas present from his Osterhagen grandparents. He told Aia that they counted the number of circles the skunk spun. It ended up to be fifty-eight rotations from the time they started counting, but he has no idea how many more circles the skunk turned before the counting began. Thankfully, it was not long before the county's animal control vehicle showed up and captured the skunk. After that the entire neighbourhood came outside to discuss what they had seen. We noticed that Aia was fascinated listening to Clement speak about this fluky skunk experience. We wondered if she was speaking Trinitarian lingo once again when Ruby and I heard her say, "So, the skunk plunked in the driveway, had a lot of spunk, plus he stunk."

Dr. Vallee examined Clement's hands, thoroughly cleaned his wounds, and because he had already heard about Nip and Tuck's exposure to rabies, vaccinated Clement. When Clement arrived back home he told Aia additional thoughts that he had while waiting in the doctor's office. He remembered the painting in the Louvre, "The Stigmata of St. Francis" by Giotto in which St. Francis received the marks of the crucifixion of Christ on his hands, the first recorded Christian to experience the stigmata. He also thought of the Bible verse from Galatians in which Paul reveals that he bears on his body the marks of Jesus. Aia told him that he is a complicated man, a terribly deep thinker, and that she thoroughly loves him, especially his heart and his mind. She added that there is no one on earth like him and that when his hands are healed and return to normal, he can use them all he wants on her. We mice are not sure exactly what she meant, but those words put a twinkle back in Clement's eyes, the first time since he got injured, hopefully wiping away most of the thoughts he had about rabies.

At 11:30 p.m. Ruby and I travelled to the parsonage and nibbled on a tiny potato lump from a pierogie as well as a kernel of rice from a cabbage roll. We agreed that Aia is up to her neck when it comes to taking care of the family. She does not have spare time to assemble a batch of homemade cabbage rolls or to stuff pierogies. We assume the cabbage rolls came from the freezer department at Grocer Dan's, in all likelihood purchased on an in-store special. Being not nearly as tasty as the Polish food Aia knows how to prepare, we ranked them with a seven-and-one-half star based on a scale of ten. Ruby and I batted around the various spellings of pierogies. Putting our noggins together we spelled out the following ways: perogie, pierogi, perogi, pierogy, perogy, pyrohy, pirogi, pyrogie, or pyrogy. Perhaps there are even more ways for them to be spelled. We decided that it might be of value to contact Ruby's second cousin, Cyril, who resides in Hamtramck, Michigan, to find out if he could add any details to our knowledge. Possibly we'll do that one day when we are feeling breezy, just as free as the wind.

– F.N.

Tuesday, October 6

MANY WEEKS AGO PARISHIONER IRMA GLEESEN DROPPED BY THE PARSONAGE TO EXPRESS cheerful congratulations to Aia on the safe arrival of the twins, probably hoping that she might get an opportunity to hold either precious Marc or Luc. This was Irma's first chance to drop by because she and her husband, Gary, have just returned from spending six months up north at their summer cottage. Irma presented Aia with a very generous, practical and much needed item for both babies: one-piece infant winter snowsuits. Another gift was a luscious-looking German chocolate cake. When attempting to place the cake on a kitchen counter, Ruby noticed Irma's uneasiness as she turned around and instead placed the cake on the dining room table. We have noticed that Aia has been short of time since the twins arrived to keep up on the ever-growing amount of dishes to wash. After Irma noticed that the kitchen counters were crammed with unwashed dishes, pots, and pans, she offered to be of help. Sitting down with Aia, Irma revealed her plan to wash up all of the dishes and get the kitchen back in shape. She said that she remembered well how difficult it was to keep up on everyday chores because of the vast amount of time newborn babies need from their mothers. We noticed that Aia could not have been more delighted or thankful to receive Irma's help since their dishwasher is broken and they cannot afford to replace it. Irma also added that when the dishes were washed, put away, and the kitchen counters were spotless, she would put on the coffee and then they could sample the German chocolate cake. While Irma was occupied at the kitchen sink, Aia fed the twins and got them in their cribs. Robinwing, a very capricious mouse, was visiting Ruby and myself during this time and overheard their conversation. Since that moment we have noticed that Robinwing has been following and observing Irma on Sunday mornings, probably because of her curiosity to find out the purpose of Irma's numerous top secret conversations she is having with many members of St. Peter's.

After Irma washed the dishes at the parsonage, her secret conversations hatched a helpful plan. Speaking with various members, she convinced them to contribute to a collection – a fund to purchase a new dishwasher for the parsonage. After church one Sunday Pastor and Aia were delighted when they were presented with a gift certificate for a dishwasher at Ingall's Appliance Centre. The very next morning they met with Orville Ingall and put the gift certificate to good, clean use. Because of the certain type of dishwasher that they selected, it had to be special ordered, but it was worth the wait. It was installed on Wednesday, September 30. Ruby and I cannot even express how many words of praise Aia has said about their one-of-a-kind dishwasher.

Unfortunately, this particular dishwasher has become the topic of much scuttlebutt. It has nothing to do with the quality or brand of the appliance, but the vibrant colour, candy apple red. Robinwing reported to us that Irma is the person most vocal about the colour, since she must have assumed that Pastor and Aia would choose either a white or ivory-coloured dishwasher. Irma even questioned Aia to find out if the dishwasher was not available in white or ivory. Aia looked as though she thought that was a very strange question. She responded by saying that they chose the dramatic bold colour red because it is cheerful and adds whimsy to the kitchen, including the thought that this energetic-looking red dishwasher will be delightful to load and unload. Aia once again rang true Trinitarian when she said that it will run daily, twice daily, or perhaps thrice daily, as this colourful appliance will have constant use.

Since Irma seems unable to wrap her head around the parsonage now having a flaming red dishwasher, Robinwing has overheard her suggest to other parishioners that Pastor Osterhagen will probably accept a call to another parish soon. When that time comes, she explained that the property chairperson will have to re-paint the dishwasher white. When Aia overheard this prattle, she surmised that Irma wanted them to leave St. Peter's. Since her feelings were hurt, Clement pulled her close and told her that there is either a right or wrong way to handle this. First of all, he suggested to Aia that she not paint Irma as her enemy because of her opinion that white is best. He added that living with a red dishwasher is a bold thing to do, suggesting that life is to be lived to the fullest, which Clement said describes Aia. We thought Clement gave Aia some solid advice when he told her to let it go, to let it bounce off of her. He reminded her to keep her skin thick and her heart tender. Ruby and I noticed that after Clement spoke loving words to Aia, she was able to settle her kettle. Aia told Clement that she hopes Irma will stop pushing the panic button about their flaming red dishwasher, be thankful that they had the common sense to not special order one in petal pink, bashful blue, opaque orange, go-getter green, egg yolk yellow, or passionate purple. Most importantly, she hopes Irma will put an end to suggesting to others that it is time for the Osterhagens to move away from Historic St. Peter's to another parish simply because of a red dishwasher.

At 10:15 p.m. Ruby and I travelled to the parsonage and found one tiny piece of Italian orzo that was delicately dressed with browned butter, parmesan, and basil. It was cooked perfectly, al dente. We split it. We also discovered and broke a red cinnamon heart imperial we found under Gretchen's chair. We were correct in predicting that there would be something red to eat at the parsonage today.

– F.N.

Wednesday, October 7

An out of the ordinary council meeting, or more correctly, emergency meeting was convened at St. Peter's tonight. A few days ago a large monetary donation was given to the church in loving memory of Forest Broderick by his two daughters, Ivy and Fern. Since Fern and Ivy reside in Northern California, they mailed a large envelope to St. Peter's with a letter describing the details of their father's exact wishes for this monetary donation. Additionally, the package included professional architectural blueprints for the construction of a large freestanding open-air picnic pavilion to be built on St. Peter's property. Most council members in attendance recognized that the plans are somewhat similar, but far smaller, than the sturdy and practical pavilion stationed at the Oswald County Fairgrounds.

Being that Forest spent his career as a state forest ranger, he often quipped to others that he was meant to be in that profession. Simply because he was born on Christmas Eve in the charming English hamlet of Forest Green, his folks gave him the first and middle name of Forest Green. This also was the tune name of his mother's favourite Christmas carol, "O Little Town of Bethlehem." Going on further he would add that the text of this carol happens to have another tune named St. Louis. Being that his mother favoured the Forest Green tune, having sung it every Christmas season at Holy Cross Parish, it made complete sense to name their newborn son Forest Green Broderick.

Paul Bunion was the village mouse on duty tonight to hear the special news at the emergency meeting. Paul, who suffers with pain and swelling due to the misalignment of his left big toe, used to be known by just plain Paul. But since this bunion has developed he is now known as Paul Bunion, not to be confused with the lumberjack Paul Bunyan and Babe the Blue Ox.

Paul Bunion overheard many details and shared them with Ruby and myself after the meeting. Forest's desire for the picnic pavilion included a stunning California redwood ceiling and a stone fireplace. This shelter would house picnic tables to be used for numerous church events. It would be the location for the church picnic, the ladies' summer potluck, Vacation Bible School, and even a Fourth of July celebration. Plus, it could be rented out for other social gatherings which would bring in additional income for St. Peter's.

After the plans were unveiled, council member Bruno Bettendorf had plenty to say. Paul Bunion revealed to us that whenever positive comments were offered, Bruno expressed his displeasure so vividly that if his attitude got any hotter he just might have burst a blood vessel. His mind is obviously against the outdoor shelter plans. Each time a person praised the idea, Bruno's displeasure grew. He announced that it would be a better choice for St. Peter's to construct an outdoor skating rink instead of a picnic pavilion. Paul Bunion mentioned that when Bruno was trying to convince the other council members to vote for the construction of a hockey rink, most of the members just looked down.

The vote to build the picnic pavilion passed, after which Bruno brought up a new topic. He suggested that whatever money remains from the construction of the picnic pavilion, it could be used to construct an outdoor cedar smokehouse for producing delicious homemade sausages. Mentioning that volunteers could gather together for some great camaraderie while working at a hands-on event, the smoked sausages could cleverly be named, "Best Wurst, Second to None, the One and Only." Bruno added that they could even prepare sausages for the church picnic as well as periodically offer advance take-away orders. He also volunteered to oversee the care and usage of the smokehouse. Everyone agreed that Bruno would be the best qualified person since he is a professional firefighter. This time while he was talking, the council members all looked at him directly in the eye and raised their hands to vote for Bruno's idea.

At 10:30 p.m. Ruby and I hurried to the church nursery where we savoured a small piece of a flavourful baby biscuit. Tonight we saved wear and tear on our teeth as the biscuit straightaway dissolved delightfully in our mouths.

– F.N.

Thursday, October 8

Aia had a doctor appointment today. After her examination she returned home and told Clement everything. If her test results turn out fine, all is well and she will not hear anything from the clinic. So, as it is often said, "No news is good news."

Aia told Clement that just before Dr. Vallee was about to leave the examining room she gathered up enough courage to ask him an embarrassing question. She explained to Dr. Vallee her timidity in bringing up the subject, but went on to say that ever since the twins were born she has had trouble getting her tummy flat. She is disappointed that her waistline is much larger than it used to be, questioning if she would be a good candidate for a tummy tuck. That really surprised Dr. Vallee, but he smiled and kindly answered all of her questions. She told him that she would appreciate a tummy tuck, if they really do work, but guesses that they could not afford one. She was seeking his advice as to whether or not he knows if the procedure actually brings about a flatter tummy. Instead, he advised her to just give it more time and that her tummy will get a bit smaller in the months to come by using sensible eating habits and daily exercise. She was happy with that news, thanked him, and left the clinic no longer dreaming about having a tummy tuck. Ruby heard her tell Clement that she really is going to try to shed the blubbery chubs that are clinging to her mid-section.

At 11:30 p.m. Ruby and I travelled to the parsonage and licked a spoon that was accidently dropped on the floor by Gretchen after supper tonight. We are certain it had been used to eat roasted acorn squash drizzled with brown sugar and butter.

Ruby and I shared with each other that we have no idea what a tummy tuck is, trying to figure it out. We wondered if it is similar to something called a ladies' body shaper that we saw advertised in a magazine. Ruby suspects a tummy tuck is sort of like a body waist cincher or shaper, but far more expensive and only available in California or Toronto. We agreed that it is hard to keep up on everything nowadays because of overflowing information. Lately we heard that one of the pear-shaped parishioners is scheduled to undergo something that is called a M.R.I. We visualize that it might have something to do with transforming an egg-shaped body frame into a svelte, willowy body shape. Ruby also suggested in a Trinitarian way that M.R.I. might really be decoded as Micro-Racketeering Inquiry, Missouri Radio Institute, or Maddux's Rheumatology Initiative. We'll sleep on it and wait until tomorrow to hear about the meaning of this acronym, after Dr. Simonsen has had a chance to decipher it.

– F.N.

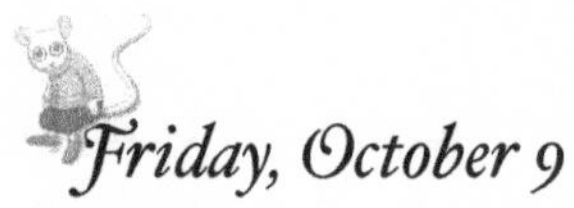

Friday, October 9

Clement received a telephone call from Rydel Stone, husband of the medical secretary who works full-time at Doctor Vallee's clinic. He mentioned that yesterday his wife, Janis, typed up Dr. Vallee's notes regarding Aia's appointment which included Aia's inquiries about the possibility of having a tummy tuck. Rydel spoke very sternly to Pastor and told him that if his wife is that vain, they have no business being a part of Historic St. Peter's. He suggested that they move to Hollywood and live among movie stars. Clement told him that Aia never intended to have a tummy tuck, she just wondered if her tummy would shrink and return to the size it was before the twins were born. Rydel's conversation did not last but a couple of minutes, but it made a long-lasting bad impression on Clement and Aia.

Clement and Aia agreed that the best thing to do would be to find a different doctor, even though they really appreciate Dr. Vallee as their family physician. Both Clement and Aia talked extensively about how Janis Stone was out of line, broke confidentiality, and probably could get fired over what she had done. Aia told Clement that Janis should be more professional in the way she behaves. She should type the medical reports with an unconcerned, indifferent, and disinterested attitude, instead of being an interfering, meddlesome, prime-time snoop queen. This incident showed to Clement and Aia just how rude people can behave. Aia strongly advised Clement to never offer Rydel an opportunity to serve on the church council or it will be nothing but trouble. It would be a huge thorn in Clement's flesh resulting in a whopper of a migraine before, during, and after every council meeting. He agreed with her. This encounter unwrapped Aia's feelings, once again, about how she feels like a fish in a glass bowl. The worst part she admitted is feeling judged by a few parishioners with ever penetrating eagle-eyes who find it anything but boring to scrutinize what she says and does. Aia admitted that she feels a commonality with any introverted movie star who is having qualms about leaving the privacy of their backstage dressing room. No matter how they come across, someone will be disappointed, even though they have a big golden star with their name pounded on their dressing room door.

Together Clement and Aia made a firm decision to find another doctor. It is a relief to them that Janis Stone will never again have the opportunity to examine and judge everything that appears on any of their medical charts.

At 11:30 p.m. Ruby and I travelled to the parsonage and found a tiny puddle on the floor of broccoli/cauliflower soup. We found one-half of an oyster cracker so we took that home and finished our snack in bed. We cannot decide what is more pleasurable. Is it a midnight snack in bed or breakfast in bed?

– F.N.

Saturday, October 10

Claire Dahl arrived at Woolcox Hall this morning announcing to the kitchen crew that she wouldn't be helping today. Instead, she will be attending the engrossing historical lecture led by Finn Larssen. As soon as his name left Claire's lips, every woman figured out what Claire was up to. Ever since Claire lost her husband to cancer a few years ago, she has acquired the nickname Ladyhawk by being on alert looking for the right manly man.

Hiding on the floor behind the church stove, two from our village, Bisque and Moccasin, were on their first date. They refrained from visiting in order to listen closely to the conversations in the kitchen. Hearing the ladies remarks about Claire's physical transformation, they were puzzled how she accomplished this within the last six days. Totally revamping her style from head to toe, Claire's brown hair now had strands of caramel and blonde highlights that adorn an edgy modern cut. Her clothing is pristine and looks like it's from a fashion magazine, accentuated with matching jewellery. Especially noticeable is the lack of her wedding ring on her left hand. It has been replaced by an oversized fashion cocktail ring that has a large London blue centre stone, complete with professionally manicured fingernails painted in a deep, dark, and mysterious shade of red. This cocktail ring spoke loudly on her left hand, communicating without words, that she is single and available. Most noticeable, however, is that she has shed some weight, maybe five to seven pounds since last Saturday. That must have been accomplished with a great amount of suffering, especially if she was on one of those unhealthy, strict, lose weight quickly plans.

Before Claire left the church kitchen, the ladies complemented her on her new flamboyant physical appearance. After that the ladies discussed how in the world Claire could have accomplished her transformation in such a short amount of time. Several of the ladies wondered if they could possibly pull that off themselves, but said that they doubted it. They all thought she must have consumed very little food, drank gallons of water, spent a fortune at the hairdresser, the nail salon, and shopped in every nook and cranny of the fashion stores located in nearby Liberty Mall. More importantly than all of that, they talked about what the possible outcome will be of Claire's flirting attempts with Finn Larssen, at which time Bisque and Moccasin started to visit about that juicy topic, too, but ever so quietly.

The tour bus arrived at 10:30 this morning with Finn getting off ahead of the group of history buffs travelling from the northwest portion of the state. The first two Saturdays in October belonged to the upper section of the state, the northeast and the northwest. This was done to avoid any unforeseeable snow, not likely to happen, but since Finn has seen it snow every single month of the year, he thought it best that the Northern tour groups be scheduled early in the month. He repeated everything that he did last Saturday at St. Pete's and so did Josie while she was posted at the keyboard with her tea tumbler and tissues.

Nearing the end of the presentation, Finn once again offered the group a chance to experience firsthand resting in the hiding place, spending a very brief amount of time in there. Claire was the first one to accept the offer, asking Finn if he had had the chance to do that yet. When he said that he hadn't yet had an opportunity, she asked him to go along with her and the two other people who had volunteered. Pastor Osterhagen was asked to lower the floor boards so that Finn had a turn to experience the hiding spot for himself. Finn and Claire were side by side resting in the hiding place. When the introduction to the spiritual finished, Claire sang along on the words of "Shall We Gather at the River," which she might have recently memorized. The mice marvelled at her trained artistic singing voice, wondering if she hoped Finn would notice her musical skills. When the spiritual came to an end, she told Finn that she was a chamber singer during her university days. Ruby said that Claire must have hoped that her words might be a conversation starter for the two of them to get to know each other better.

After the presentation, everyone enjoyed lunch in Woolcox Hall. The luncheon was identical to last week except that there were different people in attendance. The Ladies' Guild agreed last week that the menu was just perfect, and due to the fact that many of the supplies were donated which controlled costs, they were able to make a splendid profit from their labour. They visited about their hopes for profiting from the lunch today and also about the upcoming two Saturdays. For now, they will squirrel their money safely away in their treasury. Soon they will make a decision on just how to spend it, or true to their tradition, just keep saving it and letting it pile up.

One somewhat zany member of our village, Tiffin, has become intrigued to keep a steady eye on Finn Larssen. With absolutely no chagrin, Tiffin grins when he speaks of Finn, even guessing that Finn might play the violin. Most villagers think Tiffin's notions are preposterous, assuming that his interest in Finn is simply because Finn's name is embodied in his own name. Making observations while hiding in Woolcox Hall, Tiffin reported to us that Claire steadily remained in close proximity to Finn. Sitting alongside him during lunch, they exchanged a bustling conversation. Claire ardently communicated to Finn that today's presentation was absolutely engrossing, adding that she will surely be in attendance next Saturday. Finn's demeanour appeared as though he felt almost bashful when Claire fawned over his breath-taking personal presentation skills. After receiving the glowing compliments, Finn jumped up from his chair, excused himself, and vanished. After all, it was time for the visitors to board the bus, journey towards home, but, most importantly, stop halfway for some gambling excitement at the casino.

At 11:30 p.m. Ruby and I travelled to Woolcox Hall and snacked on the same thing we had last Saturday. It looks like this wild rice soup luncheon is becoming an October Saturday tradition here at Historic St. Peter's that we wish would never end.

When we were returning home, we had to take an alternate route due to flooding in the hallway that was coming from both washrooms. I guess that the flood of people arriving to view the Underground Railroad spot has put a heavy strain on the existing plumbing system. Unfortunately, Ruby and I do not know how to help, but we are expecting that there will be many people perturbed when they arrive at church tomorrow morning and see a torrent of water in the hallway that is reaching far beyond the doors of the washrooms.

– F.N.

The Twentieth Sunday after Pentecost ~ October 11

When altar guild volunteer Freya Stephens arrived at church today to set up Holy Communion, she discovered flooding. She quickly printed signs and attached them to numerous doors at St. Peter's. The information on the signs read:

THE WASHROOMS AT ST. PETER'S ARE
"OUT OF ORDER" TODAY.
SORRY.
IF YOU NEED A WASHROOM,
USE THE ONE AT THE PARSONAGE.
THANK YOU FOR YOUR PATIENCE.

Today property chairperson Will Anderly needed to handle a church property calamity. Straightaway he dealt with a steady stream of water flowing from both main floor washrooms. It was as though the headwaters of the mighty Mississippi River were located at St. Pete's and well on their way to the Gulf of Mexico. Obviously he was tied in a knot before coming on the scene. After arriving at church Will darted to the basement to turn off the water main. One refreshing mouse in our village, H2O, listened as Will spilled forth plenty of cash related words concerning the needed plumbing repairs: money, safety, hard cash, moolah, greenbacks, dough, the budget, lack of finances, loot, and once again, money. His final words as he threw his arms up in the air were, "How in the shekels are we going to pay for this?" H2O was thankful when Dave Pennington, owner of Pennington's Tool & Die, approached Will and told him to calm down and breathe. Dave suggested that Will hire a professional to fix this problem, adding that he would be happy to pay for the entire expenditure himself. Will was so thrilled that he not only hugged Dave, but kissed him on his left cheek. H2O mentioned to me that the hug and kiss seemed to completely flabbergast Dave. After that, Dave told Will to order two Rent-A-Biffies, placing them in plain sight, one on each side of the main church door for use until the washrooms are back in working order.

After the parishioners left church today, Will focused on another matter by carrying out a mysterious project. He was busy placing four inexplicable contraptions in four different locations throughout St. Pete's. He put one in the pots and pans cupboard located in the church kitchen, one in the breezeway, one in the church office, and the last one in the janitor's closet. These devices all had a small square of cheese attached to them, but no one in our community wanted to be the first one to eat the cheese because we wondered if we were faced with a safety issue. Because our safety might be at risk, the village could not wait until tonight to call a meeting. Instead we gathered together as soon as we heard Will Anderly exit the back door of the church.

Two of our mice, Tawny Bragg and Bella-Button, were the first ones to come upon the apparatus that was placed in the pots and pans cupboard. Tawny is boastful and often blows his own horn, but Bella-Button is quiet, usually pressing her lips tightly together when it is time to speak. Tawny said that after spotting the mechanism, they nearly went for the lucky chance to enjoy tasting the cheese, but refrained and backed off because they knew to put safety first. Even though the cheese was a mild-cheddar with an irresistible bouquet, they were able to garner up enough restraint to resist taking a mouthful. The entire mice village was overjoyed and proud of Tawny and Bella-Button for using their brains instead of giving in to their cheese cravings.

Round and round the discussion roamed, until most concluded that the contraption must be a mouse exercise machine intended to reduce stress, improve one's health and happiness, and of course, to get a rockin' bod. It was concluded that the cheese must be there as a reward to be enjoyed after a workout. Our village's oldest member, Methuselah, made known to us that long, long ago he witnessed a death due to one of those contraptions. Methuselah warned us that the mechanisms might be part of a ploy to trick us. He added that they are definitely not an exercise machine but a way to bamboozle victims to step into a death trap. He mentioned that in the old days it was called an eradication snare. After the village heard Methuselah's words, all became frightened, followed by pandemonium. Our only sure way to calm down was to join together in singing "Safety First." Methuselah urged everyone to stay far, far away from the death traps so that we will all be kept in safety.

Singapore, a mouse in our village who dreams of one day having endless opportunities to travel, observed Aia's expression when she read one of Freya's signs posted on the breezeway door before worship this morning. He said that after Aia read the sign she and Gretchen turned around and zoomed down the breezeway with Marc and Luc, heading back to the parsonage. Ruby happened to stay home from worship this morning due to a headache. But, because of the commotion she posted herself near the crack in the dining room wall noticing an unusually energetic Aia. She said that the first thing Aia did was to secure Marc and Luc in their wind up baby swings so she could plow ahead into breakneck housekeeping chores. Secondly, she improved the washroom by replacing the old towels with fresh ones, put out a roll of paper towels, wiped the sink, scrubbed the toilet, emptied the garbage, swept the floor, washed the mirror, shut the shower curtain, and misted the room with lavender air freshener. Thirdly, she vacuumed the living room. Fourthly, she wiped up the kitchen counters and cleaned off the dining room table. Fifthly, she tidied up the bedrooms. Ruby remarked that for Trinitarian Aia, this seemed unusual behaviour. Ruby asked me if Aia might be turning away from being a Trinitarian and instead becoming a one-person quintet.

When Clement arrived home after the worship service, he found an exhausted and discouraged Aia. She mentioned that she was happy to help supply a clean washroom, but wondered if thirty-three people really needed to go during the worship service, or if they just were curious and wanted to see the parsonage. Aia told Clement that there was such a lineup that parishioners were seated in the living room chairs and at the dining room table waiting for their turn to use the washroom. She also mentioned that she was worried about the twins being seasick because they spent so much time in their infant swings, thanks to Gretchen's excellent help in keeping the swings wound up so she could accomplish the housework. It was when Aia told Clement about their mahogany coffee table that she started to cry. We saw her reach out for Clement's hand to head to the coffee table. One parishioner had written in the dust, "to dust you will return." Aia told him that she was in such a rush that she did not have time to get out the feather duster to do a quick once over before the mob arrived. Clement was impressed that whoever wrote the "dust" words on the coffee table was familiar with Genesis 3:19. Aia added that she also is well aware of that particular Bible verse because the speedy cleanup that she accomplished this morning produced on her a sweaty brow, plus it is now lunchtime. She concluded her thoughts by saying that if she had known in advance about a tidal wave of parishioners arriving at the parsonage, she would have at least purchased fresh flowers to beautify the dining room table. Gretchen brought the Holy Bible over to her daddy and asked him to read what is found in Genesis 3:19. Clement read, "By the sweat of your brow you will eat your food until you return to the ground, since from it you were taken, for dust you are and to dust you will return." Gretchen thanked him and reported that there is a lot of dust on the floor under her bedroom dresser. After that she asked her mama what was for lunch.

Clement told Aia that the church council gathered together for a "brief" meeting after church today regarding the flooding church washrooms. Unfortunately, "brief" slid into "drawn-out," all because of the way Stig Madsen recorded the minutes of the meeting. We all know that Stig is a sought after cabinet maker throughout Oswald County who carries his carpentry pencil and buck knife everywhere he goes. Recording today's minutes took longer than usual because Stig took notes using his carpentry pencil. Plus, several times Stig stopped writing and manually sharpened his pencil with his buck knife. Ruby pointed out to me that Stig's behaviour was better than when Deborah Poole would take notes and place her fancy pen down on the table where it would roll each time to the floor. Ruby pointed out that a carpentry pencil is superior because it remains flat when placed on a table. The council decided to open a maintenance fund and distribute donation envelopes in next Sunday's bulletin. Already Dave Pennington has offered to foot the bill for the plumbers and the Rent-A-Biffies. All agreed that the funds given can be applied to the cost of the new toilets. Frankie North suggested that we name it the "St. Pete's Bowl-A-Thon," which the council thought was a fitting name. Secondly, Frankie offered to contribute a discarded pink toilet that has a resin toilet seat embellished with an attractive flamingo decal, confiscated from one of his home renovation projects. He offered to give the toilet a "real good scrubbing" before dropping it off at church. His master plan was for donation envelopes to be dropped in the toilet bowl. When we heard that he was certain the pink toilet would dress up the Narthex, plus give extra attention to the maintenance fundraiser, Frankie had obviously taken the idea too far, because no one agreed with his idea. Lastly, the council decided that since Pastor lives on the premises, he was appointed to be the "Church Bailiff." This new task is to be an overseer of the entire church building. From now on every evening he will be making rounds throughout the premises to make certain everything is in dandy shape. After Aia heard this news she asked Clement if they could move.

At 10:30 p.m. Ruby and I were more than thrilled to come upon a small sliver of Double Gloucester cheese underneath Gretchen's chair at the dining room table. However, our jubilant feelings quickly diminished when we remembered Methuselah's warnings about death traps. Even though a death trap was not located under Gretchen's chair, somehow just the thought of it seemed to sizably diminish our cheese craving. So, instead of tasting the Double Gloucester, we savoured several alfalfa sprouts that had dropped to the floor from the Osterhagen's tuna fish sandwich platter.

– F.N.

Monday, October 12 ~ Canadian Thanksgiving Day

Aia's folks, Arni and Juliette Nygaard, telephoned the Osterhagens this morning to wish them Happy Canadian Thanksgiving. After hanging up, Aia told Clement that she felt deeply homesick even though she was already at home and physically felt fine. Ruby heard Clement ask her why she felt so dismal and downhearted. Aia waited a minute before responding to him. She said that her mood sunk when her mother told her about their Thanksgiving dinner menu. Clement lovingly offered to help her out by going to Grocer Dan's and returning with a bucket of fried chicken, mashed potatoes, gravy, cranberry sauce, and a pumpkin pie. Aia told him that his intentions were really kind, but added that she wasn't a bit hungry for any of that, just hungry for seafood. Aia said that when her mother told her about their special appetizers, the heavenly two-bite and delightfully pleasing seafood sensation that her mother prepares, the "Itty-Bitty Lobster Rolls," that was enough for her to fall into a deep crater. For a second time Clement asked her how he could help, so she thought for a minute and told him her idea. Ruby heard Aia ask Clement to drive down to Grocer Dan's to pick up a big box of fish sticks which would provide a nearly satisfactory substitution for the lobster rolls.

At 11:30 p.m. Ruby and I travelled to the parsonage searching for a snack, but did not find one. Instead we sat down and quietly visited about fish sticks because we have never heard of them before. We wondered if fish come in all sizes. Perhaps fish sticks got their name because their body frames are as skinny as a stick.

– F.N.

Tuesday, October 13

Pastor Osterhagen was noticeably crestfallen when he read the contents of an anonymous letter in today's mail, witnessed by Larkspur, one of the most likeable mice in our village. Larkspur noticed that Pastor could not shake this single piece of mail off of his mind all morning. At lunchtime he took the letter home and showed it to Aia. Ruby and I felt deeply disturbed when she read the letter out loud. It said: "Pastors get a welcome when they first arrive at a church. It isn't very long before they wear out their welcome. At that point they need to go away! So, get busy and start packing boxes. You don't belong here anymore!"

After Aia read the letter she needed to take a look at the envelope. Immediately she talked about the fancy return address label containing the name and address of Conrad and Molly Goddard, faithful members of St. Peter's. Aia was quick to respond what she suspects happened. She surmised that Conrad wrote the letter intending for it to be anonymous. He must have left it on the side table in their entryway, ready to be mailed on his way to work the next morning. However, before he woke up, Molly was on her usual early morning walk where her route takes her right by the neighbourhood post box. Before she left home, she must have noticed that the envelope was missing a return address label. So, extremely helpful Molly got out one of their colourful address labels printed with vintage love birds surrounded by fancy scrollwork and stuck it on the envelope addressed to Pastor Osterhagen. Aia said that Molly might not have even told Conrad that she put an address label on the envelope, but only mentioned that she mailed it as a favour to him.

The discussion was far from finished when we heard Clement and Aia try to surmise why the Goodards want them to leave Historic St. Peter's. Thinking back, they recall that Conrad was upset about the recent sanctuary eternal light electrification. Before that modernization, Conrad was solely responsible for lighting the eternal light and later on extinguishing it. The minute the Benediction ("The Lord bless you and keep you . . .") began, Conrad would exit his pew to retrieve a ten foot ladder. Holding a candle snuffer in his left hand made him fully prepared to extinguish the burning candle suspended from the high ceiling during the singing of the closing hymn. For years parishioners have been whispering that Conrad should be told to wait until the postlude has begun to extinguish the eternal light, but no one has been found to be brave enough to break that news to him. Instead, Vince Estes, a professional electrician, was hired to electrify the eternal light by putting it on one simple light switch.

Trying to connect the hate letter and the electrification of the eternal light was a stretch for Clement until Aia recalled that Vince and Conrad exchanged angry words in the parking lot the day Vince electrified the eternal light. In the middle of that flare-up, Clement came out to the parking lot, greeted both of them, but immediately Conrad huffed and puffed and headed to his car, hastily driving away. Aia surmised that Conrad must have concluded that Clement was behind the eternal light electrification, a sure way to take his candle snuffing position away from him. They both realized that Conrad must feel that this was a slap in the face, doubled with the unspoken message that the church does not "need" him anymore. Clement told Aia that he will talk to Conrad because he must be wrestling with not being appreciated, adding that it is best to love people even when they are unlovable. However, he added, it might already be the eleventh-hour as Conrad probably has Molly convinced that they should belong to a different church.

Aia, speaking Trinitarian, said that she has never understood the point of the eternal light at Historic St. Peter's, noticing that it is anything but eternal, continuous, or never-ending. She is of the opinion that it should be burning continually to honour Christ's presence. But, she is sure that she is the only one who looks at it that way. At St. Peter's it seems to be reasonable to intermittently shine an "eternal" light by flicking it on and off with a light switch.

At 9:45 p.m. Ruby and I travelled into the very dark sanctuary at Historic St. Peter's. If the eternal light was going perpetually it would have been far easier to find a snack. We were extra lucky, though, as Ruby came across a little "o" that a toddler must have dropped. Ruby did not see the little "o" but while she walked forward her back foot went right through the little "o" as if she was wearing an ankle bracelet. She headed home with the little "o" on her foot and we shared our snack. We joined together in saying one of our favourite expressions, "Oh, my stars, our lucky day!"

– F.N.

Wednesday, October 14

After kindergarten today, Clement and Gretchen headed towards Carpenter's Apple Orchard. Unbeknownst to them, McIntosh, a village mouse that has an especially tart personality, hitched a ride with them. Finding an opportunity to scurry into the van, he hid out behind one of the infant seats until they all arrived at the orchard. Thankfully, McIntosh did not miss out on any of the afternoon's details, so Ruby and I became well informed when he visited our dwelling. McIntosh mentioned that Gretchen was appropriately decked out for today's crisp autumn weather by wearing her emerald green fleece parka and a soft, feather-weight toque. Just a few days ago Gretchen received a gift from her Granny Juliette, a green and blue knitted tweed toque adorned with a faux fur creamy-coloured pom-pom. Gretchen was thrilled with the present. She was also elated to be invited by Cassidy Carpenter, her Sunday School friend, to pick apples at Carpenter's Apple Orchard. It turned out to be such a red-letter day that it was the only topic Gretchen talked about during tonight's supper.

Gretchen relayed how Cassidy's daddy parked his pickup truck directly underneath an apple tree. The two girls stood in the bed back of the truck finding no difficulty reaching the apples. Cassidy told Gretchen that the best part of apple picking is when they find a rotten apple. Each time they picked one, they were allowed to throw it as far as they could into the field where the cows were grazing. Cassidy said that the cows eat apples even if they have brown spots or a worm. The two girls had so much fun throwing apples, some of which directly struck the cows. The cows did not even flinch, appearing utterly unaware that they had just been hit by a miscellaneous flying object.

Gretchen and Clement returned home with three large bags of apples along with a stack of professionally printed recipe cards, thanks to Cassidy's mother. Ruby and I noticed that Aia was simply fascinated by the various tempting recipes including apple dumplings, pies, strudel, crisps, and apple butter. While waiting for Gretchen, Clement shopped in the adjacent store and purchased smoked sausage, inquiring if it needed to be refrigerated. The clerk at the meat counter told him that he could store it in the refrigerator, but it is smoked and could be stored on top of the refrigerator, that is, unless he owns a cat. If they own a cat, he had better put it in a container so that the cat won't get at the sausage. He also purchased a narrow long-necked bottle of Carpenter's dessert wine, planning to save it for Thanksgiving Day, plus an eighteen pack of farm-fresh brown eggs, knowing that Aia would especially be pleased. McIntosh said that Clement later on sat down with Anton Carpenter and they had a good conversation. Before leaving, Clement went back to the store and purchased cheddar cheese. When Anton noticed Pastor's final purchase, he reached into the cooler and gave him another wedge of cheese. Anton told him that he and his family will be in church on Sunday.

For dessert tonight Aia prepared the Carpenter's apple dumpling recipe. She was grateful for the large apple supply and also delighted that Gretchen had so much fun being a country girl, or a farm girl today. During supper Aia played a tape that she was given of country music performed by "Honesty from the Heart," a group of three women who frequently sing at their church in Barnhart, Missouri, while the offering is gathered.

At the supper table, Gretchen asked a Q & A regarding Mr. Carpenter's neck. She told her folks that she noticed his Adam's apple going up and down over and over again. She wondered if Mr. Carpenter might be in danger due to a little apple being permanently stuck in his throat. Going on, she wondered if Adam's apples might be Adam and Eve's fault. Revealing that she learned about their disobedience in the Garden of Eden when Eve picked a piece of fruit from the tree of good and evil, she wondered if Adam was the first man to have a small apple stuck in his throat. Clement and Aia told Gretchen that Adam's apples are a common feature in grown men. Also, they noted that the topic is very complicated because it concerns the voice box, medically referred to as the larynx. Ruby noticed that Gretchen lost interest when she heard them use a medical term. After that, Gretchen asked another question that involved tonight's apple dumplings. Explaining that her tummy was currently full, she wondered if she could have a dumpling later on before she goes to bed. Aia smiled and told her that it would be better if she instead had one-half of a dumpling. Gretchen smiled so brightly that we noticed the glorious colour of her cheeks identically resembled the shade of a Pink Lady apple. Part of that beauty just might be due to Gretchen spending an entire afternoon breathing in fresh country air.

At 11:30 p.m. Ruby and I travelled to the parsonage expecting to snack on morsels of apple dumplings, but we came up empty. We noticed that the three Osterhagens so keenly enjoyed their apple dumplings that they actually licked their plates. Rarely, but once in a while when Aia cooks something more than ever so luscious, the Osterhagens do lick their plates. Each time that they use this improper table etiquette, Aia sternly warns them to never repeat that behaviour at a restaurant because the owner might cast out, evict, or banish them from ever returning to that establishment. But she assured them that licking their dessert plates tonight was necessary since the brown sugar butter sauce was stuck to the bottom of their plates. Wasting a single drop of such a scrumptious sauce was not an option.

– F.N.

Thursday, October 15

The parsonage doorbell rang at 4:30 this morning. Clement was so startled that he loped out of bed to answer the door. On the stoop stood their next door neighbours, Jim Keller and eight-year old son, Travis. We heard distress in Jim's voice when he spoke about his ten-year old daughter, Ashley. He said that she became violently sick during the night. He and Kathleen, his wife, needed to rush Ashley to the emergency room at Our Lady of Lourdes Hospital. Jim wondered if Travis could stay with the Osterhagens while they were away. Clement agreed, but before Jim took off, Clement said a quick prayer for Ashley which brought Jim to tears. We heard Jim blowing his nose, after which he said he needed to skedaddle as Kathleen and Ashley were in the car.

Even though Clement and Travis were very quiet, the day had already begun. There might as well have been a rooster's cock-a-doodle-doo right outside the bedroom windows because even the twins woke up. After Aia changed both diapers, Gretchen held Marc, while Travis held Luc. Clement started up the coffee pot and Aia prepared scrambled eggs and buttered toast points. As they sat at the dining room table, Travis began to speak about his sister, revealing that he felt afraid. Gretchen spoke to Travis assuring him that God lives at the hospital and will help the doctors, nurses, and Ashley. Gretchen offered to say a prayer. This seemed vitally important, so I wrote it down. This is what she prayed: "Almighty God, Heavenly Father, please help Ashley to feel better. Right now Mr. & Mrs. Keller need Your help, because they probably feel more afraid than Ashley. Help the other people in the hospital to get better, too. Thank you for Travis being here today, a day where we will have a bunch of fun! We ask everything in Jesus name, Amen." Travis thanked Gretchen for her prayer. She said that she was happy to help.

Gretchen then asked Travis if there was something he wanted to do for fun today. He quickly said that he would like to play cards. Gretchen, Aia, and Clement were pleasantly surprised hearing his idea because their favourite card game requires four people. Quickly the breakfast dishes were finished and the cards were dealt, boys against the girls. Travis is a whiz at cards because of a Keller tradition: Bring out the card table, set it up in the living room, get snacks ready, and deal out the sticky cards. Travis informed everyone that sticky cards are the ones that are covered with popcorn butter or cheese-flavoured puff crumbs. He also said that the "good" cards are the ones that are very clean and slippery. They are saved for when Mr. & Mrs. Armstrong play Rummy with his folks.

After three hands were dealt, it was evident that Travis is a "kitty hog." The contents of his hand do not matter nearly as much as discovering what is in the kitty. After outbidding everyone, even his partner Pastor Osterhagen, Travis captured the kitty a fourth time. He again ducked under the dining room table to sort out his cards. When he was finished, he returned to his chair and announced trump. This was repeated hand after hand until Clement looked at his watch and said he'd better get ready to make a shut-in visit to see Mrs. Addington. He remarked that there are but two immovable times of the day, 10 a.m. and 2 p.m., when he can call on her. After he broadcast that news, Aia, Gretchen, and Travis urged him to stay home and continue playing cards, advising him to call on Mrs. Addington at 2 p.m. We heard Clement sadly mention that he has not played cards much since his university days. When Travis heard that, he quickly volunteered his services as a fourth player to come over any time to play cards at the parsonage. Clement thanked him and said that when they have time, they will play cards again. Gretchen was helpful in that she wants to be the one to notify Travis. Travis then suggested that they construct a tin can telephone between the two houses, positioning it up on the two backyard decks. Mentioning that it needs only a few supplies from the hardware store, they could build it together. Excitement was overflowing at the parsonage as they prepared a shopping list while Aia emptied two cans of stewed tomatoes into a bowl, put the contents in the refrigerator, and rinsed out the empty cans. Already they were on their way to creating a tin can telephone line where Gretchen will be the primary telephone operator.

The card-playing craze continued until noon when it was time to stop for lunch. Because they were so occupied playing cards, Aia did not have a chance to prepare lunch, so they resorted to peanut butter and jelly sandwiches. Following lunch, several more hands of cards were played. A brief break was taken to head to the hardware store. The afternoon was absorbed with tin can telephone line construction. When the project was finished, they tested it out. Clearly celebration was in the air because it worked! It was not until 4:30 p.m. that Clement realized that he had forgotten to call on Mrs. Addington at 2 p.m. By then it was too late to visit her. We heard him telephone Mrs. Addington and apologize. She mentioned it was OK that he did not come over today because an annoying cousin dropped by and stayed for hours. She mentioned that this relative's intentions are good, but that she grates on her nerves. When the cousin finally left her house today, Mrs. Addington admitted that she needed a stiffener to help her return to normal. After telling Aia about that conversation, Clement went to the hospital to call on Ashley. At 6 p.m. he returned home with the good news that Ashley will be fine and will return home in a few days. It certainly was a good thing that Jim and Kathleen got Ashley to the hospital in time because she was suffering with appendicitis and needed an emergency appendectomy. Travis and Gretchen both nodded their heads up and down because they have heard of that type of operation before. After tonight's supper of individual meat and vegetable pies, heated up because there was no time to cook due to today's card playing marathon, the four returned to their spots to play more hands of cards. It was not until 8 p.m. that the parsonage doorbell rang. Jim and Kathleen were there to pick up Travis, profusely thanking the Osterhagens for their help.

At 11:30 p.m. Ruby and I travelled to the parsonage and came upon a variety of snacks. There was a kernel of popcorn, a cheese-flavoured puff, one green pea, two potato cubes, and one square of cooked carrot all found underneath the dining room table. We doubt that we will ever witness another card-playing monomania like the one today, but the time was not wasted. Travis is gung-ho about being a fourth player. He can instantly be notified when Gretchen, the chief operator, calls into the newly constructed tin can telephone line located between the two decks and asks him to hoof it over to the parsonage to play cards.

– F.N.

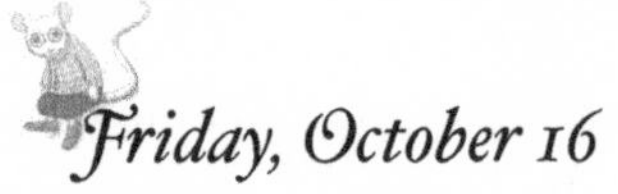

Friday, October 16

Late last night, Big Ben, one of our villagers who used to be called just plain Ben, dropped by our dwelling to seek professional advice. Even though Ruby and I were drooping from the day's activities, we sat down and carefully listened to Big Ben tell his story. We did our very best to support him and give him words of encouragement.

Big Ben revealed to us that his great grandfather Benjamin was born and raised at a clock museum somewhere in Iowa where there was an ever-present and ongoing variety of bewitchingly beautiful tick-tock sounds. Even though Big Ben has never even visited the State of Iowa, he has somehow developed an addiction to constantly watching the time, fully lacking the restraint to ignore any and all clocks, especially ones that make the tick-tock sounds. He does not know how this frivolous behaviour has come into being, but thinks it is perhaps natural, something he inherited from his great grandpa Benjamin that flows deep within his being and bloodstream.

Since Big Ben has an addiction to being on clock patrol at HSP, he refers to himself as Historic St. Peter's "Timekeeper of Timepieces." Having counted every clock at St. Pete's, that total comes to a whopping eighteen. This comes from adding up those hanging in the entryway, the breezeway, Woolcox Hall, the kitchen, all six of the Sunday School classrooms, the narthex, the chapel, the choir room, both offices, the sacristy, the basement, plus the one in the janitor's closet. Big Ben said he suffers from both physical and mental fatigue from perpetually running from room to room to check to see if all of the clocks are working. When talking about his exhaustion, he uncovered some information that Ruby and I did not know anything about. He said that he overheard Alfie Quittschrieber suggest to the property director that a prominent clock needs to be placed in St. Peter's sanctuary to keep the worship service down to one hour, never running a minute over. Alfie has volunteered to head up a committee to raise funds for this valuable and timely undertaking.

Fear was revealed in Big Ben when he talked about how much an additional clock will increase his stress and hypertension because he will have another clock to watch. He said that he could try to go cold turkey, to just let the clocks go, but he added that he is not one to let any moss grow on his stone, emphasizing that he is not a quitter. Perhaps he could go to our therapist, Jasmine, but he imagines that when the one hour appointment nears the end, she would just say, "It's time to wrap things up." Big Ben assumes that therapists are all about time equalling money.

After listening carefully to him, I offered Big Ben some simple advice: Go to the corner of Woolcox Hall where donation items are accumulating for the upcoming garage sale. Search for a wind-up clock, one that is a really good tick-er-tocker. Get help from your friends to haul the clock back to your dwelling. After that, wind it up and let it run. This practical idea would enable Big Ben to hear the continual tick-tock, tick-tock, tick-tock sound without ever leaving the comforts of home. I added that this one clock alone could satisfy all of his tick-tock needs. Big Ben was so excited to hear this solution to his problem that he hugged me. When he hugged Ruby, he picked her up and twirled her around three times exclaiming gleefully, "tick-tock, tick-tock, tick-tock!"

It was after midnight when Big Ben left for home. At that point it was too late for us to travel anywhere to search for a snack. We fell into bed and reminded each other that we must eat to live, not live to eat. After that we sang "Hickory Dickory Dock." That was a gentle way for us to unwind from such a lengthy day. We did admit to one another that if heaven was on earth, we would have savoured one-hundred-percent a tiny cube from a hickory smoked cheese log.

– F.N.

Saturday, October 17

Claire Dahl skipped out on helping the ladies today in the kitchen. Several from our village noticed that she had something far more overriding to do. After arriving at St. Pete's she headed straightaway to the sanctuary. She quietly sat in a pew composing her nerves while waiting excitedly for the tour bus to arrive. More specifically, Claire was eagerly anticipating Finn's arrival.

Another week has passed and Claire must be continuing her weight loss method. She simply looked a size smaller in her attractive new clothing and eye-catching jewellery. Because she was dressed to the nines, Darla Bungard caught sight of Claire which brought out deep frowns forming on Darla's forehead. Until now, she herself has been known as the best dressed woman at Historic St. Peter's and she must not let Claire Dahl, of all people, steal that spot away from her. So Darla left the event early today, explaining that she needed to get some shopping done.

Josie repeated her prepared repertoire of a few spirituals, clearly enjoying getting paid for playing music that she doesn't need to practice anymore. She already has two Saturdays of playing familiar spirituals under her belt, so from now on she doesn't need to do any preparation, but just coast along. She also has something else, a bit stronger, under her belt. Pastor Osterhagen is no longer the only one that notices her tea tumbler and tissues – other parishioners are detecting the smell of Josie's whisky breath.

Again Finn was the first person off of the tour bus. When he entered the sanctuary he was affectionately greeted by Claire. She has confided in her friend, Janet Woods, the truth about her attraction to Finn, adding that on these Saturdays she is hoping to warm up their acquaintance. After Finn arrived, Claire told him that they have something in common because they are both are history buffs. Because of him, this past week she has been reading everything she can locate pertaining to the Underground Railroad. She shared that she has so many questions about the topic that only he could possibly answer. Claire proceeded to admit that her questions are far too complicated to be answered right here and now. She asked him for his telephone number so she could contact him. After that he handed her his business card that contained his work telephone number, a logo of the State Historical Society, and most importantly to her, his handsome photograph printed on the back of the card.

After Finn finished his presentation this morning, everyone moved to Woolcox Hall for lunch. Claire told Finn to sit down and relax while she brought their lunch to the table. Sitting this time across from each other, she complimented him on several points regarding his lecture, emphasizing that it was even more fascinating to listen to him the third Saturday in a row. The mice who witnessed this said that Claire was very clever to avoid too much boldness by coming on too strong. She was also skillful at constant eye contact, all the while being certain to never let an awkward silence spoil their time together. When the group from the southeast part of the State was about to get back on the tour bus and head towards a bingo parlour for some entertainment, Claire walked alongside Finn. She told him she'd contact him soon, adding that she would see him next Saturday at the same place, same time.

At 6 p.m. Ruby and I travelled to Woolcox Hall and snacked on morsels of the same lunch we have had the last two Saturdays. Three Saturdays in a row we've enjoyed wild rice soup, chicken salad sandwiches, egg salad sandwiches, and brownie sundaes. We wish we could eat like this every single Saturday for the rest of our lives.

– F.N.

St. Luke, Evangelist ~ October 18

THESE LAST SUNDAYS A HARDSCRABBLE MAN BY THE NAME OF HUDSON SHAW HAS attended worship at Historic St. Peter's. On his first visit to St. Pete's, Pastor Osterhagen met and welcomed him to the church. Each Sunday he has returned to church, just like he promised Pastor. Hudson sits by himself and does not mingle with any of the parishioners. Yes, his appearance is scruffy and he has a bit of an odour, but Clement overlooks that. No one sits very close to Hudson in worship, mostly because he is a newcomer.

After today's offering was collected in the antique vintage silver offering plates with the inner centre lined in purple velvet, the ushers set them down on the altar in thanksgiving to God. During the postlude, Ralph Pfalzgraf, known by many parishioners as a real "pillar" of the church, trotted up to the altar and, unfortunately, emptied the collection plates on the pure white fair linen. This happens to be a very fine piece of white fabric imported from Switzerland with three hand-embroidered golden crosses, but to Ralph it doesn't appear to be any better quality than a sheet of oilcloth decorated with brimming baskets of fruits and vegetables. Unfortunately, Ralph equates this spot with a work table, not even respecting that it is the place where the bread and wine are consecrated for Holy Communion. Ralph proceeded to separate the offering envelopes from the cash, making four piles of currency; the ones, fives, tens, and twenties. Ralph has a good reputation at the church, but a few are keen enough to realize that although he is considered a pillar, the contents of his pillar are frequently empty. It is just as though his pillar is hollow instead of solid and of high quality. His emptiness is apparent from maliciously written letters he writes when he is irked or because he is upset at someone and simply will not let it go.

Ralph gathered up the offering piles he made, placed them in a large envelope, folded the envelope in half, and tucked it into his jacket pocket. His predictable Sunday morning pattern is to transport the envelope to the church safe and lock it up. He and his wife Denise are pattern people and return to the church office every Monday morning. After arriving, they open the safe, remove the envelope, count and record the weekly offerings, and prepare the bank deposit. While they are doing this work, they usually talk about what they are going to order for breakfast at the newly opened Captain's Choice Café. After depositing the offering in the bank, they usually head to the café.

Charity Borgman stayed behind after church today to speak with Pastor Osterhagen. Earlier this morning, Avondale tracked down a great hiding spot behind St. Pete's guest book podium. From there she was able to peek out and get a glimpse of the two bonny-looking newborn babies attending church today. Earlier on Avondale listened carefully to Charity's conversation with Shelly Taylor. Both young women were lovingly holding their newborn daughters, Abigail and Desiree. They were comparing birthdates, weight and height, recent sleeping patterns, and so on, when the subject of Holy Baptism came up. Charity mentioned that Abigail's baptism date is next Sunday. Avondale looked up in time to see astonished Shelly open her mouth as broad as a wide-mouthed frog, or more like Chesapeake Bay. Avondale mentioned to me that this must have been the first time that the two mothers realized that Abigail's and Desiree's baptisms are scheduled for the exact same Sunday at Historic St. Peter's. From that point on, it was clear to see that the two do not have the same attitude or viewpoint regarding sharing a baptismal day.

Avondale reported that Charity was delighted and overjoyed that Abigail and Desiree would have the same baptismal day, adding that she wants every single baby to be baptized. However, it was clearly not about the Sacrament of Holy Baptism itself for Shelly, but about having to share this special day with another family. Shelly said that her daughter is like a bride and that the focus needs to stay on her, making hers a cherished infant baptism, that not being possible when she has to divvy up the occasion. Shelly said that she has even hired a seamstress to create a baptismal gown fashioned out of fabric from her own wedding gown for little Desiree to wear on her "baby bride" day. Adding that she has never even heard of a double baptism, she does not intend to let anyone else participate or take part in Desiree's day. Avondale reported to us that Charity became speechless at that point, somewhat shell-shocked at Shelly's selfish tirade.

Some therapy was essential for Charity after Shelly's words. Pastor Osterhagen told Charity that she has the Christian focus on what Holy Baptism is all about, the receiving of God's promise of salvation through faith in Christ our Saviour. Pastor told Charity that the baptism plan is still on schedule and that he will give Shelly a telephone call to point out what a privilege and delight it is to have two baptisms on the same day.

After Charity, her husband, Rick, and their baby Abigail left St. Peter's today, Pastor Osterhagen went back to his office, waited awhile, and then called

Shelly. Bliss was in the room hiding behind the carillon when he heard the conversation sloping downward faster than an Olympic skier racing downhill on New York's Whiteface Mountain. Bliss clearly heard Shelly's words because she was using her outdoor voice indoors. Shelly told Pastor that she had already called another pastor in town and he agreed to do a "single" baptism next Sunday, where her baby will be the centre point of the worship service. She firmly told Pastor that she is flying the coop from Historic St. Peter's and they will be transferring their church membership over to Beautiful Saviour Chapel, a newer church located on the western edge of Oswald County. Before Pastor could say anything, Shelly clanked the telephone receiver down on the cradle. It was at that point that he got out the time worn church record book and turned to the baptismal recordings that it contained. Patiently counting Sundays where more than one baptism had occurred, he came up with one hundred and thirty-seven Sundays with more than one baptism. After that, Pastor walked down the breezeway, arrived at the parsonage and unloaded to Aia, mostly his frustration that he was not given even a minute to change Shelly's mind. Ruby and I heard good-hearted Aia remind Clement that church members will not stay forever, that some of them come and go, adding that it is not worth scratching your head over that subject. In this instance, Aia said that Shelly was all wrapped up in looking out for number one. Aia also advised Clement not to go after her, but to simply let her go. Clement listened to Aia and told her that she is a fountain full of common sense and more level-headed and cool than the water in Chicago's Buckingham Fountain. We saw Aia grin from ear to ear after Clement gave her that compliment.

At 11:30 p.m. Ruby and I travelled to the parsonage and snacked on Hawaiian macadamia cookie crumbs, a tiny taste treat from the lushly jungle-green islands. Aia did not bake the cookies, they were a gift from Wally and Ruth Walford who just returned from a week in Kauai celebrating their golden wedding anniversary. I mentioned to Ruby that I wish Aia would hunt for that cookie recipe and make them often. Ruby told me to not set my heart on this happening because macadamia nuts are far too high-priced to be included in the Osterhagen's grocery spending plan. Plus, she doubts that they are even available at Grocer Dan's. She is certain they can only be found at far away deluxe grocery stores that actually sell saffron and vanilla beans.

– F.N.

Monday, October 19

At six o'clock this morning Twilight and Goldenrod were in the middle of a deep slumber behind the office copy machine. They were abruptly awakened by Tim Sadler and Darrin Weimar when they flicked on the lights. Both Twilight and Goldenrod perked up to listen to the early morning activity in the church office. Tim and Darrin had arrived to count yesterday's offering before going to work. Being responsible for counting the offering for the next two weeks while the Pfalzgrafs are away, they had the fright of their lives after opening up the safe to discover that yesterday's offering was not there. Goldenrod reported to Ruby that they assumed the offering was either missing, or worse, had been stolen. At that point Darrin quickly telephoned Pastor Osterhagen and reported their findings hoping that Pastor would have an explanation as to what happened to the offering. He did not. After that, Darrin telephoned Simon Thompson, the current church treasurer, and also Duane Albright, the former church treasurer, waking them both up from a sound sleep to find out if they knew anything about the offering's disappearance. They did not. After that, Twilight said that both Tim and Darrin appeared to be panic-stricken.

The missing offering caused such a disturbance that by supper time today many of the parishioners (and a portion of the community) had heard about the stolen offering at St. Peter's. Some focused the blame on the newest attendee, Hudson Shaw. In no time it had spread around town that newcomer Hudson was the one responsible for the offering's disappearance, noting that the police will surely find it if they hurry over to search his house. Being that Hudson is quiet in nature and doesn't mingle at church, his only friend so far at St. Peter's is Pastor Osterhagen. There is much curiosity about him coming from the fellow worshippers who might assume that he is a drifter who moves from place to place. They wonder what his story is, who he is, where he comes from, his past, and namely, why he is attending St. Pete's. A few villagers have heard members whisper about his unshaven face and unkempt clothing, wondering what kind of a meager life he has, and how in the world he can scrape up enough money to live on. The buzz was that he stole the offering to meet his daily needs.

The police were called around seven in the morning and arrived shortly afterwards to meet with Pastor Osterhagen, Tim, and Darrin. Pastor told them that he had no idea what happened to the offering. It was helpful that he explained Ralph Pfalzgraf's usual Sunday morning pattern of locking up the offering in the safe. He added that on Mondays Ralph and his wife, Denise, tally up the offering. After the police heard about the husband and wife duo touching the offering, they strongly advised the three men to bring an end to a married couple counting the offering. One of the officers said that offering counters should not be related and that just the mention of that practice sounds suspicious and slippery, something without any controls put on it. They further explained that having a married couple in charge of church contributions is too risky and tempting and might lead to stealing, adding that Historic St. Peter's might already be losing cash every single week that is quietly slipped into a pocket or a handbag. Anyone at anytime could start up a rumour that the couple is stealing from the church. Pastor agreed to bring the matter to the Council to put some controls on this practice. However, he mentioned that he will be challenged and run into a lot of quibbling from the Council because the Pfalzgrafs seem to be above reproach.

Darrin mentioned to the police that a scruffy man named Hudson has recently been attending worship that just might be a homeless person, suspecting that he could be the one who stole the offering. Pastor said that he is just getting to know Hudson, but does not think he would ever steal from the church, adding that he is definitely not homeless because he has an address and a telephone number. The police asked Pastor to telephone Hudson and ask him to come over to the church. Hudson arrived in just a few minutes. While the officers questioned Hudson about the missing offering, he said that he didn't know anything about it and that he didn't take it, adding that he has plenty of money and would never steal from a church or from anyone else.

Everyone there could see how distressed Hudson was that he was suspected of stealing the offering. Hudson's eyes welled up but he did not cry. Instead, he said that he has begun attending church because of his late wife, Sarah Mae, who died last December of cancer. He talked about finding a fresh start in life. Noticing that it was far too difficult to live without Sarah Mae in the big house that they shared together for forty-three years, he said that there were far too many memories so he sold the house and moved away. Hudson further said that he hoped a change of scenery would help ease some of his sadness. He walked into Historic St. Peter's because of his wife and the way she lived her life. She attended church every single Sunday while he relaxed at home. Even though she persistently and lovingly invited him to go to church with her, he never did. Hudson said that he deeply regrets turning down her gentle invitations because he knows it would have meant the world to her if he had gone along, even if it was just once in a while. He told them that he often encouraged her to skip church so that they could spend time together. Hudson said that he wanted every Sunday to be slow paced and quiet, one that would begin with coffee in bed. Later on they could make an omelette and eat it on the front porch.

All listened as Hudson explained further that he is a recently retired university professor of statistics and statistical methods. Even though that was his expertise, he admitted that he never gave much thought or time to analyzing Christianity. Sometimes he briefly wondered about religion on Sunday mornings when Sarah Mae left for church. Since her death, he is now questioning if there might be life after death. After she passed away, it was a time of immense sadness that still remains with him. As a result, he doesn't bother to keep himself cleaned up and his appetite is gone. He has difficulty resting and sleeping and has lost any feelings of hopefulness. Mentioning how she made everything so inviting and special in their home, he shared that nearly every day of their marriage was simply a trip over the moon. All of the men seemed to sense the hurt that came pouring forth from his heavy heart.

Hudson continued talking, sharing that although he and his wife did not have any children, Sarah Mae was naturally childlike in the way that she found pleasure and fascination in the ordinary things of daily life. She made life fun by creating little moments. They would go to the local drive-in for twisty ice cream cones, watch old and new movies, sit under the tree in their backyard and read books, have winter picnics on the living room floor with the fireplace ablaze, and share the daily newspaper to find out what's happening, followed by discussing what they had read and learned. Nevertheless, when Sarah Mae picked up a newspaper, her first goal was to hunt for grocery store specials and give them a thorough going-over. If she discovered any seafood specials or seasonal fruit on sale, she would be in pursuit to bring home those items. Hudson admitted that he could not possibly count the number of peach crisps, cobblers, pound cakes, and trifles she made when peaches from Georgia were to be found on a seasonal special.

After Hudson revealed his deep sorrow about losing Sarah Mae, there were tender eyes and hearts among the men in the room, even in the police officers. Tim and Darrin apologized to Hudson for suspecting him of stealing. The police officers said that there wasn't anything at this point that they could do about the missing offering, but added that perhaps it will turn up later. Mostly they reiterated that major controls need to be put on the offering procedures at St. Peter's, especially making sure that the counters are not related.

After the police and Tim and Darrin left the church, Clement brewed a pot of coffee and sat down with Hudson to go over all that had just transpired. Hudson said that he no longer can attend Historic St. Peter's because some members will suspect that he is a thief. He explained to Pastor that he's lived in town for only one month and already he has gotten into trouble, emphasizing that this is the very first time he has been questioned by police officers. He is sure that his reputation will be ruined, but Pastor assured him that everything will be fine and to keep attending church. Pastor seemed to feel awful about what happened to Hudson. He reassured him that he was his friend, that he is there to help him, and that he will try to get to the bottom of the missing offering. Hudson finished his coffee, thanked Pastor and stood up to go back home, looking down-trodden. But, before he left, Pastor asked him to sit back down because he wanted to help him with his life-after-death quandary. Twilight and Goldenrod told me that they listened carefully to Pastor when he explained that Jesus Christ promised that believers in Him will live forever, finding heavenly joy. Pastor told of a Bible verse from John 3:16 that Hudson seemed to embrace which says: "For God so loved the world that He gave His one and only Son, that whoever believes in Him shall not perish but have eternal life." He explained to Hudson that God did not mean for us to die, but everybody turns his or her own way without God. This is sin, and it means our lives end unless God stepped in. Jesus died in our place and rose again. Because of Jesus, God gives the gift of everlasting life to all who believe. This is what Sarah Mae believed and why she went to church and wanted him to go. Pastor suggested that they should join together in prayer. After the prayer, Hudson revealed to Pastor that he had never been prayed for by anyone except Sarah Mae, but somehow this seemed so right. Hudson thought that maybe today's troubles happened to point him towards faith in Jesus Christ, to trust in God to help him through his grief by assuring him of life everlasting.

Ruby and I did not travel to the parsonage tonight since we heard Clement moving about in the house. He didn't seem to be able to sleep because he was so troubled about Hudson. We heard him wake Aia around four in the morning telling her that he thought he knew where the missing offering was. He has a notion it might be in the church pillar's suit coat pocket.

– F.N.

Tuesday, October 20

This morning Ruby and I listened intently through the crack in the dining room wall when Pastor attempted to contact Grant Pfalzgraf, Ralph and Denise's oldest son, concerning the gone astray offering. Grant wasn't home, but Pastor did get in touch with his conversational wife, Penny. Penny said that her in-laws are currently in Spain, part of a packaged sightseeing tour group. Mentioning that the journey has a jam-packed itinerary, she added that one highlight will be to attend a bullfight at the Madrid arena. Clement later told Aia that Penny is convinced that her mother-in-law will be jittery and jumpy throughout the bullfight because she is unable to handle any amount of gore. But, even though there will be violent bloodshed, she will be a good sport and participate in the fanfare of the event. Penny further explained to Pastor that her in-laws were lucky enough to purchase their tickets "two-for-one." Penny went on to comment that they are crackerjack cheapskates but never, according to Penny, admit that they are tightwads. Even though she confessed that it is an unpleasant way to speak about her in-laws, she is just being open and telling the truth. When returning home, she added that they will certainly bring back a couple of souvenirs. Most likely it will be a traditional hand painted floral Spanish folding fan accentuated with sequins, plus a pouch of specially roasted beans from a famous coffee plantation.

Penny provided Pastor with her in-laws hotel telephone number, adding that if it is an emergency, he could call him. After he hung up, Clement was suffering from listening exhaustion. Aia is convinced that Penny is an actual yakkety-yak machine. Clement wondered if her gift of incessant talking could somehow be put to good use by leading something at St. Peter's since she shows absolutely no signs of being a quiet wallflower or ever needing a moment to take a breath.

Holding Ralph's hotel telephone number in his hand, Clement conferred with Aia about whether or not to call Spain, knowing that it would be expensive. Considering that Spain's time is seven hours ahead of theirs, Clement decided to call him to see if Ralph knows anything about the missing offering. We heard him tell Aia that since it is nearly five o'clock in Spain, he may be able to catch him before they leave for supper. As soon as Clement dialed the telephone number, Denise answered the phone, listened to Pastor's concerns about the offering and assured him that Ralph definitely placed the offering in the safe. It was far more important to Denise to babble on about their action-packed day. She said that they were already tuckered out, but they had just enough strength to enjoy the evening's plans. Denise reported that they had been on a Spanish winery tour earlier today and had also seen a mountain hideaway that was occupied by Spanish bandits during the eighteenth century. They were looking forward to dining in a restaurant where they were expecting the flamboyant foot stomping of a flamenco dancer accompanied by an electrified classical guitar. She would turn the phone over to Ralph, but Denise told Pastor that he was busy watching a flamenco dancer on the television right now and it wouldn't do any good anyway, as he wouldn't be able to hear him with all the noise the television is making. Clement later told Aia that Denise was so busy telling him about their amazing trip that she even began to describe the upcoming meal that this small countryside, regional restaurant is well-known for that will serve roast lamb, grilled seafood, and gazpacho. She next described what they were looking forward to seeing the next day. Clement communicated to her that he needed to hang up the phone because of the expense, but Denise was so enthusiastic about their experiences that she kept on talking until Clement wisely hung up. Clement mentioned to Aia that Denise also has the gift of incessant talking, just like her daughter-in-law, Penny. The bottom line was that Denise is confident that Ralph locked up the October 18 offering in the safe.

Moving on, Aia told him that she invited Hudson Shaw over for supper tonight. She is ready to serve a roast beef dinner with carrots, mashed golden potatoes and gravy, along with green beans and Yorkshire pudding. When Hudson arrived at six o'clock he let Aia know that he was thrilled to be invited for dinner. Arriving at the front door of the parsonage, the Osterhagens noticed that Hudson had made a dramatic change in his appearance. He had a fresh haircut, was showered and shaved, and wore attractive clothing for a man in his late sixties. In one hand he held a colourful mixed European floral bouquet and in the other hand a bottle of Italian red wine. Pastor and Aia remarked at how fine he looked, mentioning that he looked like a very distinguished gentleman.

It was crystal clear to us that the Osterhagens and Hudson became special friends during supper tonight. Before they sat down at the dinner table, Gretchen invited him to sit next to her. Ruby and I saw Hudson's eyes water a bit as they all joined hands during the dinner prayer. Hudson told them that he had never held such a little hand before. Noticing that Mr. Shaw did not join in on saying the dinner prayer, Gretchen offered to teach it to him. After three tries of Gretchen's instruction, Mr. Shaw had it memorized. We saw Gretchen hug Mr.

Shaw and praise him for learning it so fast. She mentioned the next time he comes over for supper she will teach him another one because she knows three different dinner prayers, as well as *"Komm, Herr Jesu"* in German. Plus, on days when her mama prepares fish or meatballs, they always say the Norwegian dinner prayer, *"I Jesu Navn."* Ruby and I noticed that Hudson spoke to Gretchen in a grownup way, as though she was a university student and not a little girl. After he listened to her contribute to the dinner conversation, he mentioned to Pastor and Aia that Gretchen's conversational dialogue often involves statistics, his speciality. He pointed out how she relayed to him the number of children in her Sunday School class, in kindergarten, her dance class, and how many attend story hour at the Oswald County Library. Gretchen revealed to Mr. Shaw that she sees the most children of all at the library.

After enjoying coffee and warm cranberry cake drizzled with butter sauce, Hudson thanked the Osterhagen's and said it was time for him to go back home. When Hudson said goodbye, Gretchen and Aia hugged him, after which Gretchen told him that she wanted him to sit with them in church on Sunday, and to be sure to wear something that is coloured red. He said he would do that, adding that he has a red sweater vest he will wear. Aia told Clement that she is certain that "Ladyhawk" Claire Dahl will check out Hudson on Sunday. Soon she will be after him, too, and not just limit herself to Finn Larssen.

At 11:30 p.m. Ruby and I stayed home. It has been a very long day for everyone and we are simply too weary to travel to the parsonage to locate any munchies. We got worn out tonight because we quietly and persistently peered through the crack in the dining room wall, concentrating on watching and listening to tonight's dinner conversation. Mice are nature lovers, but occasionally we stay indoors because there is more action on the inside than anything that is happening outdoors. Both Ruby and I could hardly wait to close up shop tonight aiming to get an abundance of shuteye.

– F.N.

Thursday, October 22

September 4 was St. Philycis Day (pronounced Fill-a-sis) when we paused to honour the Patron Saint of All Micedom. Recalling the extravagant merrymaking of that day, Cayenne, a perfectly peppy and peppery village mouse presented a suggestion during the last village meeting. She proposed that we have a repeat performance of the fun we all had on St. Phil's Day. All were in favour. Everyone cancelled their plans for today to replace it with something far more exciting, attending another shindig. Thankfully Longfellow had saved his speech from September 4 and read it to the group once again, reminding us of the heroic excellence of St. Philycis. Following Longfellow's speech, the feasting began with the opening up of a full bag of little fish crackers that were found on the bottom shelf in St. Peter's Youth Room. The fish crackers were excellent tasting, not as if we feasted on restaurant-worthy seared scallops, but far above all of our expectations. Such an abundance of unparalleled things marked the celebration of St. Phil's Day that it could not have possibly gone any better. Once again, our favourite part of the day was when we joined the entire village to hum Sir Edward Elgar's "Pomp and Circumstance" twice, once when the celebration began and secondly when it concluded. There is far too much to write about the repeat performance in my journal, so I'll skip most of the details. Enough is, after all, enough.

Ruby put her foot down and proclaimed we would not search for a treat tonight. She pointed out that we did not need any more sustenance because we ate like horses today, having really packed it away when we gourmandized at today's gathering. Once again, I noticed Trinitarian speech popping up in Ruby's lingo due to time spent listening to Aia. Ruby was so pleased to accept my compliment that she performed her first ever perfect forwards somersault, an acrobatic move that she has been practicing for the last three days. After we got settled down for the night, Ruby told me that she also hopes to learn two other somersaults that are called the backwards and the sideways. I pointed out that she even has a three-point goal of learning somersaults. After that, we jumped into bed and Ruby quietly sang "Keep on the Sunny Side" until I fell deeply asleep.

– F.N.

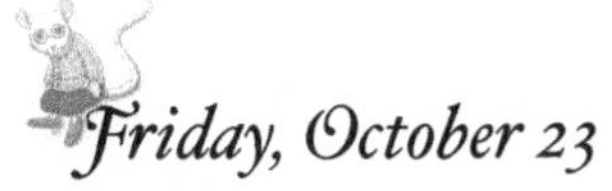

Friday, October 23

Lately Zippy, a delightfully energized mouse in our village, has been observing the new substitute volunteer, Judith Schellenberger, who is currently folding St. Peter's weekly bulletins. Judith is temporarily taking over the position from Leona Wilkes. Unfortunately, Leona tripped, fell, and broke her hip when she exited the Dr. Floss Dental Clinic following a root canal procedure. Zippy heard Judith tell Pastor that Leona has complained to her about her never-ending dental and medical expenses. She added that when Leona recovers from her hip surgery she might have to earn extra money either by delivering newspapers, pumping gas, or as a last resort, standing on a sleazy street corner to see if anyone wants her. They both laughed at that.

Zippy announced to our village that Judith arrives at St. Peter's early on Friday afternoons to fold the bulletins equipped with her prized hand tool, a bone folder instrument that creates perfect creases in the bulletin covers. The first thing that she does is to ask if the bulletins are ready, which they often are not. Then she asks how long it will be before they are ready and if she should wait or come back later. When they are finally ready, she hunts for typing, spelling, and grammatical errors, all the while rolling her eyes in disgust. Lastly, she presents Pastor Clement with a copy highlighted with all mistakes and bloopers she has found before taking them home to fold. Although Judith is quite new at this, Zippy is convinced that she has had plenty of training on how to do the job properly from Leona Wilkes.

At lunchtime today, Clement returned home and talked about the pros and cons of having volunteers, telling Aia that he thinks the cons might outweigh the pros. At that point, he did admit that at least Judith is task-oriented. The bulletin folder prior to Leona was Cloyd Hackley. Clement remembered that Cloyd would stop into the church several times during the week asking if there was anything ready to be folded. When he heard that it was too early, he would drive away to pick up a cup of coffee, returning later on to see if any progress had been made. When the bulletins were finally ready for folding, he would begin the task, but soon would wane from being overwhelmed by the undertaking. At that point, he would come to Pastor and ask for his help to finish the task. Upon leaving the church, he would take eight bulletins along with him to distribute and discuss at the Friday night card party that he and his wife, Florence, attend.

After Aia listened to Clement, she came up with a practical solution to these theatrics. She suggested that he simply work from the parsonage on Fridays. That way Judith will not be able to locate him in his office. Clement thanked her and said that he is going to put that recommendation into effect. He emphasized that from now on Judith will have to handle all bulletin typos by herself. They began to recall all the funny bulletin typos they remembered or heard about: "A worm welcome to everyone in attendance today." "All coats from the lost and found are hanging on the oat rack." "Please pick up you new box of suffering envelopes in the narthex." "The Hymn of the Day is, 'Before You, Lord, We Box.'" "Tickets are now on sale for St. Peter's annual ish fry." "Join us at the Toffee Hour." "The shushers will seat latebloomers." "Man shall not live by dread alone." "Ink lemonade and poopcorn will be provided at the Youth Group's movie night." "There will be a drunk tank featured at the upcoming church pickings." And finally, "Those interested in taking a refresher cateclism class are reminded that it will begin on Thorsday."

At 10:50 p.m. Ruby and I travelled to the parsonage and located a sliced black olive under the dining room table from the Osterhagen's Happy Friday pizza party. We wondered about typos, an unfamiliar word to us. We are aware that there is a type of human blood that is called Type O, positive or negative. After logically thinking about it, we still cannot put together how a person's blood type has anything to do with the mistakes in a weekly bulletin. Following that, we discussed the possible reaction of Francis Scott Key, if he were alive, to the misprint in the title of his hymn, "Before You, Lord, We Box." After all, the combat sport of boxing, whether amateur or professional, does not match Scott's buoyant hymn text that is combined with the exuberant and joy-filled tune of Darwall's 148th (or is it Drywall's 148th)?We are aware that church hymns lack any similarity to boxing entrance songs. They do, however, have one thing in common. Both serve to bouy up the crowd, whether during a worship service or in the boxing arena.

– F.N.

October 24 ~ Saturday

This was the final Saturday that the tour bus arrived at Historic St. Pete's for the Underground Railroad Historical Tours. Being that it was very chilly this morning, Claire Dahl arrived at St. Pete's prepared to be faced with whatever ice-cold weather came her way. She looked fashionable in a nut-brown leather coat with winter white faux fur trim, a matching toque, amber coloured leather gloves, and dark brown leather fashion boots. Because she was so well bundled up, she waited in the church parking lot for the charter tour bus to arrive. As soon as the bus turned into the lot, the mice gazing out of the basement window saw Claire searching for Finn. She must have expected that he would be the first person off of the bus, identical to his movements the other three Saturdays. History buffs from the southwest part of the state poured out of the bus, but Finn was at the tail end. As soon as Claire saw him, she waved to him and gave him a big smile. While they walked together into the building, one of the mice heard her thank him for answering her two questions this past week, conveying to him that she wished this wasn't the last time he was giving a presentation at St. Peter's. They walked together into the church building, but he separated from her to beeline his way to Clement's office.

After Finn found Clement, he greeted him, shut the door, sat in one of the office chairs, and began to speak very quietly but quickly. He indicated that he just had a few moments before his presentation was to begin and that he would appreciate some help right away. Butternut, one of the village mice that hangs out in Pastor's closet, heard Finn confide in Clement that he had personally experienced an "aha" moment this past week. He said that he suddenly realized that Claire Dahl has a flame for him with serious intentions of the two of them developing a romantic relationship. He emphasized that her communication style has charming, amorous subtleties that he, so far, has been blind to notice. Finn also said that he was troubled because he received an admiring card from her suggesting that they meet up and see each other after the Underground Railroad Tours have been completed at St. Peter's. Finn also divulged that Claire seems to be fixated on him, watching him like a hawk, or in this instance, a ladyhawk. He mentioned that while they visit, Claire constantly gazes at his lips and steadily eyes his facial features, in which she reveals a desire that she wants him to kiss her.

He asked Clement if he was familiar with that look a woman can give. Before Clement could even answer his question, Finn went on to say that he feels like he is standing under a bunch of freshly gathered mistletoe, face to face with Claire and her lips not more than three inches from his. Noticing how uncomfortable this has made Finn feel, Clement eased and consoled him by emphasizing that this was the last tour he will be giving at Historic St. Peter's and that it will be over with before he knows it. Finn asked Pastor to give him a few quick suggestions so he could make it through the morning and avoid all of Ladyhawk's advances.

Pastor told him that Claire has probably noticed that he doesn't wear a wedding ring. Pastor asked Finn why he doesn't wear a ring because he knows that he is a happily married man. Finn explained that he owns a wedding ring but that he suffers from a syndrome called "restless finger syndrome," which makes him constantly fiddle with it and spin his ring round and round his finger. He says it feels as though it is cutting off proper blood circulation, noting that every time he tries to wear it, he can't wait to take it off. He's tried to wear the ring, but found out that it is impossible. Finn told Pastor that this syndrome is far more common than you would think, mostly occurring with men. Pastor reminded him of his marriage vows and his lovely wife, Peggy. He said Claire probably has a crush on him because he is the best looking man that has come to town in a very long time. Pastor knows that she is hoping to share her life with the right man. Pastor advised Finn to be careful of temptation, adding that Claire's admiration of him is actually a compliment. But, Pastor added that he should be wary of falling for Claire's flirtations by remembering that he has a loving wife back home. Butternut glanced out and saw Finn nod his head in agreement with Pastor, thanking him for his help. Pastor and Finn prayed together for God to help him safely sail through the morning. Finn said that his time was up and that he better get a move on, since it was nearly time to give his lecture.

When today's presentation was finished, Claire left her pew and made her way to be near Finn, standing alongside him. Like the previous three Saturdays, they walked together to Woolcox Hall, sat down together, and chatted warmly while eating their lunch. Claire alluded to the idea that she would like to contact him if she has any additional questions about the Underground Railroad. Without carefully and deliberately thinking it over, Finn told Claire that would be OK. She reached in her pocket and handed him a small slip of paper with her information on it, including her home address. She told him that she would love to get together for a cup of coffee or a glass of wine at her place. She called it a casual "What's new with you?" type of getting together. One of our mice, Thistle, was hidden behind a portable folding partition that is only used during the Sunday School hour. She heard every word of their conversation clearly. At this point Thistle peeked out to see the expression on Finn's face when he heard Claire's tempting and enticing words. Thistle told me that Finn looked like Claire had gotten him to bite on her alluring bait. It seemed to Thistle that Finn was submerged waist-high in quicksand and, unfortunately, did not have the skill or knowledge of an escape plan. In other words, he had the various looks of temptation, enchantment, being seduced, guilt, delight, and remorse on his face concurrently.

When it was time for the tour bus to depart, Claire again walked alongside Finn to the parking lot. At the last minute they said goodbye and Claire embraced Finn with the type of hug that is often seen in an epic drama-romance film. The mice peered out of the window and gasped, astonished that we were witnessing a record-breaking embrace, very much as though Finn himself was Dr. Zhivago and Claire, the lovely Lara. Claire resembled Lara in her fashionable ensemble, but it was the faux fur that was wildly blowing in the chilly wind that gave her the Russian chic romantic appearance. It was evident from Finn's facial expression that the amorous caress pleased him very much, because he closed his eyes and deeply breathed in the aroma of her sophisticated perfume. The mice whistled "Lara's Theme – Somewhere My Love" in unison, feeling like we'd just seen something that only happens on the big screen created in Hollywood.

At 5 p.m. Ruby and I travelled to Woolcox Hall and snacked on morsels of what we called "The Last Lunch." Our tummies will truly miss the presence of the State Historical Society tourists savouring the wild rice soup lunch at Historic St. Peter's. These last four Saturdays we were simply spoiled.

– F.N.

Reformation Day (Observed), The Twenty-second Sunday after Pentecost ~ October 25

FABIAN, A MOUSE VILLAGE RESIDENT, SPENT MOST OF THE SUMMER DAYS BASKING IN THE Osterhagen garden by twiddling away time waiting for the green beans to grow. When they were perfectly tender he became a frequent picker. His favourite hour of the week to spend in the green bean patch was on Sunday mornings while parishioners were attending the worship service. He revealed to me that he once had aspirations of becoming a bean grower but never found the right pathway to make that dream come true, so he cast that aside. Since bean season is long past, Fabian has started attending church instead. He comes away with umpteen observations that I am able to include in my writings. I thanked him for his keen eyes and perceptive listening ears, after which I asked him if it would be acceptable for me to call him "Fabulous Fabian." He responded that I could simply call him Fabuloso, or Fab, for short.

It was not until last Sunday that the entire mice village at Historic St. Peter's had paid attention to the words Reformation and Lutheran. Several mice noticed those words while reading the contents of the October 18 bulletin. Usually there are a few bulletins that have been dropped on the sanctuary floor, so it is a cinch for the village to keep up on the latest news at St. Peter's. The bulletin stated that St. Peter's, a Lutheran church, would celebrate Reformation Sunday on October 25 even though the historical date of the Reformation is actually October 31, 1517. A Reformation service was held today at St. Peter's with most parishioners wearing red, the liturgical colour of Reformation representing the Holy Spirit moving all believers towards grace and mercy. Pastor Osterhagen wore his white robe and red stole while Aia wore a vintage cashmere red sweater that she luckily happened upon and purchased at Olden T'ings Antique Shop, along with a pleated black skirt. Gretchen wore her Little Red Riding Hood cloak with a red dress underneath it, while Marc and Luc each wore a white long-sleeved creeper with blue jeans and red slipper socks. On the front of each creeper were the words "Little Lutheran."Hudson Shaw sat right next to Gretchen wearing his red sweater vest. When it was time to pray "Our Father, Who art in heaven . . ." Gretchen reached over and held Mr. Shaw's hand while he tried to say the words but didn't know the entire prayer. After it was finished, Fab overheard Gretchen quietly tell

Mr. Shaw that she will teach him the words and he will be able to memorize it in just three tries, similar to how he learned the supper prayer last Tuesday.

One of today's attendees, Sister Bernadette, confounded everyone when she turned up wearing a red cardigan on top of her nun's habit. Parishioners appeared perplexed buzzing as to whether or not Sister Bernadette just might be saying farewell to the Catholic Church in order to fully embrace Lutheranism. One of our village mice, Huey, overheard Frank Roth mention to others that Katharina von Bora had already laid the foundation on that subject, so Sister Bernadette could do it, too. It would be far easier for Sister Bernadette to leave Catholicism that it was for Katharina von Bora to escape from the convent riding in a horse-drawn cart while hiding in a foul-smelling herring barrel. Huey told me that he agrees with Frank that Sister Bernadette might be someone who thinks things through with her heart. She came for a reason, at least, maybe the spirit of the Reformation.

Most parishioners wore red clothing today. Huey reported at our village meeting tonight that he spotted two berry red coats, three scarlet red sweaters, four pairs of lipstick red shoes, six raspberry jam red neckties, four cherry red vests, five candy apple red handbags, and one ruby red sweatshirt. Rueben and Evelyn Newmann wore matching grey sweatshirts with a prominent circular symbol on the front. The emblem was a decorated white flower with green leaves, a blood red heart, and a black cross in the centre. The background was blue, with a golden ring encircling the symbol. There was a discussion at tonight's meeting concerning the meaning of this emblem because we assume it must be of some significance to Lutherans. We are certain of that because it also appeared on the front cover of today's bulletin. I have sketched, in black and white, what this symbol looks like to include it in my journal. It is commonly called "The Luther Rose."

Our village is beginning to unravel a few characteristics about Lutheranism since noticing that the rose symbol appears in several other places at St. Peter's. One of the old historic stained glass windows contains the Lutheran flower symbol. Also, the symbol was printed on Marc and Luc's long-sleeved creepers today. Too, there was a large colourful banner that hung proudly on the wall in the chancel this morning with the symbol. It was also on the grey sweatshirts worn by Rueben and Evelyn Newmann, which included these words, "Grace Alone, Faith Alone, Scripture Alone."

Dr. Theodore Simonson's investigation of what "Lutheran" means pointed him to the existence of a large book entitled *The Book of Concord*. It seems that long ago important statements were written down. Those writings did not match up with what the other Christians believed, which resulted in conflict over these "confessions." This was fascinating to the mice, especially when Dr. Simonsen read to us something from a book called the *Augsburg Confession,* Article IV:

> "Also they teach that men cannot be justified before God by their own strength, merits, or works, but are freely justified for Christ's sake, through faith, when they believe that they are received into favour, and that their sins are forgiven for Christ's sake, Who, by His death, has made satisfaction for our sins. This faith God imputes for righteousness in His sight. Rom. 3 and 4."

The village concluded that Lutherans must know what is recorded in the Bible very, very well.

This morning before Ruby and I got settled in the tummy of the organ, we scooted through the choir room but slowed down to carefully examine the wording that is artfully painted near the ceiling edge on one wall. Numerous times we have passed by those words, but for some unknown reason, today we stopped in our tracks to read, ponder, and consider their meaning. We said to each other that these words must be of importance because someone took time to paint them on the wall. They are a quote from Dr. Luther which says, "Next to the Word of God, the noble art of music is the greatest treasure in the world." Ruby and I asked each other, "What does this mean?" Because we were short of time, we decided to bring the question up at the village meeting tonight. It is safe to assume that Dr. Luther must have adored fine music. Now that Luther is living in heaven, he must thoroughly enjoy hearing all the angels sing, not just with musical notes that exist here on earth, but with a multitude of musical notes that exist only in the heavenly kingdom.

Following worship, a Reformation dinner with a German flair was held in Woolcox Hall. Since this was a special event, single red roses were arranged with a green fern and a sprig of baby's breath to form floral centrepieces. The room looked extra elaborate with crisp white placemats and red napkins. All food, except for the donated desserts, had been catered by The Black Forest Inn in nearby Romberg County. Pastor Osterhagen led the dinner prayer with these thankful and heartfelt words:

> "The eyes of all look to you and you give them their food at the proper time. You open your hand and satisfy the desires of every living thing," says the Psalmist.
>
> "We ask You, O Father, for your blessing upon this Reformation Sunday. Sometimes we are like baby robins with beaks pointed heavenward looking and chirping for food – and you see to it that we are fed. Sometimes we are like clueless disciples, looking and coming to you saying, 'Look at all the hungry people,' and you reply, 'Give them something to eat.' And suddenly we find that you have provided for them through us. Bless every agency that helps feed the hungry, helping many in need.
>
> "Bless the food today, and those who grew the food and who cooked it, for our use and bodily strength, coupled with the spiritual strength you give us to live forever through Jesus' death and resurrection. Bless these tables that they may become thanksgiving tables, laden with gratitude and overflowing with joy, trusting in your mercy and providence, through Christ Jesus our Lord, Amen."

Since everyone in our village has been slow to notice the key words, Reformation and Lutheran, we assigned our village librarian and his assistant to probe into finding out what these words actually mean. Tonight they shared their findings at our village meeting. Dr. Theodore Simonsen, along with Dr. Christoff Kikkunen, presented their report, speaking in detail about the word Reformation. They mentioned that Reformation Sunday is a celebratory day that marks the beginning of the transformation of the church that began on October 31, 1517. On that day Dr. Martin Luther, a German monk and theologian, nailed "The Ninety-five Theses" to the door of All Saints' Church, the Castle Church, in Wittenberg, Saxony, Germany. More importantly, Dr. Luther was the outspoken one who talked about "Grace Alone, Faith Alone, and Scripture Alone," exactly like the words written on the big and beautiful banner displayed in church today. Dr. Simonsen and Dr. Kikkunen also pronounced to everyone that our entire mice village might be Lutheran too, since we reside in a Lutheran church. Dr. Kikkunen added that Reformation also has something to do with an Archbishop named Albrecht, perhaps nicknamed Al, but he will research that later on.

Ever since we took up residence at St. Peter's we have been referring to HSP as Historic St. Peter's. Today we learned that the parish is actually formally named, "Historic St. Peter's Lutheran Church," part of the Lutheran church worldwide with millions of members. Every mouse was stunned that none of us had figured any of this out. Dr. Simonsen and a few helpers managed to open up a hymnal to hymn #298. After that, Dr. Simonsen and Dr. Kikkunen explained to us that this song is known as the "Battle Hymn of the Reformation." We also noticed that the same text is printed in the hymnal twice, #297 and #298. After Dr. Simonsen and Dr. Kikkunen had closely examined both hymns they informed us that hymn #297 is set to an Isorhythmic metre while hymn #298 is set to a Rhythmic metre. We all were curious about Dr. Martin Luther's song so we gathered around the hymnal and sang the song called, "A Mighty Fortress is Our God," first in Rhythmic and then in Isorhythmic. Unanimously, we agreed that it is a fine song, voting later that we will sing it at every one of our meetings. The only decision left was to determine which metre to use. There was a very brief discussion as to which one we all favoured, but it was evident that it was best to use the original, the one Dr. Martin Luther originally composed. So, we prefer to sing it in the Rhythmic metre. The Isorhythmic metre was written later on by J.S. Bach, and that is good, too, but it is not the original. When I heard that, I thought that I personally would prefer to sing "A Mighty Fortress" J.S. Bach's way, but I kept quiet. I think I only had that preference because the cover of my journal I wrote in, "*Finley's Tale – Book I: In the Beginning,*" had a painting of J.S. Bach sitting at the organ bench. Anyway, it was just a selfish feeling on my part, a small detail that won't matter in the long run. The village intends to sing the battle hymn with as much fervor, fire, and gusto as we sing our "Safety First" song. I will sing as loudly as I can, even though it will be sung in the Rhythmic metre. Hymn #298 is now treasured among us. It was one of the factors that led us to finding out who we truly are. Because of the knowledge gained today, our village now calls themselves "Junior Lutherans."

There was one slightly disturbing ruffle that took place at Historic St. Peter's today. When parishioners were arriving in the sanctuary they noticed a sign made of white poster board suspended from the pulpit. Written on the poster was the following message: "Spread the Word. Make St. Pete's a Non-perfumed Parish." During the last voters' meeting Mandy Stonecroft proposed discouraging the use of perfume or cologne at HSP, but she failed. She has attempted to bring about this change so that the air at church is kept free of all scented products that can affect a few parishioners health by triggering their allergies and asthma, as well as being the cause of booming headaches. The village mice agree that even if St. Peter's voted positively for this change and declared itself odourless, it would not do a lick of good when it comes to parishioner Aimée Beaulieu. Aimée happens to be the best smelling woman at St. Peter's, perhaps born wearing a fancy eau de toilette spray from France that has the number five on the bottle's label. Our entire mouse village would so miss this lovely, gentle, and sophisticated fragrance if the church adopts this change. Thankfully, the scent of French perfume lingers in the sanctuary for a couple of days. It is not until Wednesday morning that the aroma has fully dwindled and dissipated. By then St. Peter's no longer is perfumed with an elegant and luxurious aroma, a masterpiece of a pleasurable scent, but returns naturally to what is in its DNA, the seasoned and occasionally musty-dusty church smell. Ruby and I asked ourselves if the unventilated historic natural church smell just might bring on asthma and trigger allergies.

At 9 p.m. Ruby and I travelled to Woolcox Hall and snacked on morsels of today's Reformation Dinner. We, too, had something coloured red, as we found a sliver of red cabbage, a yummy sweet and sour side dish which is an outstanding way to use the very humble red cabbage. It simply bursts with supreme German cooking flavour. We told each other that we feel deeply honoured to be members at Historic St. Peter's Lutheran Church in Oswald County.

– F.N.

Monday, October 26

At nine o'clock this morning, Ruby and I heard the parsonage telephone ring, so we swiftly hurried over to the crack in the wall to listen to the conversation. We figured out it was Finn Larssen. He must have explained to Pastor that he had misplaced his briefcase, wondering if he had accidently left it at the church on Saturday. Clement told him he'd take a look and if he found it, he'd call him right back. Clement did find Finn's briefcase in the front pew of the sanctuary and relayed to Aia that it is a good thing that Lutherans do not sit in the front pews during worship services because Finn's briefcase was left there completely undisturbed. Clement called Finn right back to pass on the good news. Finn said he'd drive down to the church right away to pick it up. He said that he cannot even begin to do his work without all of the information that his briefcase contains.

Shortly before noon Finn Larssen rang the parsonage doorbell, present and ready to retrieve his missing briefcase. He was so thankful that it was back in his possession. Aia was finishing up lunch preparations and asked Finn to join them. He was glad for the invitation. Today's lunch was Italian minestrone soup and garlic cheese toast followed by strong coffee and lemon bars. After lunch, Finn wondered if he could take one more look at the Underground Railroad hiding spot before heading home. Clement encouraged him to do just that.

Finn headed towards the sanctuary, that being the last time that Pastor and Aia must have expected to see him today. However, Finn promptly returned to the parsonage all worked up about something. He explained that he lifted up the Underground Railroad floorboards and espied several mouse droppings. Finn stressed that this dilemma could damage a national treasure, plus if this doesn't get taken care of, the historical spot will fall into ruin. Clement assured him that he will get on it right away by contacting Will Anderly, Board of Property Chairperson. Clement assured him that professional exterminators will take care of the problem. After Finn calmed down, we were absolutely shocked when he sought some outlandish advice from Pastor. Finn mentioned that since he is in town he hoped to meet up with Claire Dahl. After all, on Saturday she gave him her address and telephone number, plus an open invitation to stop over anytime for a cup of coffee. He asked Pastor which was best, to call her or to just stop over. We observed that Pastor, too, seemed utterly stunned at Finn's desire and intention to see Claire. Pastor invited Finn to sit down in the living room while he went to the kitchen and poured two cups of coffee. Returning to the living room, Pastor had some serious words to say to Finn. The conversation lasted a good thirty minutes. We were so proud of Pastor for helping Finn turn away from temptation. When Finn stood up to leave, he reached into his pocket, took out the slip of paper Claire had given him containing her telephone number and address, tore it up, and placed the shreds on the coffee table. Pastor and Finn shook hands and Finn thanked him for getting his head back on straight. Pastor watched him point his car north to journey back to the State Historical Society.

After Ruby and I heard about professional exterminators, we knew our village was in deep danger. We immediately determined which mouse was responsible for this disaster. It was Weegee. Weegee is our village troublemaker who has a few followers that are mesmerized into doing whatever he asks of them. Our entire village is extremely clean and tidy except for Weegee and his gang. We believe that being clean prevents discovery and allows us to live among humans. Weegee must have had the foolish idea of rebelling against some of the rules that our village has put into place, being able to compel his band of followers to do the same. Now, as a result of their misbehaviour, our village is on high alert. An emergency village meeting was promptly called to order. It was decided that the entire village will have to move away from St. Pete's until the exterminators have finished their operation. Plans were made for our mouse patriarch, Eli, to meet individually with Weegee to try to talk some sense into him. Lewis and Clark went exploring this afternoon to find a new place for all of us to live, as our lives are in danger. We are desperate for a new location.

By 4:45 p.m. today, Lewis and Clark returned to Historic St. Peter's with A1 news that they located a residence for our village's relocation. The Bavarian Bed & Breakfast is located only two blocks down the street from St. Peter's. Our mice village can be set up in the unused basement. Ruby and I overheard that the exterminators will arrive on Monday, November 3. The entire village plans to make an exodus from St. Pete's the evening before, late at night after all of the Bavarian Bed & Breakfast guests are sound asleep. We have already shortened the name of the establishment to the BB&B.

Tonight Ruby and I skipped our snack. So many in our village are unable to eat or sleep. Several of the mice have had panic attacks from overwhelming fear and anxiety, including us. Jasmine, our Mouse Anxiety Therapist, spent the day helping mice that are suffering. She told us that some are calming down just knowing that they are not suffering alone. This realization helped some of the mice find comfort because no one wants to be alone. Jasmine taught several relaxation exercises to the afflicted mice. This helped settle their agitation, giving them a practical skill to work through their fears. There was an abundance of slow, calm, and thoughtful breathing going on among the village today, thanks to our Anxiety Therapist, Jasmine.

– F.N.

Tuesday, October 27

After Gretchen finished breakfast this morning, she asked her mama if she could go outside to play. Since Aia agreed, Gretchen raced to put on her play clothes. Today's weather was a stunningly beautiful autumn day with vibrant coloured leaves and sunshine abounding.

Ruby and I hurried outside, too, to keep an eye on Gretchen. She busied herself with a child-sized hula hoop, rode her training wheel bike, and went for a little walk around the perimeter of Historic St. Peter's. It was during that hike that Gretchen had the discovery of her life and so did we.

On one side of Historic St. Peter's brick wall is a brand new plaque that reads:

State Historical Society
Historic Saint Peter's
Lutheran Church
Erected 1842
Underground Railroad Site
"Ye shall be free indeed."
John 8:36

Underneath the plaque was a nameplate that reads "TO THE CHURCH" with an arrow pointing towards the right. Since this is new signage at St. Peter's, Gretchen saw it for the first time today. She studied the words, could not read them, but she clearly understood that the arrow pointed to the front door of the church. While she quietly stood there, she eventually looked down at her feet and discovered Ruby and myself sitting motionless underneath the shrubbery. Gretchen was not afraid of us. She waved at us, said hello, and we reciprocated. After that Gretchen sat down on the grass and introduced herself. We still did not speak. She wanted to know if we were trying to hide from everyone. Ruby and I nodded our heads up and down. We were too reluctant to speak because we did not want to frighten Gretchen. Gretchen continued by telling us about her brothers, Marc and Luc, and that she holds them and also helps her mama in many ways by trying to be a mini-mama.

After Gretchen asked us another question, I could not contain myself so I spoke to her. I told her that we are "Junior Lutherans" living at Historic St. Peter's, mentioning that we are quiet about it because we want to stay safe. She told us that she wants to be safe, too, and that we should not worry because the Bible says, "He will cover you with his feathers." We told her we had not heard that before. She said that she would be right back and to stay hidden under the bushes. We watched Gretchen's little legs run as fast as she could. When she returned, she told us that her mama said the Bible verse is from Psalm 91:4. She reached in her jeans pocket and pulled out three mini pretzels, one for each of us. While we talked and chewed on our snack, she asked us if we had any questions about being a Lutheran, but we did not even know what to ask. Gretchen then offered to tell us much of what she knows about being Lutheran. We told her that we would be happy to learn from her.

Gretchen began explaining Lutheranism to us by saying that there is a big book called the Holy Bible. It is the place where you can read about Jesus, God's only Son, dying on the cross to forgive all people's sins. She said that Jesus is the way to know the Father in heaven. Adding numerous other details, she said that her baby brothers received Holy Baptism last summer, her daddy "consecrates" Holy Communion, and when her mama receives Holy Communion she gets to kneel alongside her. She added that she and her baby brothers are given a special blessing, promising them that Jesus loves them and that they are Jesus' little lambs. Very important is the Holy Trinity, which is God, Jesus Christ, and the Holy Spirit, which happens to be her mama's favourite part because she is a graduate of Trinity College. Her family says prayers every day, especially The Lord's Prayer, a prayer before each meal, plus bedtime prayers. There are lots of Lutheran songs to sing that are very pretty. She also attends Sunday School, adding that one time she knew the answer to a question that the teacher couldn't answer. We asked her what her favourite part is about being a Lutheran. She told us that she likes to invite people to church. She said that inviting people is part of something called "witnessing" that includes letting your light shine. Gretchen finished by telling us that the two words, "witnessing" and "consecrate" are the biggest words that she knows.

Soon after we received Gretchen's crash course on Lutheranism, we heard Aia call out for Gretchen to come home. Ruby and I waited for a few minutes, but soon got a wiggle on and returned home. We couldn't wait to pin our ears next to the crack in the dining room wall during the Osterhagen's lunch conversation. We were deeply inquisitive to see if Gretchen would mention us. Gretchen did tell her folks that she met two "Junior Lutherans" named Finley and Ruby Newcastle, who are mice. Since they just became "Junior Lutherans" on Reformation Sunday, Gretchen was proud to tell her folks that she told us everything that she knows about being a Lutheran. She said that Finley and Ruby live at St. Peter's but she does not know where. Clement said that they probably live in the church garden shed with the riding lawn mower and the snow shovels. After lunch Gretchen played in her room. Ruby and I overheard Clement's and Aia's conversation, which happened to be about us, while they were cleaning up the kitchen. They spoke as though we are non-existent, made up in Gretchen's imagination. Ruby reminded me that even though this was the experience of a lifetime, perhaps it is best kept quiet for safety reasons.

At 10:30 p.m. Ruby and I travelled to the parsonage kitchen. We located a broken pretzel underneath one of the kitchen cabinets. Most likely it dropped to the floor when Gretchen fetched us a snack. Ruby and I surmised that today was simply out of this world. After we got in bed Ruby sang, "This Little Light of Mine." Because of our encounter with Gretchen today and her sincere desire to invite people to attend church, we concluded that she certainly is not hiding her light under a bushel, but shining it all around the neighbourhood. We are so proud to know her! We now call her our newest friend.

– F.N.

Wednesday, October 28

Since Pastor Osterhagen is friends with Father Tim at Holy Angels Catholic Parish, Father Tim stopped at the parsonage two weeks ago to ask Clement a favour. Ruby and I were active listeners that day, wondering if it might be about something religious, perhaps participating in a joint worship service at the Oswald County Fairgrounds next summer. We were off target about that idea. Father Tim said that he would be flying on Wednesday, October 28, to Philadelphia to officiate at his niece's wedding on Saturday, which, of all days, is Halloween. Father Tim asked Clement if he was available to help out at the food bank while he was out of town. Explaining that the food bank opens at 9 a.m. on Wednesdays, he added that many people are lined up at 8:30 a.m. Father Tim revealed that the first people in line receive the limited amount of fresh fruits and vegetables, those arriving later receiving mostly canned and packaged goods. Before the food bank doors are unlocked, Father Tim stands outside on the top step of Holy Angels and delivers a brief devotion, prayers, and the Lord's Prayer. Clement told Father Tim that he would be happy to fill in for him while he is away.

When Clement returned home from delivering today's food bank devotion, Aia asked him many questions. Clement had lots to say, but he pointed out that he saw one disturbing sign that read, "These cans are out of date. Give these away first of all!"He also noticed the first person in the lineup. Her facial expressions were transformed from forlorn and downcast to eyes that twinkled. She broke into a broad smile as bright as the sun when she received three different pints of berries; raspberries, blueberries, and strawberries. Ruby thought that Aia seemed a bit jealous of the lady, adding that if she were to receive those berries they would immediately become the main ingredient in a mixed berry cobbler. After that, Aia asked Clement if their income level is low enough to receive free food at the food bank. Without batting an eye Clement told her that he would check into it.

At 10:45 p.m. all was tranquil at the parsonage so Ruby and I hotfooted our way to the kitchen. We were immensely hungry. Our tummies were actually reverberating warm-up drones that sounded as though they were flowing from a bagpipe. With delight we found a smidgen of a zucchini tart underneath Gretchen's chair. We assumed that Aia was yearning to make a mixed berry cobbler but could not afford to purchase the berries this time of year. So, she instead made a vegetable tart. We especially enjoyed the tiny squares of red bell pepper that she incorporated into the recipe that added appealing colour to the otherwise pale zucchini. When Ruby and I discussed the food bank and the Osterhagen's interest to find out if they qualify, we once again wondered if they are poor. They could very well be strapped for cash due to the church turning a blind eye every year to the district salary guidelines. It is a stretch for us to understand how Clement and Aia are expected to live paycheck to paycheck. We know that this is sad, shameful, and not one bit praiseworthy. We think it is sad that Clement has to take care of his family using money when we mice are provided for so well by God without any dollar bills.

– F.N.

Thursday, October 29

Historic St. Peter's Cemetery is located on the grounds next to the church parking lot. Ruby and I decided to be adventuresome today. So, we took a brisk walk around the grave sites. We felt as though we were painting the town various shades of brilliant orange and yellow while we walked on a carpet of crunchy maple leaves. Since we are both history buffs, we spent quiet time reading the gravestones. Noticing that many of the last names were familiar, we made the connection between some of St. Pete's parishioners and their kin that are buried in the graveyard. Ruby and I hope their relatives visit their gravesites, brush away debris, and bring fresh flowers. We noted that it would be so sad if they let too much time pass between visits. Those loved ones might just become nothing but a blurry memory. Ruby spoke tenderly about the people buried in St. Peter's Cemetery, mentioning that their lives had meaning and purpose. A mother and daughter were there placing flowers on their father and grandfather's grave. We heard her say that a cemetery reminds the living that someday their lives will end, unless they are with Christ our Saviour. He has promised to take them from their earthly death to live forever with Him in heaven.

At the far corner of the cemetery were some ancient tombstones. One that fascinated us was where Oscar Johannessen was buried in 1886 at age thirty-four. Something surreal was written on his tombstone. Ruby and I studied it carefully. The lettering was worn and aged but we were able to decipher the message which read, "Died while being rolled down a hill to alleviate his suffering." Below that were the words from Romans 8:18, "I consider that our present sufferings are not worth comparing with the glory that will be revealed in us."Standing there for several minutes, Ruby and I concluded that Oscar might have had appendicitis when someone thought that rolling him down the hill would miraculously make him better, but that the opposite happened when his appendix burst and killed him.

At 11:15 p.m. we travelled to the parsonage and found a pimento stuffed green olive. I enjoyed the green olive, while Ruby favoured the pimento. After that we went home and enjoyed our hobbies. I read a book while Ruby knitted mitts with a pair of toothpicks.

During the middle of the night, Ruby woke up screaming from a nightmare involving Oscar Johannessen. Mice have nightmares about falling overboard an ocean liner with no hope of being rescued, being sprayed by a frenzied skunk, being chased by a grizzly bear or a cat, or walking in the forest with a foreboding feeling that Sasquatch is watching. The worst nightmare I have ever heard was about a group of hikers heading down a wretched trail located deep in the heart of Africa. After they set foot on that path, not one of them was ever seen again. But, Ruby's nightmare was simply a reaction to not understanding how rolling someone down a hill would produce a medicinal cure. Before drifting back to sleep, I decided it would be best that my Ruby not go on any more day trips to Historic St. Peter's Cemetery.

– F.N.

Reformation Day ~ Saturday, October 31

Aia had her hands full this morning at the Oswald County Library juggling both Marc and Luc. She later told Clement that it would have been far easier to transport two dinner plates of fancy wedding food, along with two flutes of champagne, safely through a crowded reception buffet than it was handling the twins during today's outing. Ruby really admired Aia when she mentioned that she could not have handled the day without Gretchen's assistance. Gretchen has become a real teammate when it comes to lugging around the heavy diaper bag, offering moral support to her mother when challenges arise, and noticing when her help is needed. Ruby mentioned that Gretchen has basically taken on a volunteer job as a professional diaper bag caddie. It must be strenuous work for a young girl since it contains so many baby supplies. Several times we have noticed that she announces repeatedly that the most important item in the diaper bag is the container of baby wipes that are needed to keep her brothers clean from head to toe.

Gretchen received a postcard invitation last Friday to attend the Halloween party held at the library today. The invitation suggested that the children wear costumes. Gretchen arrived in her Little Red Riding Hood cape, refused to hang it up on one of the coat hooks, and sat down on the floor listening to story books about pumpkins, scarecrows, and trick-or-treating. After several stories were read, each child was presented with a small jack-o'-lantern paper bag. They were invited to stop at six candy collection stations throughout the library to gather goodies. Each costumed Oswald County Library adult volunteer passed out candy to trick-or-treaters when they arrived at their station. Gretchen was delighted with her bag of candy. When the party finished, Aia checked out two family Halloween films hoping to watch them tonight. During lunch, Gretchen told her daddy all about the fun that she had at the library while Ruby and I sat quietly and listened to their conversation. After their lunch of turkey noodle soup, the entire family was sleepy so it was naptime, even for the grownups.

After Clement and Aia got under the covers, they chatted briefly about Reformation Day in 1517. We heard them chuckle when they came up with an idea of how Dr. Martin & Katharina Luther might have spent every single Reformation Day in the years following the posting of the Ninety-five Theses. Deducing that the Luther's were simply exhausted, just like they are, the only logical thing to do would have been to take a nap. In a nutshell, Aia remarked that being severely scrutinized during the Reformation probably frustrated, frazzled, and fatigued Luther. She added that he must have felt as though he was continually on view for the remainder of his life. It is little wonder why Luther had a magnitude of stress and health problems. Just consider for a moment, Dr. Luther's immense unpopularity with the highly disapproving and annoyed Pope Leo X, not to mention half the realm of Christendom. Now, that's one heavy millstone, hefty albatross, and burdensome strain to carry through life according to Trinitarian speaking Aia.

Aia brought up that during story hour this morning she glanced over at a newspaper headline featuring a woman aboard a passenger train. The peculiar part was that the woman was apprehended for lighting matches and tossing them under her seat, one after another. Passengers reported that they smelled smoke in the train. For safety reasons, the train made an emergency stop. All passengers stepped off of the train. After that police dogs entered the empty cars. It turned out that the match woman was afflicted with a rare medical condition that results in an uncontrollable expelling of intestinal gas. Lighting matches was her ineffective attempt to eliminate the nasty odour. The article stated that from now on the match woman is banned from riding on passenger trains in North America. Aia said she pitied her poor husband and hopes, for his sake, that he has Anosmia, a complete or partial loss of smell. Even better would be if he had a medical condition called Traumatic Anosmia which is a permanent loss of smell. To conclude, Aia said that if his sense of smell is intact, they must probably have a mighty strong marriage. Even the lighting of a luxury highly-fragranced balsam fir Christmas candle could not begin to infuse, transform, and clarify the air quality.

Gretchen received plenty of Halloween candy from the library this morning, so trick-or-treating never became a priority. Keeping lights low at the parsonage, the family watched one of the two films Aia checked out from the library. Ruby and I were very disappointed because we had our hearts set on watching the other film. On the cover of that movie jacket happened to be a mouse named Crikey. Excitement about this film has travelled to us via the mice that reside at the Oswald County Library. From reading the back of the video cover, the library mice ascertained that the main character is an Australian mouse who became an honest-to-goodness hero by rescuing a baby kangaroo named Jaxon after he accidently fell out of his mother's pouch. Crikey relentlessly tracked down Jaxon's mother, Charlene, who was so emotionally distressed and scatterbrained about losing her baby that she was not thinking clearly. At first she hopped away at full speed in the wrong direction. It was not an easy task for Crikey and Jaxon to catch up to Charlene, but well worth the effort just to see the immense joy on both of their faces when they were reunited. Just moments after that, Jaxon climbed into his mother's pouch. Ruby and I have a deep yen to see the film, so we hope that Pastor, Aia, and Gretchen will have time to watch it before it is due back at the library on November 4. As always, being posted at the opening in the parsonage dining room wall gives us supreme opportunities to see and hear the Osterhagen's television as well as observing the compelling, captivating, and charming way of life that happens inside St. Pete's parsonage.

At 11:30 p.m. our regular evening plans were interrupted in order to attend an emergency village meeting. Two of our badly behaved mice, Hanky and Panky, revealed to all in attendance that they had discovered a "kissing corner" at St. Peter's. It seems as though at tonight's Youth Group Reformation Party there was more activity going on than Bible baseball and musical chairs. Hanky and Panky are keen on observing the youth's entertaining evenings, so they hide just outside the door at every meeting. At one point they noticed Bryan Schmidt and Jenna Powell quietly sneak out of the youth room and dash down the hallway. Hanky and Panky followed them to see where they were going. They arrived at a room located above the sanctuary that Hanky and Panky did not know existed. The first thing that Bryan and Jenna did was to sit in the far corner of the last pew and hold hands. Secondly, their two lips (or is it tulips?) touched for two seconds. Thirdly, the pair hurried back down the steps to return to the Youth Room before anyone noticed that they had briefly disappeared. After hearing this news, many from the village got a move on and followed Hanky and Panky to see this undiscovered area. When the village arrived at the so-called kissing corner, Hanky and Panky were informed that it is the choir loft, the place where praises to Almighty God are sung during Thursday rehearsals and on Sunday mornings. Hanky and Panky were clearly disappointed that St. Peter's does not have a kissing corner, but the majority in our village agreed it was for the best.

– F.N.

All Saints' Day ~ Sunday, November 1

BEAMING WITH COMPASSION IS HAZEL, A VILLAGE MOUSE WITH RAVISHING CINNAMON-coloured eyes. She happened to be in the right spot at the right time when Ralph Pfalzgraf arrived at church this morning. Hazel trailed Ralph's footsteps as he sheepishly headed toward Pastor's office. Skipping to even say "good morning" to Pastor, Ralph blurted out that he needed to confess a mistake that he had made. While Pastor and Hazel listened to him, Ralph admitted that he was the person responsible for the missing offering on October 19. Putting on his suit coat this morning, Ralph revealed that he unexpectedly came across an envelope in one of the pockets. Realizing that the envelope contained the collection from October 19, he said that the mistake happened on the day that he and Denise hastily left church to head to the airport to catch their flight to Spain. Ralph said that he had worn this particular suit coat all the way to Spain, simply forgetting that he was carrying the offering. Because the temperature was so pleasant during their vacation, there was no need for him to wear his suit coat, so he stuffed it into his suitcase and it remained there until they returned home. When he put it on to wear it to church this morning, he discovered the missing offering in one of the pockets.

Ralph seemed so distraught about his stellar reputation of being a church pillar that he asked Pastor if the offering could be counted on the sly so he didn't have to admit to anyone that he had it in his pocket all of this time. Pastor didn't think that was a very wise idea, besides he needed to notify the police to inform them that the offering had been found. Advising Ralph that it is far better to honestly admit a mistake than to try to hide it, Pastor reassured him that he will have a better reputation because he openly acknowledges his error. Ralph listened carefully to Pastor, nodded his head in agreement, and then unlocked the safe and placed the October 19 offering envelope in the spot where it should have been placed fifteen days ago. Hazel reported to Ruby that she was proud of both Ralph and Pastor in the manner in which they handled this sticky situation with truth and grace.

After church today Clement spoke with Aia about the materialized offering and Ralph's eagerness to conceal his part in the offering's disappearance. Clement mentioned to Ralph that it was best to be honest, admit his mistake, and that everyone will forgive him. Aia smiled as she revealed that through this humiliating boo-boo Ralph must feel sin-sick and in need of some balm from Gilead. She added that because of this blunder he is already beginning to develop the ticklish balance needed to have both thick skin and a gracious heart.

At 3 o'clock this afternoon, Pastor Osterhagen left town for the installation service of Pastor David Klug at King of Glory Lutheran Church, a young mission parish thirty minutes north of St. Peter's. It was scheduled for 4 p.m., followed by a dinner to welcome the new pastor and his family to the parish. Clement has been on the telephone frequently these last weeks while Pastor Klug has been contemplating and praying fervently to decide whether or not he should accept this call or remain at his current parish in Oklahoma. After his decision was made to accept the pastoral call to King of Glory, he became unusually involved in the installation service by selecting the hymns, reminding the Altar Guild that the paraments and chancel flowers need to be the colour red, and even selecting George Frideric Handel's composition, "How Beautiful are the Feet," for the choir anthem. He has gone so far as to request roast beef instead of chicken for the installation dinner. Clement quickly got very tired hearing all the fussy details and spoke to Aia about this. It was not long before we heard Aia nickname the new pastor, even though she has not yet met him, "The Bride of Christ." Aia mentioned that Pastor Klug is acting far too involved, adding that his enthusiastic behaviour might seem extreme to the members of his new parish. Lastly she added that he might benefit from a refresher course on who exactly is the Bride of Christ.

At 11:30 p.m., the usual time for our snack, Ruby and I did not have time to stop and enjoy a treat because we were in such a rush to move with the others to the Bavarian Bed & Breakfast. Before leaving St. Pete's tonight we needed to hide my journal in a spot where no one would find it. This relocation came about because Weegee and his followers made a big mistake last Saturday night by holding a wild party in the Underground Railroad hiding spot. After their party was over, they did not clean anything up before going to bed, being too weary from having superabundant fun. Weegee said that they had planned to wait until the weekend was over to tidy up the spot, but that plan didn't work. They had no idea that Finn Larssen would show up and take another look at the hiding place. Saturday's party was super fun, but Weegee admitted to Eli that they never should have partied in a historical location.

Before we all left St. Pete's tonight, our village gathered together and held paws while we sang our theme song, "Safety First." I will not be able to write in my journal for awhile, but I will return to it as soon as we can come home. There is talk that we might be able to move back to St. Pete's by November 5 or so.

– F.N.

Friday, November 6

Expert mice explorers Lewis and Clark scurried back to the Bavarian Bed & Breakfast two nights ago after a trip to St. Peter's. Having extensively canvassed the church, Lewis and Clark revealed their favourable findings. Even though the exterminators came out with their big guns, they did not find any evidence of mice except in the Underground Railroad spot. Our village was all ears, plus smiles, upon hearing that the exterminator has completed his work. We were warned, however, to stay away from the traps that are still set up behind the church kitchen refrigerator, stove, and along the wall underneath the sink. Jubilation erupted from the go-ahead to return home. Firm plans were formed to travel under the cover of night, hoping that no one will see us. All were in one accord knowing that it is worth the danger of travelling back to HSP. We are all yearning for our church home.

Lewis and Clark also spoke about their comfort and joy with the living accommodations at the Bavarian Bed & Breakfast. Announcing that they intend to spend Christmas at the BB&B, plans are to return to St. Peter's on New Year's Eve. After they gave out that information, a sizable group of mice asked to join them and remain at the BB&B. In order to keep current on news at our village gatherings, they guaranteed two representatives will be sent to attend each meeting. In turn, those representatives will keep us versed on the happenings at the Bavarian B&B. We will miss them, but respect their wishes, looking forward to hearing news from the BB&B. Our village was extremely thankful that Lewis & Clark discovered a temporary place for all to live while St. Pete's was off-limits. Before leaving, we thanked them for leading us to a safe location.

Just minutes before we moved away from the BB&B, Ruby and I shared our final treat in the *"Küche"* (German word for kitchen) consisting of a few dropped morsels of a soft pretzel. Ruby pointed out that it was unfortunate we were lacking Bordeaux mustard to accompany our treat. It was a good time to bring up that my journal is nearing completion. In just a few weeks I will have achieved my goal of recording the news and events at Historic St. Peter's for one solid liturgical church year. Ruby suggested that since I have dedicated many a moon scripting the whole kit and caboodle of the manifold nuts and bolts at St. Pete's, I might feel run-down, bone-weary, and dog-tired. (Again, I noticed Ruby speaking Trinitarian.) I appreciated it when my fine wife lovingly recommended that I should take some time at that point to recharge my batteries by simply not accomplishing a thing. I agreed. Yes, there is a time for everything.

Tonight everyone made it safely back to St. Peter's. Ruby and I were the last ones awake. She was kind enough to help me retrieve my journal before going to bed. I needed quiet time to catch up on my writing so I stayed awake all night. The absence of my journal led to a void in my life, similar to a loss or a death. After all, this is one of my goals. Now that I have my journal back, I hope to write down the things that happened at the BB&B before any more time passes and I forget the details. One time I heard a parishioner, a clear-sighted lawyer, say that we write things down so we don't forget. That made utter sense to me.

Now let me acquaint you with the Bavarian Bed & Breakfast . . .

The Inn has been majestically restored and renovated to overflow with an abundance of European ambiance. "The Radiant River Rhine" is the name of the formal dining room where the guests delight in breakfast served continental-style. In the evening the dining room is open to the public, reservations required. Residents from as far away as seventy-five miles do not hesitate to travel the distance to occasionally dine at the BB&B. During several months in 1957, artist Helmut Braun was the artist-in-residence. Having been commissioned to paint all four walls of the dining room, his work depicted various breathtaking views of castles, the Rhine River, and the countryside. By simply beholding the views, one might be tempted to include a trip to Germany and Bavaria on their personal bucket list. After Helmut completed his paintings, he returned to Germany. Later on he was privately commissioned to paint a large religious mural portraying the Baptism of Jesus in the chancel of a small historic church located in Garmisch-Partenkirchen, Austria.

Hanging from the centre of the dining room's cathedral ceiling is an immense ruby red crystal chandelier. When evening arrives the chandelier sparkles with an outpouring of the crystal's crimson light, providing an atmosphere of sheer elegance. A six foot bronze replica is positioned in one corner of the room, just to the left of the big bay window. Ruby and I heard that it is not as colossal as the one located in New Ulm, Minnesota's central park, but it is equally impressive. An antique sturdy china cabinet built out of cherry wood contains dozens of green stemmed goblets that are said to be the exact same style that are on board luxury boats travelling up and down the Rhine River.

Five bedrooms are within the BB&B, each one having a distinctive name and decorating theme. There is the "Fraulein Adelphi Room" showcasing red poppies, the "Fraulein Margit Room" with bright yellow Marguerite Daisies, the "Fraulein Gisela Room" has clusters of delicate Edelweiss, the "Fraulein Brigitte Room" displays blue corn flowers, and the "Fraulein Wilhelmina Room" is blooming with mountain wildflowers. Each bedroom has its own flair because of the Bavarian flowers skillfully painted on the ceiling's border.

The current owners of the BB&B, Les and Lily Hirschfield, are partially retired, spending winters in New Mexico. While away they leave their two dependable daughters, Carissa and Claudia, to attend to the daily detailed activities of running the BB&B. Being their daughters are married and have children of their own, the sisters rotate schedules in order to have adequate time with their families. When Les and Lily purchased the estate in 1963, the original owners stipulated that they would sell the Bavarian Bed & Breakfast to them if it retained the original name. Les & Lily were happy to keep it the same. We have heard Carissa and Claudia often tell visitors that their folks are the ones who came up with naming every single room within the BB&B.

There are six other employees at the BB&B, but by far the most important member of the staff is the renowned Dieter Nussbaum, a chef trained in Germany with supreme culinary skill and expertise. Dieter is also a well-versed herb gardener, overseeing the inn's herb garden that provides him with superbly fresh flavourings to enhance most of his cooking creations. Because of his competence in this particular area, he is now the newly published author of the cookbook, *The Quintessence of Küche Herbs*. No matter how charming and splendidly attractive the BB&B appears on the outside, as well as the on the inside, guests remember it as a setting where Chef Dieter creates sumptuous and memorable meals. He is famous as a master of gastronomy who refuses to be intimidated when using fresh herbs to enhance his creations in a wide variety of ways, even in his dessert creations.

Ruby is sleeping like a baby while I am deep in thought writing in my journal, only to momentarily be interrupted by the Osterhagen's chalet cuckoo clock striking midnight, followed by the playing of "The Happy Wanderer" and "Edelweiss."It reminded me of the cuckoo clock in the entryway at the Bavarian Bed & Breakfast. At that moment a twinge of homesickness entered my heart because we, too, fell in love with our home away from home, the never-to-be-forgotten Bavarian Bed & Breakfast.

– F.N.

Saturday, November 7

Lewis and Clark informed us that last January the newly hired employee at the BB&B instantly caught Chef Dieter's attention, probably because of her warm friendliness and beauty. Bonnie Blue Habberstadt has a twinkle in her eye each time she sees Dieter and it is reciprocated in Dieter's sparkling big blue eyes. Dieter faithfully attends St. Pete's worship services and now is bringing Bonnie Blue to church with him. The village mice think it is so precious that Dieter and Bonnie Blue hold hands throughout the worship service. It is crystal clear that Dieter is of the view that Bonnie Blue is a spellbinding American woman, someone completely authentic, not too serious like a few of the German women he knows back home. Bonnie Blue adores Dieter's thick German accent. We've noticed that she is swept off of her feet while watching him speak using robust hand gestures. The mice at the BB&B can tell that true love is budding. During coffee breaks Bonnie Blue enters the *Küche* to sit at the round table. Dieter prepares two cups of creamy coffee and places them on a tray along with a little white china plate that is lined with a red heart paper doily. On top of the doily are two very small decadent European-style sweets. For just a few minutes they enjoy a mini-date. Both of them look forward to their shared coffee breaks. During this time Dieter keeps his under-chef busy with a tower of vegetables to wash, chop, and dice. That way he'll be far out of sight and their intimate conversations will not be overheard.

Dieter is daily getting to know Bonnie Blue with acceleration. At one point he inquired about her unusual name. We overheard the long and the short of it. She mentioned that when her mother was thirteen-years old, her family took a trip to the Smoky Mountains. Along the way they stopped to visit her Mother's aunt and uncle. The two couples were so overjoyed to see each other that they decided to dine together at a trendy steakhouse. To keep Bonnie Blue and her two sisters and one brother occupied during that time, they were dropped off at a movie theatre.

After the film began, Bonnie Blue's mother became sick with a fever and the chills. Running like lightening to the washroom, she made it just in time for the displeasures of the flu to be deposited not only in the toilet bowl but also in the waste basket. Having missed the entire feature film, she remembered feeling guilty that her folks had wasted money on her unused movie ticket, uneaten popcorn, and untouched lemonade. She spent two-hundred and thirty-eight miserable minutes freezing in the theatre washroom while her siblings enjoyed the film. Her oldest sister never even checked on her during the intermission even though she was the one designated to be in charge. Worse than that, after the film was over, they were angry at her for getting sick while they were on vacation. Because her mother's siblings wanted to avoid getting the flu, all of them refused to sleep anywhere near her in the hotel room. She slept on the floor in a sleeping bag, one of two lugged along to save costs on hotel rooms.

Bonnie Blue's mother never actually saw that particular film until she was an adult. When she watched it, there was a piece of brokenness that was put back together and healed. It lifted her spirits when she saw Scarlett holding baby Bonnie Blue. She told Dieter that this was the simple explanation of how she got her name. She also mentioned to Dieter that her mother still is hopeful that someday Bonnie Blue will marry, give birth to a daughter, and name her Scarlett. Dieter listened to this part of Bonnie Blue's past and told her that he wanted to learn much more about her life. He looked into her blue eyes and told her that he loved her. Bonnie Blue reached her hand over to his and said that she loved him, too. Dieter added that he adores the name Scarlett. Bonnie Blue's cheeks turned rosy when Dieter said that he hopes one day they can have a baby girl together and name her Scarlett. Flame, the mouse in our village whose fur has the brightest luster, reported all of the above to me. He listened studiously to their conversation while hiding behind the fifty-pound sack of potatoes temporarily located in one corner of the BB&B's kitchen.

The most atrocious experience the mice had at the BB&B was when family from Wyoming were guests for one week. Because they specifically requested to have the BB&B all to themselves, no other guests were present. The family, Will (William) and Winnie (Winnifred) Lawson and their four boys Willie, Weston, Wyatt, and Walker, live on a ranch that they refer to as the "W-6 Ranch." Will drives to the heart of Cheyenne five days a week to earn oodles of money at an investment firm. On the weekend he enjoys his freedom at the ranch with his wife and the boys. Winnie was nicknamed "Pooh" very early on in their marriage by Will. Pooh prefers her nickname to any other endearing names like sweetie, honey, or babe. She isn't aware of any other woman named "Pooh," which makes her feel that she is in a class all by herself.

Pooh spends an abundance of time during the weekdays doing exactly what her personal trainer advises her to do, working out and staying hydrated by sipping on refreshing Italian bottled water, probably the finest sparkling natural mineral water on earth. Pooh is not a natural woman by any means. There is her multidimensional hair colour, her sun parlour suntan, her painted fingernails and toenails, along with salon waxing treatments. The result in her appearance makes her anything but one of those naturally hairy-legged women who bathe only twice a week to save on water while washing with homemade goat milk soap. No baggy, long, floral print hippie dress, practical dull brown leather sandals, and a 1960s jute bag with the long strap worn over the shoulder would ever fit into Pooh's chic fashion teacup. It appears that all the trips to the salon, combined with her exercise routine seem to be worth the expense and effort by keeping Pooh, the mother of four, well-groomed, svelte, and youthful. Pooh enjoys flavourful meals that their cook prepares and is successful at retaining her trim figure.

The four boys, nicknamed "The 4X4's" by their dad, have four distinct personalities and do not get along very well with each other. Because they occasionally act entitled and are always competing, it is common for swear words to spill out of their mouths. They only are careful about their language when they are near grownups.

The Lawson family is clearly not a church-going family. Because of that, they miss out on so many benefits that come with being part of a church, like confession and absolution, hearing that God loves them, along with the reassuring words about eternal life. Instead, their weekends are spent riding horses or dirt bikes, swimming, shooting their guns, arrows, or basketballs, watching movies, fishing, and ordering take away pizzas and chicken wings. The boys are missing out on the classic work ethic that is based on diligence and hard work producing a variety of wonderful virtues. Unfortunately, the Lawson Family theme can be condensed into three words, "money brings happiness."

Pooh told Bonnie Blue that they have several hard working employees that handle the ranch responsibilities. The ranch hands live year round in the house located at the back corner of the property. Besides the ranch hands, there is a gardener, a cleaning team that keeps the house spotless (including washing the laundry), plus a runner who is available to transport the boys back and forth to school and sporting events. Even a special cook arrives daily at the ranch at 2:30 p.m. to prepare the evening meal. Later on Dieter mentioned to Bonnie Blue that there is a quote from Shakespeare's "The Merry Wives of Windsor" that seems to apply very well to all six Lawson's at the W-6 Ranch which is, "The world is your oyster." The mice talked about that for a minute. We decided that we prefer to be humble little earth dwellers who enjoy the simple things in life, like our loved ones, fresh air, a sound sleep, and snacking on crumbs.

Chef Dieter daily prepares cocktails for Will and Pooh at 5 p.m. that they enjoy in the grand room of the BB&B. Along with their fancy drinks he prepares a little something to nibble on, a tiny hint of what will be featured in the evening's main course. This has created fun and games when the Lawsons guess what will be served on their dinner plates. The Lawson boys all head to the BB&B library, the Bibliothek, during cocktail hour to sit at the round whisky barrel table and either spend the next hour playing Hearts or a game that they brought along with them. The 4X4's work together to assemble their favourite game and then they spend the next thirty minutes being against each other in order to trap the game pieces which happen to be mice.

Dieter provided the boys with a treat for their happy hour, too. Being it was currently "Chocolate Week" in France, he prepared tiny sugared mice, a decadent creation with whimsical details including chocolate eyes, almond ears, and black licorice lace tails. In his childhood memories, chocolate mice were one of his favourite Christmas treats that he helped make under Oma Muttersbach's guidance. Placed on a shiny silver tray was a six-inch white paper doily with four chocolate mice. Every day the mice looked the same, but it was their filling that changed. The boys enjoyed the strawberry, mocha, lemon, orange, cinnamon, raspberry, and white chocolate flavours. When Wyatt saw the chocolate mice he started singing the English folk song, "Three Blind Mice," and so did the other boys. It wasn't long before they were singing it in a round, lifting up their voices loudly and enthusiastically about a farmer's wife who yielded a sharp carving knife and cut off the tails of three blind mice. Not only were the mice blind, but now they are amputees. Ruby and I wondered if those three blind and crippled mice could be any of my relatives that reside at the brewery in the UK. I am hoping that my English relatives have short tails indeed, so they can quickly make it into hiding when a cutthroat old farmer's wife comes after them feverishly swinging her razor-sharp carving knife.

When evening dinner is served at the BB&B, the Lawson boys do not seem to appreciate Chef Dieter's European cooking style. It's a shame that they only consume the potatoes or noodles, pushing the other food round and round their plates. After supper one of them will dial up Maria-Rosa's Pizzeria and order an extra-large thick crust barbeque chicken pizza. Fifteen minutes later, the 4X4's head down to the pizzeria that is located just a few blocks from the BB&B. Once they are seated, they dive in and consume the entire pizza, washing it down with as much pop as they can hold. This news was passed along to our village by one of our members, level-headed Luca. Luca is hoping to marry the beautifully angelic

Bianca, a resident at Maria-Rosa's. To charm her, he travels to the pizzeria after it is closed each evening, entering the restaurant through a sizeable crack in the foundation. The dining area is where the wooing takes place, plus, it is the area where the most grated parmesan cheese can be found. When Luca passed along information about the 4X4's, he was far more excited to tell us that Bianca has agreed to go steady with him. The entire village is happy for Luca and is eager to meet Bianca.

After the Lawson Family went to bed the first evening at the BB&B, the mouse community had an emergency meeting. We questioned just what kind of parents Will & Pooh might be that they allow their children to eat mice, sing a song about cutting off their tails, and let their boys play a game designed to trap mice. We decided that if the 4X4's attended Sunday School or knew anything at all about the Italian St. Francis of Assisi, they would have developed some respect for all of God's creation. Together we joined in singing "Safety First" which helped to calm down the terror among us. Somehow, someday we too might be blinded. That angry farmer's wife could show up at the BB&B and cut off all of our tails using one of Chef Dieter's premier extra-sharp German kitchen knives. We were upset, but also had compassion on the 4X4's. Perhaps they do not know any better than to behave like this.

Putting our heads together, we voted to send Lewis and Clark, along with our courageous and spirited Sacagawea, to St. Pete's to bring back four little "Cross in My Pocket" crosses from a box located on the bottom shelf in the Sunday School office. We were undivided in our thinking that the 4X4's could really benefit from owning one of them. Certainly we could come up with a way to place the four pocket-sized crosses on the round whisky barrel table. That way, when they arrived at the Bibliothek at five o'clock the next day they would each find a cross, hopefully placing it in their pockets. In the future when they would reach for coins, maybe they will think there is something much more valuable in life than money. Our mouse head librarian, Dr. Theodore Simonsen, mentioned that Will and Pooh could join together in writing a book on how to raise spoiled children. Dr. Simonsen suggested a title: *How to Raise Four Children on $1,000 a Day*. We were startled at hearing Dr. Simonsen's sarcastic words, but realize that no one can be sweet and nice round the clock.

At 11:30 p.m. Ruby and I travelled to the parsonage and snacked on one flake of cold cereal and one raisin. We talked about when we were at the BB&B and how we could have snacked on a few morsels of chocolate mice but refused to do so because we feared we would have been committing cannibalism, something that is just plain wrong. We can't eat our own kind, even if it is in the form of a chocolate effigy.

– F.N.

Twenty-fourth Sunday after Pentecost ~ November 8

Attendance at today's worship service was so high that many of the older parishioners commented that it was just like the "good old days" when family units filled up an entire pew. Perhaps the swelling attendance was due to the glorious autumn weather combined with the "Annual Apple Reception" held after church in Woolcox Hall. Owners of Carpenter's Apple Orchard, Anton and Amy, provided both hot cinnamon apple cider and chilled apple cider, along with fresh apples. The Quanbecks, Abe and Andrea, were busy deep-frying doughnuts that had apple cider incorporated in the batter. All windows in Woolcox Hall were wide open providing a pleasant exchange between abundant fresh air and apple/cinnamon-scented air. One of the parishioners guessed that the scent might be detected from at least fifty feet away from the church.

St. Peter's grand front entrance was enhanced over eighteen years ago. Our village agrees that the architect did a spectacular job of incorporating six plain glass windows looking out on the front yard of Historic St. Peter's. It is a picturesque spot to watch the rain or snow fall, or just the autumn leaves dancing and rushing about. A few parishioners prefer the sunshine that pours in from these windows compared to the historic sanctuary with highly-detailed stained glass windows that prevent them from seeing the up-to-the-minute weather conditions.

Clyde Ingelbrand, head usher for the month of November, was on duty today in the back pew keeping an eye on anything and everything. During the offertory, Buckwheat, the largest male mouse in our village, was hiding in the narthex behind the devotional book rack display. He spotted Clyde rapidly jolt out of his pew as though his trousers might be on fire, looking like he was close to combustion. Buckwheat later told me that there actually was a real emergency at St. Pete's. Overcome with fear and combined with lack of common sense, Clyde pulled the fire alarm. The sound of the alarm spread panic throughout the assembly. This resulted in the parishioners hastening to the doors, reminding one another while they were moving not to push or shove in their hurried attempts to escape the building. Buckwheat explained to me that it was a "false" alarm, noting that Clyde simply made a mistake and that there was no fire to be put out. Nevertheless, everyone could clearly hear the fire engines zooming to St. Pete's prepared to put out a real fire.

Clyde quickly stood with his arms flapping up and down to prevent the opening of the front door. Parishioners were crowded around the windows. Looking out, to their shock and disbelief, they watched a black bear roam around Historic St. Peter's front yard. Gretchen squeezed her way through the grownups so that she could gain a front row viewing spot. Buckwheat said that Gretchen immediately gave the bear a name, Ramble. This was because he was slowly strolling around the yard, in a gentle and unhurried manner. Ramble continued dilly-dallying until he finally rested on the church cement steps that lead up to the front door. After the fire engine arrived, the firefighters appeared confused because they did not spot a fire, but they did catch sight of a bear. At that point they looked even more puzzled, perhaps wondering why a black bear is resting on the church steps. Buckwheat mentioned that many members said that they would remain in the building until the bear headed towards the forest. Foolish others thought they should make a run for it and exit by the side door. At that point, Buckwheat said that the parishioners divided into two groups, the larger group wisely choosing to put safety first. The other group decided to preposterously risk their lives by rushing to their vehicles. Ruby and I shuddered at the thought of a bear chasing a member of St. Pete's. The smaller bunch went ahead and lined up by the side door. On the count of three, Clyde opened the side door and alternately shouted two save-yourself survival phrases: "Run for your life!" and "Every man for himself!" The members who were left behind watched as every runner successfully made it to their vehicles. Not fifteen minutes later, Ramble got up on all fours and leisurely tootled down the street, heading out of town, back into the forest.

Most discussions at the apple reception dwelled on the odd news that Ramble the black bear appeared at Historic St. Peter's property today, especially since the church is not in a remote area like Copper Harbor located in Northeastern Michigan. As the discussion grew, Anton Carpenter added that it might be his fault, supposing that Ramble was drawn to the strong apple/cinnamon aroma, perhaps being ravenous or even starving. Everyone dismissed that thought and assured Anton he was not to blame. During a quiet moment at her table, Gretchen put down her apple cider doughnut to inform everyone seated near her that today's Sunday School Bible verse mentioned a bear. She said it is from Colossians 3:13 where it begins by saying, "Bear with each other." It is not so very often that any of our mice have seen such amazement on grownup's faces after a child has spoken.

At 6:30 p.m. Ruby and I travelled to Woolcox Hall and found doughnut crumbs. We talked about how frightening it was at church today when a bear was in the neighbourhood. Ruby wondered if we have been spelling the word neighbourhood incorrectly, thinking that the correct spelling might just be neigh-bear-hood. Tomorrow I will pose that question to Dr. Theodore Simonsen, village head librarian.

– F.N.

Monday, November 9

During breakfast today, Aia conveyed to Clement that she would like to enroll in an intermediate knitting class to be held at the Oswald County Library on two Saturday mornings, January 10 and 17, from 10 a.m. until noon. She explained her desire for some time away from the family in order to do something that will be personally satisfying. Plus, all of her life she has been interested in knitting. The classes are $10 each which includes some private instruction. She said that she is determined to learn skills which will open up endless knitting possibilities, especially if she is taught exactly how to read knitting charts and patterns. Emphasizing that there is much more involved in the world of knitting than just the garter and purl stitch, she is excited about these classes. Ruby and I are very confused trying to figure out how garter snakes, pearls, and knitting share any commonality.

Clement listened to Aia, but commented that he was puzzled as to why she doesn't just attend the weekly church knitting group where gatherings are populated with highly-skilled knitters. A fringe benefit of joining them is that the church knitting club is free of charge. After a fraction of an explanation from Aia, he quickly understood that she feels suffocated if she spends too much time with church people, plus she welcomes the opportunity to get to know other people in the community that don't pigeonhole her as "The Pastor's Wife." Clement said it was a healthy idea and that he will gladly watch the children while she is away on those two Saturdays. After reaching to pull out his pocket planner, Clement immediately wrote down the two Saturdays, which seemed to make Aia very pleased.

At 11:30 p.m. Ruby and I travelled to the parsonage and diligently searched the kitchen and dining room floor hoping to find a morsel of something, anything. We were unlucky, which led to feelings that we might be a pair of sad sacks. However, the pleasant aroma in the parsonage was similar to Aia's oh-so-flavourful shepherd's pie. It's too bad we couldn't even come up with one petite green pea or cube of cooked carrot. Oh well, we will stay positive by keeping our heads up while standing tall, knowing that tomorrow is a new day with fresh possibilities and, hopefully, a treat.

– F.N.

Tuesday, November 10

After lunch today, Clement called on Florence Hobson, a parishioner whose medical condition took a turn for the worse yesterday. Last night she was taken by ambulance to the large hospital fifty miles away from St. Peter's. In addition to Florence's acute illness, she has the beginning symptoms of dementia. When Clement returned home late this afternoon, he and Aia sat at the dining room table talking about this very peculiar hospital call. We noticed that he appeared anxious to reveal all that had happened during this unorthodox excursion.

With our ears pressed against the crack in the dining room wall, Ruby and I listened to Clement speak about parishioner Lenny Kirby. Clement said that when he was in Florence's hospital room, she informed him that Lenny had just called on her and had given her Holy Communion. After that she told him that St. Peter's should be more organized, pointing out that there was no need to send two clergy at two separate times to make a single hospital call. Hazel pinpointed that it was a shame Clement wasted his time and also used up so much gasoline to come and see her when Lenny was already one step ahead of him. The last thing she added was that one pastor was plenty enough to call on her as she is definitely not at death's door.

Lenny's presence in Hazel's hospital room utterly baffled Clement. He wondered if this was from Florence's dementia. But just before driving back home, Clement stopped for gas at Fitzsimmons' Fill-Up. While he was standing there, he looked over and spotted Lenny at one of the other gas pumps. Lenny did not see Clement, but Clement said that he did a double take because Lenny was oddly dressed in a clerical shirt, even though he is not an ordained pastor or priest. Obviously, he told Aia, that anyone can purchase a clerical shirt, the garment meant to be worn only by clergy. He added that a person wearing hospital scrubs does not automatically make them a doctor or a nurse because of their apparel, just as a person in a heating and cooling uniform doesn't make them qualified to repair furnaces and air conditioners. After those thoughts, Aia quickly interjected that Lenny must have purchased his clerical shirt and communion kit at Stefano's Church Goods where they have the best apparel selections while combining it with incredible customer service. Over two cups of coffee along with toffee bars, they strived to make sense of the rationale as to why Lenny would impersonate a pastor by wearing a clerical shirt, call on one of St. Pete's members at the hospital, plus bring her Holy Communion.

We heard Aia speculate that anyone who would voluntarily wear a clerical shirt where the plastic neckband uncomfortably rubs against the skin must be desperate to adopt a new, distinctive, and powerful identity, pretending to accomplish that by wearing a black clerical shirt. She also mentioned that Lenny's escapade could have easily remained anonymous if it was not for Clement's sighting at Fitzsimmons' Fill-Up. Since Lenny lacks theological training, pastoral qualifications, and is not an ordained pastor, Aia concluded that Lenny had no business wearing a clerical shirt. Lastly, and most importantly, she added that Lenny was deceiving all who saw him into believing that he is actually clergy. Aia highlighted that Lenny has no need whatsoever for a clerical shirt at his place of employment. She pointed out that he is a night maintenance custodian at Gaetano's Feta Cheese Factory.

At 10:30 p.m. Ruby and I sat under the dining room table delighting in a taste of a toffee bar crumb. It tasted so rich that it briefly kept us from talking. We scratched our heads as to Lenny's wardrobe decisions today. Somehow we felt downcast for him when we wondered if he is a pastor "wannabe." Or, he might possibly lead a double life or even possesses a split personality. To put the best construction on it, he is surely acting out his reverence for the Office of the Ministry like a security guard who dreams of being a police officer. Ruby simply refers to Lenny as "HSP's Wackadoodle." I realize that calling someone a name is unkind, but sometimes the naked truth just has to be told.

– F.N.

Wednesday, November 11

Long before Gretchen, Marc, and Luc woke up this morning, Clement was on his way to St. Ansgar's Spiritual Retreat Centre located in the northernmost portion of the state, being named after missionary St. Ansgar, known as the "Apostle of the North." He recalled entering the centre last fall when he drove down the long straight road with thickly forested pine trees on both sides. One can look ahead and spot the mighty statue of St. Ansgar solidly holding a church model close to his chest while carrying a shepherd's staff in his other hand. We could hear excitement about attending this three-day pastors' conference not just because of the thought-provoking topics delivered by highly-regarded professors, but that the centre's location is deep in the woods on crystal clear Lake Laren. The meals are the only part of the conference that he is not eagerly anticipating because they are meager in size, plus only nutritionally healthy foods are served. Aia then asked him what he would like to eat for supper the day he returns from the conference. Without taking a breath, the words "sauerkraut hotdish" flew out of his mouth. He did tell Aia that he is well prepared for this ball game because several candy bars, a bag of potato chips, peanuts, and two packages of cookies are the most important items in his suitcase.

While he was saying goodbye to Aia, she started to cry. It was clear to Clement that she was short on confidence about facing the upcoming days without his help. Clement showered Aia with warmth and love by pointing out that he has measureless faith in her. He added that she has the ability, along with a plethora of oomph, to handle full-time parental duty. Aia stopped crying when they held hands and Clement prayed: "Dear Heavenly Father, Thank you for my wife, my lovely Aia. It is a blessing from above that she is continually willing to put abundant effort into lovingly taking care of our family in both big and small ways. All day long stay with her. When she is exhausted, be with her while she rests. Please protect us when we are apart and bring us back together. We ask everything in Christ our Saviour, Amen." (FYI – Recently I have been keeping my journal close at hand so I can immediately write down important things. Clement's prayer today seemed very powerful because Ruby and I noticed how it launched and transformed Aia's confidence level. Ruby marvelled at Aia's new self-assurance and wondered if perhaps prayers are so powerful that they can change things.)

Before Clement left the parsonage there was an extra-big kiss and sturdy hug shared by the two of them. Three hours later the parsonage telephone rang and it was Clement saying that he arrived safely at the retreat centre but he had some bad news about his suitcase. Because he was in such a scramble this morning he forgot to put it the van, so it is still sitting on the floor in their bedroom. He mentioned missing many essential items like clean clothing, his toothbrush and shaver, but the cardinal things missing were his snacks. Clement must have been in a hurry to hang up. We heard Aia tell Gretchen about her Daddy's forgotten suitcase. Aia hoped that if he stepped on the gas he would be able to pick up those items at a nearby drug store before the opening worship service begins at noon.

Later on today, while Aia was taking care of the twins in the living room, an emergency arose. She assumed that Gretchen was simply playing with her doll in her bedroom. All of a sudden a bird was flying around the living room and Gretchen was squealing with delight. Earlier today, because the weather was pleasant, Aia had opened up a few windows to let fresh air inside. Gretchen managed to slide open the screen on her bedroom window which resulted in a White-throated Sparrow flying into the house. After panicking, the first thing Aia did was to place the twins, who were now crying, in their cribs and quickly shut their bedroom door. Then she ran like the wind around the house to close every door, hoping to trap the bird in the living room. After she successfully had the bird confined, we heard her telephone up a member of the church, Nettie La-Fontaine. Briefly Aia explained to Nettie the overwhelming panic she was feeling, asking her to please hurry over and bring along her cat, Midnight. Nettie agreed that she and Midnight would be there without delay to help in any way that they could. When Ruby and I heard that a cat was going to arrive at the parsonage, we sent out a red alert to our entire village urging them to go deep into hiding to avoid any confrontation with Midnight. Midnight would put all of the mice into a state of alert just with his presence.

After Nettie arrived at the parsonage, Aia and Nettie put their heads together and came to the conclusion that the best *modus operandi* would be to open up the top part of the living room window screen, place Midnight in the living room where the bird was freely flying, and to pin their hopes on the bird getting frightened and darting out the window. That was their plan and they were sticking to it. Within a minute of their course of action, Midnight had successfully accomplished his job by scaring away the sparrow.

Aia was so relieved due to Nettie and Midnight's presence that she put water on to boil and brought out the cream and sugar set along with three Nanaimo bars. Gretchen got out her play tea set and Aia poured milk in the little pot. Aia placed a bowl of half-and-half on the kitchen floor so Midnight would be well-rewarded for a job well done. Nettie told Aia many times that she was glad that she and Midnight could be of help, also offering to be there if she needs any other help while Pastor is away.

After Nettie and Midnight headed toward home, Aia asked Gretchen why she slid her bedroom window screen open. Gretchen explained that it was because of a conversation she had a last week with Mr. Shaw. After church she was looking out the narthex window when Mr. Shaw told her that his wife would stand on their deck and put one hand in front of her that held a bit of bird seed. When Mrs. Shaw remained still and quiet a bird would land on her hand and begin pecking away at the bird seed. Gretchen told her mama that she wanted to do the exact same thing, but she did not have any bird seed, so she used breakfast cereal instead. Aia clearly understood why Gretchen opened the window screen, but strictly warned her to never do that again. Gretchen finished off the conversation by telling her mama that it was better that a bird got into the house instead of a squirrel because they are never-ending chewers. She was certain that if a squirrel was in the house it would have gone right for one of the legs of the dining room table and chewed away until the leg broke in half. The result would be the entire table collapsing. Gretchen told her mama that squirrels persistently chew to keep their front teeth trimmed because their teeth continue to grow their entire life. Aia wondered how she knew that uncommon piece of information. Gretchen told her that Mr. Shaw explained that to her in a nutshell. While the two of them were observing a squirrel eating dropped wild bird seeds from the church's cathedral bird feeder, it led to the bird-in-hand subject. Mr. Shaw and Gretchen named the squirrel Phooey-Chewy.

Today had enough turmoil. The sparrow in the house hysteria tuckered Aia out so she had no energy left to cook supper. Gretchen advised her to order chicken dinners from Deb's Friendly Chicken Shack, paying three dollars extra to have the food delivered to the parsonage. That convenience helped her get through this particular meal, plus there would be leftovers for tomorrow's lunch. While they were eating supper, Aia spoke about the name of the restaurant, Deb's Friendly Chicken Shack, wondering why the word "friendly" is included in the actual name of the place. She continued her speech by telling Gretchen that the hallmark of a really great church seems to be measured by their friendliness level. Surely a church is about the good news of salvation, but with so much talk about a church needing to be friendly, she wondered why that word never appears in the name of any church, emphasizing that churches are not named "Historic St. Peter's Friendly Church," "Grace Friendly Bible Chapel," or "Hobson Corner's Friendly House of Faith." She told Gretchen that she would have to talk to her Daddy about this when he gets back home. We watched Gretchen speak with a puzzled expression on her face when she told her mama that she did not know what she was talking about. Immediately Gretchen changed the subject and asked if they could drive to Bill's Dollar Bill tomorrow to purchase hair bows and pink nail polish. Aia replied that they cannot go shopping for three days because their van, along with her Daddy, is spending three days getting renewed, rejuvenated, and reinvigorated at St. Ansgar's Retreat Centre. Once again, Gretchen looked bewildered so she changed the subject and asked if the two of them could play a game.

At 10 p.m. we travelled to the parsonage because all of the lights were turned off and we assumed Aia was sound asleep. After we got there we heard her crying. We felt badly because we love her but have no way to comfort her and help her to feel better. All we can do is hope that tomorrow is a happier and easier day.

– F.N.

November 13 ~ Friday

Even though today was Friday the thirteenth, a day some might think is clouded with superstitions, activity was shining extra brightly at St. Pete's. Many ladies were there to prepare for tomorrow's annual fall bazaar. Tweak, a member of our village who is keen on seeking numerous ways to make improvements, was on duty for this gathering. He was accompanied by one who possesses the finest auditory range in our village, Earshot. Between the two of them, they do not miss much at St. Peter's. Posters in town advertising the event call it "Historic St. Peter's Bazaar, Lunch and Talent." Insiders, or members of the church, simply refer to it as "St. Pete's Annual BLT."

The team of women browned many, many pounds of ground beef, diced bunches of celery, chopped onions, and assembled all ingredients to fill up five electric roasters of homemade chili. The actual recipe is called, "Chili, Not Too Bland, Not Too Spicy," a trusted recipe they have used since the very first bazaar was held in 1963. The recipe turns out perfectly every single year and is known far and wide as a mild chili that all ages of people can enjoy. The ladies have contributed their signature baked goods, an item of junk for the white elephant table, along with something homemade and unique for the crafty talent table. Several weeks ago Aia volunteered to help, but she has since regretted her offer. Clement had just returned from St. Ansgar's Spiritual Retreat Centre, but he, too, was helping set up tables and chairs for tomorrow's lunch. Aia is once again agitated that they have left the three children at home with a babysitter. Whenever they shell out money for a sitter so that they can volunteer at church, she gets downcast and announces that she would rather spend the money going on a pizza date with Clement. That was her recurring theme today, especially since it is "Happy Friday," which others sometime refer to as "Pizza Friday."

Most of the ladies have an assigned task, the same familiar duty that they perform year after year. This was Aia's first time helping with the bazaar so a beginner task was farmed out to her, that of chopping onions. She performed this unpleasant duty alongside a partner, Sheila Strongmeier. Sheila is not a member of Historic St. Peter's but a friend of Rachel Timmons who was absent tonight. Sheila was only doing Rachel a favour by filling in for her. She explained to Aia that Rachel was out of town tonight attending a friend's fiftieth birthday celebration.

While they were chopping onions and simultaneously shedding buckets of tears, Earshot, due to his acute hearing, got a real earful. Sheila secretly whispered to Aia that Rachel was absent because the birthday party was being held forty miles away at a male strip club. Sheila said this info is hush-hush, not for circulation, so she urged Aia to keep quiet so that the church ladies won't find out about it. Sheila mentioned that Rachel would simply die of embarrassment if anyone at the church found out her whereabouts. Obviously, Sheila never imagined that she was speaking directly to the pastor's wife. If she had known that, we assume she would have zipped her lips shut and not divulged any information about Rachel's participation in a birthday party where the guests were sowing wild oats.

After final preparations were completed, Clement and Aia returned to the parsonage. Immediately Aia took an extra-long shower to wash away her acquired onion odour. Tomorrow will be a long day at the church. More money will be spent on purchasing the chili lunch, paying the babysitter, in addition to money already spent to prepare her baked goods and a crafty item. We heard Aia blurt out to Clement that she should actually be named a "BLT," which stands for a "Burned-out Lady that is Tearful." Aia has prepared her favourite homemade sweet, Cathie's cashew caramels, for the bazaar and is hopeful that some younger people will purchase them since they still have good strong teeth. She knows that most of the older people will avoid them because of their dental work that includes implants, crowns, and bridges. Aia said that the caramels were a lot of work to make and that the ingredients weren't cheap either. She finished her complaining by saying that this weekend can be titled a "cost-a-lot" weekend, but she would much prefer to have a "save-a-lot" weekend.

At 11:30 p.m. Ruby and I travelled to the church kitchen and snacked on two red-coloured treats, a kidney bean and a diced canned tomato that had been dropped on the floor. The colour supposedly has an aphrodisiac affect on males, which I found out to be true. Between the red kidney bean, the red canned tomato and my precious gemstone, my wife Ruby, a triple true love story was in the air tonight. Romance and attraction certainly is a puzzling and pleasurable part of one's life story. Ruby and I hope that Rachel wasn't wearing the colour red tonight when she attended her friend's birthday bash. We fear that it just might have led her down the wrong path.

– F.N.

November 14 ~ Saturday

The doors of Woolcox Hall opened at 10:30 a.m. for "Historic St. Peter's Bazaar, Lunch, and Talent." A flood of attendees eagerly arrived to selectively purchase items from the baked goods table, the talent table, and the white elephant resale table. St. Peter's smelled like a twirling combination of chili, garlic toast, and coffee.

Ruby and I noticed Pastor and Aia arriving at the "BLT," leaving Gretchen, Marc and Luc at home with a babysitter. When Aia asked how she could help, she was assigned to wash dishes. Unfortunately, she worked at the deep sink from 10:30 a.m. until 1 p.m. before taking a fifteen minute break for lunch. After that she resumed washing dishes until 2 p.m. It was a good thing that Aia was wise enough to bring along rubber gloves. If not, her hands would have instantly resembled an eighty-five year old woman with a hard-working past. Thanks to the gloves, she can remain a thirty-two year old woman who is looking ahead to a hard-working future. Nutley, one village resident who cracks killer jokes and clever one-liners, was out of sight in the breezeway when he spotted Aia leaving the event. Guessing that Aia had her fill of the bazaar, Nutley revealed to us that this might be her first and last bazaar. Walking down the breezeway she pulled of her rubber gloves while looking as though she was daydreaming about living someplace far, far away from St. Peter's, most likely at a church that steers clear of bazaars. Ruby and I heard her ask Clement the one question she periodically asks him: "Can we move far away from here?" Clement usually replies, "Not today, tomorrow, next week, next month, or next year. We'll likely move a year or two after that, maybe."

At 8:30 p.m. Ruby and I travelled to Woolcox Hall and snacked on morsels of blonde brownies, chocolate chip cookies, and the Southern aphrodisiac, red velvet cake. Ruby and I can hardly wait for next year's bazaar since the red velvet cake had such an effect on us that we felt like we were a honeymoon couple.

– F.N.

The Twenty-fifth Sunday after Pentecost ~ November 15

Joey Cabot and Jocelyn Murray were united in Holy Marriage in this morning's service. Pastor Osterhagen delivered a wedding message based on John 2:1-10, the wedding in Cana. The music was vibrantly glorious, especially when Jocelyn walked down the aisle to "The Prince of Denmark's March," composed by Jeremiah Clarke, with Jeff Van Deren as the trumpet soloist.

Joselyn was truly radiant dressed in her long-sleeved wedding gown. Carrying a bouquet that included bright red, yellow, and orange Gerbera daisies and bittersweet perfectly accentuated the autumn-themed wedding. Joey looked handsome in his black suit and amber tie, along with a bright orange daisy fastened on his lapel. Ian simply wore black slacks, a crisply ironed white shirt, and a little clip-on bow tie. Several weeks ago his grandparents, Sean and Betha Murry, sent Ian a package from Kinsale, Ireland. Because they were unable to attend today's wedding due to Betha's ill health, they made certain that Ian would represent their family by wearing an argyle bow tie in three shades of brown, the traditional "Murray of Atholl" weathered plaid. A deep golden taffeta flower girl dress, along with bronzed metallic Mary Jane shoes were worn by little Maisie. She was too precious when her little hands gently tossed colourful maple leaves on the white aisle runner. After that, Joselyn walked down the centre aisle escorted lovingly by her dad, Jamie Hanson.

Last week two of the mice in our community, Savannah and Hecktor, attended our village meeting to announce their marriage intentions. They shared with the assembly their hopes to get married by Pastor Osterhagen on Sunday morning, November 15, during Joey and Jocelyn's wedding, making it a double wedding. Hecktor kindly requested a little bit of help from the mice community in order to avoid being spotted by any parishioners during the ceremony. Desiring to find a remote place in the choir loft where they could quietly hide, they would be ready to make their wedding promises to each other when Pastor asks Joey and Jocelyn the momentous wedding questions. They plan to whisper their promises to each other in two languages, English and Mouse. After hearing about their wedding plans, the entire mice community was very supportive. Many came forward to offer help.

Yes, volunteers are helpful, but it can work the other way, too. One of the volunteers, Bennett, is far too eager to assist Hecktor and Savannah, wearing heavily on their nerves. Not seeming to get the message that they want an extremely simple wedding free of all doodads, doohickeys, and thingamabobs that Bennett thinks are an absolute necessity, none of this seems to register with him.

Bennett is a newcomer to our village having miraculously travelled in a parishioner's suitcase from the picturesque town of Clovelly, located in North Devon, England. While the elderly Auggie and Viola Olafson were preparing to leave the Neville Manor in Clovelly, Bennett was absolutely dead set to hide in the depths of Viola's suitcase. Being that the Olafson's live directly across the street from St. Peter's, it was a cinch for Bennett to leave the Olafson's dwelling to join us. All realize that he has had unique experiences in England that simply don't happen in the U.S. He is actually one of the very few British mice that had the pleasure of attending a royal wedding. As a result, he has far too many viewpoints about what exactly should be included in a proper wedding. Bennett immediately found a prominent position in our community by appointing himself the village wedding consultant/coordinator.

Though he assumed that his services would be sought-after by Savannah and Hecktor, Bennett was mistaken. Straightaway he quizzed them about their decision to have a simple, plain church wedding. Without pausing, he brought forth several other options like a beach wedding, a destination wedding, a wedding at a winery, and a number of other venue ideas that were far from practical. Because he cannot wrap his head around their determination for an easy as ABC wedding, he has spoken non-stop about many sparkling wedding details involving the following: the vows, the ceremony, decorations, etiquette, food, the reception, wedding traditions, the guest list, musical selections, the honeymoon destination, soloists, flowers, and even the throwing of rose petals as an alternative to the traditional tossing of rice, which is now frowned upon because somebody's auntie could slip, take a fall, and break her hip. Hecktor finally lost his temper and told Bennett to shove off, his words not being at all kind. When he hollered at Bennett, Hecktor imitated Bennett's British accent and said, "Bennett, chap, we don't want to hear about all the bits 'n bobs you have suggested for our wedding. We don't care a tickety-boo about all that fancy stuff. We just want a simple wedding, not the awesome, bee's knees kind of wedding that you have planned for us. Just back off and let us have our way. If we change our minds and decide we want a royal wedding, we'll give you a shout. Otherwise, get a wiggle on and clear off!"

After Bennett was lambasted by Hecktor's roughshod words, his feelings were crushed. At that point Bennett announced his resignation from being the village's wedding consultant/coordinator. Instead, he has decided to appoint himself the baby shower consultant/coordinator. Hecktor and Savannah looked upset when he said that, but didn't say anything. They realized that their days of receiving Bennett's advice are not nearly over, because after they are married they want to have quite a few babies.

After arriving home from the wedding reception, Aia talked a lot about the day. She told Clement how simply beautiful the wedding was. Aia said that she wished all weddings would be held on Sunday mornings, adding that she applauds the inclusion of the wedding service in their hymnal. She liked how tender it was that the first thing Joey and Jocelyn did after becoming husband and wife was to kneel together at the communion rail to receive Holy Communion.

For several months a crew of employees at Cabot & Sons Lumber Yard have been constructing a reception hall on the lumber yard's property using materials that were conveniently right next door. It was built especially for Joey and Jocelyn's wedding reception but will be rented out in the future for other events. It is a classical Swiss-style chalet with richly finished woodwork, dark beams, vaulted ceilings, a large fireplace, and a sizable area for dining and dancing. The dance floor was especially unique at today's wedding reception mostly because of the creativity of the lighting guy who really lit up the place with a dazzling array of twinkle lights. A decadent wedding buffet dinner, prepared by Chef Dieter, consisted of everything from mini-crab cakes to a beef carving station along with plenty of other scrumptious foods.

Hecktor and Savannah got married this morning, too, and seem to be every bit as happy as Joey and Jocelyn. Their extremely simple wedding reception was held in Woolcox Hall after the ceremony. Bennett was a grumpy old twit for most of the day until he was introduced to the lovely Miss Galaxy. All in attendance observed that each time Bennett looked at Miss Galaxy, clusters of dazzling stars were in his eyes. Maybe soon he can be his own wedding consultant/coordinator because it looked as through fate or destiny has shined brightly upon Bennett and Galaxy.

Ruby and I stayed home tonight and skipped our snack not only due to overeating at Hecktor and Savannah's wedding reception but we were simply "miced-out." We imagine it is similar to human beings when they have had far too much socializing and say they are "peopled-out."

– F.N.

Monday, November 16

A wise elder in our village, River Birch, visited us this morning bringing along a heavy heart. The topic on his mind was something he hopes will be placed on the agenda at our upcoming village meeting. He expects that if the problem is stamped out at an early stage it will not have a chance to become ingrained in our community.

River Birch revealed to us that the entire village has become far too proficient in the English language simply due to listening closely to St. Peter's parishioners visit with one another. Because of this, a giant hornets' nest has developed. It has come to the point that it is affecting our culture and traditions when it comes to naming offspring. River Birch pointed out that the village is swinging away from choosing traditional earthy names. Instead, a trend is developing to select unusual, creative, and stylish names. River Birch's idea is a challenging one because he wants there to be an official "NO-NO" list to regulate the choosing of names. His thinking is that this will get the village to return to their roots by encouraging them to use traditional names from the good old days. I asked him to reveal to me a few names the mice think might be awesome choices for their babies. He then unfolded a "NO-NO" list he has created that includes the following names: Teabag, Candlewick, Cheeseburger, Irish Oats, Light Switch, Beefeater, Copy Machine, Rice Cake, Bare Budget, Swiss Cheese, Fondue, Car Wash, Snowblower, Mustard Seed, Hymnal, Rosemaling, Chip Dip, Pneumonia, Hairdryer, Advent Calendar, Youth Group, Spring Rolls, Bach Cantata, Guest Pastor, Shingles, Toothbrush, Breadsticks, Wallpaper, Hotdish, Blessed Assurance, Dishtowel, Surf & Turf, Sandy Beach, Dill Pickles, Sign-up Sheet, Greeters, Turtle Doves, Light Bulb, Choir Loft (or Anthem, Room, or Robes), Oven Cleaner, Shish Kabob, Confirmation, Thermostat, Cranberry, Door Knob, Cape Cod, Matchstick, Foot Odour, Guest Speaker, Coffee Urn, Rømmegrøt, Half & Half, Magazine, Chow Mein, Dental Floss, Fruit Soup, and Silent Night. River Birch lastly revealed that there is a couple in the village that is currently considering naming their newborn twins Wander and Lust. When I heard the name Lust, I was momentarily at a loss for words. River Birch and I see eye to eye on this being an urgent matter to stop this poppycock by advocating the use of nature names and setting up some strict boundaries. After all, to name someone Lust is beyond any doubt appallingly distasteful. Just the mention of that suggestive word can evoke all sorts of visions of being overcome with temptations. Besides, it just might be one of those offensive four letter words.

Together we decided to replace his "NO-NO" list with a "YES-YES" list, one that is comprised of acceptable names, with plans to present it at the upcoming village meeting. After all, I told River Birch that we have a rich heritage and to name a loved one with a name like Dishwasher or Light Bulb would dishonour our tradition of blessing loved ones with appropriate and time-honoured names. River Birch was so pleased with our discussion that while he was tearing up his "NO-NO" list he began to cry like a river, fully opening up his waterworks. Within just a few minutes he composed himself, got control over his emotions, which made it possible for his equilibrium to return to normal.

At 10:45 p.m. Ruby and I travelled to the parsonage kitchen where we found three shreds of sauerkraut from the pork roast Aia prepared today. It smelled so wonderful in the parsonage all afternoon that we could hardly wait for Clement and Aia to go to bed in hopes that we might find just one shred of Polish sauerkraut for our snack. It was truly a piece of gold. While we ate we closed our eyes and imagined we were on a sightseeing trip to the old town of Warsaw, Poland, along the banks of the Vistula River. When I mentioned the Vistula River, Ruby's eyes widened and she revealed to me that if we ever have a baby and it is a girl, Tula would be a breathtaking name. I highly agreed with her and mentioned that Tula would be the first name that I put on the "YES-YES" naming list.

– F.N.

Tuesday, November 17

Clement returned home this morning from the post office with today's mail that contained a letter from the Restoration Committee at the Oswald County Fairgrounds. When he unfolded the letter, a pile of raffle tickets fell to the floor. The letter asked for the church's financial support to help restore a newly acquired tiny historic church. While Aia gathered up the raffle tickets, Clement read the letter out loud. This is what we heard:

Dear Pastor Osterhagen and Members of Historic St. Peter's Lutheran Church,

The Oswald County Fairgrounds is proud to announce the addition of a small historical church building to the Heritage Village. Shepherd of the Pines was originally located twenty-three miles north of the fairgrounds surrounded by a grove of pine trees. Now that the building has been donated and transported to the fairgrounds, it will receive the richly deserved tributes of hundred of visitors who will pause for a moment to enter this small-scale place of worship to meditate and pray.

The dimensions of the church are six feet by eight feet. The interior includes an altar, pulpit, baptismal font, cross, a round stained glass window depicting the Good Shepherd, and four wooden pews. The church will be open for viewing during the annual fair, as well as being available for very small (ten people or less) weddings and baptisms.

The Restoration Committee is seeking financial support for a new roof, construction of an outdoor sign to display information about the church's history, and to plant a pine forest to surround the church's new location. We are asking for your help and support to bring this project to fruition.

Enclosed are twenty-five raffle tickets for this purpose. The winning ticket will entitle the prizewinner to a weekend stay for two at the Honeysuckle Bed & Breakfast. Included will be an evening meal served in the Trellis Dining Room where prime rib and sky-high popovers are their speciality. Another take-away gift for the winner will be a handcrafted willow picnic basket crafted in Maine that contains seven bottles of premium top quality liquor. The drawing will be held on New Year's Eve during the Oswald County Fairground's midnight brunch. The winner need not be present to win and will be notified by mail. Raffle tickets are

$25 each and are also available at several locations throughout Oswald County if you need more.

We are thanking you in advance for your help and support. The $625 dollars you send us for the tickets will keep in motion the preservation of Shepherd of the Pines Church. If you have any questions, please do not hesitate to contact any one of us at the Oswald County Fairground main office.

On behalf of the Heritage Village,

Jenny Mitchell, Grant Weaver and Chevonne Gibbs

Oswald County Fairgrounds Heritage Restoration Committee

Clement conveyed to Aia that he doesn't have the first idea what to do with this information that expects him to promote a church restoration project by selling raffle tickets where the winnings include booze. If the church office sells raffle tickets or puts an announcement in the weekly bulletin that even mentions that precise word, several of the church teetotalers will surely bristle, which is never a pretty sight. Aia's Trinitarian advice to Clement was simple, practical, and understanding. She told him that if he doesn't know what to do in this situation, then do nothing. Adding that it is his choice whether or not to be manipulated by the letter, she advised him to procrastinate what he is asked to do. She suggested that he simply stuff the letter under a pile of papers on his desk. In a couple of weeks, place the letter on the church bulletin board and get rid of the raffle tickets by taking them to the bank to add to their supply, advising them that they will sell far better at the bank than at the church. That way, if anyone asks you if they can purchase a ticket from you, simply point them to the bank. Aia explained to Clement that there are many benefits of procrastination and often they can be your best friend. This is not laziness or goofing off, but a delayed way to finish a task that you did not want to be given in the first place.

After those good recommendations, Aia spoke out of the other side of her mouth by asking Clement if she could purchase a raffle ticket from him. She explained that they could use a new deluxe wicker picnic basket handmade in Maine, because that must be the best quality picnic basket produced in the United States. She also told him that she has heard that the Prime Rib Dinner in the Trellis Dining Room is so famous that even the Governor of the State has dined there. Clement asked her what they would do with all of the moonshine if she won the raffle. She quickly came up with a three-fold solution to divvy it up between her folks, Clement's folks, and to keep some. At first she thought of giving it all to

Josie the organist for her tea tumbler, but thought better of it because Josie always seems to have a plentiful supply of hooch-juice.

At 11:30 p.m. Ruby and I travelled to the parsonage and snacked on a few sesame seeds. Aia baked homemade sesame seed dinner rolls today and a few of the seeds dropped to the floor. We talked about the word booze, a word that is brand new to us. After putting our heads together, we concluded that Clement and Aia were talking about firewater. We will bring the word booze to the next village meeting for educational purposes so everyone can learn a new word and discover what it means. Besides, learning a new word is a good for healthy brain activity.

– F.N.

Wednesday, November 18

This morning Ruby and I were sweetly awakened by listening to Aia's angelic singing voice combined with the pleasing aroma of buttermilk pancakes. Ever since Ruby and I took up residence next to the parsonage, we have wholly delighted listening to Aia sing songs from her vast melodious repertoire. One particular folk ballad has often been sung that has sorrowful words along with a hauntingly bewitching tune. Ruby and I have it memorized. Each time Aia sings it, it gets stuck in our heads. We have done our utmost to dismiss it from our minds, but have failed. We figure it is one of those songs that simply demands not to fall between the cracks. Ruby suspects it might be a historic song, perhaps linked to a war that involved a big tea party that was held in Boston, Massachusetts. Since the song is a real tear-jerker, she suggested that we turn to whistling the melody instead of singing the melancholy words. We have surmised that life is too brief to spend a lot of time shedding tears when there are so many opportunities for merriment. After all, in Job 8:21 are the uplifting words, "He will yet fill your mouth with laughter and your lips with shouts of joy."

It was not until today that Ruby and I pieced together the connection between this particular song and Aia's frequent use of buttermilk. Her recipes for pancakes, fried chicken, salad dressing, Irish soda bread, and corn dogs all have one ingredient in common, buttermilk. When Aia prepares these recipes she often sings a song about a place called Buttermilk Hill. It is the spot where two sweethearts were parted because the woman's true love has gone off to war. She sits alone on Buttermilk Hill crying and waiting for her sadness to go away. We are not familiar where this hill is located in Oswald County. But, in our minds, it might no longer be a sad place, but a cheerful spot that has several outdoor lawn benches that just beg a person to sit a spell while taking in breathtaking mountain views. During the winter it might even be a toboggan or sledding hill. Perhaps it is an official location where Olympic downhill skiers do their training. The next time I see our head librarian, Dr. Theodore Simonsen, I will put in a request for him to investigate Buttermilk Hill, a spot so noteworthy that it even has a song written about it.

At 10:15 p.m. Ruby and I travelled to the parsonage hoping to find a tiny nibble of a buttermilk pancake, but we were unlucky. We went home with empty tummies, crawled into bed and whistled the buttermilk song before we went to sleep. After that we tried to figure out who Johnny is that is mentioned in the song. We concluded that Johnny must have left his girlfriend behind and travelled back home to County Cork because he yearned for his mother's scones that incorporate fine Irish buttermilk. The buttermilk in Ireland must be of supreme quality because the cows graze on the vibrantly lush, salt-kissed, verdant grass and clover that cannot be found anywhere else on earth.

– F.N.

Thursday, November 19

After numerous months of the parsonage's water softener tank failing to perform the job it is intended to do, Clement was so fed up that he telephoned Roy Morgan of Morgan & Sons Plumbing & Heating to set up an appointment. Prior to this, Skip Spencer, owner of Skip's A-Plus Plumbing & Heating, and also a faithful member of St. Peter's, has come over at Pastor's request to check the water softener levels. Each time Skip gladly reports that there is absolutely nothing wrong with the unit, claiming that it provides plenty of soft water.

Last week Clement stayed home with the children so Aia could get a haircut. After she returned home from the beauty parlour, Aia was completely distressed. She mentioned to Clement that before the beautician picked up her scissors, she examined Aia's hair and found it to be chlorine damaged. Assuming that Aia is an avid swimmer, the operator pointed out that too much exposure to chlorine can even turn the hair green, urging her to be certain to wear a swimming cap each time she hits the pool. Aia told her that she only goes swimming once in a blue moon, so that cannot be the cause of her hair lacking luster. She, too, has noticed that her hair is dull, dry, and full of tangles because their water softener unit is not working properly. After relaying all of this to Clement, Ruby saw him open up the telephone book to search the yellow pages to find a plumber who is not a member of St. Pete's.

After checking the levels on the suspected non-functioning water softener, Roy reported to Clement that he needs to say farewell to this tank and say hello to a new unit in order to have soft water. Roy went on to say that there are abundant disadvantages in having hard water. He mentioned that there are so many minerals found in hard water that they get in the way of any type of soap or hair products working properly. Soap scum becomes difficult to remove, plus it is hard on clothing and the pipes. Roy's final point was that hard water is not only tough on people, but on the house, along with the sufferer's pocketbook.

After that, Roy pulled the paperwork out of his briefcase and Clement signed the rental agreement for a brand new water softener. Roy had an available time this afternoon for his workers to install the unit. He added that the adorable Osterhagen children will have a very soft bath tonight. Aia was so thrilled about this news that she threw her arms around Roy and hugged him. Ruby and I were struck by this because up until this point Roy and Aia were complete strangers.

Victory was accomplished on the water softener problem, but there remained one bummer of an obstacle. Clement and Aia discussed the predicament of Skip's non-functioning water softener. We listened to their conversation as to whether or not they should tell Skip about the replacement, ask him if he wants the softener back, or just ignore the subject for now. We heard their plan. They were going to place the old disconnected water softener in one corner of the laundry room and cover it up with an old sheet. Sometime later they will figure out what they should do. Until then they will drag their feet.

Everyone in the Osterhagen home was pleased about this improvement. Clement is happy that he does not have to haul forty-pound bags of salt pellets down the basement steps every time he turns around. Gretchen was happy because she took the longest bath she has ever taken. The twins were content because their clothes were softer. But we noticed that Aia was smiling most of all. She even found an applicable Bible verse and cleverly inserted the word "soft" before the word water: "As (soft) water reflects the face, so one's life reflects the heart." – Proverbs 27:19

At 11 p.m. Ruby and I travelled to the parsonage and broke one of our rules. We promised never to go anywhere in the parsonage but to the kitchen and dining room. Tonight we could not resist going down to the basement to see the new water softener. Innocently thinking that a water softener would be similar to a cascading fountain, we discovered it is only a metal tank that quietly hums a very plain one-note tune. After that we hurried upstairs and found three petite green peas under the dining room table. We each ate one and split the other. During suppertime at the Osterhagens we had heard them discuss Emily Dickinson's quote about green peas: "How luscious lies the pea within the pod." So true.

– F.N.

Saturday, November 21

After lunch today, Aia telephoned her mother, Juliette Nygaard, asking her for her salmon spread recipe. Ruby saw Aia write the recipe down. Aia repeated it back to her mother to make certain it was correct. I quickly got out my pen and notebook. We agreed that it must be of out-and-out importance to be worth the cost of a long distance telephone charge just to obtain it.

Salmon Spread
1 can (14.75 oz.) salmon
1 8 oz. cream cheese, room temp
½ cup sour cream
5 finely chopped green onions
½ tsp. salt
2 drops hot pepper sauce
2 T. Fresh lemon juice
1 T. Worcestershire sauce

In a medium bowl, mix together the cream cheese, sour cream, green onions, salt, hot sauce, lemon juice, and Worcestershire sauce. Add flaked salmon (bones and skin removed) to the mixture and incorporate. Cover and refrigerate eight hours or overnight before serving. Spread on flatbread or crackers.

Just as I finished writing down Juliette's recipe, there was a rap on our door. One mouse in our village, Crash, came over to relay information regarding Ginger Mulready, the newly appointed person in charge of St. Peter's Lost & Found Box. Even though Ginger is a volunteer, she surely takes action and is inclined to think that she is on staff. We are inclined to think that she has crowned herself Queen Bee of the Lost & Found.

Crash happens to be a very weary mouse due to his rare physical condition. Ruby and I feel so sorry for him. Unfortunately, Crash has an uncontrolled balance disorder that results in him colliding, clanging, clobbering, and actually careening into objects, several times a day. He is covered with bumps and bruises.

We, too, wonder if this condition might be coupled with an inner ear problem, since his ears hurt and he suffers from dizziness. Anyway, we welcomed him into our dwelling and listened to his apprehensions regarding Queen Bee's plans.

A couple of weeks ago Crash sideswiped one of the pew's wooden platforms. After he composed himself, he found, in that very spot, a dropped bulletin underneath the pew where Ginger Mulready sits each Sunday. Crash relayed that Ginger had written notes on the margins of the bulletin. Included were the following phrases: "Vanished & Appeared," "Misplaced & Pinpointed," "Disappeared & Unearthed," "Adrift & Gathered," and "Departed & Discovered." Together we discussed, "What does this mean?" After hashing about several ideas, the three of us concluded that Ginger intends to revise the classic old-school name of the Lost & Found Box. A little later Crash overheard the newfangled name that Ginger hatched when she was speaking to Sister Bernadette, adding that she will notify the entire church of this improvement by means of next week's bulletin. Crash, Ruby, and I somewhat approve of Ginger's fresh idea to name the Lost & Found Box "I Once Was Lost, But Now I'm Found." Nevertheless, Ruby mentioned that the name sounds too recognizable, wondering if the phrase is from an overused song with a far too familiar tune. We will have to deliberate over the new name because we are certain we have heard that terminology before. Crash suggested to us that a superior new name for the Lost & Found Box would be to call it "The Lord's House Hodgepodge Hamper."

Crash has also noticed that Ginger is attempting to find a home for every item that is currently in the Lost & Found Box. After hearing Crash's comments, we fear that some of Ginger's behaviours might come across as offensive and ill-mannered. For example, one item in the box was a woman's extra-extra large spring jacket. Ginger was on a mission to find the owner, so she asked every plump woman in the building to reveal to her their clothing size. It is probably fair enough to do that if the jacket is toddler-sized, but when it involves adult well-upholstered women, it is a good long way from being hunky-dory. Another example is the pink pacifier that Ginger hopes to match up with the appropriate baby girl. Crash witnessed her asking April Taylor if the soother belongs to her baby daughter, June. April appeared stone-faced, but her words were calm when she asked Ginger if she was trying her Sunday best to be comical or just bothersome. After that Ginger asked Sister Bernadette her habit size, even though we thought it would be a stretch to envision St. Peter's one and only nun wearing an immense jacket. When Ginger held the jacket up to show Sister Bernadette, Crash noticed the embroidered patch sewed on the back that had a Guernsey cow logo along with the words, "Rupert's Fried Cheese Curds – A Squeak of a Treat!" Crash reported that Ginger did successfully pick Sister Bernadette's brain to find out if there happens to be a patron saint that you can pray to when something is lost. Sister Bernadette was beaming when she told her that many Catholics turn to St. Anthony in prayer when they are in that type of predicament.

We decided that despite Ginger's idiosyncrasies, she is managing the lost and found items well. After that, we wondered what St. Peter's would be like if everyone behaved like Ginger Mulready.

At 10:10 p.m. Ruby and I travelled to the parsonage and happened upon a butter-flavoured cracker crumb. We chewed over in our minds what it would taste like if it was topped with Juliette's special salmon spread. We are aware that the term "luxury tin can foods" includes canned delicacies like lobster meat, escargot, and tiny shrimp. Assuming that canned salmon fits also in that category, today's salmon spread must have tasted simply sumptuous to Clement, Aia, and Gretchen.

– F.N.

Christ the King/The Last Sunday after Pentecost ~ November 22

Bernard Fleischacker, the town Deputy Sheriff and head usher at Historic St. Peter's, was in church today displaying a broad self-important smirk on his face. Bernard, or "St. Bernard" as Aia refers to him, is someone who sometimes lets his authority go to his head. This is not just due to his official title as Deputy Sheriff, but it seems to be a prevailing degree of superiority that he naturally possesses.

This egotism in Bernard showed itself clearly yesterday afternoon. After Clement received an emergency telephone call from Kathleen Whittington about her father, Edmond, Clement hurried to Our Lady of Lourdes Hospital. It was clear that Edmond had taken a turn for the worse and was said to be near death. While Clement was driving down Bantner Road, Deputy Sheriff Fleischacker pulled him over and issued him a ticket for speeding thirty-five miles per hour in a thirty-mile-per-hour zone. Clement must have dreaded knowing he would have to shell out money to pay for the ticket. He told Aia that he put it in his suit pocket and decided to deal with it later, after he was finished at the hospital.

Ruby and I listened carefully when Pastor said he made it in time to Edmond Whittington's hospital room to give him Holy Communion, pray with him, and to help his family. The Whittington family held hands while standing around Edmond's hospital bed. Together they prayed Our Father, but most of them cried, finding it hard to get the words out. After that the six daughters beautifully sang "I'm But a Stranger Here, Heaven is My Home." The sound was clear and natural, made up of six singing voices that sounded like one voice, probably because they are related. It was so beautiful that even the hospital staff on the floor stopped what they were doing and just listened. Not long after that, Edmond peacefully died and left his wife, Esther, and daughters Kathleen, Katrina, Kimberly, Kristen, Kayla, and Kitty on earth while he went to his home in heaven.

When Clement returned home he sat down and spoke with Aia, mentioning that there will be a funeral the early part of the week. Then he pulled out his speeding ticket and revealed to Aia that Bernard Fleischacker had a smug sweetness on his face when he handed him the ticket, even though he told him that he was speeding to get to the hospital because parishioner Edmond Whittington was on his deathbed.

It was at this point that the Osterhagens realized that Bernard Fleischacker was behaving foolishly. They recalled that Bernard used to be employed as a security guard at the State University, but, understandably, quit his job because it was far too stressful to deal with vandalism, drugs, theft, and drunkenness. Thankfully, he likes his current job far more in this slower paced, but rarely sleepy town. Obviously, issuing speeding tickets is an outstanding feature, a real highlight of St. Bernard's job.

Aia told Clement that he should issue a ticket to St. Bernard for his poor ushering techniques on Sunday mornings. St. Bernard must speculate that the only job of an usher is to pass out two things, the bulletins and the offering plates. Clement told Aia that he would like to issue a citizen's arrest, but being this is not Medieval England he will instead order a guide book on ushering. After St. Bernard reads that information, they agree that his pride might drop a notch or two when he sees how much of the usher job description he is not even aware of.

At 8 p.m. Ruby and I travelled to the youth room. We were terribly excited to discover two treats. Underneath one table was a kernel of caramel corn and under another was a chocolate covered peanut. We assume that the youth must have had a super good time tonight playing Bible Charades followed by two different melt-in-your-mouth treats. Too, we questioned this: If Deputy Sheriff Bernard Fleischacker had been asked to chaperone the youth event and had discovered two treats dropped on the floor, would he have pulled out his notebook and issued littering citations to the Youth Group?

– F.N.

Monday, November 23

This morning the Circuit pastors that serve churches in Oswald County, along with the retired pastors, gathered at Historic St. Peter's to attend a Pastors' winkel. Winkel is a German word which means corner or nook. So, from throughout Oswald County the pastors came to meet in one corner, this time the corner being at St. Peter's. A winkel is held every other month, hosted by one of the churches, taking turns in a rotation. Today Historic St. Peter's took its turn in the sequence.

After the pastors arrived at St. Pete's, they enjoyed coffee and donut holes before worshipping together. All were eager to view the Underground Railroad hiding spot because they have heard a great deal about it. Comments about envy and jealousy were spoken in jest because their parishes are not honoured to be listed on the State Historical Register. Clement told them that it was very fortunate for St. Peter's to receive this acclamation from the State Historical Society but their churches are just as special in many, many other ways.

Clement was honoured to host his fellow pastors, including Bishop Fillmore. Our village thought he was a knight in shining armour at delivering a sermon to so many highly-educated clergy. Following the worship service there was a circuit meeting which lasted until lunchtime. A noon meal was provided by a few ladies from the Seniors' Group. Today the pastors enjoyed chunky potato bacon soup, buns, sliced cheddar cheese, and frosted pumpkin bars. After lunch the pastors changed location and met in the cozy Fireside Room. This was time for discussion, questions, and for working out a solution regarding a current hot topic, the primary reason the Bishop was in attendance. The discussion ended at 3 o'clock. Then it was time to change locations once again by walking to the parsonage for a cup of coffee and treats before returning to their corner/nook of the circuit. Most of the pastors need to get back to their church because they have a meeting of some sort tonight that will usually last until 9:30 or 10 p.m.

Aia has worked ahead, the only possible way during these years, to host today's winkel. Burning midnight oil was her only solution to get everything ready. The dining room table was dressed in a lovely amber coloured tablecloth, topped with special treats that consisted of homemade baklava, brownies, Granny Smith apple slices with caramel dip, and coffee. The dining room chairs were placed throughout the living room, which provided a place for everyone to sit down. Today the parsonage was so squeaky clean everything sparkled. Aia and the children were dressed as though it was a Sunday morning and they were ready to attend church.

Yesterday Aia stopped in at Serena's Floral Shoppe to look for fresh flowers to create a colourful centrepiece. Carefully she carried their Swedish crystal vase into the shop to ask Serena for some advice. While looking at the refrigerator stocked with amazingly beautiful flowers, Serena suggested filling the crystal vase with white flowers instead of autumn blooms. Serena was certain that paperwhites would look stunning in this Swedish vase. Aia explained that the vase is a treasured wedding gift that she and Clement received from her Aunt Berdie Fuglestad, her Dad's only sister. Serena offered to arrange the paperwhites for Aia, honoured to be the chosen florist for this big event to be held at St. Pete's parsonage.

Aia, being very practical, was out of her element spending money on fresh cut flowers, but somehow this was the right time to do it. When she pulled her billfold out of her purse, Serena told her that she will chop the bill in half because she knows that pastors don't earn a lot of money. Aia was delighted about her successful trip to Serena's. Serena mentioned to Aia that she could not even imagine hosting so many pastors who are all so "connected" to God. She would be so anxious that she would not sleep the night before for fear that the wrong thing would accidently slip out of her mouth. Serena said that she couldn't do it, but she told Aia that she has all the skills she needs to pull it off. They hugged each other and Aia walked away with the prettiest centerpiece she has ever seen in her life.

The pastors decided to enter the parsonage, not from the breezeway, but through the front door. They must have needed some fresh air after being cooped up all day. A couple of the pastors lagged behind because they needed a smoke. Minutes before they arrived, the doorbell rang at the parsonage. Aia opened the door expecting to welcome the pastors into the house for afternoon coffee. Unfortunately, Ladonna Kazlauskas, dressed in overalls where the bib was soaked with fresh blood, commanded Aia to fetch a cake pan. Aia quickly returned to the door with a glass oven–proof casserole dish. In the bed of Ladonna's truck was a load of fresh liver. Ladonna dropped open the tailgate and grabbed a very scary-looking butcher's knife, proceeding to slice off a big chunk of liver, placing it in Aia's cake pan. Since Ladonna's hands were bloody, Aia asked her to come into the parsonage to wash her hands, but she refused. The worst thing about the whole liver delivery experience was that Ladonna bent down and washed her hands in the snow, right by the front door of the parsonage. The snow turned bloody red. It looked like the scene of a murder.

Ladonna then hit the road. Within a minute, the pastors were heading towards the parsonage. Aia panicked, ran into the house carrying the cake pan containing the big slab of liver. She was in a flurry to get the liver out of sight, so she ran down the basement and placed it in the clothes dryer. When she came upstairs the pastors were curious to find out what gruesome thing had transpired by the front door that caused the snow to be awash with fresh blood. Aia explained the unfortunate circumstances, followed by a room full of hearty laughter. This opened up conversations about quirky things all of the pastors have experienced.

One pastor told about a member who rang the doorbell at 9:30 in the evening to drop off two big boxes of zucchini, the extra-large sized ones. Timing was unfortunate because their suitcases were packed and they were ready to leave on a two-week vacation the next morning. His wife got the preposterous idea that because they couldn't use the zucchini, they should cut it up and flush it down the toilet. Unfortunately, he agreed with her. It was not even an option to throw them away because of several odd experiences with a kooky parishioner rummaging through their garbage can. To make a long story short, the zucchini stopped up the plumbing system, which brought out the worst in the church property director. By the time the plumbing was finally repaired, the entire church was privy to all the details regarding the parsonage toilet, which, by the way, cut several days out of their vacation because they had to stay home and deal with the repairs.

Another Pastor told of coming home from church on Sundays and finding an old bread bag full of stale donuts placed between the screen door and the front door, a little something to help him and his family lower their grocery bill. This older couple invited them over for supper one evening. The Pastor and his family had never encountered being in such a filthy house before. The dining room was filled with fine crystal brought back from many, many trips to Europe, but everything was blanketed with thick dust. During dinner they were served plenty of fine Italian wine in multi-coloured cut-crystal goblets. Before the wine was poured he noticed that the goblet had collected dust. While the hosts were in the kitchen his wife hastily pulled a tissue out of her purse and wiped down the interior of their wine glasses. He remembered his wife whispering to him a sensible suggestion: temporarily pretend that you are visually impaired.

Another Pastor spoke of a Christmas gift he and his wife were given, that of an expensive Bamboo salt chest that contained six flavours of gourmet salt. Just several days before that, he began taking medication to control his high blood pressure, being warned to stay away from salt. He did admit to experimenting with the smoked salt, finding out that it is perfect rub for roast chicken. The best use of any of the salts was to add a little bit of it to ground beef to season the hamburgers. That gift was received nearly ten years ago and they still haven't made much of a dent in it.

After the Pastors left the parsonage, Aia needed some therapy from Clement. Her main complaint was that Ladonna didn't even ask her if they liked to eat liver, but just assumed that they did. Aia told Clement that Ladonna is way too commanding and rough in her behaviour, exactly like she was today, but her attitude is especially turbulent at voters' meetings. They decided that they can't do anything to soften Ladonna's behaviour, and neither can anyone else, not even her poor husband. Apparently it is quite simple. Ladonna is Ladonna and that's that.

When Aia began cleaning up, Clement told her he would put the washed diapers in the dryer. Shortly after his words actually sunk in, she raced to the laundry room to fling herself in front of Clement and the clothes dryer. Thankfully she was there to prevent Clement from loading the dryer with diapers. One bad habit that Clement has is that he doesn't physically look inside the clothes dryer to see if it is empty before he tosses the washed clothing in there and pushes the start button. Opening the dryer, Aia pulled out the cake pan of fresh liver. All they could say was that it was a good thing Aia got the liver out of there in time because they really can't afford to purchase a replacement clothes dryer and another supply of cloth diapers. Also, they don't want Marc and Luc wearing pink diapers. While Aia cleaned up the kitchen, Clement sliced the mountain of liver into thin slices. We noticed Aia stand still for a moment and watch Clement sporting a white apron while he was busy at work using their largest carving knife. She mentioned to him that he resembled a meat market butcher who is blessed with fastidious carving skills. He turned his head and smiled at her. When he was finished he began frying bacon and onions to go with their liver supper. Now there are several plastic containers of liver in the freezer for future meals.

Aia was very tired from simply living the day and asked Clement if he could instead be a pastor in North Carolina where they could live close to the coast. She explained that if a parishioner gave them food, perhaps it might be blue crab, sea bass, kingfish, clams, snapper, bluefish, oysters, sea trout, shrimp, or flounder. Another option would be to live in Oregon where they might once in a while receive Pacific wild salmon. Clement told her that this is where his pastoral call is right now, and neither one of them knows what the future will bring. They held each other and both said, "I love you." Aia admitted that taking care of the twins and

Gretchen, she really doesn't have the strength to move, so liver is tolerable now, hoping that perhaps seafood might replace liver in the years to come.

At 11:30 p.m. Ruby and I travelled to the parsonage. We were so anticipating a new taste experience, a morsel of liver, bacon, and onions, but we couldn't find any. We did come upon a small crumb from a brownie so we considered ourselves temporarily satisfied. That all changed when Ruby's tummy grumbled, so we split from the parsonage and headed to the church kitchen to find an additional snack. Thankfully, we came upon a crumb of a frosted pumpkin bar from the lunch at today's Pastor's winkel. That bit of nourishment completely quieted down Ruby's tummy rumbles.

– F.N.

Tuesday, November 24

Two weeks ago Bishop Fillmore telephoned Clement and had an extensive conversation with him. Bishop frequently turns to Clement for advice with problems, appreciating Clement's pastoral common sense approach. Bishop told Clement that he deals with one problem time and again, that of retired pastors remaining members of the church that they served. Many of them remain immersed in their church relationships and friendships. One church in particular that he is working with has the retired pastor elected to the council, serves on the Board of Elders, plus has an extroverted wife who is the head of the Altar Guild, Ladies' Guild, and sings in the choir. Both the retired pastor and his wife attend the Seniors Group where he has been appointed the group's "Pastoral Advisor." All three of their adult children are active in that church, lead various groups, and one son currently is the Chairperson. Even their twelve grandchildren constitute half of the Sunday School enrollment. Bishop refers to the place as their "Little Kingdom."

Bishop explained that the current pastor is frustrated with the continual hovering done by the former pastor. Even if the retired pastor does not say anything, just his presence prohibits the church from moving forward. The retired pastor has even gone so far to turn his family room into a mini-office where members are welcome to stop by and chat.

Clement advised Bishop that the Council of Bishops needs to create a policy regarding the role of retired pastors. Bishop agreed. The Council of Bishops will meet soon and he is certain that they will create guidelines concerning retired pastors, reminding them that their time is completed at the church in which they served. Because this problem is so common and also steadily increasing, they may require that retiring pastors simply move forward by joining another church.

After breakfast this morning, Clement took off for the District Office, a forty-five mile drive, to fill in for the Bishop. Bishop Fillmore is across the District attempting to calm down the turbulent waters the newly called pastor is trying to navigate while the retired pastor is glued to his every move.

After Aia successfully got the twins down for their afternoon nap, she returned to the kitchen and washed up the lunch dishes. While standing on a kitchen chair, she reached up on her tiptoes to place a rarely used bowl on the shelf above the kitchen cupboard. Instantaneously the chair gave way and she came crashing down, first painfully hitting the side of her body on the kitchen table corner before she fell to the floor. Gretchen witnessed the accident. Her first reaction was to immediately run to her bedroom to remove the quilted coverlet from her twin bed. Then she raced back to the kitchen and placed it on top of her mother. Aia told Gretchen that she simply could not move or get up from the kitchen floor because she was in a tremendous amount of pain. She fell so hard it was as though she ran head first into a brick wall without wearing a helmet, only it was her chest, side, and back that hurt, including her head.

Gretchen immediately picked up the wall telephone and dialed 911. The dispatcher wanted to speak with her mother, but Gretchen told her that the telephone cord was not long enough to reach her mama. She said that her mama was on the kitchen floor and could not get up. The dispatcher told her to stay on the telephone, but Gretchen told her that her baby brothers were crying. She said that she needed to give them each a clean pacifier. She also needed to hit the play button on the cassette player so they could listen to their baby lullaby tape. She promised the dispatcher that when she was finished she would run right back to the telephone and talk with her again.

When Gretchen returned to the telephone the dispatcher kept her on the line and told her that the doorbell would soon ring with people there to help her mother. Before the ambulance crew arrived, I sent Ruby to fetch Snowdrop, our only albino mouse, because we needed her help. When Ruby returned with Snowdrop, I showed Snowdrop the way to enter the parsonage, urging her to quickly hunt down the diaper bag and hide in it. Due to the fact that she is completely white in colour, I thought she would be safely nestled among the white diapers. Snowdrop was able to accomplish this mission. So, when she returned from the hospital later today she reported to us the abundant details that happened at Our Lady of Lourdes Hospital.

Not just Aia was taken by ambulance to the hospital, but Gretchen, Marc, and Luc were along because there was no one at home to take care of them. During the ambulance ride Gretchen was extremely concerned about everyone's safety because no one was buckled up. She told the crew that she knows a song about car safety, so she sang it to them while they were on their way to the hospital. Snowdrop said that Gretchen's singing made her mama and the crew smile when they listened to her. Once they arrived at emergency, the children were separated from Aia and were taken care of by two hospital volunteers. By that time, another volunteer was able to get through to Clement to notify him at the district office.

Clement must have dropped what he was doing when he heard about Aia's broken ribs to hurry as fast as he could to the hospital.

After Clement arrived he was able to take Aia and the three children home. He told Aia that it is so typical of ministry that while he is helping someone else his own family needs his help even more. He wanted to squeeze her for being such a wonderful and understanding wife. Aia told him that she didn't want a squeeze and will not want any hugs for about six weeks, that is, until her ribs are healed.

After the Osterhagen Family arrived home, Clement and Gretchen pitched in and got the babies fed, changed, and to bed. He also helped Aia do the same. After that he and Gretchen sat at the dining room table and took a break. Clement enjoyed a gin and tonic. Gretchen was fascinated with a kiddie cocktail decorated with a paper umbrella while they waited for a frozen pepperoni pizza to bake. Over their drinks, Gretchen gave him an in-depth account of her mama's accident and how she tried to be helpful. He complimented Gretchen for all she had done. She praised him for how he came to pick them up at the hospital and take them home. Gretchen talked about the hospital ladies dressed in yellow flowered outfits that took very good care of the twins by holding and rocking them, even singing a song that began with the words, "Hush, little baby." The song included something about a mockingbird, but she is certain that Marc and Luc are far too small to be given a mockingbird. Gretchen did notice that the volunteers were unaware of exactly how to properly put on a disposable diaper. During their first attempt, Gretchen observed that they put them on backwards. Since Gretchen was certain that Marc and Luc would end up feeling terribly uncomfortable, or might get a nasty big diaper wedgie, she took over and gave the volunteers a lesson on how to properly diaper a baby. They thanked her and remarked that the next time they need to change a diaper they will know how to do it correctly. Gretchen's last thoughts were about the volunteers and their own undies, wondering if they put them on backwards and might not even notice. After she said that, Clement doubled up with laughter and told Gretchen to stop talking because he might split his side. She warned him to please calm down as she refuses to telephone 911 two times in one day.

At 11:30 p.m. Ruby & I travelled to the parsonage and munched on a teeny, tiny, perhaps even nanoscale-sized piece of pepperoni that we discovered on the kitchen floor. It was absolutely delectable! We expected pepperoni to taste like pepper, but it did not. When we returned home we crawled in bed and Ruby sang me to sleep with a remarkable song about blue lavender that includes the silly words dilly dilly.

– F.N.

Wednesday, November 25

Tonight's Thanksgiving Eve Worship was held at 7:30 p.m. Earlier in the day Clement needed to scrutinize his Thanksgiving Eve sermon, so he went to his office intending to find some quiet uninterrupted time.

Long before the Osterhagens arrived at St. Peter's, it was decided to discontinue having a worship service on Thanksgiving Day, but instead have one on Thanksgiving Eve. The reasoning supporting that idea was that many members of their parish might not like having too much fall on one day. Attending church, preparing a Thanksgiving turkey dinner with all the trimmings all the while entertaining relatives would require a person to be a real ball of fire, plus have a constitution as strong as an ox.

At four o'clock Pastor Osterhagen was floored when three members of St. Peter's unexpectedly arrived at his office and wanted to meet with him. He wondered if it could possibly wait until after tonight's worship service, but all three said they were unable to attend church tonight, so right now is a more suitable time. The men were Denny Young, a forty-something architect who has designed quite a few buildings in Oswald County; Ryan Cox, a local contractor; and Kevin Morgan, a certified electrician. Together they brought forth a proposal that they have created for the betterment of St. Peter's.

When two of the village's mouse scouts, Juniper and Cloudberry, were listening to this conversation, they detected that the men have put together a proposition to redesign and remodel St. Peter's sanctuary and narthex. Cloudberry said that all three of the men were trying to raise Pastor's awareness by telling him that the sculptured crucifix suspended above the altar, along with the baptismal font, pulpit, lectern, and pews are simply outdated and clearly behind the times. Kevin added that when several visitors have attended worship they remarked that the sanctuary is far too full of antiques for their modern tastes. They hope to equip the chancel with modern, sleek accoutrements. Their formal proposition and verbal explanations crossed the "T's" and dotted all the "I's" by assuredly pronouncing that they have an M.D. on their side. He is not a doctor but a "major donor" who is ready and willing to fund the entire project.

They continued voicing their thoughts that when their remodeling plans become a reality, the upkeep will be much easier for the janitor because it will eliminate having to dust all of the detailed carved walnut woodwork that currently is in the chancel. By removing and selling off all of the old liturgical hardware, the new ones would be much slimmer and would make room for a needed band area. There would be plenty of funds to purchase a baby grand piano and a professional drum set. They mentioned that the M.D. would like to see the church music modernized instead of hearing the antiquated and stuffy sounding organ music that is currently being played during each worship service by Josie.

Juniper and Cloudberry noticed that Pastor had so many thoughts going round and round in his head that he looked like he had a bad headache. Juniper imagined that the gears in Pastor's head were working overtime, running at nearly a thousand miles per hour. Pastor was amazed that these three educated men would even entertain tearing down the historical regalia and craftsmanship at Historic St. Peter's only to replace everything with trendy church furnishings that will look outdated in three or four years. The men even advanced an idea that there could be individual comfy theatre chairs in the sanctuary once the old squeaky wooden pews were removed.

Pastor took the safety first approach in his opening comments and said that when something is torn apart in a church it is usually because of a safety issue, not because of a desire to change the type of decor. Emphasizing that Historic St. Peter's is actually historic and has that particular word included in its proper name, Pastor called to mind that the church is on the State Historical Register, reminding them that it is essential to preserve the church's historical features. He told the men that he knew the design and craftsmanship of the chancel cannot be duplicated or replaced, and if that is lost, so will a big part of Historic St. Peter's character, integrity, and originality. He highlighted that most of the parishioners are certain that they belong to the most beautiful church in the world, treasuring everything about their historic church.

Denny, Kevin, and Ryan revealed to Pastor that they do not share his thoughts. They are determined to proceed with their proposal by taking it first to the church council followed by taking it to the voters' assembly. Dennis mentioned that money can move mountains and that this is just a little mountain, actually a hill. The three men are confident that they can accomplish this renovation because they have the M.D. tightly on their side. Kevin mentioned that he would appreciate it if Pastor were on their side, but even though he is not, it is still their church and they will put into process the plans that they have carefully drawn up.

After the little ones were in bed following tonight's worship service, Aia asked Clement to sit down and tell her what was bothering him. She grabbed a cold beer from the refrigerator and gave it to him along with a soup bowl of potato chips, asking him to spell out the agitation he was holding inside. Clement immediately explained his thoughts from an unexpected meeting he had with three members before the Thanksgiving worship service. He disclosed details of what they were proposing for St. Peter's. Clement said something to Aia about how parishioners can sometimes be bumbling, fumbling, mumbling, and tumbling fools that come up with ideas and plans that lack common sense. Aia told Clement a comment she had just heard that goes like this: "Would you like to hear God laugh? If so, tell Him your plans!" When Clement heard her words, he laughed and it was the first time since lunch that he had smiled.

The three men had communicated to Pastor that they intend to work on this improvement in the New Year. Clement confided in Aia that he is not looking forward to ringing in the New Year at Historic St. Peter's, not with destruction on the horizon. Right before Clement fell asleep tonight his last words were, "God help us," to which Aia replied, "He already is."

At 11:30 p.m. Ruby and I travelled to the parsonage and snacked on morsels of a square of cut up stale bread. It was not one bit tasty. We wondered if it is to be an ingredient in tomorrow's Thanksgiving meal. We were surprised at the drab taste of it. Aia's superb cooking is never that plain tasting. Perhaps she is upset about the proposed remodeling of St. Pete's that might take place in the New Year. We surmise that preparing food might be the last thing on her mind.

– F.N.

Thanksgiving Day, Thursday, November 26

Early this morning an urgent telephone call interrupted a flurry of turkey preparations at the parsonage. After attending last night's Thanksgiving Eve worship, Bob Jackson called to lodge a complaint about the "lowly" new location of the four solid walnut planter boxes that his Dad built for St. Peter's back in 1951. Now they are simply chucked in the hallway outside the church kitchen. Pastor Osterhagen attempted to give him an explanation about the planter relocation, but he bit his lip and waited until Bob had said his fill. After the telephone conversation ended, Clement sat down at the dining room table with Aia and told her about a new group that has been formed at Historic St. Peter's that calls themselves "The WASP's." Aia could see how upset Clement was due to his contorted facial expressions. We were glad Aia was there to listen to him, to provide words of encouragement to keep his thankfulness level from dropping down any further, especially since thankfulness is what this day is intended to be focused on. After Clement felt a bit better, Aia returned to the kitchen and stuffed freshly chopped herbs underneath the skin of the bird, mentioning that she hopes this will be the most succulent turkey they have ever prepared. After that, she actively focused on several side dishes, which she proclaims to be the most supreme part of the Thanksgiving meal.

Clement found out from Bob that on the sidelines of St. Peter's there are four retired men that meet weekly to discuss current church issues. Just eight miles from town is Harv's Pancake Haven where Bob, Bart, Barry, and Bernie gather every Tuesday morning for an all-you-can-eat pancake special. It is there they enjoy old-style barbershop-like camaraderie. Aia interjected that while the men are away from home their wives most likely are baking seven-layer bars. Having been friends for a long time they call themselves "The Four B's." Bob even shared their four-part code of behaviour that they recite before their pancakes arrive. It goes like this:

1. BE PROMPT: Do not make anyone wait for you. Remember that pancakes cool off very quickly.
2. BE RESPONSIBLE: Bring enough cash to pay for your breakfast. Remember that Harv's Pancake Haven is a cash only café.

3. BE PRODUCTIVE: Eat plenty pancakes to fill up. Follow that suggestion so that you will not be hungry again until supper.
4. BE RESPECTFUL: Leave all cuss words behind. Remember to use pleasant words like please, thank you, excuse me, and above all the most important word, sorry.

Unfortunately, Bob was extremely agitated. It is because he discovered that the planters not only have been demoted from their revered position in the sanctuary, but now have a new lowly use – that of collecting donations for the needy. One planter is for canned goods, another for non-perishables, one for toiletries, and the last one for new socks, mitts, and toques. Bob is certain that his Dad would roll over in his grave if he could see what has happened to his well-designed handcrafted planters. His mother, too, would surely be so shocked and saddened that she also would twitch in her grave because she was the one who selected and artfully arranged the planter's artificial greens. Bob questioned Pastor as to why this was done without even asking for his permission. He even pointed out twice that his folks had freely done all of this without any expense to St. Peter's. As a boy he remembers well the Sunday of the "Planter Dedication." The called pastor at that time was Pastor Handt. It was such a meaningful Sunday for his family when Pastor and Mrs. Handt and their son, Davey, were invited to his folk's home after church to mark the occasion with a special dinner featuring baked ham topped with warm cherry pie filling.

Clement mentioned to Aia that he has heard complaints about the artificial, dusty plants needing to be replaced with real plants, backed up with the thought that fake greenery cannot possibly be considered symbols of life when they are made of green plastic. Of course, Historic St. Peter's sanctuary does not have enough natural light for live plants to thrive, so Jody Framm, the Director of Social Involvement, presented a creative use for the planters during the last council meeting.

Bob also brought up that "The Four B's" have emerged from being a leisurely pancake eating group to a defense-minded, ready-to-rescue-the-church-from-ruination squad. Last night Bob could not sleep due to the relocation of the planters, but time was not wasted because he had a chance to think and formulate a plan. He is now determined that "The Four B's" will rename their group "The WASP's," an apt acronym for "Worried About St. Pete's."

Pastor helped Bob but he told Aia that he felt like he had been stung by a mad swarm of wasps. Bob did admit that the artificial plants had seen better days and that he is not against collecting goods for the needy, but revealed his sadness that he did not get to say goodbye to the planters. Pastor gave Bob an idea that he thought might help him feel better. He offered that "The WASP's" could return the planters to their original place in the sanctuary, fill them with Christmas greenery adorned with little white lights. That way they would add a tremendous amount of beauty to the sanctuary during the upcoming Advent, Christmas, and Epiphany season. After that they would be transported back to their new location and be used as collection boxes. Bob was so thrilled by this idea that his tone changed from a stinging wasp to pure honey. Both agreed that this could be repeated in the years to come.

By the time Clement told Aia all of the above her mouth was open so wide that Gretchen told her mama to shut her mouth tightly so that a bee will not fly in there and sting her tongue.

It was nearly midnight before Ruby and I travelled to the parsonage. Thankfully we found a morsel of a creamy French-style green bean underneath Gretchen's place at the dining room table. Ruby and I discussed exactly why the beans are called French-style, wondering if it was because they were sliced into very thin strips. We concluded that Aia must have used the time-consuming *chiffonade'* slicing technique on the green beans. Now we understand exactly why this out of the ordinary casserole appears at every single holiday dinner. It is so fancy it might be an actual recipe from *Le Cordon Bleu* where all is perfection in the culinary arts.

– F.N.

Friday ~ November 27

Custodian Chuck Brownton's retirement party was held tonight in Woolcox Hall. A catered dinner was delivered from Grocer Dan's Deli consisting of fried chicken, macaroni salad, relishes, dinner rolls, along with a large decorated sheet cake. Two brothers in our village, Lonesome Pine and Mountain Pine, were on duty to observe the celebration so that they could provide a report at our village meeting. Thankfully, the two found a hiding place just underneath the hem of the floor-length stage curtains. It was a perfect place to remain invisible since the only time the velour drapes are actually opened and closed is during St. Pete's Annual Talent Show. Recalling last year's event, parishioners can still be heard speaking words of praise about Candace Pedersen's stunning singing performance of "You Can't Get a Man with a Gun." Candace even used another one of her talents to sew an Annie Oakley sharpshooter-style dress accentuated with suede leather fringe, perfectly coordinating with her walnut brown felt cowgirl hat and leather boots.

This evening was meant to recognize and thank Chuck for all his years of faithful dedication at St. Peter's. Along with his wife Jayne (the gatherer of Toothpick Ted's toothpicks), Chuck has done a first-rate job at keeping the church clean and tidy. The Brownton's son Chuck, who goes by Skip, and his wife Kimmy, were formally welcomed tonight as the new custodians. Kimmy was busy telling people that they intend to clean the church every Saturday, planning to bring along their children, six-year old Nolan and four-year old Taylor, as well as Nolan's training wheel bicycle and Taylor's tricycle. Skip and Kimmy are evidently looking forward to earning extra cash. Their children will be able to ride their bikes throughout the many hallways at the church while they are occupied with their custodial work. Mountain Pine heard Kimmy tell one parishioner that no matter what the weather is like outside the children will be able to bike ride inside the hallways of St. Peter's.

Two couples willingly made all the arrangements for tonight's celebration. Prior to the dinner, Myrtle Cunningham attempted to warm the dinner rolls in the oven. But in no time flat a foul smell began gliding throughout the church kitchen and then swirled throughout Woolcox Hall. Mountain Pine reported to me that the parishioners were whispering to one another with confused looks on their faces. Even those seated at the head table located on the curtained stage were speaking in hushed tones, until Lonesome Pine overheard Jayne Brownton use her regular voice to tell Chuck that something reeks to high heaven. It was not long before all in attendance heard a bloodcurdling scream erupt from Myrtle when she opened the oven door. Grabbing hot mitts, she instantly removed the burned buns, but immediately found out that was only a teensy-weensy part of the problem. Sadly, on the bottom of the oven were two roasted mice that were burning to a crisp. Myrtle's husband, Harry, left her in the dust to deal all alone with the pandemonium. He must have decided it was far more important to dash to Grocer Dan's to purchase replacement buns. He did his best, but the bakery area of the store was completely out of buns so he instead returned with eight loaves of white bread.

Most conversations at the dinner tables centered on the very expensive industrial oven that was installed in the church kitchen two years ago, generously paid for by HSP's Ladies' Guild. After two mice from our village perished in the oven, most parishioners think it best to take the oven to the dump and then purchase a new one. Many agree that the odorously rank smell could never be eliminated from the oven. Some thought it might be worth a try to keep the temperature at 450 degrees for an entire twenty-four hour period to see if that might burn off the stench of death. Looking ahead, though, we assume that no human being would ever want to bake an angel food cake or a meatloaf in that oven after it became a crematorium. Lonesome Pine and Mountain Pine are certain that the oven topic will consume the heart and soul of the next voters' meeting. But, they were not sad about a new oven needing to be purchased, but were sorely glum about their two friends, Binky and Mitzy, that went up in smoke because Myrtle turned the oven up to such a high temperature.

The evening ended very quickly due to the unpleasant aroma. Most in attendance gobbled down their fried chicken and then hurried to leave the building. Some others filled their paper plate and took food home with them. A few left empty-handed with unsatisfied tummies.

At 9:30 p.m. Ruby and I, along with several others in our village, gathered in the church kitchen for a moment of silence to pay our respects for the lives of Binky and Mitzy. They were young mice that did not know it is best to stay out of an oven. Unfortunately, they did not use sound judgment. Just like that they lost their chance to ever become old and wise.

– F.N.

Saturday ~ November 28

Four weeks ago St. Peter's Sunday bulletin included a "We Still Do!" wedding vows renewal invitation from Samuel (Sam) and Samantha (Sammy) Witcombe. The Witcombes were thrilled to invite the entire congregation to witness their marriage renewal commitment to one another.

Last month Wizzy, one member of our village who is always keen to discover what is new and unusual at Historic St. Peter's, overheard Sam & Sammy when they met with Pastor Osterhagen to plan their special day. It was at that meeting that Wizzy discovered that the purpose of this "We Still Do!" event is truthfully to make up for a church wedding that they never had. Twenty-five years ago money was so tight that the Witcombes were joined in Holy Marriage at Sammy's family home. Sammy mentioned that she wore a short white dress purchased on layaway at the local department store while she carried a single pink rose encased in a bunch of baby's breath. After the "I do's" a homemade lunch consisting of egg salad sandwiches and frosted spice cake comprised the frugal wedding dinner. Both Sam and Sammy mentioned to Pastor that they very much enjoyed their wedding day, but these twenty-five years later they are financially well off and really want to have a genuine church wedding that includes everything from "A - Z."

One and all enjoyed the Witcombe's renewal of wedding vows today. Sammy wore a lovely bridal gown and carried an enormous floral bouquet. The ceremony even included special music from a professional soloist and harpist. Due to inviting all of their relatives and friends, along with the entire congregation at Historic St. Peter's, the sanctuary was overflowing. Afterwards everyone was treated to a catered reception consisting of a variety of deli sandwiches, fruits and vegetables, salads, and one unexpected type of food, Alphabet Soup, which Whizzy said fit in nicely with the "A - Z" wedding theme. Front and centre was a royally decorated wedding cake with dozens of pink icing roses.

Wizzy revealed to the village that the most interesting part of the day was the tender "A - Z" poem that the creative couple had composed. Sam and Sammy took turns reading it. Because Wizzy has a mastermind memory capacity like that of a brainy scholar, he recited their words to all of us attending tonight's village meeting. Everyone listened attentively to these words:

Amore is what the Italians say
But I just call it love.
Cause ours is plain and simple,
Don't you think so?
Everything about you is
Fun when we're together.
Good for me that I
Have you around.
In the past I was lonely,
Just existing day by day.
Kindly did you come along with
Love to give and love to take from me.
Money cannot buy it,
Nor can you earn its favour.
Only as a gift it comes.
Perfectly it casts out fear.
Quietly it fills the room,
Reminding me how
Special it is
To have love.
Until the earth and heaven
Vanish and are gone,
We will share our love.
X's and O's, honey.
You're the one who puts the
Zing in everything!

At 11 p.m. our meeting was finished so several in our village scurried to Woolcox Hall to find a treat. All were stone silent when they tasted the decadent chocolate wedding cake crumbs. Dr. Theodore Simonsen, village head librarian, broke the silence when he informed everyone about a special cake he read about in an old St. Pete's church cookbook called "Scripture Cake." He informed us that the recipe incorporates Bible verses that pinpoint specific ingredients needed to prepare the cake, such as "finest flour" (Leviticus 24:5), "sweet calamus" (Jeremiah 6:20), "fragrant cinnamon" (Exodus 30:23), and "olive oil" (Exodus 30:24). There are several other ingredients, but he said that was all he could recall. When we returned to our dwelling, Ruby touched on a good point by saying that preparing Scripture Cake would encourage people to open up their Bibles. She wondered also if there are Scripture appetizers, Scripture soups, Scripture salads, Scripture vegetables, and Scripture main entrées. After all, cake is not meant to be eaten daily but is reserved for special occasions, unlike the Holy Bible that is meant to be read seven days a week. For a brief moment Ruby wished that she was a human being so she could discuss Scripture recipes with Aia. But, that hankering swiftly vanished when she considered how terribly complicated it must be to be a human being.

– F.N.

First Sunday in Advent ~ November 29

Today marks a brand new church year. I have completed my goal of recording one full liturgical church year at Historic St. Peter's in Oswald County. However, I feel compelled to keep going since so much is happening here that is worth recording. Plus, there are still a few empty pages in my notebook. I am determined to carry on until I run out of room in my journal. It won't be long from now before I will put down my pen.

Following today's worship service, Mamie Patterson firmly gripped her walker, the type that has a seat, a backrest, along with two trusty saddle bags and headed straightaway to her car parked in one of St. Peter's handicapped accessible parking spots. Thermador, a village resident who is partial to spending time outdoors when the weather is nippy, was thoroughly hidden behind a good-sized shrub when he noticed Mamie arriving at her car. Spotting a flyer underneath the driver's side windshield wiper blade, she reached out her arm to scoop up the paper. After that, she headed back into the building to track down Pastor Osterhagen to show him the leaflet. Upon locating Pastor, she reached into one of her saddle bags and removed the advertisement, handed it to him, and explained that she was not certain if he had already seen one. Mamie told him that this was the second Sunday in a row that the same flyer has been deposited on the front window of her car while she was in church attending worship.

Blizzard and his wife, Midwinter, share an awe-inspiring interest in observing any variation of winter weather conditions while stationed at their favourite viewing spot, the window ledges in St. Peter's Fireside Room. This pastime developed after they heard a catchy song about snow falling at the last youth group gathering. It was a bit difficult for them to make out every single word that was coming out of the tape player because popcorn kernels were noisily exploding inside the flashy-red popcorn machine. Even though the apparatus was twirling away at full speed, they somehow memorized the song's snappy refrain. The two of them are a real blessing to our village because they are not only interested in only the outside winter weather conditions, but are just as much concerned about the emotionally charged weather conditions among the members at St. Peter's, especially those openly displayed.

Today Blizzard and Midwinter were hiding behind an institutional-sized pail of sidewalk salt while they witnessed the conversation between Mamie and Pastor Osterhagen. Mamie explained that last Monday she telephoned her niece, Stacey Graham, who is a faithful member of Holy Angels Catholic Parish, to discuss the flyer. Stacey told her that the parked cars at Holy Angels received leaflets under their windshield wipers, too. Because Mamie has difficulty seeing regular-sized print, she asked Pastor to kindly read the words to her, adding that she didn't bother with it last week because she assumed it was an annoying flyer advertising residential snow removal services. Mamie surmised that because the handout was distributed two Sundays in a row, it must be of significance. She added that it might be especially noteworthy since the flyers were also distributed at Holy Angels, and that's a way bigger parish than little St. Pete's. Blizzard and Midwinter reported to us that Pastor Osterhagen looked at the glossy flyer with the eye-catching Christmas artwork and then read it to Mamie. This is what it said: "Join us for a different kind of Christmas Eve! This spectacular celebration features internationally known Swedish soprano, Ulrika Jönsson, who has the voice of an angel that will fill your heart with the true spirit of the Christmas season. This community-wide Christmas Eve Candlelight Service will be held at the Oswald County Armory, 6317 Jefferson Road, on December 24, at 5 p.m., sponsored by Grace and Truth House of God. A festive reception will be held afterwards with abundant Christmas cookies and hot beverages. All are invited!"

After reading the handout, the whole subject matter of Christmas Eve ate up the remainder of Clement's day. Feeling perturbed, he told Aia that he cannot figure out when deplorably bad etiquette has became acceptable behaviour in church circles. He appeared unable to get past the blatant nerve of Grace and Truth House of God to descend upon St. Peter's parking lot to place leaflets on every parked vehicle. He has a sneaking suspicion that their primary goal is to lure members away from Historic St. Peter's on Christmas Eve by inviting them to their colourful different kind of Christmas. He pointed out that this new church, led by Pastor Matthew Wheeler, might be guilty of sheep stealing, an unethical way to grow their church. He further told her how renting the Armory for the event, which seats hundreds of people, is almost the size of a concert hall. Because international Swedish soloist Ulrika Jönsson will be singing "O Holy Night" and other touchy-feely Christmas carols, no one will want to attend St. Peter's on Christmas Eve. Historic St. Peter's will have a Christmas Eve Candlelight Service with only six people in attendance, the five members of the Osterhagen Family plus Josie, the organist. Aia chirped in by saying that if that is the case it won't be the end of St. Pete's and that she would enjoy a merry little Christmas for a change very much.

Since Clement couldn't settle his kettle, he decided to telephone Father Tim at Holy Angels, followed by calling Pastor John Ernst at Berea Baptist Church. But before making those calls, Aia encouraged Clement to keep in mind the meaning of his name, which is merciful, one who is good and forgiving. Clement took a deep breath and thanked Aia for reminding him of that info. While comparing notes with Father Tim, it was confirmed that Holy Angels parking lot was attacked by flyer distributors the last two Sundays as well. Father Tim has also heard that many of his parishioners, along with others in town, are planning to be at the Armory on Christmas Eve. Clement told Father Tim that his next move was to telephone Rev. Ernst. While listening to him, Clement found out that the leaflets had been distributed at Berea, too. Rev. Ernst hadn't heard about this event, but after church today he picked up a flyer that was littering the church parking lot and read it. He is not aware that any of his members will be at the Armory on Christmas Eve. His plan is to ignore the flyer and assume that his members will attend Berea on Christmas Eve.

Clement's next step was to call Father Tim back and discuss Pastor Matthew Wheeler's "sheep stealing." Their conversation momentarily even went so far as to wonder if they should cancel their Christmas Eve worship services. Both agreed that was not an option. They even mulled over how their parishioners were reacting to being invited away from their own churches on Christmas Eve. After all, this is designed to lure the sheep to where the grass appears to be greener, but this grass just might be artificial turf. Together Father Tim and Pastor came up with a solution. They decided that the strongest move is to actually do nothing. They have chosen to avoid talking about it, mentioning it, or being concerned with it. The one thing they will do is pray. They will encourage their parishioners to attend church on Christmas Eve, be prepared to deliver a solid Gospel-based sermon, all the while expecting that their sanctuaries will be overflowing with people. Maybe even some in attendance will need to sit on folding chairs to accommodate the overflow.

After Clement's conversations with Father Tim and Pastor Ernst, Ruby and I noticed that his outward demeanour improved. He thanked Aia for listening to his concerns about sheep stealing. Aia said she was happy to be all ears, always wanting to support him. She said that since he is now feeling better, she would appreciate the chance to share a brief personal opinion about the entire issue, as she, too, has thought about it most of the afternoon. Aia told him how she has a lot of faith in the good people of Historic St. Peter's because they dearly love their church. If they do choose to attend the Armory event, it is not the end of the world. Anyone who does that will end up missing out on what it is like to spend Christmas Eve at Historic St. Peter's, a feeling similar to being away from home at Christmas. After that Aia walked to the piano and beautifully sang and played a tender Christmas carol just for Clement about being home for Christmas. She finished by telling him that the handout from Grace and Truth probably won't do much good. It is comparable to passing out flyers in the sunny state of Florida for free sun tanning minutes, which would be a completely ineffective marketing tool for that business. In Florida people can stay home in the comfort of their own backyards and get all the free sun tanning minutes that they could ever desire. Aia's last words on the topic were spoken Trinitarian-style when she said, "Don't be troubled, have no fear, and it'll be alright." Once again, their tulips (or is it two lips?) came together and smooched so tenderly that Ruby and I had to look away, it was more than we could handle.

At 11:30 p.m. Ruby and I travelled to the parsonage kitchen and snacked on red, white, and green cookie crumbs that had dropped to the kitchen floor from this afternoon's pinwheel cookie baking jamboree. Especially pleasing was the inclusion of pure vanilla extract in the pinwheels. Ruby pointed out that the flavor delightfully swirled, swooshed, and spiralled around in our mouths when we taste-tested these Christmassy creations. I appreciated Ruby's Trinitarian observation.

– F.N.

St. Andrew, Apostle ~ Monday, November 30

SINCE THERE WAS SO MUCH UNEASINESS ABOUT ST. PETER'S MEMBERS BEING INVITED TO attend Christmas Eve worship at the Armory, I ran out of time to write down other events that occurred on the First Sunday in Advent. I feel badly that I slipped up, but find some comfort in two phrases, "Better late than never" or "Being tardy is better than not arriving at all."

Due to the predictable weekly offering shortfalls at St. Peter's, combined with the calendar year soon coming to an end, Brent Wood, one member of St. Peter's Stewardship Team arrived at church yesterday carrying a red plaid umbrella, even though it was a sunny winter day. After hanging up his parka on the coat rack, everyone noticed a sturdy paper sign pinned to the front of his long sleeved shirt that contained the words, "We must make our budget!" Apparently this was part of his creative original giving plan to purposefully combat the budget shortfall before it is time to ring in the New Year. Two mice in our village, Quaker and Shaker, happened to be stationed behind the plastic tower that is located near the coat rack. From that central position they clearly heard Brent's conversations, or more correctly, his repetitive chanting as parishioners arrived for worship. After everyone left the church yesterday, Quaker and Shaker hurried to our dwelling eager to reveal all that they had seen and heard. After the opportunity to hear about Brent's eccentric three-part chant, we wondered if he was also a Trinitarian speaker like Aia, or if he might be a graduate of Trinity College.

Quaker and Shaker are not high achievers, go-getters, or trailblazers. Simplicity, combined with lives of quiet harmony is what has solidified their brotherhood. In fact, when Brent forcefully opened his trusty umbrella, both mice gasped and shook terribly at the thunderous noise. They were thankful for good fortune because the ear-piercing noise did not blow them to kingdom come. The clangor from Brent's umbrella being sprung into action could have easily scared away a bear if one happened to be hiking in the Adirondacks on a misty morning. Too, Quaker and Shaker revealed that they were concerned about Brent being unaware of the old superstition about bad luck will happen when an umbrella is opened indoors.

Shaker told us that Brent announced to the arriving parishioners his new Stewardship Drive, which he called, "Rainy Day Cash." From the interior of his umbrella Brent had knotted long strings of skinny Christmas ribbon. As he stood there holding the open umbrella, in his other hand he held a tape dispenser. Already taped to one ribbon was a fifty dollar bill, obviously Brent's donation to get his stewardship plan kick-started. While he stood there he repeatedly chanted, "We must make it! We must make it! We must make our budget!" Parishioners caught on to the fundraiser, but the first few people timidly taped one dollar bills to the ribbons. After Brent observed this, Quaker and Shaker heard him intensify his rallying call by using phrases including these words: "General Operating Budget," "Make up the difference," and "Where the axe is likely to fall." It is sad to say that he once actually asked someone if they were a "giver" or a "non-giver."When Brent saw one of the wealthy members, we noticed she became uneasy when he mentioned her lifestyle that has included trips to Europe. Shaker revealed that after currency came in and was taped to the "Rainy Day Cash" umbrella, a whopping $785 had been collected to go towards the general operating budget.

Frank Williams approached Brent after worship yesterday and frankly told him that he was initially upset that he had carried this stewardship drive out on his own without the council's approval. But, since the umbrella brought in so much cash, he was pleased with the result and even thanked Brent for the tremendous amount of pluck he had garnered to pull this campaign off. Frank also told Brent that he smiled when he heard his chant, "We must make it! We must make it! We must make our budget!"

At 7:30 p.m. Ruby and I travelled to the church kitchen to see if we could find crumbs from yesterday's coffee hour. Thankfully, we found a tiny bit of a maple frosted doughnut. Ruby mentioned that Quaker and Shaker would refrain from tasting a choice doughnut that includes expensive pure maple syrup from either Vermont or Quebec. Instead they would favour a simple, but classic, old-fashioned plain cake doughnut. While chewing, Ruby and I tried to imagine how many leaves drop from a typical maple tree during autumn. Ruby chose the wide-ranging number of 200,000 while I decided on a more conservative number of 127,482. Tomorrow we will call on Dr. Theodore Simonsen, village head librarian, and see if he is able to calculate that information, or at least give us an informed guess or a ballpark figure.

– F.N.

Wednesday, December 2

Early this morning, two members of our village, Pembroke and Polly, watched Aia step lively down the breezeway to the church storage room. Within just a few minutes she returned to the parsonage carrying an old-fashioned manual typewriter. Pembroke and Polly hurried to our dwelling to report all that they had seen. Ruby told me that Aia placed the typewriter on one end of the dining room table as soon as she returned home. Clement seemed confused as to why she got out the old dusty typewriter. Aia responded that she is going to write a book. Asking what the topic of the book was going to be about, Clement seemed surprised to find out that it was about the silly side of church life. Clement said he would have guessed it was going to be a daily devotional book, a faith-based book for women, or one about Christian motherhood. Instead, she conveyed three quick words, "noteworthy church humour." She also told him that she better get click-clacking because she is serious about this endeavour. Admitting that she was not just talking about the sound a woman makes while walking in high heels, but that the parsonage will be filled with the click-clacking sound coming out of this old ticker. Another sound produced by the typewriter will be the bell ringing each time she touches the carriage return. Aia appeared as though she cannot wait another minute to begin this undertaking, even if she has to move heaven and earth all by herself to get it done. Revealing that her head is so full of chapters, she said she had better get it on paper because she cannot hold it all inside her brain any longer. She finished by telling Clement that she will snatch every fragment of time to work on this undertaking.

Aia was thrilled to begin her writing, but it came to a stop when Marc and Luc awoke from their naps. Clement was inquisitive about her ideas, so she informed him that the book's setting will be located at a historic church similar to St. Peter's where a village of tiny gnomes secretly reside throughout the building. Their main form of entertainment is to peek out and watch the way human beings behave. Finally, she said that she will persistently hammer away at it, but with the family occupying most every moment of her time it might take years to accomplish it. Clement said that he was proud of her, appreciated her new undertaking, and that he loved her. Because of his kind support and the love floating in the air, she gently put her hand to her lips and blew him a kiss. We thought that was sweet!

The first page of the book must not have gone very well. Ruby saw Aia pull a sheet of paper out of the typewriter, crumple it up and throw it like a softball towards the kitchen garbage can. Fortunately, for us, it missed the can and landed just behind it.

At 11:45 p.m. Ruby and I travelled to the parsonage and to our delight we found Aia's crumpled up paper. Carefully we opened it up. After reading the words we wondered if Aia actually had the potential to be an author. Her opening words were, "She was faced with a heart-sickening choice." We love Aia, but that did not sound like a very catchy way to begin a book; an opening phrase is meant to grab the reader's attention. We are confident that particular sentence might already be in fifteen or more other books. However, Aia did throw this page in the rubbish, so maybe her second attempt will be better. We did relish hearing her tell Clement about the characters Miki & Bitsy Isaksen, two church gnomes who observed parishioner Maureen Phillips and her umbrella bad habits. Maureen somehow thinks that umbrellas are communal property, something to be shared, certainly not a personal possession. Whenever it is raining on a Sunday, umbrella snatcher Maureen grabs any one of the umbrellas that are suspended on the coat rack and takes possession of it. Parishioners have tried to talk to her about this being inconsiderate, but she ignores their words.

Since no snack was found tonight, we instead chewed, actually discussed, the contents of author Aia's initial attempt at writing a book. Extrapolating on the fact that her opening sentence was far from amusing, we found it to be frightful and unnerving. Perhaps we misunderstood her intention to write a book about church humour. But, we know that Aia often changes her mind. She could very well have chosen to write a scary crime thriller filled with various types of murder instruments involving firearms, knives, or stirring cyanide into the murder victim's coffee cup. We determined to wait a second, hold on, and count on time passing before we will know which direction Aia's book will head towards. Hopefully, she will be inclined to settle on the far more pleasant path by writing about church humour.

– F.N.

Thursday, December 3

Ruby and I basked in the aroma whirling throughout the parsonage this morning. Aia was baking a round loaf of sourdough bread. Ruby and I are familiar with one of the phrases from the Lord's Prayer, "Give us this day our daily bread." Also recognizable to us is the expression, "staff of life," as we have observed that bread is a mainstay of the Osterhagen's daily diet.

Lately the homemade bread production does not seem to bring Aia much joy because she struggles to keep pace with the demands of the starter. Today she sat down with Clement and revealed another one of her Trinitarian plans. First of all, she told him that she cannot keep up with the "Mother," the sourdough starter. She expressed that Mother needs to find another dwelling, an apartment, home, or mobile home. But, there is no reason for Mother to be without a roof over her head. Together they thought of giving their starter to the Cook Family, simply because they have seven children, the last two being twins. Aia said that the Cooks could easily polish off an entire loaf of bread during supper. While the second part of her reasoning was communicated to Clement, she said that Gretchen is finding the bread completely irresistible slathered with butter. It has become the only thing that she wants to eat. Thirdly, Aia carefully pointed out to Clement that he has gotten a bit thick around the middle from all of the bread consumption. Clement did not appear offended, but told her that it was probably true, adding that every bite was worth it.

So, the Osterhagens decided to discontinue sourdough production at the parsonage and move on to food flavours that are less demanding. Tonight's supper was a farewell to sourdough, but still a celebration of loaves and fishes similar to what is found in Matthew, the feeding of the five thousand. Even though Aia prepared delicious pan-fried fish with green bean amandine, Gretchen still preferred to eat only bread and butter. We saw Clement wink at Aia from across the table to silently communicate that they are going in the right direction by chucking the sourdough production at the parsonage.

At 11:30 p.m. Ruby and I travelled to the parsonage and surprisingly found sourdough bread crumbs under both Clement's and Aia's places at the dining room table. We assumed that Gretchen enjoyed her bread and butter most of all so she was careful not to drop even one crumb. We also talked about the sadness of farewells. Quick as a wink the sourdough baking is now finished at the parsonage. But, Ruby and I will not be sour. We will put on our smiles and remember that for a brief time we were privileged to live right next door to what we had begun to refer to as "Sourdough Lane."

– F.N.

Friday, December 4

Ruby and I were interested when Aia announced that today is "Grandma Nygaard's Noodle Day." Plans were to prepare homemade noodles while Marc and Luc were napping. Just after Aia and Gretchen donned their aprons, Aia realized that she is short on flour and eggs. Clement hurried down to Grocer Dan's to pick up supplies. After returning home, he divulged that he had heard some outlandish scuttlebutt. We were downright spellbound listening to their intriguing conversation.

Clement recalled that the last time Aia shopped at Grocer Dan's she came home with a new tube of skin moisturizer. On that particular day parishioner Leigh Ann Turner was the checkout clerk that rang up Aia's items. What she did not expect was the disapproving expression that was on Leigh Ann's face. Apparently Leigh Ann was puzzled about one of Aia's purchases, but did not say anything. Clement revealed to Aia that when Leigh Ann rang up the flour and eggs today she asked if he liked Aia's tattoo. She also wondered if he might soon be getting a tattoo, perhaps one to match Aia's. Clement told her that Aia does not have a tattoo and that they both never intend to get one. After hearing those words, Leigh Ann exclaimed an awkward, "Shucks!" Clement asked Leigh Ann why she thought Aia had a tattoo and she replied, "I assumed she had just gotten one because that particular brand of skin moisturizer is the number one lotion recommended by tattoo artists for skin aftercare." We came to find out that news of Aia's supposed tattoo has spread far and wide at St. Peter's. Many parishioners have a strong opinion that their pastor's wife, of all people, should not have a tattoo. Aia proclaimed that fewer fabricated stories would have been spread around if she had just boarded a jet and headed towards California. There she could go under the knife to obtain an expensive neck lift, a total nose job, or some other type of cutting-edge plastic surgery that she has not even heard of.

Clement realized that Leigh Ann must have told her folks about Aia's supposed tattoo and then it catapulted into a whispering campaign. He said that he would not be surprised if it comes up at the next council meeting. The rumour has even gone to a new level with those who favour tattoos. Those who appreciate tattoo art might hope that their Pastor's wife had the common sense to choose a Christian symbol, perhaps a cross, or the word "Faith" on her forearm, or "Walk by Faith" tattooed on one or both of her feet. Practical Aia had a solution. Ruby and I listened carefully to her plan: This next Sunday she will wear summer attire to church, even though it is freezing cold outside. When the parishioners notice her dressed in a sleeveless tank top, a short skirt, and sandals, they will observe that she does not have any tattoos on her arms, legs, shoulders, or feet. Aia is convinced that this simple action on her part will put an end to the pastor's wife disgracefully sporting a tattoo or two. Clement made certain that Aia knows he thinks she is brilliant, creative, and brave when it comes to problem-solving.

Aia is hurt about this gossip. She did mention to Clement that it is not as bad as one pastor's wife in Beeker County, Kimberly Scott, whose entire congregation assumed she was suffering from a mental illness. This happened when an invitation was published in the weekly bulletin encouraging members to come and hear Kimberly speak about the topic of depression. The speaker was actually Kimberly Lane, a representative from the Beeker County Mental Health Association. Although it was an entirely different Kimberly, everyone assumed that it was their pastor's wife simply because the bulletin announcement lacked a last name. Unfortunately, tittle-tattle about Pastor Scott's wife and her depression is still mushrooming throughout Beeker County. Aia said that it is a real "tornado in a teacup" for Kimberly Scott, but not for Kimberly Lane.

We noticed that Aia seemed to put the gossip aside by keeping on top of the noodle production. Cotton string was suspended from the kitchen drapery rod to one of the door hinges. This provided a clothesline to drape the noodles on until they are completely air dried. On Christmas Day these special old-world noodles will be served with Wiener schnitzel and gravy.

At 10:30 p.m. the Osterhagen household was stone quiet. Ruby and I hurried over there and ate a dropped noodle on the kitchen floor. Even though it was uncooked, we understand the reason why Aia makes these for Christmas dinner. We are already looking forward to the feast on Christmas Day.

– F.N.

Second Sunday in Advent ~ December 6

NEARLY EVERY SUNDAY AFTER CHURCH, FOUR COUPLES FROM ST. PETER'S ENJOY A MEAL together at Ollie's (cash-only) Corner Café, just kitty-corner from the church. Recently two mice that previously resided at Ollies, Greasy and Spoon, have joined our village because Ollie's has been temporarily shut down by the health department. Greasy and Spoon are concerned about many of Ollie's faithful and daily customers, noting that they will have to adjust being without Ollie's daily blue-plate specials that are served on a blue dinner plate. Even though the blue-plate specials change daily, one item that customers could always count on is the inclusion of baked beans. Just before the shutdown, Greasy and Spoon hurried over to join our community. We are happy that they are here. Both can tell larger-than-life stories that they have accumulated from overhearing customer's conversations. They have noticed that the most faithful customers always sit at the counter and listen to Ollie's knee-slappers while he flips pancakes, chicken-fried steak, eggs, and hash browns.

The Schlossers, Fendricks, Browns, and Nostadts all brought boxed lunches with them today, placing them in the kitchen refrigerator before the worship service. After church, they sat together at a round table in Woolcox Hall and shared a lively conversation. Greasy and Spoon hid behind a stack of chairs and listened carefully to their conversation. Not only were they chewing their hoagies, they were finding fault with Pastor Osterhagen. The predominant topic was regarding a recent change that has been made at HSP – the removal of one particular wooden church pew to make way for a brand new baby grand piano.

Gerome and Cally Schlosser were the most outspoken couple, trumpeting that the removed side pew had long ago been donated by Gerome's great-grandparents, Gustav & Annaliese Schlosser. Throughout the history of St. Peter's their pew has remained in this place of honour with one generation after the next of Schlossers worshipping in their family pew. To make matters worse, it has been relocated to an unimportant place, a spot by the seldom used back door of St. Peter's, which is technically an emergency exit. Gerome expressed that his great-grandparents would be heartbroken about this if they were alive because they were the original founding members of the church. Reminding parishioners of their donation is a bronze engraved plaque that proudly heralds the Schlosser name. Now the cast off and abandoned pew is up against a wall where the plaque is no longer visible. Cally pointed out that this is an aesthetic disgrace at Historic St. Peter's since the sanctuary is practically a religious museum. She noted that plaques are on all of the pews, the windows, the baptismal font, and many other visible places, but now the Schlosser name has been dishonoured by the Schloser pew removal.

Gerome and Cally changed the subject by telling their friends that the only reason the church purchased a baby grand piano was so that Pastor's wife, Aia, could show off her musical skills in style. Cally told everyone that she does not look forward to hearing embellished piano renditions of the hymns, but prefers Josie's plain old-fashioned organ playing.

Just as the Schlossers were sharing their thoughts, Pastor headed toward the church kitchen. Earlier on Aia asked Clement to retrieve the ketchup bottle from the church kitchen because she was making sloppy joes but didn't have enough ketchup. Just as Clement came around the corner he overheard the conversation about Aia, enough to visibly sadden him. He gracefully walked up to their table and told them that the baby grand piano has been lovingly donated by philanthropist Prudy Rasmus because she believes that music has enormous power to speak to the spirit, mind, and emotions. Her generosity was driven forward during a meeting of the Oswald County Symphony Board when she learned that Historic St. Peter's is scheduled to host upcoming professional concerts, one of which is already placed on the calendar, Handel's "Messiah." Pastor informed the group that right now Aia is far too occupied with their children to be a show off. He also added that if any of them personally knew her, they would be well aware that she does not make a pretentious display of her musical abilities. Greasy said that after those words were spoken Clement fetched the ketchup bottle and exited Woolcox Hall.

At 6:30 p.m. Ruby and I zoomed to Woolcox Hall hoping to find anything that might have dropped from a hoagie. Sure enough, we were in luck. Underneath the Schlosser's place we found a slice of Hungarian salami. We reckoned that they were so upset that they forgot to use good table manners while they were complaining about the Osterhagens. After Greasy and Spoon told us what they observed, Ruby said that the behaviour of the Schlossers crossed the line and is called, "Having the Pastor for lunch" or "Eating the Pastor alive." We were both dumbfounded that Clement did not reveal to Aia any of the complaining that he had just heard, but instead asked her to teach him how to make sloppy joes. I am including it in my journal since it seemed a high-priority at the parsonage today. Aia said, "Brown ground beef with chopped onion; drain, if necessary; add enough ketchup until it resembles sloppy joes; stir in a little bit of brown sugar and mustard; and finish with a splash of vinegar. Heat and serve on buns accompanied with an abundance of dill pickles." Clement appeared glad to hear the simplicity of the recipe and thanked Aia for the instructions. Clement added that sloppy joes are a real comfort food. He revealed that right now he needs to calm down and soothe his emotions. Aia asked him what had happened, but Clement wouldn't talk about it, instead summing it up by quoting a Bible verse from Luke 10:3 which reads, "Go! I am sending you out like lambs among wolves." Aia looked perplexed but immediately hugged Clement and said, "Let's eat lunch and see if you feel better. If and when you are ready to talk about it, I can help. Remember that God will protect us from the wolves, the ones that wear sheep's clothing."

After Ruby and I were settled in bed tonight, we talked about church plaques. Currently one of the toilets in the ladies' washroom is out of order, but a replacement has been delivered and is in the church entryway waiting to be installed this week. On the box we noticed the phrases, "Excellent Choice," "Bold and Powerful," and "Quiet, with Efficient Flusher Performance!" Since there appears to be an emotional attachment to plaques at HSP, perhaps this new toilet will provide another spot to place a bronze plaque in memory of a loved one. Ruby suggested it could be attached to the tank portion of the toilet instead of on the toilet seat. Earlier today we heard Clement telling Gretchen that when the big cardboard toilet box is emptied he will bring it home and together they will make a cardboard puppet theatre. We wondered, too, if the new puppet theatre should be graced with an engraved bronze plaque.

– F.N.

Monday, December 7

Mondays are Clement's regular day off. During breakfast Ruby and I heard them merrily talking about today's "Annual Christmas Card Production," as Aia refers to it. After breakfast the dining room table was spread with cards, photos, stickers, and postage stamps. Just before launching forward with today's game plan, Aia assembled a tray containing a teapot, three mugs, and three marshmallows. Ruby was burning with curiosity to discover exactly what flavour of tea was in the pot. At that point, Ruby sucked in a downreaching breath, drawing in so deeply her oxygen level must have been at least the magnitude of a barn door. After that she lunged forward and stuck her nose through the crack in the dining room wall. Panic was in the air when we both realized that her nose was literally stuck in the crack. Thankfully, she remained calm while patiently wiggling her nose loose. On the double I examined her nose, fearful that she might have a nose splinter, but it was unscathed. At that point my spur-of-the-moment words were rather rash because she had not prioritized safety first. I pointed out that she was surely sticking her nose where it didn't belong. Her endeavour, though, did reveal that the contents of the teapot were not peppermint or cranberry spice tea, but hot cocoa. Before Clement sat down at the table, he turned on the tape deck and Christmas carols blasted forth. Ruby and I could see that the Osterhagens were not only absorbed in the annual Christmas card production but were having fun. They had not progressed very far before being interrupted by the parsonage doorbell.

After opening the front door, Clement was greeted by postal worker Bev Godfredson holding a large box. He quickly invited her to step into the parsonage so she could warm up for a few minutes. Even though her eyelashes and eyebrows were caked with snowflakes, her conversation was very toasty. Being so cheerful that her first cousin, Mila Wagner, had arrived yesterday from Germany, she said she was looking forward to celebrating Christmas with her, American-style. Before Bev headed out into the bitingly cold weather, she told Pastor that he will meet Mila on Sunday when they attend church. Later on Clement told Aia that he did not even recognize Bev fully covered in protective winter outerwear. He did see her friendly eyes, though, through her ski mask. After Clement returned to the dining room table, he announced to Aia and Gretchen that the Christmas cards will be taken to the Post Office tomorrow, doubting that their van would even start up in this fearsome sub-zero weather.

Placing the heavy box on the kitchen table, Clement, Aia, and Gretchen seemed excited to discover its contents, hoping that the entirety of Historic St. Peter's congregation had kindly given them a Christmas gift. They appeared stupefied after the box was fully open. Placed on top of the contents was an unsigned note which read, "These are new choir robes to replace the time-worn, tattered gowns. Many of the old choir robes have broken zippers and are spotted with candle wax. Consider this a gift from a loving member." Underneath the note Clement counted twenty top-quality red choir gowns with snowy white stoles each embroidered with a metallic gold cross.

Ruby began crying when she spotted the look of disappointment on the Osterhagen's faces. She could see that they would have been touched to receive a Christmas gift from the church, maybe even something monetarily substantial, a gift card to a restaurant, or even twenty-five dollars off of their next Grocer Dan's purchases. Aia mentioned that it did hurt when the Pastor and his wife in Beeker County were given a Caribbean cruise from their church last Christmas Eve. Aia remarked that St. Peter's is not very generous. Clement pointed out that they are given several plates of Christmas cookies each December.

Appearing deep in thought while he sat at the dining room table, Clement composed their family Christmas letter. After he finished, he read it to Aia while Ruby and I were absorbed listening to his words. The last paragraph went like this:

> "We continue to enjoy our family and many friends, but sometimes it is a struggle to love everyone. But, we know that God's love for us is what produces love in us. It is best to remember the words written in 1 Peter 4:8 that says, 'Above all, love each other deeply, because love covers over a multitude of sins.'"

Aia complemented him and then brought out a platter of assorted Christmas cookies given to them by a loving family in the church, the Nelsons.

At 10:45 p.m. it was hushed at the parsonage, so Ruby and I travelled to the kitchen where we found a chickpea on the floor, broke it in two, and ate it. We think it might have been an ingredient that never made it into the bowl of tonight's tossed salad. After returning home, we gabbled about what exactly is a Caribbean cruise. Since the word Caribbean begins with the word car, we assume that it is some sort of road trip, perhaps on Route 66 where one can drive by numerous cornfields. We think that St. Peter's should be generous and give a one-week Caribbean cruise to the Osterhagens for Christmas. It would be very fitting because they find abundant beauty in the run-of-the-mill parts of life, even if it is viewing miles and miles of cornfields. Also, early tomorrow we will contact our two village librarians for assistance because we have a baffling question that is far beyond our comprehension. When we heard Aia speak of chickpeas, other similar words popped into mind containing the petite word "pea." Our curiosity was piqued as to whether chickpeas are in the same category as peachicks, peahens, peacocks, or peafowls.

– F.N.

Wednesday, December 9

Parishioner Marcie Fredrickson arrived at the parsonage this morning to drop off her recipe for strawberry pretzel dessert squares. Being that Aia and Marcie are hostessing the upcoming January Ladies' Guild meeting, Marcie has decided that both of them should prepare the same dessert. We thought it was kind of Marcie, giving Aia plenty of time to make certain she has all of the recipe's ingredients.

Since Aia was expecting Marcie this morning, she plugged in the coffee pot and the two of them chatted at the dining room table. Ruby was especially interested in their conversation since it was mostly about decorating or redecorating. Marcie remarked that she had never been inside the parsonage but has seen oodles of homes throughout Oswald County because of her business, "Marcie's Creative Concepts." Marcie praised the quality of the parsonage's hardwood floors, pointing out that the parsonage has good bones. However, the tone of her words cleverly intimated disapproval when she spoke about the Osterhagen's style of decorating, the cozy way the living room and dining room were furnished and adorned.

Ruby and I perceived a tinge of shock on Aia's face when Marcie offered her professional services to redecorate the two rooms. Marcie spoke openly about the parsonage being a vital part of Historic St. Peter's property and that it should present a refined, aristocratic image. Before Marcie got too far along on her redecorating suggestions, Aia thanked her for the professional advice and assured her that she will give it some thought. On her way out of the door, Marcie turned around to add that when the parsonage redecorating is complete there could be an open house so that all of the parishioners could see the numerous improvements. Aia again kindly thanked Marcie, especially for the dessert recipe. Then she shut the front door.

After Clement arrived home for lunch, he had a lot on his plate dealing with a distressed Aia. Aia told Clement that she does not like any of Marcie's ideas, but prefers their home just the way it is. White walls, modern furniture, and contemporary adornments like purple orchids are not her style. Aia said that she likes their comfy furniture with patterned fabric and she does not want to change their home. Clement added that he surely does not want to part with the treasured arm chair that once belonged to his Grandpa. We noticed that when Aia appeared finished listening to Marcie's suggestions, Marcie still continued on about improving the look of the fireplace. Marcie suggested that three candles be placed on the mantle with an abstract, but wildly colourful painting placed above the fireplace. Aia said she felt hurt when Marcie mentioned that her Dala horse collection, in various colours and sizes, be removed. Aia thinks that they look perfect on the mantle arranged like toy soldiers, from tallest to shortest. She does not want the rural landscape painting of a village girl, a cow, and two geese being replaced by a canvas of frenzied splats of orange, purple, and black paint along with a grouping of three matching candles.

Clement put forth a practical strategy. The plan is to stick together by supporting one another, purposefully stirring in a large amount of procrastination. The two of them will avoid the renovating subject with Marcie. If she brings up her tips for showcasing the parsonage's best assets by redecorating, tell her it is not a good time because we cannot handle any changes while we are raising a young family. Aia threw her arms around Clement, thanked him, and told him to sit down for lunch. They ate clam chowder topped with crunchy oyster crackers.

At 11:15 p.m. Ruby and I travelled to the parsonage and found lots of shortbread crumbs. Aia and Gretchen spent the afternoon making these luxurious creations that are only prepared during the Christmas season. We were so delighted to end the day with a buttery treat. Ruby shared her thoughts with me that we are living a charmed-life, actually living off the fat of the land. I agreed with her because butter is definitely a fat and one of the three primary ingredients in shortbread. Earlier today Aia announced to Gretchen that they will bake sugar cookies tomorrow. We both feel elated because we are already looking forward to finding oodles and oodles of crumbs at the parsonage tomorrow night. Ah, there is nothing that can hold a candle to Yuletide baking traditions.

– F.N.

Friday, December 11

Tonight eighteen female students from Steady Steps Christian High School located in Beeker County were at Historic St. Peter's to present an evening program featuring liturgical dance. All were dressed in white gowns with purple sashes around their waistlines. Their movements were well choreographed. The audience found their graceful interpretation of the music praiseworthy.

Many weeks ago the members of St. Pete's were asked to billet the "Abundant Praise Liturgical Dance Group." They needed nine homes. No one volunteered, most likely due to it being December. Octavio, an aficionado of classical dance, perked up his ears when he heard Pastor and Aia discuss the lack of cooperation from St. Peter's in regard to housing the liturgical dancers. Since they have nowhere to accommodate the girls overnight, they decided that it would be easier for the entire group to sleep in the Fireside Room, noting that St. Pete's has three washrooms, so facilities would not be a problem. Octavio heard Aia mention that she will telephone "You Name It, We Rent It" and order twenty sleeping bags and twenty towels and washcloths. Practical Aia said that the girls could do without pillows for one night because their towels could either be folded or bunched up to substitute for a bed pillow. Mentioning that Aia also intends to prepare a treat for the dancers, Octavio said she will go to Bill's Dollar Bill to purchase two large foil roasters. One will be used for hot taco dip, the other for a big pile of tortilla chips.

After tonight's performance the girls arrived at the church kitchen to hang out, so much so that Aia was overwhelmed by the overcrowding. Apparently Aia must have instinctively perceived that the girls were very hungry. So, holding her hands on the sides of her face, she called out Clement's name. Standing at the kitchen entryway, he spotted her through the crowd. She asked him to drive down to Carlo's Pizzeria and pick up a king-sized pizza. A half-hour later Clement arrived with the pizza and placed it on the table in Woolcox Hall alongside the taco dip and chips. Everyone enjoyed their snack, followed by heading to the Fireside Room where the fire already made it warm and cozy.

Gretchen was so captivated by the dancer's rhythmic variations that after tonight's snack, several of the girls taught her the liturgical moves to the Kyrie, her favourite church song. Being tickled pink about the dancers staying overnight, Gretchen asked her mama if she could be included in the sleepover. After

Gretchen got Aia's approval, Clement returned to the parsonage with Gretchen. She ran to her bedroom closet to gather her yellow daisy sleeping bag, along with her pillow, sleepwear, and her teddy bear, Horace. Now she was fully prepared to join the bunking party that was well underway in the Fireside Room.

Ruby and I did not go to the parsonage tonight but scurried instead to the Fireside Room. It was there that we listened to all of the gentle whispering coming from the bunking party. We wondered if the liturgical dance group was practicing whispering so it could be added to one of their routines incorporating Psalm 107:29 where it reads, "He stilled the storm to a whisper; the waves of the sea were hushed." We agreed that it would be breathtaking to see this Bible verse incorporated into a liturgical dance number. The girls could make sweeping, swirling, and swishing hand waves while whispering mysterious messages. It would be spine-tingling. Perhaps our village youth would be keen on learning liturgical dance. I will add it to the agenda for the upcoming village meeting. Ruby was so inspired by this thought that she has already volunteered to be the coordinator. Selecting the Agnus Dei as the first song to be choreographed, she proclaimed that her mind is actively envisioning the movements to match this beautiful Lamb of God song.

– F.N.

Third Sunday in Advent ~ December 13

TODAY'S STEADY FALLING OF DELICATE SNOW WAS SO PEACEFUL. RUBY AND I FOUND A window ledge in the Fireside Room to rest on while spending most of the day enchanted by the sight of the snowflakes. On the other side of the room were Blizzard and Midwinter doing the exact same thing. Ruby mentioned that its beauty was so divine that a poem should be written about it. I told her that was an excellent idea. To remember and pay tribute to this dreamlike day, I promised Ruby that I would compose a piece of poetry.

This might be the shortest entry into my journal. An excess of Christmas preparations are underway within our village. Too many of our members are expecting our presence at every holiday gathering. We are exhausted, so we took the day off. It felt good to be enraptured by the beauty of the winter season. Ruby and I wonder if Clement and Aia feel as whipped as we do from being buried in social engagements. We wish we could advise them to downshift by taking some time off. They could begin by hiring a babysitter so they could go for a walk in beautiful Bryson Woods, appreciating the peacefulness of God's nature. If they are lucky, perhaps they will even spot a deer or see a few pheasants. Afterwards, they could go to Dino's Diner for coffee and French fries. Aia could slip a small jelly jar of her zesty homemade ketchup in her purse to use for dunking the fries. Her creation far excels all of the far too sugary commercially made varieties available at Grocer Dan's.

At 11 p.m. we travelled to the parsonage following our usual pattern. We did not intend to eat anything, but we did spot a whole walnut. We have already consumed far too many cookie crumbs this Christmas season, plus it is only the middle of the month. Oodles more crumbs will be available before the New Year arrives. We simply have to cut back and curb our consumption of sweets. Because we are in such a habit of going to the parsonage before bed, it didn't feel right not to spend time there, so we went anyway and just sat and rested on the kitchen floor. Ruby whispered to me that Aia and Gretchen baked a type of cookie today that included chopped walnuts. She is almost certain Gretchen referred to the cookies as snowballs. We are confused. We wonder if the batter actually contained some of today's fresh snowfall. Before we left the parsonage, Ruby picked up the stray walnut and took it with her. She will put it in safekeeping in case we need sustenance later.

After returning home from the parsonage, it was pointless to fall asleep because I was so set on composing a poem. It was an opportunity for me to do something creative by using my imagination. I am not a poet and know it, so I didn't want to blow it. In my stomach was a pit, trying to find poetic words to script. Now the pain has split, because the poem is knit with words that fit.

It took me six hours and thirty-seven minutes of burning the midnight oil to compose a brief, but fitting Haiku poem that captured the blissful emotions Ruby and I experienced today while watching snowflakes gently fall. Predominately in my mind were inspiring words I remember hearing from Psalm 51 where it reads, "Wash me, and I shall be whiter than snow." Here is my composition that commemorates today's celestial snowfall.

Snowy winter's day,
Snowflakes veil imperfections
As God covers sin.

After completing the Haiku poem, I fell fast asleep. Being not a poet and knowing it is exhausting. From now on I will stick to completing my journal. It is far easier to just tell it like it is, instead of condensing very selective words into a 5/7/5 syllable Haiku formation.

– F.N.

Saturday, December 19

Perhaps you are aware that I have taken a few days off from making entries in my journal. Ruby has not been feeling well, being frightfully tired, ravishingly hungry, and extraordinarily thirsty. Each morning she has awakened feeling sick to her tummy. Thankfully, it goes away as the day progresses. I am hesitant to even announce this, but perhaps she is expecting. I am keeping my hopes up and so is Ruby. This is the reason for the cessation in my writing, but now I am determined to continue until my notebook is filled to the brim.

At 10 a.m. today Historic St. Peter's council met to sort out some small but pertinent issues before the upcoming New Year begins. Fairly new on the council is Blake Dunn, a twenty-four year old man that is highly vocal about making improvements at St. Peter's. Several in our village have observed that Blake is thrilled to be on the church council. Petunia, the most hopeful mouse in our village, dashed into hiding before council members arrived for the meeting held in the board room. After the meeting was finished, she arrived at our dwelling to report all that she had heard.

Petunia declared that Blake has taken it upon himself to be somewhat of an expert on *Robert's Rules of Order,* ever since he purchased a used copy of it at the library's annual book sale. Apparently he has studied its contents to help properly govern council meetings. However, Blake's main concern today was about the substandard quality of the minutes that the council secretary, Michelle Greene, records at each meeting. After Michelle read the minutes of the prior council meeting, Blake lambasted Michelle's ability to take minutes, claiming that she is obviously unqualified to perform the job properly.

After Blake behaved in this manner, many of the council members challenged him by expressing appreciation for Michelle's fine reporting abilities. Blake ignored their words of praise, after which he suggested that it is time for the church to move forward by getting a new council secretary. Blake recommended that his wife, Bethany, who has recently finished schooling to become a legal secretary, is ready and willing to replace Michelle. Because Bethany hopes to obtain a legal secretary position at a nearby law office, Blake said this opportunity and experience would tremendously enhance her resume. So far, Bethany does not have any experience to place on her resume.

Michelle pointedly asked Blake if he was aware of her occupation. Blake responded negatively, but thought perhaps she worked at a big-box store. Michelle told him that he is incorrect and that she is a professional court reporter. She added that she has twenty-four years of background in the field, going back to when he was swaddled in diapers. Michelle pointed out that she has experience in family court, divorce court, and traffic court, of which she recollects being in the courtroom when someone by his exact same name was in the witness box facing the judge. That particular day the nineteen-year old Blake Dunn appeared in traffic court for a speeding ticket along with reckless driving. Michelle then let slip to everyone that she also was the court reporter for the bloodiest murder case ever conducted in Oswald County. Petunia revealed to us that after Michelle spoke about her vast experience, Blake became very quiet and looked down at the table for the remainder of the meeting. Ruby and I think his behaviour might be what is described as shame or humiliation.

At 11:15 p.m. Ruby and I travelled to the board room where we found an abundance of Christmas cookie crumbs. The council meeting lingered on far too long today, so they stopped and took a coffee break. Clement headed to the parsonage to pick up a plate of Christmas cookies that Aia and Gretchen made first thing this morning. Everyone savoured the star-shaped stained glass cookies. Petunia thought the cookies were really appropriate for a church meeting because they were very ecclesiastical in appearance. Ruby asked me to explain the word ecclesiastical, so I told her that it simply means having to do with church. She still did not understand, so I told her another way to say it is churchy-churchy. That hit a bingo with her so she nodded her head upwards and downwards in agreement.

– F.N.

Fourth Sunday in Advent ~ December 20

IT WAS USELESS TO EVEN ATTEMPT TO ATTEND THE WORSHIP SERVICE THIS MORNING. Ruby was not a bit like herself. Since we spend every Sunday morning in the tummy of the organ, the last thing we needed to have happen was for the contents of Ruby's tummy spilling forth in that sacred place because of morning sickness. We are both convinced that Ruby is with child. We have struggled with the disappointment of not having a baby, but now there is a real possibility that we might become parents.

At 11:15 p.m. I travelled alone to the parsonage in search of a treat to take back to our dwelling. I found a bit of a soda cracker and gave it to Ruby. She remarked that it tasted better than anything she has ever eaten, including the one time that Aia's folks visited them and brought along a bakery box of Canadian beaver tails, the sweet pastry that is formed in the shape of an actual beaver tail. After the soda cracker crumbs settled Ruby's tumbling tummy we were able to rest, sleeping like babies.

– F.N.

The Nativity of Our Lord/Christmas Day ~ Friday, December 25

After we listened to a fine concert of Christmas carols in the tummy of the pipe organ this morning, Ruby and I returned home and I began a new journey, something on my bucket list. I picked up a paintbrush. My recording days are at an end, but I fancy that you, the reader, probably would appreciate a report about what happened on Christmas Eve at Historic St. Peter's Lutheran Church.

Last evening a few parishioners who belong to St. Pete's, some from Holy Angels Catholic Parish, and various others in town attended the Christmas Eve, "A Different Kind of Christmas" celebration that was held at the Armory. It began at five o'clock with a Christmas carol sing-a-long. However, by 5:20 p.m. it was announced that Swedish soprano, Ulrika, had cancelled at the last minute with no explanation given as to why she scrapped this gig. Because of that there was a mass exodus of people exiting the Armory, hurrying to their vehicles in order to return to their own churches. Most were hoping to catch what remained of the 5 p.m. Christmas Eve Candlelight & Carols at St. Peter's and the 5 p.m. mass at Holy Angels Catholic Parish. Pastor Osterhagen and Father Tim probably gave their very best Christmas sermons to those parishioners who had not been caught up in a "sheep-stealing affair." The sheep who went astray also found out that they clearly saw the star in the east shining brightly over their own church and followed it to where the Christ Child lay, that is, at Historic St. Peter's and at Holy Angels Catholic Parish.

At 11:30 p.m. Ruby and I travelled to the parsonage and snacked on morsels of figgy pudding topped with an unforgettably delicious sauce. Surprisingly, we also found a tiny piece of a canned oyster. For a moment, I imagined that we were spending Christmas in Merrie Olde England. Just moments after that I became dizzy, probably from the inclusion of French brandy in the figgy pudding sauce. Ruby held me close to support me, suggesting that we return to our dwelling. After we arrived home she tucked me in bed and whispered *"MgJssqpo Cdpovihn-qaeiofh,"* which means "Happy Christmas" in the mouse language. The last thing I remember was Ruby crawling in bed and sweetly singing "What Child is This?" While listening, I realized that the perfectly well-written carol is actually a Q & A. A question is asked, while the refrain provides the answer: This is God's Son, Immanuel, God-with-us. The holy night of Jesus' birth included not just the

Holy Family, but angels, shepherds, and their sheep. Those at the crèche bowed down low and worshipped the Christ Child. The nativity is recorded in two gospels, Matthew and Luke. The Gospel of St. Luke contains far more details, so I would point you in that direction. By the way, any mice in the stable that holy night would have also marvelled to see God lying in a manger.

– F.N.

The Holy Innocents, Martyrs ~ Monday, December 28

Today was a snappy, ice-kissed, snowy day throughout Oswald County. Because of the record-breaking nippy winter weather, I made a faulty assumption that people would stay put in their warm homes to avoiding venturing into an outdoor icebox. But, my mistaken expectation did not apply to the ever-hearty and stalwart Aia because she and Gretchen were piling on layers of winter gear to go out and about. Gretchen spoke during breakfast about how she was excited to be mama's helper, but also reminded her mother of her promise to spend time at the fish area of the grocery store watching the brand new display of lobsters that live in a bubbling tank. We heard Gretchen mention that she was the most excited about going outside in the cold weather to hear the crunching sound that her snow boots make when she walks on the crackling snow. Ruby and I remember the day Clement and Aia had a short discussion about this topic and appropriately graced that particular sound with a name. Since that time they have referred to the sound as "arctic crunch."

You are well aware that the church year came to an end about a month ago. However,Ruby and I were so engrossed overhearing something that happened at the parsonage today that I decided to add an additional entry to *Finley's Tale - Book III: The Bond of Love*. Also, there are several blank pages in my journal, so I might as well keep going and use up every single sheet. It would be wasteful not to use the paper for what it is intended. After I run out of paper, I for sure will call it quits.

Aia and Gretchen left the parsonage early while Clement stayed home with Marc and Luc. Before noon they returned home and unloaded a van full of supplies, temporarily placing them in the parsonage kitchen. Ruby and I noticed Clement's bewildered facial expression as he surveyed their purchases. Trinitarian Aia was obviously primed, poised, and prepared to ease Clement's initial shock regarding the copious amount of items sprawled on the kitchen counters, table, and floor.

Resting at the dining room table for a few minutes, Aia spoke of the inherited antique French clock that has sat on their piano year after year. Referring to it as a sizable knickknack, she mentioned that it was nothing but an impractical, fanciful dust-catcher. Going on to further explain, she pointed out that the clock was in need of extensive repairs because it has not been ticking since she received it. After logically thinking about it, she chose to take it to an antique store for an appraisal.

Many weeks ago she spoke with Humphrey Chandler, a long-time member of the Antique Clock Dealers' Association. He agreed to have the clock professionally appraised. Within days he called her back to reveal the appraiser's findings. Explaining to Aia that it is a rare Parisian clock built sometime prior to 1750, it even has the maker's name engraved on the lower portion of the clock's face, a real beauty of an antique. Aia said Humphrey urged her to sell it to a museum to be included in a clock collection so others would have a chance to appreciate it. Humphrey offered to help her locate the right museum, adding that for a small fee he would be happy to handle the transaction details. Since Aia was anxious to get this clock off of her hands, she agreed to Humphrey's suggestion. When Humphrey telephoned two weeks ago, he told her that a sizeable cheque was on its way to her. He was pleased that the clock had been purchased by a museum in Montreal. Soon it will be permanently housed in a glass case, located in a room called "The Chamber of Heirloom Timepieces," which contains rare antique clocks from all over the world.

Continuing on, Aia spoke to Clement about her family's history with the mantel clock. Mentioning that her great-grandmother purchased the old clock from a fancy shop in Sainte-Anne-de-Bellevue, Quebec shortly after she and her great-grandfather were married, it has been in their family ever since. The clock was handed down to her grandparents, then to her parents, and finally ended up with Aia even though she did not want it. Because the clock is highly ornate and overly-embellished with detailed gilt bronze figures that stand on four scrolling feet, she has never taken a fancy to it. So far, no one in the family has cared for the look of it either. Her great-grandmother who hand-selected the "beauty" is the only one who has treasured it. Aia told Clement how thankful she was to get rid of it.

Admitting to Clement that she has kept all of this a secret because she wanted to surprise him, she unveiled the purpose and means of obtaining today's purchases that were now temporarily parked in the kitchen. Aia said that after she and Gretchen entered the grocery store, they headed for the lobster tank where Gretchen was completely captivated watching lobsters for the first time. Aia instead scanned the free fish recipe cards that were on display near the fresh fish case. She mentioned to Clement that most of the recipes were impracticable, just fancy ways to dress up a fish dinner with a bit of flare. Before leaving the fish department, Aia did pick up a family-sized box of fish cakes along with a bag of fresh lemons and carried them to the front of the store. Placing the food into one buggy, she grabbed another buggy so she and Gretchen each had one. Aia went on to say that Gretchen was a topnotch helper when they shopped for disposable diapers, in all available sizes, along with diaper wipes and diaper rash ointment. Aia filled both buggies to the top with boxes of disposable diapers. Because Gretchen knows how to count, she placed thirty containers of diaper wipes in her buggy. After that, Aia led the way to the cashier by manoeuvring her buggy with one hand while holding on to the front of Gretchen's buggy. Gretchen brought up the rear while Aia swung her head from the extreme left to the far right to see how their journey was proceeding. She mentioned to Clement that she was careful not to bash into anyone, especially someone being wheeled in one of the complimentary wheelchairs. The diaper boxes were so high up in the air that Gretchen could not see anything in front of her but trustingly and blindingly followed her mama.

After they loaded the van full of their purchases, Gretchen told her daddy that they drove to the drive up and ordered a hot chocolate and an oatmeal cookie while her mama got a coffee with double cream. Gretchen said that they listened to music in the van all the way home. Her favourite song was about a chicken that knows how to dance. Clement heard Gretchen say that her mama called it an "oom-pah" wedding song. Gretchen said that the song sounds so happy it should not be used only for weddings, but it should be sung in church. She asked her daddy if they could sing it in church on Sunday, but Ruby noticed that Clement remained speechless.

Later on Clement wondered about Aia's plans to store the dozens of diaper boxes in the parsonage. She explained that she intends to stack them floor to ceiling against the one empty wall in the twins' bedroom. Clement laughed when she said that the bedroom might resemble the Great Wall of China, the Berlin Wall, or maybe even the Wailing Wall. But, the "Diaper Wall" will come down box by box as the babies grow. We observed that Trinitarian Aia is delighted beyond words about their purchases because it now means that her cloth diaper days are now finished, have bit the dust, simply a thing of the past, which will vastly cut down on the towering amount of laundry she is continually confronted with.

Explaining to Clement that the best reward from closing the deal on the clock was that it increased their savings account, there being enough to save for a vacation. Aia suggested taking a trip to Prince Edward Island after the boys can walk. If they travelled to P.E.I. they could stop at Sainte-Anne-de-Bellevue, Quebec, to see for themselves the home her great-grandparents lived in so long ago, a part of their ancestry. While in P.E.I. she hopes that they can purchase tickets to see a performance of "Anne of Green Gables," plus take an eerie walk through the haunted forest. On other days they could stroll barefooted along the beach where the children would be busy building red sand castles. Aia went on to mention dining at one of the many seafood restaurants. She added that even if they have to rough it by camping in a tent for a week to save on lodging costs, enjoying a Maritime dinner will be worth every single loonie and toonie. Gretchen piped up at that time and added to the conversation that when she is a grown up and has a baby girl she is going to name her Anne, that is, Anne with an E.

Following their conversation, we heard busy footsteps walking back and forth to the twins' bedroom while they transported the boxes of disposable diapers. There was a happy mood while they were building the "Wall of Diapers." After they were done working, Gretchen asked her folks if they could go out for "hangkeburgs," as she calls them, at Nancy's Lunch Wagon. Ruby and I think she really means hamburgers, but Clement and Aia don't ever correct her pronunciation of that particular word. It was then that the family got all suited up in winter gear and left the house, heading to Nancy's. Once again, my assumption about people staying at home when the weather outside is arctic cold was mistaken. Ruby concluded that weather conditions are rarely mentioned by the able-bodied, strappingly hardy, weather-resistant Osterhagens. I noticed, once again, that Ruby is more and more becoming a Trinitarian speaker just like Aia.

At 12:30 p.m. Ruby and I travelled to the parsonage. Since the Osterhagens went out for hangkeburgs, we felt safe to peek into Marc and Luc's bedroom. We were curious to catch a glimpse of the "Wall of Diapers." We ended up seeing even more when we noticed a much smaller wall, a "Wall of Diaper Wipes," located in one corner that Gretchen must have built. We thought both of the walls were very impressive and well-assembled. It also was enjoyable to look at the assortment of diaper boxes. Each and every box had a picture of an adorable baby, not nearly as darling as wee Marc and wee Luc, but pretty close to it. After that, Ruby and I hurried back home and tried to imagine what our baby might look like.

– F.N.

Tuesday, December 29

For several weeks Nelda McBride has chosen to sit in the very last pew during the worship service instead of in her usual spot located near the front. Another change is that she now leaves during the last hymn to stand by the drinking fountain. Albert Coulson also sits in the very last pew, which has led to the two of them becoming acquainted, especially during the lengthy sharing of the peace. Whippersnapper, a young but confident member of our village, has been watching their friendship develop. He reported to us that last Sunday Albert exited the sanctuary at the exact same time as Nelda. Whippersnapper is confident that romance is blooming, probably due to the fact that they have one health concern in common, arthritis. While Nelda and Albert were standing at the drinking fountain comparing arthritis symptoms, medications, and potions, they discovered that both of them sit in the back pew because it has become too difficult to turn their stiff necks around to see who has shown up for church. Both agree that if they stand by the drinking fountain, every single person leaving the sanctuary will walk by them on their way out of the building, a form of monitoring church attendance, just for fun.

Prior to the postlude last Sunday, Whippersnapper heard Albert ask Nelda to join him for brunch at Coralee's Cranberry Cove Café. After she replied positively, he suggested that she try a new arthritic pain reliever called Arthritis-Away. Albert said that he highly recommends it as it calms down his neck pain. The product can be found at Tippecanoe & Tyler Too Pharmacy, whose catchphrase is "A Quality Pharmacy Good Enough for a President." Albert added that when he first tried Arthritis-Away, all he could say was "Oh, my land, this is a miracle!"

At 10:30 p.m. Ruby and I were snuggled under the covers. We discussed the health ramifications of arthritis. When Whippersnapper told us some of the pains that Nelda and Coulson share in common, it sounded very similar to what Stiff, a warm-hearted member of our village suffers with daily. Stiff's demeanour is anything but smug, starchy, or stuffy, since she refuses to let her attitude be affected by her health condition. In Stiff's better days she was lithe and springy, a real joy to watch. Her given name is Lindy and in her better days many called her Limber Lindy. Changing her name to Stiff seemed appropriate when her joint affliction set in. In our bones we feel so sorry for Stiff when she suffers. Sometimes when she moves her joints make a creaky-crack sound. She no longer can go out and about at St. Peter's because the sound of her clamorous joints might present a safety issue for the village. But, she is a good sport and throughout it all she triumphantly wears a smile.

– F.N.

Tuesday, January 5

Last Sunday Aia was the substitute organist while Josie Johnson was on vacation in Iowa. In preparation for Sunday's worship service, Clement and Aia set up the baby swings in the choir loft on Saturday afternoon. Each time the swings came to a stop it was Gretchen's responsibility to wind them up. Aia was so flustered at being both an organist and a mother simultaneously that she accidently headed off to church wearing one black shoe and one brown shoe.

Unfortunately, both Clement and Aia have had a tickle in their throats. During worship today a coughing flare up began. Prior to the organ prelude, Aia opened up a brand new box of Dutch mints. She has found that these drops are far more soothing than any of the plain old drug store varieties of cough drops. Upon opening the blue and white box decorated with delftware painting, one of the peppermints accidently dropped to the floor, landing underneath the row of organ pedals, making it impossible to retrieve. Patti, a real sweetie in our village, came upon the peppermint drop just prior to tonight's meeting. It was sensational to experience how her fresh breath significantly altered the aroma of the entire meeting area, transforming it into a place of complete freshness. Because it was decided that Patti has the freshest breath in our entire village, it was brought to a vote to honour her with an official title. Ideas spilled forth as to the exact naming of the title. After a short discussion, Patti was called to the front and awarded the title, "Patti, St. Peter's Peppermint Princess."

Gracie, a village mouse who seems to do everything with little effort, was on duty last Sunday morning. While Clement was delivering his sermon, he broke into a humdinger of a coughing fit. After the sermon, she was keen to observe Aia while she was on her knees at the communion rail waiting to receive Holy Communion. Fishing out a fresh peppermint from her pocket, Aia slyly handed a Dutch mint to Clement while he was serving Holy Communion. Gracie mentioned that he looked as though he was not expecting to be given anything and, unfortunately, he dropped it. Quickly Aia fetched out another one and gave it to Clement. He put it in his mouth, which immediately curbed upcoming coughing. After worship that day, Gracie heard one parishioner ask Pastor if his cough was coming or going. Gracie said that he didn't respond with an answer, but instead heartily laughed, which unfortunately brought on another whopper of a cough.

After everyone left St. Peter's last Sunday, Gracie retrieved the dropped Dutch mint from the chancel floor.

Since both Patti and Gracie lucked out and came upon a peppermint, they now have something in common, fresh breath. After spending so much time together, Gracie decided it was time to have a heart-to-heart chat with Patti. Admitting that she was envious of Patti's official title, she wondered if Patti could help her receive a title, too. Patti was eager to help, but reminded her that it will take some serious brainstorming, which would accelerate even faster if they put their heads together. Patti soon suggested that they simply share her title. All they would need to do is make a few changes in the title's wording. After a two-minute silence, Patti recommended an improved title that is a bit lengthy, but fitting: "Princess Patti and O Day Full of Gracie, Official Aficionados of Dutch Mints." Gracie was so delighted that she might receive a title that she imagined herself wearing wooden clogs. While humming a simple tune she performed a brief clog dance. When Patti saw Gracie's clog dance involving numerous heal and toe taps, she asked Gracie to teach her the moves. Within minutes they were a dancing duo. This lead to a yearning to obtain wooden clogs that will allow them to make percussion sounds while striking the floor in rhythm to the music. If they can find a cobbler in the village to carve them wooden shoes, then they will be able to entertain the village with their newly developed talent. Until then, they will go to the next village meeting to explain the reasoning as to why they want to share the official title, hoping to receive approval of the title's new wording.

Josie, the organist, stopped at the church today having returned from her trip to Nashua, Iowa. While visiting the famous Little Brown Church, Josie purchased twenty-five souvenir pencils to begin a new collection after her original assortment of pencils was stolen from the organ. Later on, Clement revealed to Aia that this is the first time that he has spoken with Josie that she did not cover her mouth with a tissue, or have booze breath. Instead, she smelled like peppermints. Aia quipped back, "From now on, let's give Josie this title: 'Queen Josie, St. Peter's Official Aficionado of Using Peppermint Pastilles to Camouflage Liquor Breath.'" Ruby and I could tell that Aia felt guilty after saying those words, because she quickly decided to scrap that idea and award Josie with a better title, "Organist Josie Johnson, Peppermint Schnapps Aficionado."

Today Ruby and I witnessed a tiff between Clement and Aia, and believe it or not, it was over crunchy potato sticks. Aia made it very clear to Clement that she enjoys the sandwiches that St. Peter's serves at funeral luncheons that are a tuna fish mixture spread on buttered bread topped with potato sticks. Attempting to keep a steady supply of potato sticks in the parsonage pantry, she is usually unsuccessful. Today she blamed Clement for their disappearance. She emphasized that the best part of funeral sandwiches is the crunchy topping. Ruby thinks Aia was overly upset because she is not feeling well. After their little quarrel, Aia picked up a green apple and bit into it so hard that we were concerned that her front teeth might fall out. Gretchen looked so stunned at what was happening that she, as a young Lutheran said, "What does this mean?" Clement wrote the words "purchase potato sticks" on a sticky note, showed it to Aia, and assured her that she will not have to wait for someone to die before she will have her next funeral sandwich. She crumbled up his note, hugged him and apologized, adding that the loss of potato sticks is nothing to cry about.

At 10:30 p.m. Ruby and I travelled to the Osterhagen's kitchen and found a tiny chunk of albacore tuna. We could easily imagine what it would taste like if it contained a crunchy potato stick topping. At 11 p.m. Gracie came to our dwelling revealing that she now has a royal title. However, it appears receiving a title is not quite enough of a distinction to satisfy her desires. She asked our support because she wants her first name to be changed at the next village meeting to "O Day Full of Gracie." She warned us that it is not to be shortened to "Grace" or worse, "O Day." She did mention that it would be acceptable if everyone called her "Ful-la." I will speak in approval of her desire at the next meeting. Gracie hugged and thanked us, leaving our dwelling with a radiant smile. After Ruby and I turned in for the night, we visited about Gracie's desire to change her name. We wonder if somehow her distant relatives might have dwelled at Pastor N.F.S. Grundtvig's Danish home in the mid-1800s when he authored the hymn "O Day Full of Grace." Gracie's new name sounds strikingly akin to this dearly loved hymn sung throughout the Pentecost Season and is often requested at funerals. Her new name does not sound very original, but it is a fine new name, reminding everyone to ponder the grace that God daily bestows on His believers. No wonder there are so many churches graced with the name "Grace Lutheran Church."

– F.N.

Friday, January 8

Last Friday afternoon Ruby observed Clement sitting in his green leather recliner with his feet up. Due to Ruby's splendiferous eyesight, she was able to see what he was reading, a book from the church library. On the cover of the little beige book were the words, *The Oberammergau Passion Play 1970*.

We have found it to be very uncommon to see Clement reading a book while at home, but he obviously snatched this quiet opportunity while Aia, Gretchen, and the twins were napping. He was reading this particular book until Marc and Luc awoke, needing a diaper change. Up until that point the house was so quiet that we could hear the numerous clocks tick, something he later told Aia he had not heard in a very long time. Ruby and I were inquisitive about the contents of this little book, so we asked our two village librarians to research the word Oberammergau. Yesterday their research was completed so they stopped over to reveal their findings. Dr. Simonsen and Dr. Kikkunen explained that Oberammergau is a quaint town located in the Bavarian Alps where a world famous passion play is held every ten years. Being that Pastor is reading the text of this book, it is the next best and cheapest way to experience the Passion Play rather than flying to Bavaria to take in a live performance.

Thoughtfully I have placed the subject of the Oberammergau Passion Play on the agenda for the next village meeting. Hoping that Banjo, who prefers to be known as Jo, will keep his keen eye out for the book's return to the library, our village would then read the text, divide up the parts, form a musical chorus with selected soloists, resulting in our very own passion play. We would not be able to perform it every ten years. In that amount of time we will all have turned to dust. But, perhaps we could repeat it every ten weeks.

For the last three days, Aia has altered her eating habits. Even though she is still preparing regular meals, Ruby and I have noticed that during their mealtimes Aia has made three noticeable changes: 1. The plate that she uses is not a regular dinner plate but a sandwich plate; 2. Her consumption of black pepper has increased; and 3. She no longer uses regular cutlery but chop sticks. As we visited about her new behaviour, we decided that Aia might be implementing a self-created diet, Trinitarian style, another example of being a graduate of Trinity College. Now it looks like things are back to normal since Aia ate tonight's supper using a regular dinner plate with her food sprinkled with a moderate amount of black pepper, using regular cutlery. Aia admitted to Clement that during the last few days she has been "Mrs. In-a-Funk Curmudgeon Grump" while striving to get back into her smaller slacks. She added that from now on she will have to be content wearing her big girl pants because she cannot accomplish the mountainous amount of daily work being fueled by so little food.

At 11:20 p.m. Ruby and I travelled to the parsonage and ate well. At supper this evening Gretchen accidently dropped a forkful of Stromboli on the floor. Ah, the combination of salami, ham, mozzarella cheese, pizza sauce, and homemade dough were *eccellente* (excellent), *splendida* (splendid), and *indimenticabile* (unforgettable). In our original language, all three of these descriptive words are combined to fit effortlessly into just one word that is easy to get one's tongue around, called "*azsdifnqe-Gixymswethbmoeinrgbniopaer-Ogbvniokdptkvvnqwero-infoaiwngvy.*"

– F.N.

First Sunday after Epiphany, January 10

Several weeks ago Belinda Johnson spoke with Wanda Cage while she was washing up St. Peter's communion vessels in the sacristy. Two village mice, Wiggly and Piggly, were hiding under the sink when they heard the women discussing the subject of disposable plastic communion cups. Belinda simply needed some information about where to purchase the special cups, noting that she hopes to use them at an upcoming event at St. Pete's. Since the special order would take several weeks to arrive, Wanda offered to give Belinda a box of cups in return for a donation to the Altar Guild. Wanda said that she would soon place an order for more cups from Reed's Church Supply, noting that right now there are plenty cups on hand so there is no worry that St. Pete's will run out of them.

Today's event after church was hosted by Patrick and Belinda Johnson, commonly known as the "P.B. & J's." Their unique nickname stems from the way they sign their names on volunteer sign-up up sheets. They are quick to sign up to donate flowers, to help with the fall and spring cleanup, to provide treats for coffee hour, etc. The P.B. & J's are the long-time owners of PBJ Boat Sales & Rentals located on Lake Harvey.

Just recently the Johnson family started a small independent business called "The Pizzazzy Peanut." Their goods feature a wide variety of peanuts seasoned with various flavours. Barbeque, garlic and onion, chili, honey, salt and vinegar, hickory, and no salt, are just a few examples of the flavours. Also sold are raw peanuts for boiling. Their son, Brady, is in high school showing an interest in accounting, so keeping the books for "The Pizzazzy Peanut" provides him with valuable hands-on training.

Following the worship service today, everyone was invited to Woolcox Hall for a "Peanut Party." Several long tables were dressed with white linen tablecloths and table skirts. Displayed on the tables were signs denoting each flavour of peanut. Adjacent to each sign were dozens of plastic communion cups containing a few peanuts for customer sampling. Wiggly and Piggly told me that they have been anticipating this event since they heard Belinda's and Wanda's communion cup discussion several weeks ago. Both mice listened to many conversations today while they hid underneath one of the tables, the table skirt keeping them out of sight. They also had high hopes that a peanut might be dropped and roll under the table skirt. To their delight, a honey flavoured peanut suddenly flung in front of them when it was accidently shoved forward by someone wearing brown penny loafers. Wiggly and Piggly quickly split the nut in half, noting that it tasted sweet with warm notes of a distinct flavour, similar to dark brown sugar.

Aia and Gretchen were in attendance at today's event with Marc and Luc content in their double stroller. Gretchen voiced her opinion about the flavours of peanuts that she sampled, but had the most praise for the plain salted cocktail peanuts. Aia sampled most of the peanuts, but purchased only a bag of the raw ones. We felt sorry for Clement because once again he missed an entire event. It was reported to me that after today's worship service a parishioner was crying in Pastor's office so loudly that it could be heard through the door. Someone must have needed his attention, help, a listening ear, and most importantly, prayer.

When Aia and the children returned home, Ruby noticed that Aia got out a large kettle and filled it with raw peanuts, water, and salt and placed it on the stove. Gretchen wondered what her mama was cooking. Aia told her that she was preparing goober peas for tonight's snack. After that Aia started making lunch while singing some words that yearned for a country road to take her home where she belongs. The melody was magically lovely, but Ruby and I were perplexed by the words and their meaning. First we wondered if Aia does not feel at home in the parsonage. Secondly, where in the world are the Blue Ridge Mountains? And, thirdly, where is the Shenandoah River? It was at that point that I stopped asking questions as I was aware that I, too, was beginning to sound Trinitarian.

At 11:15 p.m. Ruby and I travelled to the parsonage. We were overjoyed to find a boiled peanut under Gretchen's chair at the kitchen table. Goodness, how delicious it was! After we were finished, we were confused as to what to do with the peanut shell to avoid leaving any mess, any trace of our presence. Finally we figured it out. Together we used our tails as though they were hand brooms and swept the shell to the kitchen door. There happens to be a gap under the door which leads to the garage. (Thankfully, Clement has not made this repair yet, but we know he intends to install a new threshold when he has time.) We gave the shells a sturdy heave-ho, flinging them under the door, out of sight, and into the garage. Trinitarian Ruby mentioned that it was a grand slam, a clean sweep, a real hole-in-one.

– F.N.

Tuesday, January 12

St. Peter's Ladies' Quilting Group gathered together today after taking a break over the holidays. The first ladies to arrive at church this morning came upon a big box sitting by the back door that must have been dropped off earlier today. It had big black letters on the box that read, "For Mission Sewing." It contained clean, but used, bed sheets that are to become the underside fabric of the colourfully vibrant quilts that the ladies create. While Silvie Berger was unpacking the box, she became unglued at finding a good-sized plastic bag that contained a mysterious white powder. Because this has never happened before, she needed the other quilters to help her examine it. The bag was passed to and from each member while they sought to figure out its contents. After many minutes, one of the women suggested that it just might be an illegal drug, probably heroin or cocaine. After those scary words were mentioned, the entire group was terror-stricken and ready to push the panic button. Silvie even questioned if there could be someone in the church who is part of a drug smuggling operation. After that, not even thirty seconds passed before it was pointed out that everyone's fingerprints were on the bag. Audrey Fassbender was so overtaken by envisioning that she might be sent to the state penitentiary for being part of an illegal drug operation that her heart pounded wickedly, she became short of breath, and she began to pass out. Two of the ladies came to Audrey's rescue by guiding her to a chair, telling her to close her eyes, and talking about the beauty of her glorious pink and white peony garden. When Audrey felt better she quoted her confirmation verse from Psalm 46:1 in the KJV, which says: "God is our refuge and strength, a very present help in trouble." She told the ladies that she has said her verse out loud nearly every day since it was given to her sixty-two years ago, revealing that it helps her to have control over being a jumpy jittery jellyfish. One of our mice, Farley, was not so far away because he was hiding in the church kitchen behind the push broom. When he heard the troubles going on, he scrambled to Woolcox Hall to hide behind the base of one of the portable basketball poles to witness the fearful hullabaloo.

Not one of the women knew exactly what to do, so Peggy Hayward ran as fast as she could to Pastor Osterhagen's office for his help. Pastor told the quilters that the first thing they were going to do was to call the police. The second thing was to wait for the police to arrive. The third thing was to not be alarmed. Farley told me that Clement is now beginning to speak Trinitarian, just like his wife, Aia.

It was a long wait at Historic St. Peter's for the police to arrive since they were dealing with a real emergency. Some of the women could not wait that long. Two needed to hurry home to take their medication that had to be taken with food. Three others were expected at the bowling alley. Even one woman had to race home to give her diabetic dog a shot. When the police arrived they heard the full story before they gathered up the bag and took it with them to the station.

It was not until tonight that the contents of the bag were revealed when Pastor received a telephone call from the police station. The plastic bag did not contain illegal drugs but was composed of a joint compound called gypsum dust to be used on interior walls when putting up sheetrock. It is still mysterious how the bag got nestled between the donated sheets.

At 5:30 p.m. Ruby and I travelled to the church kitchen hoping to find a snack from today's Ladies' Quilting Group. We were in luck when we found a few crumbs of a cranberry coffee cake. We talked about the events of the day at St. Peter's, concluding that any plastic bags nestled between sheets just might be illegal drugs. We also came to the conclusion that Clement handled everything so well today. Unfortunately, most pastors cannot possibly learn everything at the seminary they need to know that will fully prepare them for the oddities of parish life.

– F.N.

Wednesday, January 13

Overnight a humdinger of a snowstorm pummeled Oswald County resulting in school closures. First thing this morning Clement received a telephone call from Lance Farber asking him to call on his dad, Grover, to bring him Holy Communion at Loving Arms Nursing Home. Clement revealed to Aia that he had just called on Grover last Friday and he seemed to be doing well, but something must have changed. Scratching his head, he knew he would not be able to plow the van through the driveway, let alone drive down the street that has not yet seen a snow plow. He thought he could try to hike his way there but the snow drifts would be up to his knees. Gretchen listened to his predicament, quickly suggesting that he ski to the nursing home, adding that he would be there as quick as a bunny. Clement thanked and kissed Gretchen for her sapient advice. While Clement was putting on his parka and other winter gear, Gretchen asked him what maple syrup had to do with cross-country skiing to the nursing home. Clement was perplexed at her question, but soon realized that when she heard the word sapient she thought it had something to do with the sap that drips from maple trees that ends up becoming maple syrup. Gretchen mentioned that she knows a lot about maple syrup from a book she checked out at the Oswald County Library entitled, *Sweet Sap from the Maple Tree*. Clement told her that he would sit down and go into detail about the word sapient after he returns home from calling on Mr. Farber.

This final entry into my third journal now wraps up my year long recording of church happenings at Historic St. Peter's Lutheran Church in Oswald County. Writing a journal was the topmost item on my bucket list. Looking back, I am amazed that I found the fortitude and persistence to see it come to fruition. But, as it is written in Ecclesiastes 3:1, "There is a time for everything, and a season for every activity under the heavens." Moving forward, I plan to begin the second item on my bucket list: painting miniature portraits. I can't even put in plain English how enthusiastic I am to get cracking on this endeavour. My plan is to paint a likeness of each member of the Osterhagen Family, one of my beautiful Ruby, and lastly, a self-portrait. While browsing in the Sunday School craft room several weeks ago, Ruby spotted a box containing small oval art canvases, acrylic paint, and paintbrushes. With help from some of our strongest villagers, the box was pushed to our dwelling under the cover of night. Ruby helped me set up an art studio near the window where sunlight floods into our dwelling at midday. With supplies at hand, it's time to put my efforts into something brand-new.

In concluding my journal, I have listed all of the people and mice who have been so important to the life of St. Pete's this past year, because each one is very special and I don't want any of them to be forgotten. Their names are listed along with a brief description. I hope that when you read their many names it will bring about a little smile on your face, a memory about them, and you will be delighted that you had the opportunity to read about these fine Lutherans. It has been an eye-opener for all of us learning about what makes Lutherans tick. I had not intended to list so many names, but Gretchen inspired me to do so after I listened to her sing a Sunday School song that touched my heart. I will not forget it when Gretchen sang about the church not being about a building, but people.

Thank you to each and every one of you for reading *Finley's Tale – Book III: The Bond of Love*. At this point, I hope you clearly see the light at the end of the tunnel when it pertains to what "church life" is really like. I have dedicated *The Bond of Love* to Pastor Clement Osterhagen, a treasured man of faith. Our village, as well as St. Peter's parishioners, look up to him as a guiding servant, admiring his encouraging steadfast faith and his pastoral heart. As I close, I would like to bring to mind one of Clement's favourite Bible verses. It is from Romans 1:17 where it reads, "For in the gospel the righteousness of God is revealed – a righteousness that is by faith from first to last, just as it is written: 'The righteous will live by faith.'"

I cannot end this part of my tale in the same fashion that I ended the other two tales. Saying goodbye is often sad, we all know that, so instead of saying farewell or bye for now to you, my reader, I will say that I hope our paths meet again. You have shown love to me by following my tale and I express my thanks to you by saying *Uqqw weoi* (Mouse), *Mange Tusen Takk* (Norwegian), and *Vielen Dank* (German). I'm sending you a big X (hug) and a big O (kiss).

Your forever friend,
Finley (Tweed) Newcastle
(F.N. for short)

P.S. After reading my journal, my hope is that you wholeheartedly embrace the same admiration for your own pastor that I have for Pastor Osterhagen. An excellent takeaway from reading my journal are some kind and loving tips that are not just to be remembered but to be put into practice. That way your pastor can carry on doing the abundant work that God has placed in his hands. Please keep these wise words in the forefront of your mind: Be good to your pastor, thank God for him, show him love and respect, overlook idiosyncrasies, don't expect perfection, squash gossip, and most importantly, pray for your pastor and your church. Your pastor lives among you to spread the news of salvation in Jesus Christ our Lord. It is there that you will find the forgiveness of your sins. May God bless you and keep your faith strong until one unknown day He calls you to join him in heaven where you will be welcomed into your eternal home.

At 11:30 p.m. Ruby and I travelled to the parsonage and snacked on a droplet of brown ale. It felt like the perfect celebration for completing my long journal. We ended the evening by saying that Historic St. Peter's Lutheran Church in Oswald County is blessed to have Pastor, Aia, Gretchen, Marc, and Luc Osterhagen live among them because they brighten up this little corner of a really big and confusing world.

– F.N.

Appendix

Characters included in *Finley's Tale – Book III: The Bond of Love*

Finley Newcastle, Church mouse and author of *Finley's Tale – Book 1: In the Beginning, Finley's Tale – Book II: Heaven on Earth,* and *Finley's Tale – Book III: The Bond of Love*, a trilogy touching on church mouse musings at Historic St. Peter's Lutheran Church in Oswald County

Ruby Newcastle, Finley Newcastle's precious gem of a wife

Pastor Clement Osterhagen, Shepherd at Historic Saint Peter's Lutheran Church, a real keeper

Aia Osterhagen, Pastor Osterhagen's wife, and mother of three, fan of anything Trinitarian

Gretchen, Marc & Luc Osterhagen, cherished children of Pastor & Aia Osterhagen

Wayne & Calhoun, finders of a Yin &Yang journal for the recording of *Finley's Tale - Part III: The Bond of Love*

Humbly, a timid and easily frightened mouse

Priscilla (Cilla) Larkin, mother of the bride who asked Pastor to change the shamrock-green chancel paraments during the season of Pentecost to ones whose colours would coordinate well with her daughter Poppy's wedding colours

Penelope (Poppy) Larkin, bride whose chosen wedding colours are cameo-blush pink and metallic silver

Rita Hines, local seamstress whose skills are of such a high caliber that she is often commissioned to sew fashionable clothing for Governor Silbertson's wife, Margo

Mrs. Margo Silbertson, Governor's wife who dresses to perfection in ensembles sewed by local seamstress, Rita Hines

Hawthorne, most adventuresome mouse in the village

Raymond (Ray) Larkin, husband of Priscilla, who together purchase liturgical paraments for HSP's chancel

Harriet Larkin, Cilla Larkin's unpleasant mother-in-law

Denver Wickstrom, sweet gent who will sit next to Harriet Larkin during the wedding dinner and attempt to sweeten up her disposition

Shane Borg, Aia's first cousin who attends Purdue University, also known as P.U.

Martha Kuehnert, Clement's grandmother who was a home-made sauerkraut expert

Anders (Andy) Rasmussen, groom of Poppy Larkin

Nita Janssen, lovely soprano soloist who sang "May God Bless this Couple" at the Larkin/Rasumssen wedding

Maverick, village mouse who heard the "foul" banter between Gretchen and Mr. Beckman

Mr. Ambrose (Bro) Beckman, "The Silver Fox" tricycle rider and church gasser-passer

Dr. Theodore Simonsen, village librarian who researches many unusual topics

Bramble, mouse that keeps current on the "Rod, Line & Hook" Lake Harvey fishing report

Palmer "Pike" Hallgrimsson, landed a 24-pound northern pike on his confirmation day fifty years ago

Roland Robinson, Pike's steady fishing buddy

Hálfdan Hallgrimsson, Pike's father born and raised in Vik, Iceland, whose veins must have run with fish blood

Dorothy Hallgrimsson, Pike's easy-on-the-eyes wife and co-leader of "The Grace-Filled Re-tirees"

"The Grace-Filled Re-tirees," church group that put fishing for men on hold, instead choosing to host a "Fall Fish Fry" with all the trimmings

Jake & Georgia Lambton, hosts and providers of a keg of beer for the November Fish Fry to be held at their year-round cottage on Lake Harvey

Turner, village's most nimble and fastest mouse who overheard the fishing starting and ending time conversation

Brad & Estelle Barretto, owners of the Sweet Dreams Ice Cream Shoppe who provided complimentary triple scoop waffle cones to the four fishing contest winners

Hop & Scotch, village duo sent out to oversee the First Annual Fishing Contest

Stu Lazzarin, towed his fishing boat on a trailer behind his truck, transported three parishioners to Lake Harvey with Hop & Scotch hiding in his boat

Fishing Contestant Josh Nowak, winner of catching the first fish

Fishing Contestant Fred Berger, winner of catching the largest fish

Fishing Contestant Ava Halvorson, winner of catching the smallest fish

Fishing Contestant Stan Bakken, winner of catching the last fish

Ellis Newcastle, Finley's Scottish father

Sister Bernadette, Catholic nun of Holy Angels Catholic Church who has the desire to attend Sunday worship at St. Peter's Lutheran Church

Sister Carmella, Catholic nun who has eaten an apple for lunch every single day of her 33 years at the convent, bringing it to a whopping grand total of over 12,000 apples

Gumi, first mouse to witness Sister Bernadette attend HSP

Wheel & Barrow, two mice who listened in on Pastor's and Sister Bernadette's conversation

Mrs. Gabrielle Charpentier, one of St. Peter's shut-ins that always calls Aia "Sister" because she cannot remember Aia's name

Marie Crogan, a member of St. Pete's with possible natural nun qualities

Gully, watched Pastor tack a poster of an influential historical figure on the bulletin board, but could not put a name to it

Leona Wilkes, self-appointed "Bulletin Examiner, Bulletin Folder, Bulletin Overseer"

Elmer Walsh, parishioner who wanted to generously donate custom pew cushions for comfort

Allyn Clarke, parishioner against pew cushions who preferred kneelers to be installed in the sanctuary

Gill Green, Reid Miller, Lanny Foster, & Tim Payne, St. Pete's grass cutters who enjoy a beer after the work is completed; same people who also instituted the "No Alcohol Policy" at St. Peter's

Rosetta & Wallaby, outdoor observers of St. Peter's grass cutters

Finn Larssen, State Historical Society Representative

Josie Johnson, St. Pete's organist who sips from her tea tumbler, speaks with a tissue covering her mouth

Darla Bungard, colourful woman who is the church cruise director

Trina Darvey, donator of fancy mushrooms from the Ferguson Family Mushroom Farm

Chef Alex O'Gara, talented chef-in-residence at the Elkridge Mansion

Claire Dahl, "Ladyhawk," in search of the "right" man

Mandarin, one of the sweetest mice in our village who observed Clair's attraction to Finn Larssen

Janet Woods, Claire's friend who is happily married to her teddy bear, Ronnie

Ronnie Woods, Janet's husband who is a real teddy bear that enjoys snuggling with her

St. Francis of Assisi, Italian saint who loved all creatures

Billy Parker, owner of two little white mice

Pearly & Alabaster, Billy Parker's white pet mice

Dallas Whittingham, far too embarrassed to return to St. Pete's because of an unfortunate experience with his donkey, Don Quixote

Don Quixote, "dumping" donkey owned by Dallas Whittingham

Herman Jenkins, parishioner who crudely spoke to Chuck Brownton, which resulted in Chuck writing a resignation letter and turning in his church keys

Chuck Brownton, church janitor that keeps the premises spotless, except after Don Quixote's "accident" on the sanctuary floor at the last "Blessing of the Animals"

Hedgie & Hedgiette, pets blessed by Pastor Osterhagen

Nip & Tuck, two dogs who bit Pastor's hands

Nettie LaFontaine, proud cat owner of Midnight

Midnight, black cat that belongs to Nettie LaFontaine

Petal Duff, owner of Nip & Tuck that were accidently exposed to rabies

Goldie, Clement's childhood dog

Brucie, Clement's childhood friend who had a rabid skunk turning circles in his driveway

Cyril, Ruby's second cousin twice removed, lives in Eastern Europe and is a pierogi expert

Irma Gleeson, parishioner who decided the Osterhagens needed a white kitchen dishwasher, but to her chagrin they ordered a flaming red one

Gary Gleeson, husband of Irma whose ears are exhausted from listening to her complain about the red dishwasher

Robinwing, curious mouse seeking out Irma's plans

Orville Ingall, owner of Ingall's Appliance Centre who special-ordered a flaming red dishwasher for the parsonage

Forest Broderick, deceased state forest ranger who provided money to construct an open air pavilion on St. Peter's property

Ivy & Fern, Forest's daughters who reside in Northern California

Paul Bunion, village mouse not to be confused with Paul Bunyan & Babe the Blue Ox

Bruno Bettendorf, against the church constructing a picnic pavilion, but in favour of building a smokehouse

Dr. Vallee, Osterhagen Family physician

Rydel Stone, upset husband of Janis Stone, Dr. Vallee's office employee

Janis Stone, non-confidential medical office secretary

Bisque & Moccasin, two dating mice that heard the ladies' astonishment about Claire Dahl's improved appearance

Tiffin, zany village member who keeps a close eye on Finn Larssen simply because the name Finn is included within the context of his name

Will Anderly, property chairperson that dealt with the washroom calamity

H2O, villager that heard Will Anderly use an abundance of money-related words

Dave Pennington, owner of Pennington's Tool & Die, who kindly offered to pay for washroom repairs

Freya Stephens, Altar Guild volunteer who discovered the washroom flooding

Tawny Bragg & Bella-Button, first mice to come across what they assumed was an exercise machine

Methuselah, wise older mouse that warned the mice about a death trap mechanism that he calls an eradication snare

Singapore, village mouse who dreams of one day traversing the entire world

Stig Madsen, carpenter who slowly wrote down council minutes using his carpentry pencil

Deborah Poole, former church council secretary whose pen always rolled to the floor

Frankie North, council member who came up with the "Flush & Slush Fund"

Arni & Juliette Nygaard, Aia Osterhagen's folks who are both teachers

Larkspur, one of the most likeable mice in the village who witnessed hearing the "I Hate Pastor" letter

Conrad Goddard, composed his "I Hate Pastor" letter because he was upset that his eternal light position was terminated due to the electrifying of the sanctuary eternal light

Molly Goodard, affixed a return address label to the envelope of her husband's "I Hate Pastor" letter thinking that she was being helpful

Vince Estes, professional electrician who had unfriendly words with Conrad Goddard and appears to be personal friends with Pastor Osterhagen

McIntosh, village mouse with a tart personality combined with a tender heart, went on an outing with Clement and Gretchen to Carpenter's Apple Orchard

Cassidy Carpenter, Gretchen's Sunday School best friend

Anton Carpenter, owner of Carpenter's Apple Orchard

Jim Keller, next door neighbour who asked Pastor Osterhagen if Travis could spend the day at the parsonage

Travis Keller, son of Jim & Kathleen, card player, originator of the tin can telephone idea

Ashley Keller, daughter of Jim & Kathleen, who had her appendix removed

Kathleen Keller, wife of Jim, mother of Ashley and Travis

Mr. & Mrs. Armstrong, card playing friends of Jim & Kathleen Keller; when they get together they use the "good" cards, not the sticky cards

Mrs. Addington, shut-in that can be only called on at precisely 10 a.m. or 2 p.m.

Mrs. Addington's cousin, a "holier-than-thou" woman who annoys Mrs. Addington by being too much of a goody-goody

Big Ben, HSP's "Timekeeper of Timepieces" who is addicted to the tick-tock sound

Benjamin, Big Ben's great-grandfather who resided at a clock museum in the State of Iowa

Alfie Quittschrieber, committee chairperson to raise funds for a sanctuary clock so that the worship services will not exceed one hour

Hudson Shaw, labeled a "hardscrabble" man and suspected of stealing the offering, who fully transformed his appearance before coming over to the parsonage for supper

Ralph Pfalzgraf, church pillar who counts St. Peter's weekly offering with his wife, Denise

Denise Pfalzgraf, extremely talkative wife of the church pillar who helps her husband count the weekly offering

Charity Borgman, mother of Abigail, whose baptism is scheduled at St. Pete's

Shelly Taylor, irate mother of Desiree refusing to be part of a "double" baptism

Avondale, little mouse who overheard the ticklish conversation between Charity and Shelly

Abigail Borgman, infant daughter of Charity Borgman

Desiree Taylor, infant daughter of Shelly whose baptism will not occur at St. Peter's but at Our Saviour's Chapel

Rick Borgman, wife of Charity, father of Abigail

Bliss, mouse who hid behind the carillon and heard the double baptism theatrics

Wally & Ruth Walford, returned home with a box of macadamia cookies from Kauai, Hawaii, to give to Pastor, Aia, & family

Tim Sadler & Darrin Weimar, substitute offering counters

Twilight & Goldenrod, mice observers of the supposedly stolen offering fiasco

Simon Thompson, current church treasurer at St. Pete's

Duane Albright, former church treasurer

Sarah Mae Shaw, deceased and treasured wife of Professor Hudson Shaw

Grant Pfaltzgraf, son of "The Church Pillar" Ralph, and his mother, Denise

Penny Pfaltlzgraf, talkative wife of Grant, daughter-in law of Ralph & Denise

St. Philycis, Patron Saint of All Micedom, saved mice from extension in Malta

Cayenne, a perfectly peppy and peppery village mouse that suggested we have another shindig

Longfellow, mouse that delivered a lengthy formal address in honour of St. Philycis

Zippy, a zingy and zappy village mouse who gets a kick out of observing Leona Wilkes folding the weekly church bulletin

Judith Schellenberger, honoured to carry the title of St. Pete's "Bulletin Folder"

Cloyd Hackley, former "Bulletin Folder" who wanes during the middle of the job and calls on Pastor Osterhagen for assistance

Florence Hackley, Cloyd's wife, who attends a card party with him every Friday evening

Butternut & Thistle, two mice who listened as Finn Larssen expressed frustration with Claire Dahl's continual flirtation

Fabian (aka Fabuloso or Fab), frequent picker of the Osterhagen's garden green beans who once had his heart set on becoming a bean grower but couldn't achieve his goal

Fred & Nancy Osterhagen, a Lutheran pastor and his wife who are Clement's folks

Sister Bernadette, nun that worships at St. Peter's on Sunday mornings because she is disgruntled with the weak preaching and the poor quality of the modern music at Holy Angels Parish

Huey, village mouse who agrees with Frank Roth on his opinion about Sister Bernadette leaving Catholicism, telling Ruby and myself that Sister Bernadette thinks with both her mind and her heart

Frank Roth, parishioner who is certain Sister Bernadette will leave Catholicism and become Lutheran

Rueben & Evelyn Newmann, parishioners who wore Luther Rose sweatshirts to church on Reformation Sunday

Dr. Christoff Kikkunen, village Assistant Head Librarian of Finnish descent

J.S. Bach, deceased composer who tried to "improve" Dr. Luther's "A Mighty Fortress" to be sung to a Isorhythmic metre instead of Luther's original Rhythmic metre

Mandy Stonecroft, one who hung a poster from the pulpit in her determination to make St. Pete's a zone free of perfume

Aimée Beaulieu, sophisticated and refined parishioner known for wearing fancy French perfume

Weegee, village mouse that had a wild party with his friends in the Underground Railroad spot leaving behind a mess that forced the entire village to move to the Bavarian Bed & Breakfast

Eli, mice village patriarch, a real guiding light for the village

Lewis & Clark, official mouse explorers who have benefited the village with many discoveries

Jasmine, Mice Anxiety Therapist

Father Tim, Priest at Holy Angels Catholic Parish, leads weekly devotions and prayers at the Food Bank, good friend of Pastor Osterhagen

Oscar Johannessen, died in 1886 due to a burst appendix from being rolled down a hill

Mrs. Johannessen, Oscar's wife who rolled him down a hill to alleviate his pain and suffering

Costumed Oswald County Library Volunteers, passed out Halloween candy at story hour

Katharina von Bora (Katie), dearly beloved wife of Martin, a runaway nun who escaped the convent by hiding in an empty herring barrel, mother of several children, proud land-owner, protector of silver and wealth, constant helper and encourager to Martin, cook, gardener, and exquisite master brewer of hearty German beer, plus a gracious hostess

Dr. Martin Luther, dearly beloved husband of his wife Katie, German theologian, former Catholic priest, founder of the Protestant Reformation, composer of "A Mighty Fortress is Our God," as well as many other hymns, along with umpteen other particulars that could fill an entire "L" volume in an encyclopedia

Pope Leo X, annoyed at Dr. Martin Luther about the 1517 Reformation

"Match Woman," ignited matches in a passenger train resulting in her being banned from travelling via train ever again

Crikey, a courageous Australian mouse who became a hero when he rescued a baby kangaroo that fell out of his mother's pouch by guiding him back to his mother, which was so earth shaking it became the subject of a movie

Jaxon, Australian baby kangaroo that accidently fell out of his mother's pouch

Charlene, Jaxon's mother who could not have found Jaxon if not for Crikey's heroism

Hanky & Panky, two mice who thought they discovered a "kissing corner" at St. Peter's but it was only the choir loft

Bryan Schmidt, Youth Group member who kissed Jenna Powell for two seconds

Jenna Powell, Youth Group member who kissed Bryan Schmidt for two seconds

Hazel, compassionate village member who listened to the details of the missing offering

Pastor David Klug, enthusiastic, but thorough, newly-installed pastor of King of Glory Lutheran Church who was far too involved in planning his installation

Helmut Braun, German artist commissioned by the Bavarian Bed & Breakfast to paint scenic murals of Germany for the dining room

Less & Lily Hirschfield, current owners of the BB&B

Carissa & Claudia, daughters of the Hirschfield's, top-notch helpers at the BB&B

Chef Dieter Nussbaum, BB&B Chef and herb cookbook author, crazy about Bonnie Blue

Bonnie Blue Habberstadt, employee at the BB&B, smitten with Chef Dieter

Bonnie Blue's Mother, flu sufferer who spent 238 minutes in a theatre washroom which resulted in missing out on seeing the feature film

Scarlett, the name Bonnie Blue hopes to someday give to a baby daughter

Flame, mouse endowed with the brightest luster of fur in the entire village who hid behind a sack of potatoes to eavesdrop on Dieter and Bonnie Blue

Will & Winnie (Pooh) Lawson, wealthy Wyoming residents and the proud owners of the "W-6 Ranch"

Willie, Weston, Wyatt, & Walker Lawson, the four sons of Will & Pooh, who are referred to by their parents as "The 4X4's"

Luca, level-headed villager hoping to marry Bianca, a resident at Maria-Rosa's Pizzeria

Bianca, a mouse living at the pizzeria now going steady with Luca

Sacagawea, Lewis & Clark's female trusty guide that helped locate pocket-sized "Cross in My Pockets" to give to "The 4X4's"

Abe & Andrea Quanbeck, apple cider doughnuts deep fat frying duo at HSP's "Annual Apple Reception" that was also hosted by the owners of Carpenter's Apple Orchard, Anton & Amy Carpenter

Clyde Ingelbrand, November head usher who pulled the fire alarm

Buckwheat, largest male mouse in our village, the one who witnessed the emergency

Ramble, black bear that moseyed around St. Peter's front entrance, sat on the sidewalk, and later headed out of town

Florence Hobson, hospital patient called on by two pastors, one who was an imitator and the other, Pastor Osterhagen, the real deal

Lenny Kirby, pastor impersonator who unconventionally wears a clerical shirt who Ruby has dubbed "HSP's Wackadoodle"

St. Ansgar, a medieval European missionary referred to as the "Apostle of the North," namesake of a retreat centre

Phooey-Chewy, an outdoor church squirrel that spends time under the cathedral bird feeder waiting to nibble on wild bird seeds that have dropped to the ground

Tweak, village mouse that constantly is trying to make improvements

Earshot, village mouse with acute hearing abilities

Sheila Strongmeier, Aia's onion-chopping partner

Rachel Timmons, attendee at a wild birthday party held at a male strip club

Nutley, village mouse who cracks the most jokes

Joey Cabot, groom of Jocelyn, employed at the family business, "Cabot & Sons Lumber Yard"

Jocelyn Murray, bride of Joey Cabot and mother of Ian and Maisie

Jeremiah Clarke, late 16th century composer of the wedding fanfare, "The Prince of Denmark's March"

Jeff Van Deren, trumpet soloist at Joey and Jocelyn's wedding

Ian & Maisie Murray, Jocelyn's children and adorable attendants at her wedding

Sean & Betha Murray, Ian & Maisie's Irish grandparents who were unable to attend Jocelyn's wedding, but sent Ian a Murray plaid bow tie to wear at the wedding

Hecktor & Savannah, two mice who were married at HSP during a double wedding

Auggie & Viola Olafson, parishioners who vacationed in North Devon, England, unknowingly bringing Bennett to the United States with them in Viola's suitcase

Bennett, British-born mouse, self-appointed wedding/baby shower coordinator/consultant

Miss Galaxy, very special new friend of Bennett, who puts clusters of stars in his eyes

River Birch, mouse elder who created a "NO-NO" English naming list

Jenny Mitchell, Chevonne Gibbs, & Grant Weaver, members of the Oswald County Fairground Heritage Village Restoration Committee

Roy Morgan, owner of Morgan & Sons Plumbing & Heating

Skip Spencer, parishioner who owns Skip's Plumbing & Heating and denies that there is any problem with the parsonage's hot water tank

Emily Dickinson, poet who penned a few words of praise about the green pea inside the pea pod

Crash, village mouse that collides into things because of a physical impairment

Ginger Mulready, queen bee of the "I Once Was Lost, But Now Am Found Box"

April Taylor, questioned by Ginger if her baby daughter has lost a pink pacifier

June Taylor, infant daughter of April

St. Anthony, about whom some people believe that praying to him will help them recover what is lost or stolen, whether it is material goods or the spiritual gifts of faith, hope, and love

Bernard Fleischacker, town Deputy Sheriff and an usher, nicknamed "St. Bernard" by Aia

Kathleen Whittington, oldest Whittington daughter

Edmond Whittington, deceased husband and father who left behind his wife and six daughters

Esther Whittington, widow of her dear Edmond

Katrina, Kimberly, Kristin, Kayla, & Kitty, the younger five daughters of Edmond and Esther

Serena, owner of Serena's Floral Shoppe and one of Aia's friends

Berdie Fuglestad, Aia's dear auntie that gave Clement & Aia a Swedish crystal vase for their wedding present

LaDonna Kazlauskas, bloody liver provider who washed her hands in the snow

Bishop Fillmore, weary from helping pastors deal with retired pastors who remain at the parish they previously served

911 Dispatcher, helped Gretchen when her mother fell on the kitchen floor and could not get up

Snowdrop, the only albino mouse in our village that triumphantly hid in the diaper bag and went via ambulance to Our Lady of Lourdes hospital after Aia broke two of her ribs

Hospital Volunteers, taught by Gretchen on how to properly diaper her twin brothers so they didn't each get a diaper "wedgie"

Retired Pastors, those who retain membership at the church they previously served, hovering over the happenings"

Council of Bishops, aim to create a policy about the role of retired pastors

Denny Young, a pushy architect in cahoots with Ryan Cox and Kevin Morgan

Ryan Cox, unmovable contractor collaborating with Denny Young and Kevin Morgan

Kevin Morgan, a certified electrician that is conspiring with Denny Young and Ryan Cox

Juniper & Cloudberry, two mouse scouts that listened intently to the proposal to redo the design of the sanctuary to make it more contemporary

The M.D. (Major Donor), ready to contribute a vast amount of money, not a Doctor of Medicine or has earned any type of a doctorate

Bob Jackson, upset parishioner grieving over the relocation of the sanctuary planters

Bob, Bart, Barry & Bernie, an all-you-can-eat pancakes group who originally called themselves "The Four B's" but changed their name to "The WASP's" because they are "Worried About St. Pete's"

Pastor & Mrs. Handt, & their son Davey, invited to the Jackson's home following the "Planter Dedication" for a celebratory ham dinner

Jody Framm, Director of Social Involvement who created a new use for the four planters

Lonesome Pine & Mountain Pine, two village mice that were in attendance at custodian Chuck Brownton's retirement dinner

Candace Pedersen, singing star (and sewing star) at last year's talent show performing "You Can't Get a Man with a Gun"

Jayne Brownton, Janitor Chuck's helpful wife

Skip & Kimmy Brownton, St. Pete's new custodians

Nolan & Taylor Brownton, children of Skip & Kimmy, who will hop on a training wheel bike and a tricycle to ride the hallways at HSP while their parents are engaged in cleaning the church

Myrtle Cunningham, women who accidently turned up the oven temperature so high that she burned dinner rolls as well as ignited into flames two village mice

Harry Cunningham, drove breakneck to Grocer's Dan to pick up eight loaves of bread to replace the dinner rolls burned by his wife, Myrtle

Binky & Mitzy, two young mice that were immolated in the church kitchen oven

Samuel (Sam) & Samantha (Sammy) Whitcombe, couple who had a "We Still Do!" wedding renewal of their vows

Wizzy, brilliant village mouse who recited the "A - Z" wedding renewal vows to the entire mouse village

Mamie Patterson, recipient of a "Different Kind of Christmas" flyer

Thermadore, village resident that watched Mamie Patterson grab the flyer from underneath one of her car wiper blades

Blizzard & Bleak Midwinter, two village members that watch the snowy winter weather from the window ledges in the Fireside Room

Stacey Graham, niece of Mamie, who also received two flyers at Holy Angels Catholic Parish

Ulrika Jönsson, Swedish soprano soloist scheduled to perform at "A Different Kind of Christmas" but who bailed at the last minute

Pastor Matthew Wheeler, a "sheep stealer" who tries to snatch parishioners from other churches in order to grow the membership in his church

Pastor John Ernst, minister at Berea Baptist Church

Brent Wood, stewardship team member who created the "Rainy Day Cash" umbrella

Quaker & Shaker, simple and quiet mice who observed Brent Wood's "We must make our budget" activity

Frank & Shelby Williams, parishioners and council members who were initially displeased about the umbrella stewardship campaign

Maureen Phillips, lady who snatches umbrellas hanging on St. Pete's coat racks

Pembroke & Polly, two mice that witnessed Aia hauling a manual typewriter to the parsonage

Miki & Bitsy Isaksen, two make-believe church gnomes included in Author Aia's book

The Cook Family, blessed with seven children, recipients of the "Mother" sourdough starter

Grandma Nygaard, deceased grandmother of Aia, whose homemade noodle recipe is repeated every Christmas at the Osterhagens

Leigh Ann Turner, teenage checker at Grocer Dan's who mistakenly assumed Aia had gotten a tattoo

Kimberly Scott, pastor's wife in Beeker County, who was mistakenly thought to be suffering with depression

Kimberly Lane, Beeker County Mental Health Association representative

Ollie, owner of "Ollie's (cash-only) Corner Café" located kitty-corner from St. Peter's, now temporarily shut down by the health department

Greasy & Spoon, two mice who previously resided at Ollie's who keep the village entertained with real knee-slapper stories they heard at that establishment

Schlossers, Fendricks, Browns, & Nostads, four couples that eat together on Sunday noon

Gerome & Cally Schlosser, complainers about Pastor and Aia and the "Schlosser" pew removal

Gustav & Annaliese Schlosser, charter members of Historic St. Peter's whose donated front pew was moved to a remote location, covering up the golden plaque

Prudy Rasmus, philanthropist who purchased a baby grand piano for St. Peter's

Bev Godfredson, postal worker who delivered a large box full of choir robes to the parsonage on an arctic winter day

Mila Wagner, first cousin of Bev Godfredson that has arrived from Germany to celebrate Christmas with Bev, American-style

Marcie Fredrickson, owner of Marcie's Creative Concepts, hopes to redecorate the parsonage

"Abundant Praise Liturgical Dance Group," girls from nearby Steady Steps Christian High School that had a bunking party in the Fireside Room after performing a concert at HSP

Horace, Gretchen's much-loved teddy bear

Blake Dunn, council member who has studied *Robert's Rules of Order* and wants to replace the secretary of St. Peter's Council with his wife, Bethany

Petunia, village mouse who observed the last church council meeting of the calendar year

Michelle Green, Secretary of HSP's Church Council, Court Reporter

Bethany Dunn, recent graduate with a legal secretary degree

Humphrey Chandler, Antique dealer who is a member of the Antique Clock Dealers' Association who helped Aia claim the value of an unwanted clock

Nelda McBride, arthritis sufferer who stands by the drinking fountain to see who has attended church

Albert Coulson, friend of Nelda, who also has arthritis

Whippersnapper, young confident mouse who is interested in the subject of arthritis

Stiff, female mouse that suffers with arthritis, whose real name is Limber Lindy

Patti, voted freshest breath in the village and re-named "Patti, St. Peter's Peppermint Princess"

Gracie, officially had her name changed to "O Day Full of Gracie," but doesn't mind going by "Fulla"

Pastor N.F.S. Grundtvig, Danish poet who penned the hymn "O Day Full of Grace"

Banjo, watched Pastor select *The Text of the Oberammergau Passion Play 1970* from the church library

Patrick & Belinda Johnson, owners of PBJ Boat Sales & Rentals, new owners of "The Pizzazzy Peanut"

Brady Johnson, son of Patrick & Belinda, high school student who is interested in accounting, keeps the books for "The Pizzazzy Peanut"

Wanda Cage, member of St. Peter's Altar Guild with knowledge about how to order disposable plastic communion cups, gave Belinda a box of them to use at the "Peanut Party" event

Wiggly & Piggly, two village mice who observed the "Peanut Party" held in Woolcox Hall as well as taste-testing a honey-flavoured peanut

Silvie Berger, quilter who discovered a plastic bag containing white powder that was nestled among some folded sheets

St. Peter's Quilting Group, to their horror, touched the plastic bag full of "drugs" leaving everyone's fingerprints on the bag

Audrey Fassbender, a jumpy jittery woman who was fearful she was going to be sent to the state penitentiary for being part of an illegal drug operation

Farley, mouse who witnessed the illegal drugs police investigation

Peggy Hayward, quilter who hurried to get Pastor's help during the illegal drugs confusion

Lance Farber, telephoned Pastor after a huge snowstorm asking him to call on his dad, Grover

Grover Farber, resident at Loving Arms Nursing Home, in need of a pastoral call during a wicked snowstorm

Addendum: Thirty-one Years Later

By Chance Quigley, Current President of St. Peter's Mice Village

Ever since Finley Newcastle's three documented journals were unearthed from the deep depths of St. Peter's ever-growing church library, we are finding that they are heartfelt and historical recordings that fully follow one particular liturgical church at Historic St. Peter's. The author, Finley Newcastle, passed away decades ago, but his stellar reputation as a giant in our mouse community continues to abide. After his passing, the mice village meeting hall was dedicated to his memory by being named, "Newcastle Commons." Two current members of our village, Tab and Lloyd, are ceaselessly on watch for the latest news. After finding this discovery they brought the information to the next village meeting. In no time at all another mouse, Jiffy, successfully convinced everyone that the journals should be read aloud each time we have a village meeting. It did take a very long time, but everyone remained still as a statue when hearing about this slice of St. Pete's past. In view of the unearthing of the *Finley's Tale* series, thanks to Tab and Lloyd, combined with Jiffy's insistence to unveil its contents, the village's gratitude attitude has improved. It has become a bit like the gracious blessings found in the Beatitudes, especially the phrase, "Blessed are the meek, for they will inherit the earth." In a nutshell, interest in both the past and future among the mice community can be summed up by proclaiming wise words spoken by Dag Hammarskjöld, the 1961 Nobel Peace prizewinner: "For what has been, thanks; for what will be, yes."

Our village has heard much about the Osterhagen Family since they moved away from Oswald County to North Carolina where Clement was called to serve at Our Saviour of the Lake Lutheran Church. Gretchen, Marc, and Luc are now all grown up. Gretchen became an opera singer and resides in Atlanta. Marc and Luc studied French cuisine in Montreal and each got a position at a resort in the Laurentian Mountains. Nine years after the twins were born at Our Lady of Lourdes Hospital, Aia gave birth to a baby girl, Liesel Jeanette Osterhagen. Liesel is a student at a Lutheran liberal arts college in the Midwest studying nursing. Several villagers have heard a few St. Peter's parishioners speak about receiving Christmas cards from Pastor Osterhagen and Aia, telling that Pastor is preaching, teaching, and visiting at Our Saviour of the Lake. It is noted that Aia now has time to fully dedicate herself to her painting career that is delightfully showcased on her expressive website. She mostly paints trolls, gnomes, and other curiously mysterious things that most church people in all probability would not dream of hanging up on their walls. But that doesn't matter since she does most of her work on commission for people who live either on the East or West Coast, or more recently in the quaint village of Gimli, Manitoba, where two mischievous elves, Snorri and Snaebjorn, reside.

After finishing reading Finley's three journals, much discussion followed at our recent village meeting. It was decided that the journals should be placed in a spot where they will definitely be discovered by human beings. The Underground Railroad hiding place was a naturally perfect location because it would be found by the State Historical Society early in October when they hold their annual showings of the Underground Railroad hiding place.

Our village soon formulated a plan. Essentially, the thing to do was to come up with a very long piece of string to tie around the notebooks. Thankfully, Wolfe, the mouse with the most fortitude in our village, raced to the parsonage washroom and spotted a container of dental floss on the floor that must have been dropped by one of Pastor Matthew and Lydia Engel's five children. After Wolfe hauled the floss to Newcastle Commons, a group of our strongest mice methodically wrapped the cinnamon-flavoured dental floss all the way around the circumference of *Finley's Tale, Books I, II, & III.* By forming a mouse chain gang that consisted of every available strong mouse in the village, they were able to drag *Finley's Tale* centimetre by centimetre to the Underground Railroad spot. Their efforts worked wonders in succeeding to place *Finley's Tale* in St. Pete's Underground Railroad site, the exact historical location our mouse explorers Lewis and Clark discovered decades earlier.

Our village, without a doubt, perceives that some of St. Pete's parishioners consider changes to be an unwelcome millstone around St. Peter's neck, causing them to feel uneasy and fearful every time something new is presented. But, keep in mind that when the church proceeds forward, it does not fully throw away the past but is only seeking new opportunities and ways to spread the Word of God. One of the sanctuary stained glass windows at Historic St. Peter's depicts a boat, the ancient symbol used for the church. Long ago St. Gregory pointed out that the church is a vessel in motion that guides, protects, and transports believers from birth to death. The opposite of St. Gregory's portrayal is a cruise ship with privileged and fussy passengers aboard that hanker after entertainment and gourmet meals, one after the next, and doesn't really go anywhere.

Our village embraces new beginnings, noticing that abundant things pour forth from changes: knowledge, flexibility, appreciation, faith, diversity, renewed passions, comfort, peace, and healthy growing personalities. New routines open up mindfulness, faith growth, and even love. Yes, love. There are many things we are learning at Historic St. Peter's Lutheran Church, but the one thing we are well informed about is God's love the way it is mentioned in Psalm 136. You can read about it yourself. No matter how many experiences in life are behind you about who did what, where, when, how, or why, remember that "His love endures forever." One member of our village, Sweet-Lips, decided to rewrite that particular phrase and has translated this into Mouse: *"Mopihawefbwhg oinfw mjcbwq qwe njzpo"* which means in English, "His devotedness and affection goes on and on endlessly." I will finish by urging you to hang on to God's Word with your heart, soul, and mind. By doing that you will be fine, or is it refined?

At 11:30 p.m. My wife Daisy and I travelled to the parsonage and were far beyond delighted when we located two shreds of pulled pork and one ribbon of coleslaw. They turned up underneath the dining room table. This afternoon we noticed Lydia Engel returning from Grocer Dan's Deli carrying a small container of precooked pulled pork. Daisy and I remarked that the current pastor's wife must not have an interest in cooking. From reading Finley's journal, the mice community listened as Finley wrote about Aia's vast culinary ability every time Finley made a recording. But, pastor's wives are not formed with a cookie cutter. Each one is unique, a one and only. Even though Lydia stocks the parsonage kitchen with ready-made foods like frozen lasagne and pre-peeled baby carrots, she shines in other areas. Our village is hopeful that Historic St. Peter's parishioners will embrace their new pastor's wife and accept her just as she is. It would not be fair treatment to compare her to a former pastor's wife, concluding that she cannot hold a candle to that person.

Daisy was so thrilled at the chance to sample a bite of precooked pulled pork that when she finished chewing she popped this question: "Chance, Chance, with just a glance, I am entranced. Would you like to dance at the manse?" After we happily twirled around several times, we headed home. Daisy hummed me to sleep with the phenomenal hymn tune called Le P'ing, which is hymn #871 in St. Peter's sturdy and well-loved burgundy hymnal. I was tired, ready to get some Z's and was looking forward to waking up to the rising sun. – Chance Quigley, Current President of St. Peter's Mice Village, also known as C.Q.

P.S. For informational purposes, Chef Dieter Nussbaum and Bonnie Blue Habberstadt were united in Holy Marriage many years ago. They have a stunningly beautiful ginger-haired daughter that they named Scarlett. Scarlett is akin to Scarlett O'Hara in the well-known film when she becomes either frustrated or impatient and reacts with the twelve-letter expression, "Fiddledeedee!" This is simply a set phrase that she picked up from watching G.W.T.W. countless times. Daisy and I discussed how Finley's days, too, are now gone with the wind. However, because of his efforts during his lifetime our village has been able to follow the trilogy of *Finley's Tale*, an authentic landmark literary work. Nothing like this had ever been accomplished by a mouse, until it was fulfilled by Finley Newcastle by the sweat of his brow and the love of his heart.

Within Finley's final journal was a very small sheet of paper. It was a note that contained some life-changing words that were spoken at Finley's funeral. The note included words of wisdom, something the living can learn from. We were all glad that they were written down so we won't soon forget the insightful message it contained. It read, "To the world you may be one mouse, but to one mouse you may be the world." Now that is something substantial to contemplate and chew over as one passes through life trying to discover one's purpose and vision. I think we all question, at some point, why we are here in this place at this particular time. Currently I am questioning whether or not I should begin journaling one full liturgical church year at St. Peter's, something more current than Finley's writings. A snap decision about this I cannot make. Let's leave it at "perhaps I will, perhaps I won't."

Discussion at the village this afternoon concentrated on finding out precisely which variety of fruit tree was the forbidden one located in the Garden of Eden. It was suggested by Verner that Eve must have picked a Red Delicious Apple, while Tag-Along thought it might have been a Golden Hornet crab apple. More suggestions were from Switch and Bittersweet who agreed that it was either a Granny Smith apple or a Washington pear. Put to a vote, all villagers agreed that we do not need to be wise-apples or discerning pears and hunt down this beside-the-point Biblical fruit detail. It was also pointed out that we should not bother our busy librarian, Dr. Justin Haapala, by asking him to investigate something so trivial while he is researching the harmful consequences of excess sugar consumption. It is plenty enough information just to know that the forbidden fruit was, most likely, not a pineapple, or worse, a road apple. We do conclude that original sin came into being in the Garden of Eden and that humankind has struggled with it ever since. It's a good thing that Historic St. Peter's Lutheran Church in Oswald

County continually points to the ever-flowing forgiveness of sins all through Christ's death and resurrection.

Before I conclude, I need to sign off by writing three small words, *"Soli Deo Gloria."* I have no clue what that phrase actually means, but it must be of incredible importance since it is ever so beautifully carved into the cornerstone of Historic St. Peter's. Perhaps, in your free time, you could head down to your local library and kindly speak with the head librarian, or assistant librarian, and ask for assistance to discover what that phrase means. Until then, I must say farewell to you with words that I do understand. It is a meaningful church phrase that goes like this: "The Lord be with you," in which the response is with the sincere words, "And also with you." That seems like a greeting and a farewell simultaneously. It must stem from faith, hope, and love. Another small slip of paper was found in *Finley's Tale, Book III: The Bond of Love* which goes like this: "While waiting for God to open a door, try praying in the hallway." That is excellent advice to follow all the days of your life.

A heartfelt farewell, *adieu,* bye-bye, see you soon, cheerio, *adios,* see you later, bon voyage, until we meet again, or aloha. Dr. Justin Haapala recently taught me that the beautiful Hawaiian word "aloha" is a way to say both hello and good-bye. After gaining this knowledge, I have fully embraced the word, using it many times a day instead of a plain old "howdy" or a run-of-the mill "so long." But, please choose whichever parting word or words are most applicable to you. It is best to sum it all up in one all-embracing word, Godspeed! Numbers 6:24-26 says it far better than I ever could. It reads, "The LORD bless you and keep you; the LORD make his face shine on you and be gracious to you; the LORD turn his face toward you and give you peace."

– C.Q.

THE END

About the Author

Greetings! My name is Sandra Voelker. Originally I hail from the United States having grown up in Austin, Minnesota, a mid-sized city that is known worldwide as "SPAM Town, U.S.A." Taking up residency in Canada came about when my husband, a Lutheran pastor, accepted a call to a parish in Windsor, Ontario. For the last three decades I have held church organist positions in three different locations, Michigan, Minnesota, and Ontario. A published composer of hymn tunes and settings, I have also worked in church offices, banks, an art gallery, and Hormel's corporate office.

We have four daughters, and God has also blessed us with two granddaughters and two grandsons. Topping my daily delights of favourite things includes breathing God's fresh air, selective types of music, spending evenings at home, my Northern attempts at Southern and international cooking, reading, popcorn and movie nights watching British murder mysteries, word search, daily tea or coffee at four p.m., being a friend, home wine-making, growing herbs, thrift store shopping, writing, and painting.

My daily prayers are thankful to God for the many people I love, but included also are those who are far from loveable. I know that one day Christ our Saviour will take me home to heaven, but I hope that He procrastinates that for a while yet.

The side-splitting groundwork of the *Finley's Tale* series springs from actual and imagined "church" experiences during my lifetime. Being a P.K. (pastor's kid) and a P.W. (pastor's wife) are blessings that have provided me with a fragrant potpourri of priceless encounters and experiences, a panorama of parish life that only those on the "inside" witness. *Finley's Tale* Books I, II, and III exist because I was in seventh heaven writing about that which I know best of all, "church musings."

Soli Deo Gloria

Follow Finley's Tale online at

finleystale.com

where you can find:

• discussion questions for a book group or Bible study

• periodic blog articles about Historic St. Peter's

• recording of "Safety First," the mouse anthem and more!

Also in the Finley's Tale *series*

978-1-4866-1531-5

In the Beginning, the first book in the *Finley's Tale* series sets in motion the journal of Finley Newcastle, a literate church mouse who writes his observations of the people (and mice) who populate a small-town church. Keen to monitor, study, and write about the parishioners and his fellow mice, including what others might think of them, Finley is unaware that his account may prove comical to human readers.

His favourite humans are Pastor Clement Osterhagen, his wife Aia, and their daughter Gretchen who reside in the parsonage. They are merciful, quiet, quick to forgive, prone to worry, adventuresome, big-hearted, and extra good-looking. Finley's observations lead him to conclude that they possess a strong faith in Jesus Christ.

Heaven on Earth, the second book in the *Finley's Tale* series, brings to light more amusing adventures and further intriguing developments at Historic St. Peter's, recorded by church mouse Finley Newcastle.

978-1-4866-1666-4

Finley and the entire mice village perpetually observe the anything but boring church people, some odd shenanigans, an underground discovery, church vandalism, and much, much more—and their top priority, as always, is Safety First.

Pastor Osterhagen and his family walk by faith through the church year by doing what they do best: confidently proclaiming and trusting in Jesus Christ, their Lord and Saviour, for the forgiveness of sins, and relying on God's daily gifts of abundant grace and protection.